Breathe

NOVELS BY JOYCE CAROL OATES

With Shuddering Fall (1964)

A Garden of Earthly Delights (1967)

Expensive People (1968)

them (1969)

Wonderland (1971)

Do with Me What You Will (1973)

The Assassins (1975)

Childwold (1976)

Son of the Morning (1978)

Unholy Loves (1979)

Bellefleur (1980)

Angel of Light (1981)

A Bloodsmoor Romance (1982)

Mysteries of Winterthurn (1984)

Solstice (1985)

Marya: A Life (1986)

You Must Remember This (1987)

American Appetites (1989)

Because It Is Bitter, and Because It Is My Heart (1990)

Black Water (1992)

Foxfire: Confessions of a Girl Gang (1993)

What I Lived For (1994)

Zombie (1995)

We Were the Mulvaneys (1996)

Man Crazy (1997)

My Heart Laid Bare (1998)

Broke Heart Blues (1999)

Blonde (2000)

Middle Age: A Romance (2001)

I'll Take You There (2002)

The Tattooed Girl (2003)

The Falls (2004)

Missing Mom (2005)

Black Girl / White Girl (2006)

The Gravedigger's Daughter (2007)

My Sister, My Love (2008)

Little Bird of Heaven (2009)

Mudwoman (2012)

The Accursed (2013)

Carthage (2014)

The Sacrifice (2015)

A Book of American Martyrs (2017)

Hazards of Time Travel (2018)

My Life as a Rat (2019)

Night. Sleep. Death. The Stars. (2020)

Breathe

A NOVEL

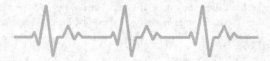

Joyce Carol Oates

An Imprint of HarperCollins*Publishers*

BREATHE. Copyright © 2021 by Ontario Review, Inc. All rights reserved. Printed in the United States of America. No part of this book may be used or reproduced in any manner whatsoever without written permission except in the case of brief quotations embodied in critical articles and reviews. For information, address HarperCollins Publishers, 195 Broadway, New York, NY 10007.

HarperCollins books may be purchased for educational, business, or sales promotional use. For information, please email the Special Markets Department at SPsales@harpercollins.com.

Ecco® and HarperCollins® are trademarks of HarperCollins Publishers.

A hardcover edition of this book was published in 2021 by Ecco, an imprint of HarperCollins Publishers.

FIRST ECCO PAPERBACK EDITION PUBLISHED 2022

Designed by Michelle Crowe

Title page art by Idrisalfath/ Shutterstock, Inc.

Library of Congress Cataloging-in-Publication Data has been applied for.

ISBN 978-0-06-308548-0 (pbk.)

22 23 24 25 26   LSC   10 9 8 7 6 5 4 3 2 1

The mind is its own place, and in it self
Can make a Heav'n of Hell, a Hell of Heav'n.

—JOHN MILTON, PARADISE LOST

How very hard, to enter an empty house.

—ANONYMOUS

Breathe

PART I

The Vigil

A Voice Out of a Fever Cloud

A hand is gripping yours. Warm dry hand gripping your slippery humid hand.

Whoever it is urging you—*Breathe!*

Leaning over you begging you—*Breathe!*

Not words but sound-vibrations rippling through water. Wavy-rippling water in which sun motes swarm in a delirium resembling joy.

Drunken delirium of joy. Scalding-hot skin, fever. At what temperature do bacteria boil? At what temperature does the brain boil?

Blink if you can hear. Blink if you are alive.

Blink squint try to see who it is leaning over you begging *Breathe!*—the face is obscured in shadow.

Darling I love you so much.

I have your hand. I will never abandon you.

The Vigil

Nothing matters except: he must not die.

He must *breathe*. He must not cease *breathing*.

Oxygen is seeping in a slow continuous stream into his nostrils through a translucent plastic tube.

IV fluids into his veins, that have been severely dehydrated.

He is neither fully awake nor is he fully unconscious. You believe that he can hear you, his facial expressions are not impassive but ever-shifting, his eyes behind the closed lids are alert, alive.

You are alert and alive as you have rarely been in your life determined that your husband *breathe*.

Pleading in desperation. In childish hope, unreason. Begging your husband *Breathe! Don't stop breathing!*

Begging as you would never have imagined you might one day beg at the bedside of a very ill man clutching at his hands which (you note, you will long remember noting with a thrill of naive hope) are warm as your own hands, and (you believe) just perceptibly responsive—when you squeeze his fingers, he seems to respond, if weakly, with the air of one whose mind is elsewhere.

Don't leave me! Please don't leave me! I love you so, I can't live without you . . .

A plea, a threat, a promise, a vow—*can't live without you.*

Words of pathos, futility. Words uttered how many times in the course of human history and never other than in futility.

Can't! The Skull God of the high desert surrounding Santa Tierra laughs in derision.

TERROR OF (YOUR HUSBAND'S) DEATH has broken you, all pride has leaked away like urine through the catheter inserted into the husband's shrunken stub of a penis.

Pride, dignity, common sense leaked away. Where?

(Into a plastic sac discreetly fastened beneath the bed.)

Begging the struggling man *Breathe!*

How it has happened, why it has happened—your life bound up with the life of this man.

Why him, and why you. In love.

Made to wonder—are we infants in our deepest selves, in our most profound memories, linked by our terror of utter loss?

What you love most, that you will lose. The price of your love is your loss.

Where a cruel and capricious god has brought your husband (and you) to die.

A mistake, coming to this remote place. An adventure, Gerard had said.

Not that Santa Tierra, New Mexico, is truly remote, less than an hour's drive from Albuquerque. A smaller and less gentrified Santa Fe.

Weeks, days you've been here in this landscape new to you. Passing with torturous slowness even as the spool of minutes is fast unwinding.

Too fast! Too fast! A fundamental principle of physics, Time accelerates nearing the point of impact.

For your husband, whom you love with a feverish desperation

that surprises you, no longer breathes normally. Not for weeks has he been able to breathe without effort, and now he has been fitted with a breathing tube, sending pure oxygen to his brain. Not for weeks has he been able to breathe without visible strain, a strain that shows in his face, and this strain has become yours as well.

For you are helping him *breathe*. You are convinced that you are helping him *breathe*.

This is not a regular breathing, a metronome sort of breathing, uncalculated, easy, rather this is a gasping sort of breathing, and in the interstices of this breathing there are pauses, caesuras, like those missteps in dreams in which you stagger, stumble, fall from a step or a curb, and jerk yourself awake.

Those silences in your husband's breathing that are terrible to hear, terrifying.

Initially diagnosed with pneumonia. Then, a blood clot attached to the (left) lung. Then, (metastasized) cancer to the (left) lung revealed in a scan.

Then: more. And now more.

Your joint fantasy has been, you will review together all that has happened since the hospitalization. Your joint fantasy has been, there would be a time, an interlude, when you might together step *out-of-time*, the better to comprehend what has happened, and is happening.

But there has not been such a time *out-of-time*.

You have begun to understand, there will not be such a time *out-of-time*.

It is all you can do to grip your husband's hand. Urge him—*Breathe!*

Where once these strong fingers gripped yours, enclosed your (smaller) hand in his hand. As your husband's soul, more magnanimous than yours, embraced and buoyed aloft your (wounded, shrunken) soul.

Now, you are comforting Gerard. It is your desperate hope to comfort Gerard. You begin to see that there is no greater purpose to your life than to comfort Gerard.

Pressing blindly into the rapidly diminishing space that is your (shared) future as if this space were not rapidly diminishing but un-bounded.

How can we comprehend an *endlessly expanding universe?*—Gerard had wondered.

Essentially, we cannot comprehend.

Cannot comprehend infinity, from the perspective of the finite.

Cannot comprehend the magnitude of our own deaths, from the perspective of our (small) lives.

You feel the loss already, the anguish to come. That you will be losing this man whom, in life, you'd struggled and (mostly) failed to know.

Older than you by nine years. Yes he has been fatherly, protective. But now you must protect him.

In a wild imagining begging the stiff-faced oncologist—*Take my bone marrow, is that possible, infuse it in him—save him!*

Crazed, pathetic. *You* would not utter such ravings, in your *right mind.*

Feel the strain of your husband's heart. His strong, durable, hope-ful heart. His will to live, to persevere in his being. You must hold him tightly! For the duration of his life, and beyond.

Transition to hospice. A turn in the road into a cul-de-sac neither of you had anticipated.

Disbelieving—*This can't be happening!*

And yet—*Is this happening? So soon?*

Acceleration nearing the point of impact. No time to plan what you might have planned—a more deliberate death, a shared death. For you have been taken by surprise. Your brain has been stunned, it is slow to react. You are limping, faltering behind. You are being pushed out onto a stage. You are blinking, blinded by dazzling light.

You have no script, no words. You cannot see an audience. You can only plead for a change in the script. For mercy.

I am here, I have your hand, I love you—please don't give up . . .

Hear yourself stammer in a pleading voice. In a faint, failing voice. In a voice that quavers with dread, yet hope: you will assure your husband that he is loved, yes he is very well loved. And because he is loved he is safe, he is being cared for, he will not be made to suffer. He will not feel any more pain, he will be protected from pain, the worst of the pain is beyond him now. He has been sedated, he is floating on a warm shimmering sea of Dilaudid dreams, a very high dosage, each day a higher dosage, and so he is safe now from further injury as he is safe from the cruelty of hope to which you have foolishly succumbed out of ignorance, naivete. But hope has vanished now, the air has cleared.

Like a train that has departed from a remote rural station and is already out of sight beyond the horizon—hope is gone.

And you are not on the train. No longer are you on the train.

As the remainder of your life together rapidly spools out.

THESE MIGHT BE MY FINAL DAYS—so Gerard said to you over the phone eleven days ago. He'd called you shortly after Dr. N___ had made his rounds that morning at 7:00 A.M.

These unexpected words, calmly uttered by your husband, a voice out of nowhere, a voice out of a cloud, these damning words which through a buzzing in your ears you'd seemed at first not to hear.

Inwardly crying—*No. No. No. No!*

The cell phone nearly slipped from your icy fingers to clatter onto a countertop.

(Will this be the last time Gerard calls you on your cell phone? Don't want to think yes, probably.)

By the time you arrived at the hospital you'd recovered from the shock of what you'd heard. You'd had time to prepare words of your own. Counter-arguments. Rejoinders.

Insisting that Gerard had to be mistaken, please would he not say such things, such upsetting things, it's distressing to you to hear such things, surely these are not his *final days*, for Dr. N___ had seemed hopeful only a few days previous speaking of *zapping* the smaller tumors, starting *immunotherapy* to shrink the large tumor—didn't he remember? Surely Dr. N___ would not have changed directions so quickly. And so it's misleading to be speaking of *final days* . . .

Trying to keep your face from shattering like glass.

I'm here. I have your hand. Can't you see I will never let you go, I love you so much.

You are angry, you will be bitter, no but you must not succumb to despair, don't allow yourself to (yet) recall how you'd had to beg the curiously terse, impassive Dr. N___ to order a scan of your husband's stomach and abdomen (for Gerard had been complaining of pain in that part of his body for weeks even as his respiratory distress was so much more critical, had to be treated immediately, the abdominal pain the oncologist dismissed as constipation and indeed yes, the patient did suffer from constipation, but this was a symptom and not a cause of his pain) and by the time the scan is taken the cancerous urethral growth is too large to be operable.

Why does Dr. N___ wait so long to order this scan? Why does Dr. N___ while nodding his head sagely seem not to hear you?

But not (yet) such thoughts. For it is another time: your husband is (still) alive.

Seeing him observing you with something like pity softened by tenderness the sudden thought came to you—*I will purchase opera tickets for August!* One of Gerard's favorite operas was Gluck's *Orpheus and Eurydice*, scheduled for the first week of August in the Santa Tierra Opera Festival.

In fact it was early April, which is months from August.

What are you to do with such a *fact*? Blunt and weighty as a rock in the hand.

A pledge that you believe Gerard will (still) be alive in August. A pledge that you have faith in whatever it is in which individuals *in extremis* have faith, that cannot be named.

Buy the tickets, show them to Gerard tomorrow! So that he will know that you have faith. (Unless he laughs sadly, shakes his head. Makes no comment at all.)

And now today is April 11. The thirteenth day of Gerard's intensive care. Doctors have convened that very morning—oncologist, pulmonologist, urologist, nephrologist. Gastrointestinal consultant. Palliative care physician, palliative care nurse practitioner.

There has been scheduled a (another/final) biopsy to check a metastasized tumor in one of your husband's kidneys. A (final) immunology treatment aimed at the (very large) urethral tumor.

Hope is the thing with feathers. But no.

Hope is the cruel thing. Banish hope!

With hope banished time will move more swiftly even as hours will move with the excruciating slowness of a clock distended by the gravity of the planet Jupiter.

You will hold your husband tighter, ever tighter. In Santa Tierra the wind comes in fierce hot gusts buffeting the windowpanes of the hospital room and so (it might seem that) you are holding your husband tight to prevent these gusts of wind from tearing you apart. Frantic to hold him, his shoulders, his torso, frantic to kiss his forehead that is both feverish and clammy, his cheeks that have become creased with fine cracks, his (beautiful) (blue-gray) (part-closed) eyes. (Will Gerard ever open his eyes fully again? And if he does open his eyes, will he see? Will he see *you*?) Declare that you will never leave him, you love him and will never cease loving him, he will never be alone, you will carry him with you forever in your heart; never have you, who take seriously a vow to speak/write truthfully,

clearly, without rhetoric or subterfuge, without resorting to such abstract clichés as *in your heart*, spoken in such a way; but then, never
have you found yourself so dazed, so unmoored, desperate to assure
your husband who is struggling to breathe that he is safe from suffering, by which you mean (of course) that the powerful opioids that
buoy him aloft will prevent him suffering the unspeakable pain that
awaits, if the opioid haze is allowed to evaporate, and so his suffering is bearable, or is promised to be bearable; it is not false for you to
claim to him that he is "safe"—as you would wish to think that you
are safe (though poised above an abyss: when this ordeal has run its
course you must decide whether you should step forward into that
abyss or cling out of cowardice to your diminished and left-behind
life) though you are (certainly) not safe for you are not sedated, you
have not been anesthetized against the ravaging torture of cancer,
cancers metastasized throughout your body; your skin bristles with
sensation, your every nerve, indeed it's as if the outermost layer of
your skin has been peeled away and you are vulnerable to the slightest
draft of air, lacerating the tender blood-tinged dermis beneath.

All this you will tell your beloved husband again, again and again
for each minute repeats itself, each hour, interminable because unfathomable as all finite spaces (like this hospital room on the seventh
floor of the Santa Tierra Cancer Center) contain infinities.

Again, and still, and again, and still with hypnotic certainty
begging your husband *Breathe!*—for you cannot imagine the world
without him, you cannot imagine any dimension of being that does
not include him; you cannot imagine your own life continuing, tormented by the possibility that each of your husband's breaths might
be his last, already your brave stoic husband has endured beyond the
expectations of the medical staff, continuing to breathe hoarsely, la-
boriously, convulsively, as a wrestler might struggle to breathe even as
his chest is being crushed in the grip of a cruel opponent; managing
to breathe though shuddering with the effort; managing to breathe

though whimpering with the effort; unless the whimpering is your own, the shuddering is your own, through hours of interminable days he will breathe, and he will breathe, as you bid him *Breathe!*—and he will pause ever longer in his breathing, each time the pause is longer, you are in torment, you are in your own private agony, holding your own indrawn breath waiting to hear your husband breathe, the gasping intake of breath, the sucked-at breath, the catch in his throat, a moist *click!*—you are desperate to bargain as a child might bargain *Don't let him stop, don't let him die*—*not yet* though you have nothing with which to bargain. You cannot bargain away your soul to any god or devil for you have no soul beyond your own faltering breath. You cannot bargain away your soul for if you had a soul, by now it is in tatters like a papier-mâché lantern battered in a windstorm. It is time for your husband to die, the medical staff has expressed amazement that he has endured so long persevering in this twilit state neither awake nor asleep, neither conscious nor unconscious; perhaps he is dreaming, perhaps he is dreaming of a frantic woman leaning over his hospital bed trying to embrace him, face wet with tears, face made ugly and contorted by tears, unrecognizable as his wife, determined to hold her husband fiercely in an embrace from which not even death can pry him.

Is this a dream? Can't be happening, must be a dream.

(But if we are dreaming together? Can we save each other!)

Not a floor beneath your feet but a kind of ice-sheet supporting the hospital bed in which your husband lies fixed in place with IV lines in his veins, ice-surface shining-blinding, your eyes blinded unable to see clearly, not daring to see clearly for you are immersed in the opioid dream that shimmers beneath your husband's bruised eyelids. Shimmering of dreams like reflections in ice. In the freezing water beneath ice. Almost, you can see these dreams. Quick-darting as fish in the luminous water beneath ice. You can feel them against your skinless arms—quivering, thrumming, heat of your husband's body in its struggle to remain alive even as it is being dragged down-ward beneath the glittering ice-surface to death and dissolution, to stammered words, grunts, dragged downward by the capricious cruel god of the high desert plateau with the name too terrible to be ut-tered aloud—*Ishtikini*. Pueblo-god of toothless laughter, god of eye-less sockets, Skull God, beast-god, scavenger-god poised to devour the body's organs as soon as life ceases to pulse through them: heart, brain, lungs, kidney, liver, stomach, intestines.

No one but you will remember—*But this man is heroic!* Struggling to breathe, to persist in breathing, even as his organs are failing. Slow realization of diminishment, loss. Gradual realization that each day, each hour the patient has been growing weaker, not gaining strength from the liquids dripping into his veins but un-nourished by them, no appetite, no longer capable of walking in the corridor as he'd done initially, not even making his way with a walker, only just able at last to sit upright in a wheelchair you push for him in the hospital corridor in a loop each day losing strength as he was not (re)gain-ing the weight he'd lost but losing more weight, his cheeks becom-ing sunken, eyes brimming with moisture when you'd squeezed his hands and assured him that he'd been a wonderful husband and he'd said *Wonderful?—but I failed you by dying.*

A wild startled laugh, a child's frightened laugh—*What are you saying? You are not dead, you are with me here. We are both alive . . .*

A spasm of coughing, your husband can't answer you, too weak to refute you as you insist he has been a wonderful husband, your life with him has been the happiest life you could imagine for yourself, it is the only life you could imagine for yourself, you do not want to live beyond this life. As he lapses into silence you will assure him another time that he is loved, he has been a wonderful husband who is loved, and he is safe because so loved, this is a safe place where he will not suffer needlessly, he will not suffer at all, you will never leave his side. As in the exhausting interminable hours to come you will hear your defiant voice wax and wane, wane and wax, growing fainter, growing stronger, and again faint, and again stronger as the undertow of your husband's dying tugs at you, tries to pull you under, still you are resolute—*Breathe! Darling, please breathe—don't stop.* And the stricken lungs suck at air, pure oxygen seeping into nostrils through a narrow plastic tube attached to the nose. Your own audacity will surprise you, the desperate strength of which you wouldn't have guessed yourself capable, as a swimmer who has never been tested in deep waters is surprised at her ability to keep herself afloat, to keep from drowning. You are determined that your husband will not give in, will not die and abandon you, not one moment too soon. Though by this time you will be so dazed with exhaustion your eyelids will droop, only barely you will comprehend what is happening in this hospital room, what an ordeal, what horror, why you are begging the man *Breathe! Breathe!—please . . .* for in this chilled space humming with monitors in this interminable interlude *out-of-time* there will be only the present tense in which you have gone without sleep and without food for how many hours since before dawn this morning, embracing the man to whom you have bravely joined your life, leaning over his body in the high bed, your neck aches with the strain, your shoulders ache with the strain, your throat aches with the strain of assuring this man tirelessly, defiantly that you love him, that he is safe, he will not feel pain, he will not be alone, how many days have passed, no idea how many days, hours, weeks while outside the hospital room the hot searing New Mexico winds continue to blow through sunlit daytime hours, gusts of wind bearing bits of mica, grit inhaled into nostrils, mouth, lungs, gusts of wind like the ferocious laughter of the desert gods, and after dusk the wind dies down, fades, and night is abruptly chill, no longer a warm terrain but the high desert plateau and you are made to realize how far you have journeyed, how many thousands of (reckless) miles to this place leaving behind your comfortable town house on Monroe Street, Cambridge, walls of books, bookcases in bedrooms and in bathrooms, bookcases in narrow corridors, stacks of books in the basement, books still boxed after the move of twelve years previous when bravely you'd vowed to yoke your lives together, laughing in very recklessness, in yearning and in love. *Do you take this man? I do, I do! Do you take this woman? Of course—I do . . .*

Sickness and in health. Till death do we part.

Recall with horror you'd uttered these words happily. As if *till death do we part* might be so interpreted: happily.

Damp with perspiration yet shivering clammy-skinned, anxious in terror of what's-to-come. In a film, ominous music. In the hospital room, only the sound of *breathing*.

Initially, first hospitalized, Gerard had been sharp-eyed, lucid.

Fits of coughing, bronchial infection, needing to be sedated because he could not sleep because unable to breathe without coughing but clear-minded, coherent, not yet subjected to a battery of tests, not yet invaded by powerful opioids that cloud his mind. Not yet transferred to the adjoining Cancer Center—a transference that dashes his spirits, and yours. Antibiotics, blood thinner, oxycodone. CAT scans, biopsies, fMRI. Initially the prognosis had not seemed ambiguous. Initially the first-detected cancerous tumors (lung, kidney) had appeared to be *slow-growing*. Even with this sobering news and in his new circumstances Gerard insisted upon working, furious at wasting so much time, goddamned bad luck, eight-month residency at the Institute and already the first month was passing with very little to show for it. Desperate to work, refusing medication that made him groggy, or anyway refusing it for as long as he could, giving you instructions what to bring from his office at the Institute, how you might assist him with the four-hundred-page copyedited manuscript of his next book provocatively titled *The Human Brain and Its Discontents*; it was Gerard's custom to answer each query from a copy editor in meticulous cursive script on yellow Post-its affixed to manuscript pages, thus a typical copyedited manuscript of Gerard's was riddled with yellow Post-its like miniature prayer flags.

Maybe I can get something accomplished here, maybe my time out-of-time *won't be totally wasted.*

Wanting to think that his hospitalization in the Santa Tierra Cancer Center was nothing more serious than a therapeutic *time-out*, an opportunity for concentrated work.

Hope is the poisoned bait. *Men eat of it and die.*

Not (yet) realizing that hope is the distraction, the deceit. Hope is what you must not allow to seep into your bloodstream. Hope is what you must never believe. Hope will break your heart for hope muffles the oncologist's carefully chosen words: *Dr. McManus, I have scheduled the palliative care physician to speak with you and your wife* but neither of you hear these words, instead you hear *CAT scan, biopsy, radiation, "zap" the small tumors, immunotherapy to shrink the urethral cancer, physical therapy, high-protein diet.* Amid the succession of tests inflicted upon your husband you come to appreciate the word: *patient.* For it is *patience* that is required if one is to become (again) well: if the bloodwork is to become normal; lungs, heart, kidneys, stomach, urethra—again (improbably?) normal. If the fine-tuned organism that is the patient's body is to function, not thrown off course by a misfiring of neurons, a brittle, thus easily broken rib; blood clots in thigh, lungs, kidney; a fit of spasmodic coughing that undoes days of recovery, like the smashing of fine crystal by an idiot. And when the appetite dims, and ceases; when the patient who has loved food shakes his head irritably—*No, not this. No*; when the patient is impatient, when the patient is "not himself"—what's to be done?

What has been done, that can't be undone?

Then, time slows. Days, nights pass inexorably yet time has slowed. Each day, each night is interminable. Each hour. There is the possibility—(is there? or is the wife of the afflicted man imagining this?)—of a blood marrow transplant if the proper donor can be found (in time). (Is Michaela McManus a proper donor? You have begged to be tested, why has Dr. N___ not scheduled a spinal tap?) A bone marrow transplant is one of the most difficult of medical procedures as it is one of the most expensive, you understand. Yet the key words seem to you *in time*. A donor must be found, the procedure must begin almost immediately, why is everything so slow in the Santa Tierra Cancer Center?

Skies of sharp-chiseled clouds wounding to the eye, such beauty unknown in the East where the cityscape devours three-quarters of the sky and the air is porous with haze. Running along the Charles River embankment, wiping your eyes of a thin suety secretion, airborne toxins from vehicle exhaust and industrial waste sucked into the tender pink tissue of the lungs, how much healthier to live in Santa Tierra, New Mexico, at a higher altitude though (in fact) it is difficult to sleep here, air and blood are so thin. Head throbs with pain for you haven't been able to sleep for more than a few fitful minutes at a time for several nights, disoriented, short-breathed, for already the vigil has begun, before you realize what is happening the terrible vigil has begun pressing toward its (inevitable) end like a landslide gaining force and momentum as it descends a mountain. As each night is identical with the others each night feels *impersonal, unrecorded*. A night when you've been at the house, not *home* (you and your husband have never called this uncomfortable place *home*, only *the house*), staggering now down the hill, like a sleepwalker descending the walkway to the Institute grounds and through the Institute grounds to the first street, and to the second street near-deserted at this hour, at last to Buena Vista Boulevard with its tall white lights and now a half-mile marching rapidly, breaking into a jog as you near the hospital, panting, praying the most abject of prayers *Dear God let him be all right, let him be alive—one more time . . .* indulging in the futility of prayer to a god in whom you have never believed but determined to try all stratagems as a desperate gambler placing numerous bets in the face of catastrophic loss.

Approach the high-rise beige stucco Cancer Center knowing yourself awaited impatiently in room 771. For Gerard has tormented you with calls that morning: first call at 5:16 A.M., second call at 6:20 A.M., third call at 6:47 A.M. by which time you are fully awake and teeth chattering with dread/excitement on your feet preparing to leave for the hospital without troubling to shower, even to change the clothes you'd worn yesterday which you had not removed when you collapsed into bed, for this is still a time when Gerard could make calls on his cell phone, express bemused exasperation with himself, impatience, not (yet) realizing that no attitude of his toward his medical condition will have the slightest effect upon that condition as no attitude however laudable, however articulately expressed, will have the slightest effect upon whether he will live beyond the next forty-eight hours, daring even to laugh, to apologize—*I'm so sorry, Michaela. That this has happened, screwing up our time here in—wherever we are . . . In New Mexico, in such a beautiful place, Jesus!—me in the God-damned hospital . . .*

And you assure him—*But you'll be out soon. Then . . .*

Interminable days slide into a rapid week, a week becomes weeks, one day you stare at the calendar astonished that so much time has passed and (yet) Gerard is not (yet) recovered enough to be discharged from the hospital even to a rehabilitation facility. You imagine yourself a determined swimmer, determined not to drown, determined to swim at slightly beyond your capacity managing to keep your head above the water, managing to keep the sun-warmed water from being swallowed when you gasp for breath, managing to keep the sun-warmed water from being inhaled up your nostrils and into your head-cavity, in a way you are (almost) proud of yourself, your endurance so much more than you might have predicted.

Yet: flee from the scene, when Gerard is taken away for a scan, an

X-ray, an MRI. Once beyond the tall shadow of the Cancer Center feel a shot to the heart of sheer adrenaline, begin to walk very fast, legs rapid as a robot's rapid-pumping legs. Push yourself until you too are panting for air, for oxygen, breathless in this high altitude where the air is thin as a razor blade for otherwise you are incapable of sleeping at night: cannot turn off your dazzled brain to sleep at night: a brain glaring like fluorescent lighting that will not let you sleep at night: a brain buzzing and crackling like an insect zapper, like the most lurid crackling fires of Hell, that will not let you sleep at night.

Exhaust yourself until you are literally staggering. Interminable days beginning before dawn, ending after midnight. Collapse onto your bed fully clothed, too tired even to unlace and kick off the pink-and-gray running shoes with the dark-rose laces, Gerard helped you pick out in a runners' store in Cambridge, Mass., a lifetime ago.

Falling, fainting. Down down *down*.

And then in the morning, waking with a jolt. *Is he——?* But no, he is not beside you.

Not in the bathroom running water. Not humming to himself. Not coughing. Not here.

(Terrified) (in a state of trance) running panting down "scenic" curving Vista Drive, keeping to the far left of the (single-lane) road as vehicles pass you headed downhill, very few at this hour. Scarcely seeing blossoming cottonwoods, cactus. Wisteria, lavender, rosemary grown to a height unimaginable in the Northeast.

Your first full day in Santa Tierra, walking down Vista Drive into the town with Gerard, holding hands like young lovers. How like a honeymoon this visit would be!—you hadn't really had a honeymoon when you'd first married.

The tale you tell yourself. The tale you tell, retell yourself.

The tale that explains nothing while (seemingly) explaining all. What had been initially diagnosed as bacterial pneumonia turns out in a vertiginous succession of tests to include a blood clot in the (infected) lung, a blood clot in the right thigh, small tumors attached to kidney, lungs; eventually, after an inexplicable delay, a tumor attached to the urethra, at 4-by-14 centimeters too large to remove surgically. A strategy is planned of radiation, chemotherapy, immunotherapy. But what of the patient's high creatinine reading, is there a possibility of renal failure? (A kidney CT reveals an advanced kidney condition of which the wife knew nothing: the husband had, evidently, ignored prostate symptoms for years.) What of metastasized cancer to lymph nodes? To the brain? What of swollen ankles, wrists, right arm? Though each hour, each day passes with excruciating slowness yet it is all happening very quickly, weight-loss, sunken cheeks, dulled eyes, opioids and delirium, a succession of doctors, a succession of tests, a succession of plastic food trays carried into the room to be presented to the patient, a succession of scarcely touched meals, a succession of untouched meals, until at last one morning you are clasping at your husband's hand crying *Don't leave me! Don't leave me!*—begging like a child, helpless sobbing like a child, how can this frantic woman be *you?*—dissolving in tears, and more tears, never an end to tears, in one who'd claimed (boasted) that she rarely cried, hadn't cried in decades, not since her parents' deaths, a beloved grandmother's death, emptied of all tears but crying now whenever she is alone, whenever she is in a private place, trying not to cry in the patient's presence because that will only frighten and demoralize him.

All is for the patient. In the service of the patient-husband. You, the wife, will make any bargain.

At the husband's bedside pleading *Can you try to eat, Gerard? Please, try to eat? The soup today is tomato bisque, it tastes quite good actually, I think you might like it . . . no? The yogurt is blueberry, your favorite, will you try some? Please?* As one might plead with a recalcitrant child. Lifting a white plastic spoon to your husband's mouth which he considers for a brief frowning moment then brushes away with a dismissive gesture that chills your heart.

Please please please try to eat. You have lost fifteen pounds, you must eat . . .

Hear yourself: beg.

Risking your husband's ire: beg.

The (woman) palliative care physician has spoken carefully to you as the wife of the patient-husband. The (woman) palliative care nurse-practitioner has spoken carefully to you. They are kindly, tactful, soft-spoken, tender. The floor nurses and nurses' aides have prepared you with their somber smiles and courtesy, the oncologist Dr. N___ under whose auspices Gerard McManus has been admitted to the Santa Tierra Cancer Center has deftly avoided you, your reddened eyes, raw ravaged gaze which is (you will see in time) just another way of preparing you for the worst for to the nattily dressed Dr. N___ who favors colorful linen shirts beneath his white jacket, at times even a bow tie, the loss of any patient is an embarrassment. And the (possible, potential) loss of a patient as distinguished as Gerard McManus of the Santa Tierra Institute for Advanced Research is an acute embarrassment, an occasion for artful circumlocution, awkward jokes and allusions obscure even to Gerard McManus who nonetheless tries to laugh politely when such a response seems warranted.

You don't laugh at Dr. N___'s awkward jokes. *You* stare hungrily at Dr. N___'s mask of a face willing the eyes in that mask to engage with you which very rarely they will do.

And now it is later. Somehow, it has become later. Days passing into weeks, and so it is *later.* You'd been meaning to go back, turn back, you and Gerard both, review exactly what happened, the sequence of events including the initial arrival at the Albuquerque airport, so much to remember, to maintain in chronological order!— with the excruciatingly slow yet swift passage of time you assume that there will be a *time-out* to allow you to comprehend what is happening, and yet—though you have been prepared for the decline, you are not (as it turns out) at all prepared for the (actual) decline, not rapid at first, yes but then rapid, and seemingly irreversible: weight-loss, dehydration, renal failure, the pressure of the (4-by-14 centimeter) urethral tumor on the stomach causing nausea, impossible for the patient-husband (who happens to be Gerard) to endure the strain on his organs much longer, heart, lungs, kidneys, liver; he has not eaten a meal in weeks, what seemed at first a snobbish disdain for mediocre hospital food in which (almost) one could take a kind of perverse pride has been revealed as a symptom of pathology, and not exquisite taste; even if he tries now, he cannot eat; has barely eaten at all for the past week; if he tries to swallow even soft foods he gags, if he tries to swallow even liquids he gags, he is clearly very exhausted, his ankles and wrists are badly swollen, his urine is being retained in his (hard, swollen) bladder, such extreme edema in itself can be lethal and so of course you must prepare yourself for the end, for his final minutes; you must prepare yourself, yet your mind drifts away in a vapor of unknowing; recall when you'd first met, at a Murray Perahia recital in Cambridge, a meeting of pure chance, introduced to each other by a mutual acquaintance who would never afterward figure in your lives.

At first sight. Well—almost.

But yes, I think we both knew.

Clasping hands with a stranger! For that is the custom.

And now, years later the catastrophic end. Nearing the catastrophic end. And now, the price that must be paid for such happiness.

Too large to be removed surgically. When you'd heard this, you'd known. Gerard had known.

Another time clasping the man's hand. That same hand. For in that instant, there could be no words. And this time, the hand that had been so warm, so strong, so welcoming years ago felt cold, and not so responsive.

But where will love abide?—you are wondering. When the husband's body has been taken from you.

Such thoughts you cannot retain. In the instant in which such a thought passes through your mind, it is gone.

BREATHE! I LOVE YOU.

Alone together now. At last alone. Not to be interrupted by the intrusion of medical staff. No more meals, all meals have ceased. No more checking of vital signs, all such routines have ceased. Tell yourself that this is desired. This is wished-for. This is the promise made to you: you alone can comfort your (dying) husband, you can rub his cracked lips with balm, you can wipe his forehead with a cool compress, he can (perhaps) hear your soft-murmured words, though he (probably) can't respond he can (perhaps) hear you as you whisper to him embracing him in your arms, murmuring to him another time how you love him, what a wonderful husband he has been and how happy you've been in your marriage; the tale you tell, tell and retell is how he has changed your life forever; even as his breathing has become a torment to him, and a torment to hear, that hoarse labored breathing, that strangled breathing, the agonizing pause of seconds between breaths, and when you think *This is the end, no more* there is another gasping breath, and still another, and another breath quavering with effort as if a great boulder were being pushed away from the mouth of a cave to flood the cave with sunshine, to free the spirit trapped in the darkness of the cave. So often during the past several days a wild elation has swept through you—*No. He will never die, this will never end. It has gone on forever, it will not end. I will not let it end.* And halfway you have come to believe, since the start of your husband's hospitalization nearly twenty days ago, that this interlude, this ordeal, will not end, very easily it might continue for a very long time, and in the interim it is (quite) possible that a new procedure for shrinking metastasized cancers will be discovered, will be made available, at the Santa Tierra Cancer Center it is (quite) possible that this radical new procedure will be adopted, perhaps there will be a *drug trial* in which Gerard McManus might be enrolled, none of this is far-fetched in the slightest, you don't need to believe in miracles, indeed you *do not believe in miracles* in order to believe this. For you love him so much, it is a torment to you. You should release him yet you cannot possibly release him but continue to beg him *Oh darling breathe! Breathe!*—you are paralyzed with fear, you are in despair of losing this man you love more than you love yourself, you have no wish to survive him, naively and vaguely you'd planned to bring sleeping pills to the room, a handful of barbiturates from your cache at the house, to (somehow) manage to swallow enough pills to cease breathing even as your husband ceases breathing, a romantic fantasy in which you'd indulged yourself in an exhausted state, yet (of course) this fantasy cannot possibly be enacted, if you'd wanted to die with your husband in your arms you'd have had to prepare a strategy, you'd have had to make arrangements beforehand to remove your husband from the Cancer Center and to establish a hospice in your residence where you would have privacy for such a (noble?) act but (of course) you'd made no arrangements, days and weeks have passed and now it is too late for you'd done nothing more than make tentative inquiries, you have been so distracted by your husband's ordeal, so mesmerized by his suffering, and by your own constant realization that you have no more control over what is happening to your husband and to you than if the two of you were dried leaves blown in the searing-hot desert winds.

Breathe! Don't. Ever. Stop.

Madness! You cannot stop begging your husband, you cannot relinquish him, in terror of losing him, even as he struggles to breathe like a fish on land convulsing as he suffocates in air. Sobbing helpless and broken, the distraught wife, bereft of all shame, all inhibition, trying now to hold his body in both your arms, pressing your hot damp face in the crook of his neck pleading still for him not to leave you, not to abandon you, paralyzed with horror at what is happening, the culmination of weeks, days, hours, the culmination of a man's life of forty-eight years; this singular interminable day that began at dawn and has continued for twelve, thirteen, now fourteen hours as you gradually realize that Death is already in the room, Death has seeped into the room without your knowing, in a corner of the room at the ceiling there is Death, a darkening shadow, a stain, a dark star-stain radiating outward like an eclipse of the sun that is an eclipse of your life.

You know, you understand. Yet you cannot know, and you cannot understand. You are crazed, hysterical. You have lost all sense of decency. Crying *No! Breathe! Don't leave me—no!* even as your exhausted husband is dying in your arms, a final sharp intake of breath and a long anguished trembling pause and a final heaving sigh of profound weariness that is the death-sigh, the last exhalation of a man's life.

This sigh, you will never forget. This sigh, you will hear virtually every hour of every day of the life remaining to you.

This sigh, and the silence that follows like the silence after a thunderclap.

3

Post-Mortem

Mrs. McManus?—you can remain with your husband as long as you wish.

We will be waiting out in the corridor.

4

Time-Out-of-Time

It was a season of hot searing winds by day. Stony-cold still air by night. A season in their (joint, married) lives that was *out-of-time*: an eight-month residency for Gerard McManus at the Institute for Advanced Research, at Santa Tierra, New Mexico, where they knew no one. Twenty-seven miles north of Albuquerque, where they knew no one.

Indeed, they knew no one in all of New Mexico where neither had ever lived or even visited.

Here was a new terrain. A high desert plateau, battalions of sculpted clouds, dark-bruised El Greco skies that drew the eye helplessly upward, intimidated by the sharp hurtful blade of beauty.

And the air, at 7,875 feet above sea level pristine-clear, white-tinged, conspicuously thinner than the (urban, sullied, near-sea-level) air to which they were accustomed in Cambridge, Mass.

In this stark lunar landscape they couldn't seem to catch their breaths. Especially Gerard who'd had asthma as a child and remained susceptible to respiratory infections.

Michaela who ran for an hour in the early morning beside the Charles River in Cambridge was discomforted to be winded within minutes when she ran along a canyon trail in Santa Tierra or climbed hillside steps too quickly. Awakened from sleep in the night by a panicky sensation of being unable to breathe as if a pillow had been placed over her nose and mouth, or a disembodied hand, or a cloth soaked in ether . . . Not realizing at first where she was, what place this could be, so sparely furnished, with stark white walls, vertical panels of glass, a moon so glaring-white it might have been radioactive visible through the bedroom wall—in fact, a window in relationship to their bed where Michaela would have sworn a window couldn't be.

But this was a new house. In a new landscape. Stark and stony sere-colors in which natural light could be blinding. And this setting incongruously festooned with exotic cacti, wisteria thick-vined as boa constrictors, hollyhocks, sagebrush, lavender and rosemary grown to heights unimaginable in Massachusetts.

A yet-uninhabited house. A house to be claimed as *theirs*.

Inside the house there was surprisingly little color. For this was a private residence built in the stark style of Frank Lloyd Wright who'd himself designed the original Institute building in 1951.

The interior atmosphere of the house was that of a museum of minimalist objects. Fierce Native American war masks, on the fireplace mantel and on walls; tall thick coarse-textured candles that looked as if they would emit clouds of noxious smoke, if lit; crude wooden carvings of various creatures ranging from Gila monsters to potbellied deities, or demons, that might be mistaken for Buddhas if you didn't look closely. A droop-breasted demon-goddess with a shrieking mouth, sharp curving claws for fingers, and what appeared to be (neither Michaela nor Gerard cared to inspect too closely) a raw gaping vagina prominent between her spread legs. A male figure with a disproportionately large skull from which strands of coarse black (human?) hair sprouted to his shoulders, gaping mouth, swollen belly and erect skinny penis curving upward like a snake—as Michaela would learn, the Scavenger God Ishtikini whose ravenous appetite can never be appeased.

In the master bedroom was a squat froglike creature with bulging pop eyes, deep slit-nostrils in place of a nose, pitted skin that looked as if it were made of calcified mud—this, a hardwood carving several sizes larger than a bullfrog. Strangest was a life-sized stag head made of myriad layered strips of leather held in place with staples resembling tiny seeds; its eyes were mismatched marbles and its twelve-inch horns were the real horns of a stag, one of which was cracked and hung askew.

"Oh, God! What is *this*!"—Michaela cried in exasperation.

These artifacts, or whatever they were, Michaela came to dislike, and so (stealthily) hid them away in closets and drawers, hoping that Gerard wouldn't miss them; if he did, she would explain that the ugly things weren't *art*, and she doubted that they were even authentic Native American.

Especially Michaela disliked the (obscene) female figure, that could only have been created by a male artist. So awful, Michaela not only hid it in a closet but draped a towel over it.

Authentic indigenous art they did want to own, certainly. Before their trip Gerard had researched the work of the most revered regional tribal artists—Navajo, Taos Pueblo—which he planned to purchase, to bring back to the house on Monroe Street, Cambridge. These were beautiful carvings primarily of animals, handwoven rugs and wall hangings, quilts that "told stories."

Yes! Michaela agreed. The household in which she'd come to live as Gerard's wife twelve years before could do with some reviving.

Her heart was suffused with hope, this *time-out-of-time* would be the honeymoon they'd never had time for.

GO AWAY! LEAVE HERE!

You are not wanted here.

Almost, Michaela could see the figure squatting on her chest—

hunched, stunted, with coarse savage hair to its shoulders and glaring eyes that were (yet) blind. As if the humanoid creature had discovered her by her smell, in the dark.

Waking panicked. Paralyzed beneath the creature's weight.

Then, managing to throw off panic like a soft spiderweb clinging to her face. Not wanting to disturb Gerard for with the rational part of her brain she understood that she had to be dreaming.

. . . not wanted here.

. . . in danger here.

The voice was distinct. A thistle-like rustling in her ear, an approximation of a human whisper.

Sitting up then in bed, cautiously. As her racing heartbeat slowly returned to normal.

Sleeping with another person is a responsibility, a trust: you must not intrude into the other's dreaming.

Above all, you must not alarm the other with your (baseless) fears.

It was the new place, the new bed, not very comfortable, yes and the new, thin air, a sense of unease, nothing more. Having to adjust the expectation that she would be waking in the (familiar) bed, bedroom, house in Cambridge where furniture had become so familiar it was virtually invisible to their eyes, walls were lined with books floor to ceiling like the interior of a cocoon, and the exterior landscape scarcely impinged upon the interior at all: if there were views in the house on Monroe Street they were modest, urban views of deciduous trees, the house next door, a patch of cloudy sky.

Stiffly beside her Gerard slept with his back to her. Michaela hesitated wanting to touch him, gently; caress his shoulder, his arm, his side, his flank; would have liked to press her lips against the smooth cool skin of his back and with her fingertips trace the archipelagos there of freckles and moles like Braille, a secret language only she, the wife, could decipher.

But Gerard did not wish to be touched just now. Michaela knew.

For several years following his divorce Gerard had lived alone. Desperately lonely at first but then by degrees beginning to feel relief—for human relations are so complicated, so resistant of interpretation. Like a foreign language when one is too old to easily learn a foreign language.

Alone had become a natural state for Gerard, intimacy was sometimes not so attractive to him.

Michaela too had lived alone for several years following the end of a relationship. But living alone, sleeping alone, defining herself as essentially alone was not a condition Michaela wished to preserve. She could not bear a life without intimacy or at least the possibility of intimacy and so she lay very still (like a bride) (a virginal bride) and waited to see if Gerard would turn to her, speak softly to her. If he might gather her in his arms as sometimes he did, unexpectedly, with a tender little laugh.

Hey. Darling. Love you!

Or—You awake? Kiss me!

But Gerard did not turn to Michaela and gather her in his arms. He did not call her darling or command her playfully to kiss.

And so how lonely, in the night! Beside a husband wishing to sleep and not to be wakened by his wife at just this moment for (it would seem) there remains an infinity of such moments in their life together.

Never come to the end of kissing.

Unthinkable

You know that I love you.
. . . will never abandon you.
My promise when we were married.

FOR IF I ABANDON YOU *that is death.*
That is the death of you, and that is the death of me.
And so, we must not let them separate us—not for a heartbeat.

YOU KNOW THAT—DON'T YOU?

A Rare Parasite

Twenty-two days after their move from Cambridge, Mass., to Santa Tierra, New Mexico, Gerard fell ill.

Wanting to blame the high thin air of New Mexico. Relentless searing winds that blew for much of each day drying their sinuses and leaving a fine film of dust in their mouths precipitating Gerard's symptoms: the harsh dry cough, the wracking but (mostly) phlegm-less cough, the cough-that-causes-sharp-chest-pain.

Just asthma, Gerard insisted. For which he (already) took medication each morning.

Michaela protested: this harsh, hacking cough did not sound like Gerard's asthma-cough, she was certain . . . She would find a doctor for him, if he wished.

"Don't be ridiculous, Michaela. It's nothing."

Nothing! Surely it was *not nothing*, the way Gerard coughed in the early morning, in the bathroom, often with the fan whirring to disguise the alarming staccato sounds like the retorts of a pistol.

Repeating, she would find a doctor in Santa Tierra, if he wished.

Well, he *did not wish.*

Eventually Gerard conceded that the cough did "sound" bad: he would double the asthma dose.

Since she'd first known him Gerard had resisted any concern of

Michaela's for his well-being. Physical intimacy did not bring with it the ease of intimacy in other regards. Michaela was not one to intrude on the privacy of others and so, with Gerard, there was a line she dared not cross, invading the man's privacy.

Excuse me: that's private.

Sorry. That's private.

Why d'you want to know? That's private.

Absurd! Yet, Michaela was made to know that Gerard felt strongly about this.

That brick wall you confront, in the other. Eventually.

The wall that is the end of intimacy. The wall that separates.

The wall of unreason, intransigence. The wall that you might laugh at, which (yet) remains, unyielding.

Michaela could not comprehend: her (genial, reasonable) husband quite enjoyed Michaela asking him about many facets of his life, dating back to early childhood; but he resisted a certain sort of attention that suggested weakness, infirmity, aging. A sort of attention that suggested prying, prurience. Unclothed in Michaela's presence, Gerard wasn't self-conscious in the slightest—but he would flare up in annoyance if Michaela discovered something about him that might be considered a health issue, a medical problem. For Gerard was not a husband who welcomed a wife's maternal solicitude. *He* was the dominant personality in the marriage, by their tacit agreement.

Days in succession Michaela was forced to listen without commentary to her husband coughing this new, harsh, hacking cough that pained her to hear. As if something had crawled into his chest and was choking him to death—*that humanoid figure squatting on her chest.*

Drawn by the heat of his blood, it was. One of the squat demon-figures that dwelled in the rented house . . .

Go away! Leave here! You are not wanted here.

Something terrible will happen to you, if you remain.

But where could they go? They'd only just arrived in Santa Tierra. Their house in Cambridge was rented through August. Gerard would never have consented to give up his appointment to the prestigious research institute, that paid its fellows more than the Institute for Advanced Study at Princeton.

Undermine a man's pride, you risk injuring his vanity. And a man *is* his vanity.

Each morning Gerard was eager to get to the Institute office to which he'd had his console computer, boxes of books, papers, documents shipped from Cambridge. It was touching to Michaela, how enthusiastic her husband was about his work, as if he were, not a distinguished historian of science, but one of his own post-docs. (Michaela had acquired an academic appointment for the spring term also but a less distinguished one, teaching a weekly memoir workshop at a branch of the University of New Mexico, for a modest salary; she had no office nearby, and would not have required one in any case.)

It was a twenty-minute walk from the hillside house to the Institute campus, on a flagstone walkway that descended to the quadrangle of buildings of surpassing beauty and strangeness, made of scorched-looking desert rocks, untreated wood and poured concrete, tall vertical glass panels in the tradition of Frank Lloyd Wright. Gerard's office in a newer building overlooked a courtyard reminiscent of a Zen garden of polished black stones, dwarf cacti, waxy colorless flowers that looked artificial—yet, Michaela discovered that these were in fact living flowers when out of curiosity she stooped to pinch a petal and it fell at once to the ground, bruised.

How strange!—Michaela recoiled, as if she'd unwittingly killed a living thing.

In this season of hot searing winds by day that blew ceaselessly by night with a high-pitched whistling that insinuated itself into the very coils and honeycombs of the brain like a rare parasite.

7

The Man Who Never Dreams

He has claimed that he never dreams. You have told him, maybe you just don't recall your dreams.

He insists: it's analogous to amnesia. If you don't remember an event, it hasn't happened.

What isn't imprinted in the brain cells doesn't "exist"—it hasn't really happened.

You protest: But of course it has happened! If you feel pain, you have felt pain . . .

No. If there is no recording of the pain in your brain it didn't happen—to you.

It may have "happened"—to a living sensate being. But if your brain didn't record it, and you have no memory of it, it didn't happen to you.

8

Respite

And then it is revealed to you: it has not (yet) happened.

Whatever it is that will happen, that will tear your life in two, not clearly and cleanly as you might tear a sheet of paper along a folded edge but roughly, horribly, as you might tear a leg or an arm from a living body, has not (yet) happened.

What relief! Still your husband is lying more or less as you'd left him the previous night in his hospital bed on the seventh floor of the Santa Tierra Cancer Center.

Quickly you see: potted begonias from the Institute, on a windowsill; a bouquet of carnations you'd brought Gerard yourself, wilting in a plastic vase; a wicker basket of fruits you'd brought for Gerard, mostly untouched; several days' accumulation of the *New York Times* and such professional journals as *Science, Nature, Journal of Neuroscience*; on the bedside table a stack of Gerard's books, notebooks, offprints as well as his laptop and cell phone. Nothing has changed in the nighttime hours you've been away—a relief!

And yet, for a moment you stand in the doorway of room 771 staring at the figure in the bed. *Is* this your husband, or is he a stranger?

An older man, of an age beyond fifty, propped up against pillows in his bed, a sprawl of notes, printed pages, professional journals about him though he doesn't appear to be perusing them. Slackbellied, listless in a hospital-issue gown. Both arms bruised, an IV tube attached to one of the arms.

The face, of an alarming pallor, especially about the eyes; stiff graying hair, white-stubbly jaws, vacant/melancholy gaze in the instant before he sees you and the eyes sharpen into focus: "Ah, Michaela! My love."

My love. Hearing these words you feel your heart suffused with joy. *Still alive! My husband is still alive.*

9

Wait

Of course you want to summon his family. His (adult) children. But quickly he says *no*.

"Not yet."

"But—when?"

"Just not yet."

He is not an alarmist. (*You* are the alarmist.)

Gerard McManus is not a person who seeks attention, wishes to interfere in the lives of others. Hesitant to contact his (adult) children for fear (you sense) that they will not rush to see him in faraway New Mexico unless it is made to appear (not by him: by you, the alarmist) that the situation is urgent.

"We can wait. If it's a false alarm, we don't want them here."

"But—wait how long?"

"I'll tell you. *Wait*."

AS HE'D REFUSED TO WEAR a hospital gown, initially. Insisted upon his own clothes: short-sleeved blue shirt of a fabric that never wrinkled even when slept-in, much-laundered jeans, white cotton socks. And when he was sitting in a chair, or walking about the corridor hauling the IV gurney behind him, sandals.

Five days, a week he'd hold out. Bravely. Stubbornly. Until finally it became expedient to surrender his own clothes, switch to hospital-issue clothing. By this time the patient was too sick to care much for appearances.

Still you would not have guessed: your husband would never wear his own clothing again.

You would not have guessed: your husband would never call you on his cell phone again.

You would not have guessed: your husband would never see his (adult) children again.

10

Spinoza

Gerard's heavily annotated paperback copy of *Spinoza: Ethics* you have brought to his hospital room at his request. As Gerard has wittily observed, he is working against a deadline.

This remark you hear, you smile to hear, you do not wince to hear, as Gerard has alluded to a *deadline* several times since being hospitalized.

In fact, the copyedited/revised manuscript of *The Human Brain and Its Discontents* is due back at the Harvard University Press within the month.

Gerard has been working intermittently on it for weeks but has been slowed down considerably by "these circumstances" as he calls the inconvenience of being hospitalized.

It is essential for Gerard to check quotations from the *Ethics* against quotations scattered through *The Human Brain and Its Discontents*. For this he has enlisted your help going through the hefty manuscript searching for yellow Post-its that reference Spinoza.

Try to listen to Gerard speak of Spinoza in some slantwise relationship to cognitive neuroscience but you are distracted this morning, you absorb little of what he says. It is the voice, or nearly the voice, of Gerard McManus's public persona, that dazzles audiences with such startling and original insights but all that you will remember

afterward is a skein of nonsense syllables that mean absolutely nothing to you.

"*Every (physical) substance is necessarily infinite. Every (non)physical
substance is necessarily finite.*"

Your head fills with static. *Infinite, finite!*

All that is crucial is the next lab report. What is the patient's
white blood cell count, what is the patient's degree of oxygen intake,
what is the patient's creatinine reading.

What is the "progress" of the tumors.

The first time you'd heard Gerard speak in public he'd told an
onstage interviewer that reading Spinoza's *Ethics* at the age of eighteen, a university freshman, changed his life forever: "Every molecule
of my being."

As later, reading Schopenhauer, Nietzsche, Wittgenstein would
further alter his life: "Made me the person I am today."

A boastful sort of humility, it had seemed. Yet sincere.

Yet now you want to protest, angrily—*No. That is not true. Your
parents who loved you made you what you are. Those who were tender
with you when you were vulnerable, and protected you, and hid from you
that they protected you, and those who love you now, and are protecting
you now—these have made you what you are. Not men you never knew,
who never knew you. And not books.*

11

Bed of Serpents

In damp rumpled bedclothes unable to sleep and when lapsing into sleep discovering yourself in a bed of writhing serpents that causes you to wake in terror—*Oh! Oh God.*

Throwing yourself from the bed, one of your knees striking the hardwood floor—*God help me . . .*

TERROR OF SLEEP.

Terror of lying sleepless through the night.

The Vigil II

But there is no beginning.
And there is no end.

RUN! MUST RUN! DOWNHILL/UPHILL. TO/FROM the Santa Tierra Cancer Center, Buena Vista Boulevard, Santa Tierra, New Mexico.

A tangle of snakes pursues you. Churning writhing snakes clammy-skinned against your arms, legs, naked belly.

. . . dreamt that I was lying in a bed of serpents, woke screaming and terrified and what d'you think it must mean? That I'm afraid of something, I suppose.

ACCUSTOMED TO REHEARSING LITTLE ANECDOTES with which to entertain Gerard when Gerard is in a mood to be entertained.

As through your life from a time before memory you have presented yourself to others through little anecdotes—"Stories." The pitch of your voice tends to lightness and airiness at such times; you do not wish to suggest to your listener(s), or to anyone, that you take yourself too seriously.

Who does she think she is?

Thinking she has a right to live!

Occasionally you require advice from your husband, or sympathy; your husband is very good with advice, but he is warily good with sympathy as if he has learned (from his experience as a parent?) that immediate and unqualified sympathy may be counter-productive, encouraging weakness in others.

And so you take care never to appear self-pitying to your husband, for Gerard has little patience with self-pity in others as in himself.

But now since Gerard has become ill, preoccupied with his own mortality, you have no one to whom you might tell such entertaining anecdotes.

No one to whom you can define yourself. No one to take note of *you*.

If there is no one to hear the narrative of our existence do we in fact exist?

What bravado in such statements composed in a void for no one to hear, no one to admire.

If there is no one to admire us, do we exist?

And the corollary: *If there is no one to love us, do we merit existence?*

Tormented by such thoughts. Invaded by such thoughts as by an infection in the blood.

Run! Must run!

Never stop running.

IN THE EARLY MORNING she walked swiftly downhill to the Cancer Center and in the late night she walked (less swiftly) back up to the house from the Cancer Center.

Good to be exhausted! Good.

Conscious of her lungs filling/emptying. Tissue-sacs. Razor-thin air that yielded a paucity of oxygen to her brain.

When not at her husband's bedside the wife is consumed with anxiety that something terrible will happen to him in her absence.

Yet, once a week on Thursday afternoon Michaela teaches a three-hour memoir workshop thirty miles away at a branch of the University of New Mexico in suburban Albuquerque.

It is a terrible risk for her. Slipping into another dimension—impersonating another self.

Not the desperate self, the desperate wife flailing arms, legs, in an effort to keep from drowning.

Managed not to miss a single class since Gerard was hospitalized and indeed rarely mentions the class to Gerard who may have forgotten that Michaela has any sort of occupation outside his hospital room.

Not wanting to think that Gerard may have forgotten, may be in the process of forgetting, exactly who Michaela is in his life.

A second wife can only be—well, second.

The first wife is the mother of the children. In the deepest area of the husband's brain, first wife/mother must be irremediably imprinted.

None of this does Michaela wish to think about. Especially when she drives along the congested freeway in the leased, unfamiliar car in a trance of suspended panic hoping not to have an accident at such a fraught time.

But my husband is very ill, in a hospital.

I can't die and leave him!—he would have no idea where I am.

A grim sort of pride Michaela is taking, determined to complete the course and not disappoint the students. Determined not to make excuses for herself, not to inform anyone associated with the workshop of her husband's condition. Not the director of the writing program who'd hired her; not the fifteen students, most of them older, who'd enrolled in the course. For the workshop has become precious to Michaela, a lifeboat bearing her aloft in a churning treacherous sea.

Terrible to be so far away from Gerard for more than five hours. She has instructed the nurses to call her on her cell phone if there is an emergency.

During the three-hour class Michaela doesn't turn off her cell phone. Often distracted by what seems to her a vibration issuing from the phone, a plea for her attention that, when she surreptitiously checks, turns out to be nothing.

Yet even when she isn't in Albuquerque Michaela isn't always at Gerard's bedside. Nights she spends alone in the hillside house. Gerard lapses into a fitful opioid sleep at about 11:00 P.M. after being given his nighttime medication and so the nurses urge Michaela to go home, to try to sleep, too.

Your immune system will crash if you don't sleep. Then you will become sick, too. Then you will be no help to your husband or to anyone, Mrs. McManus.

Mrs. McManus! Already the name is beginning to sound like a rebuke.

A SEASON OF HOT GUSTY WINDS by day, stony chill by night like the interior of a mausoleum.

In the early morning the sky is suffused with an iridescent deep purple like an exquisite bruise, that gradually lightens in the east. On most nights the moon is so prominent in the sky, Michaela can make her way up the hill to the (empty, darkened) house without needing to use Gerard's little flashlight.

The glass-walled Institute-owned house is built on a steep hillside, cantilevered over a shallow ravine in which dwell nocturnal creatures with eyes and teeth that glisten by moonlight. Nighttime insects throb and pulse in the ravine loud as madness.

By day Michaela has an occasional glimpse of gaily plumed birds amid foliage in the ravine, said to be domesticated parrots that had escaped captivity and become wild. If she listens carefully she can hear their excited shrieks.

By night Michaela is very tired and rarely looks in the direction of the ravine. Lights inside the house throw reflections onto the floor-to-ceiling windows of a ghastly-white face bearing little resemblance to hers.

And in the morning, returning to the Cancer Center. Hurry!

Whether she has slept or not. *Fuck sleep, who needs sleep*—a coarse ribald voice close beside her ear.

Get your ass moving, girl. Downhill.

Once in motion, momentum will carry you. Law of gravity, inertia.

Lungs filling/emptying/filling with air. First principle of life: *Breathe.*

She has come to fear/hate the ceaseless wind from the desert. Tasting grit on her lips. Breath sucked away by the wind. Taking refuge in the refrigerated hospital.

H'lo ma'am—the (morning) receptionist nods and smiles yet insists that Michaela sign the ledger as she has signed it unvaryingly every morning since Gerard was admitted to the Santa Tierra Cancer Center.

MICHAELA MCMANUS 771 ONCOLOGY (DR.) GERARD MCMANUS

As if *(Dr.)* will make a difference! Still, she must try.

Keeping him alive. Alive! My husband.

In room 771 it is wonderful to see how oxygen seeps silently into the husband's nostrils through a translucent plastic tube.

Wonderful to see that the husband is *alive*, and *breathing*.

"Gerard! Hello."

Grips the husband's hand which grips hers in turn, but belatedly. Not wanting to see how in recent days Gerard's reflexes have slowed, even his vision seems to come more slowly into focus. His tone is likely to be reproachful: Asking why is she *late*?

Trying to explain, she is not late.

Where has she been?—Gerard asks. Visiting her friends?

No friends here. Not one.

Gerard is distressed that he can't seem to read very well lately. Print swimming in his eyes. God-damned medications affecting his eyesight and making him groggy so would Michaela please read to him? Small-print articles in *Science, Nature, American Journal of Neuroscience & Cognitive Psychology*. Front section of the *New York Times*.

Michaela isn't accustomed to reading aloud, the effort is surprisingly stressful. Her throat feels parched, hoarse. And there is the effort not to cry. She hears her voice unnaturally earnest, "sincere": there is some doubt (she feels this doubt as impersonal, the humming of an invisible mosquito) that what is issuing from her mouth is in fact *her voice*. In the midst of the reading interludes Gerard sometimes squirms or winces with pain (?) but indicates to Michaela not to stop—he is listening, and does not wish the reading to be interrupted just yet.

Sometimes Michaela discovers that Gerard has lapsed into an exhausted sleep, mouth slack and saliva glistening in the corners of his chapped lips which Michaela wipes gently with a tissue, and kisses. (Michaela kisses her sleeping husband at risk, in dread of waking him.)

At such times his breathing is hoarse, unnerving to hear. And when there is a lengthy pause between breaths she feels her heartbeat accelerate—

Breathe! Breathe . . .

Sometimes so anxious that she reads to Gerard a sequence of words that might be foreign, their meaning lost to her, and Gerard, far from having drifted into sleep, is entirely alert, annoyed: "Michaela! You're reading too fast, I can't follow. Please start over."

"From the beginning?"

"Yes! From the beginning."

But there is no beginning.

And there is no end.

Urgent Care

"Excuse me. I need to talk with you, Professor."

Grim words: the heart sinks.

Indeed, a grim-faced young woman with sallow, sullen skin, damp reproachful eyes, a faint but distinct odor of unwashed armpits, underwear. Her hair is incongruously neon—wanly festive streaks of blue, magenta, silver, brass—short-cut, jagged and uncombed. Her clothes are shapeless, sexless, with a look of having been slept-in. Her enunciation of *Professor* is acid-tinged with irony.

Since the conclusion of the workshop at 6:00 P.M. Letitia Tanik has been waiting with forced patience for the other students to file out of the seminar room. She'd annoyed Michaela by arriving twenty minutes late for class with a muttered excuse—*Sor-ry!* She'd been distracted during the three-hour class, sighing often, glancing surreptitiously at the cell phone in her lap, as if, like a child, she imagines that Michaela isn't aware.

But Michaela is determined to smile sympathetically at Letitia, who is clearly under duress.

"Of course, Letitia. My office is on the fourth floor . . ."

"Can we just stay here, Professor? I need to leave in a few minutes."

Letitia speaks with an air of reproach. Michaela feels the sting of a rebuke but understands that the unkempt young woman is in distress and doesn't mean to be rude.

Nor is calling her adjunct instructor *Professor* meant to be mocking or ironic, Michaela chooses to think.

To assure their privacy Michaela shuts the door to the seminar room. Invites Letitia to sit down at the table with her. "What is it, Letitia?"—calibrating a teacherly tone midway between friendly solicitude and a wary sense of respecting boundaries.

It has been Michaela's intention through the semester to impersonate an individual who is not-herself: not a wife whose husband is dying: not continuously distracted, not anxious, not overwhelmed as by walls closing in upon her, floors shifting beneath her feet.

An individual who is indeed a university professor: a figure of (benign, gracious) authority.

Like breathing through a straw, it has been. Such effort. Though the straw is bent, broken yet one can breathe through it, with effort. *Breathe! Never stop.*

Of the eighteen students in the memoir workshop Letitia Tanik has been the most problematic, baffling. At the start of the term she'd been a highly vocal, sometimes argumentative presence in the workshop, virtually quivering with excitement and enthusiasm at times; then, after turning in two obsessively detailed prose pieces describing family life in a tight-knit immigrant community in Las Cruces, in the southern part of the state, prose pieces which were greeted with much praise from her fellow writers and from Michaela, and a few critical suggestions, Letitia was absent for two class meetings and has failed to hand in assignments. In a neutral voice she'd apologized to Michaela—*Sorry to miss class. Had some kind of flu.*

It is shocking to Michaela, the change in Letitia Tanik! Where previously Letitia had taken care with her appearance, far more than most of the other young women in the workshop, exuding an air of punk-style glamor, purple lipstick and purple nail polish, inky-black eyeliner, eyebrow and nostril piercings glittering against powdered-ivory skin in an eerie evocation (Michaela thinks) of the late Amy Winehouse; now her face is sallow, plain, aggrieved. Where once her streaked hair suggested the feathers of an exotic bird now it is growing out dull brown at the roots. Like the purple lipstick, the punk jewelry has vanished—the playful tinselly glitter. Without eye makeup her eyes seem to have shrunken and have become lash-less, without luster. Colorful clothes have been replaced with shapeless clothes. As if executing a harsh revenge upon her body Letitia seems to have stopped caring for herself as a physical being.

Her voice is a breathy lowered murmur forcing others to lean close to her to hear her even as her rigid body signals—*Stay away! Keep your distance.*

Michaela has picked up these signals. Indeed Michaela has no intention of drawing close to the scowling young woman.

But here is a surprise: all Letitia seems to want from her instructor is a simple favor, a grade of "incomplete" in the workshop.

She's too far behind on the assignments to catch up, Letitia says. She wants her writing to be good, and it just isn't, right now.

She's sorry, she hasn't been well. She's been missing other classes too. The reason being—*personal problems.*

Michaela understands: *personal* means *don't ask.*

Michaela tells Letitia that she's sorry to hear this—she'd been concerned that something was wrong. Since Letitia had missed two classes. And hasn't handed in work lately.

Taking care not to seem to be accusing Letitia. Not to seem to be judging her.

Hesitant to make inquiries for fear that her sympathy might be misconstrued as intrusive, overly curious. Inappropriate in an instructor considerably older than her undergraduate student.

Michaela assures Letitia that she has no objection to giving her an incomplete grade. But there are three weeks remaining in the term, it's possible that Letitia will be able to catch up before the end . . .

"Ma'am! You didn't hear me, I guess. I'm saying that I can't write at all, not like I used to. Like, there's something heavy on my chest, pressing down—just makes me so *tired*."

Ma'am strikes Michaela's ear like *Professor*, something of a rebuke.

Drawn to her, rebuked by her. Not consciously, Michaela thinks, the girl invites sympathy, even as she repels it.

As the deathly-ill yearn for us to save them, yet repel us for our failure.

"Have you seen a doctor, Letitia? If you're feeling . . ."

Letitia laughs derisively. As if Michaela has inadvertently said something very funny.

Michaela is thinking that of the eighteen students in the workshop, only Letitia has never called her by her first name as she'd invited them to call her; indeed, Letitia has never called Michaela any name at all, first-or-last name.

"Oh *shit*."

There's a sudden chattering sound like a parrot—Letitia's cell phone ringing inside her hemp-woven shoulder bag. Letitia frowns rummaging through the bag, locates the phone, answers in a vexed voice in a language Michaela thinks at first is Spanish.

Trying not to overhear. Trying not to give the appearance of overhearing.

Not that it matters, Letitia isn't speaking Spanish. And even if she were, Michaela with her limited knowledge of the language probably couldn't have deciphered much of what she says for Letitia is speaking rapidly, in a lowered, impatient voice.

How angry Letitia is! Her fury is self-lacerating, as in one clawing at her own face.

Michaela thinks: requesting an incomplete in the memoir workshop doesn't seem unreasonable. The focus should be on student work, not on disciplining students for failing to turn in work. Michaela is an adjunct in the English Department at the University of New Mexico in Albuquerque for just one term; a temporary instructor not likely to teach here again after the term ends. (If she will even complete the term.) Indeed, Michaela dislikes giving grades in courses in "creative writing"; unless a student fails to complete the minimum work she is likely to give only A's and B's.

She'd screened applicants for the course, selecting eighteen out of more than forty; she considers that everyone in the class has demonstrated talent by simply being chosen. Along with two or three others, Letitia Tanik was one of the strongest applicants.

Nor has Michaela any interest in being punitive with unhappy students like Letitia who have fallen behind the others like swimmers floundering in a turbulent sea.

When Letitia breaks off her phone conversation Michaela assumes that she is about to jump up from the seminar table and leave. Yet, Letitia doesn't move from the table but instead leans forward on her elbows, resting her head on her hands. She sighs heavily, there is something left unsaid.

Michaela wonders if Letitia expects her to ask more questions even as she has indicated that she doesn't want her privacy invaded.

Michaela sees that Letitia Tanik is probably younger than she'd seemed initially, perhaps no more than twenty. Without makeup she looks defenseless, vulnerable. Her skin is blemished at the hairline, her eyelids are inflamed. In the aftermath of the brief phone conversation, she has begun to breathe harshly; she shifts her body, smelling of rank animal rage.

"See, ma'am, what happened to me, three weeks ago, three weeks and two days, I was—I was raped—I was raped by this *friend* . . ."

Michaela listens, astonished. *Raped, friend.* In such proximity, incongruous words.

". . . in this house where I am living, off-campus, there's mostly graduate students, he's a graduate student in chemical engineering . . . Professor, you have to promise: you won't tell anyone."

Without thinking Michaela nods. Of course.

Letitia explains that the "friend" who'd raped her was not a boyfriend but he'd kind of acted like he wanted to be, hanging out in her room, walking with her on the street, he'd met up with her for drinks a few times, not just the two of them alone together but with others, foreign students like him, all of them in engineering—"Like, in this country they come from, that's what they all want to be: *engineers.*" That night there was a lot of laughing between them, watching YouTube videos, back and forth between her room and his and they wound up in his room, next thing she knew she was waking up naked in his bed, sick to her stomach and vomiting and her "friend" disgusted with her telling her to go back to her own room, she couldn't stay with him, he had to get some sleep before an early class . . .

Letitia begins to cry. Angry sobs, wiping at her eyes. Telling Michaela she hasn't told anybody, didn't want anybody to know except she has to have an incomplete in Michaela's course, she will *just die* if she fails the course, or if Michaela reports her . . .

And this guy she'd trusted, telling her what happened was *consensual.*

Don't blame me he's telling her. *Anybody's to blame it's both of us and this includes you.*

"Looking at me like—like I'm a slut and a liar and he *hates me.*"

Adding, "He'd always said he liked my 'look'—'cool'—*he's* got short-cut hair and hates heavy metal . . ."

Michaela lets Letitia talk angrily, bitterly. Badly she wants to lay her hand on the girl's arm to comfort her—but no.

The gesture might be misunderstood. Misconstrued. Sympathy misread as condescension.

Michaela tries to think: What are the university rules? She'd paid little attention to the pamphlet she'd found in her mailbox, presuming that the protocol of dealing with sexual harassment and sexual abuse would never enter into her relations with her students whom she sees only once a week and who are, for the most part, older students, part-time students.

It's unfortunate, Michaela has already promised Letitia not to report the incident, without knowing quite what she was doing.

Michaela asks Letitia if her "friend" had hurt her and Letitia says stiffly yes she thinks so last time she'd looked. But he'd just say it was an accident, they were both drunk, God damn him he'd just say, he'd repeat—*con sen sual.*

"You didn't tell anyone?"

"I said *no.*"

Can't tell anyone, Letitia says hotly. That would only make things worse.

Especially, her family can't know about what happened. *Cannot know.*

They would be so ashamed of her, Letitia says. They would be mortified. In their community you can't even—ever—say the word *rape* out loud. A wife would not utter the word *rape* even to her husband—especially to her husband.

Everyone would know what had happened to her, the family would never live it down. Parents, grandparents. *All* her grandparents. They would never forgive *her!*

Her sisters—they would never let her forget it. They'd feel sorry for her but they would never—ever—let her forget it—"That's the way they are."

Her parents hadn't wanted her to go to Albuquerque to the university, Letitia says, but to a community college in Las Cruces. So they would blame her for coming here. They'd wanted her to live in a residence hall not off-campus housing with older students so they'd blame her for that—where the rape happened. No one in her family would ever believe that it wasn't her fault, what happened to her—because she'd been drinking, drunk. Because she'd passed out. That she'd been drinking at all would totally disgust them. They had no idea that Letitia drank sometimes—not a lot, but sometimes. No more than anybody else. In fact, not so much as anyone else. So what happened to her was her own fault, they would think, they would be so disgusted some of them wouldn't even speak to her, she knew. In their eyes she had no one to blame but herself. The so-called friend who'd gotten her drunk, who'd raped her, or whatever he'd done to her when she was drunk and unconscious and naked in his smelly bed, she still has bruises on her arms and belly, her hips, thighs, all this time later just starting to fade, a bump on the side of her head like (maybe) he'd knocked her head against the wall beside his bed. God knows what happened and all he can say is it's her fault as much as his.

Also, he tries to act like nothing much happened between them. Nothing special. Seeing her, saying hello to her in the house, other people around and he'll wave at her acting like they are—still—kind of friends . . .

Bitterly Letitia says: "He isn't White, if that's what you're wondering."

Michaela has no idea what this means. Why Letitia speaks accusingly to her.

"He's from the same religion as me. *That* would really make my family sick."

But why?—Michaela wonders. Would the family expect better behavior from one of their own, than from a young White man? But isn't Letitia *White*? Isn't "Tanik" an Eastern European name?

No matter Letitia's last name, her mother's last name might be very different. Letitia is biracial, perhaps. Michaela is beginning to be anxious, like one stepping into water, uncertain of her footing, and how deep the water is.

Michaela reverts to common sense: advising that Letitia see a doctor. Even if the assault was three weeks ago. Even if she thinks she doesn't want to report the rape. Michaela will take her to the infirmary if she doesn't want to go alone, she says. Michaela will stay with her and drive her back to her residence afterward.

Michaela has surprised herself, speaking so impulsively. And Letitia is moved by this offer, it seems. She hesitates for a moment. Then shakes her head vehemently *no*.

No no no no no.

ANOTHER WORLD TO LIVE IN. *Our writing.*

And if you are writing a memoir, your actual life is enclosed in the writing like an embryo in a womb.

Michaela has written just two memoirs of childhood and adolescence in late twentieth-century midwestern-suburban America, both highly acclaimed. Her prose is impressionistic, in the style of Virginia Woolf: states of mind shifting like desert sands into ever-new and arresting forms, unpredictable.

In an era in which individual identity has become the nexus of anxiety, and family dysfunction seemingly universal, Michaela has concentrated on the small rituals of daily, domestic midwestern life, the "healing powers" of pleasures shared with relatives and neighbors, a way of life passing into oblivion by the time she began to publish in her early thirties.

In tone, Michaela's memoirs have been respectful, even reverential. She has no appetite for the harshness of satire, she has no wish to "see" with an objective camera-eye. Was it Gloucester, in *King Lear*— *I see feelingly.*

Since Gerard's illness Michaela has not been able to write nor has Michaela felt a strong urge to write. Everything about her is too fraught with *feeling.*

Too much suffering, helplessness. On all sides. She cannot watch TV news, cannot glance at newspaper headlines. Photographs positioned at the very top, center of the *New York Times*—no.

So much casual, commodified death. Deaths. Where once newspapers would never have published photographs of the maimed, suffering, dying, dead now such atrocities have become commonplace. Such sorrow.

Making her way numbly along hospital corridors. Not allowing herself to glance into rooms as she passes.

Michaela urges her students to keep journals when they can't write. For journal-keeping may be the most sincere, as it is the most intimate, kind of writing.

Yet, for Michaela, it isn't possible. For what is *writing* but a way of distracting the self from what is essential: life, death.

That is, life threatened by death.

That is, a specific life threatened by a specific death.

Such *writing* is a fraud, a delusion: the being who is the *writer* cannot know the first thing about herself except when she is under attack, and, when she is under attack, she is not able to *write*.

Like Letitia Tanik. Too distracted, too unhappy.

Michaela wants to think that one day *when this is all over, when Gerard is home again* she might write a different sort of memoir, now that she has experienced such panic, the panic of dissolution . . .

But she cannot imagine its conclusion, she can barely imagine her life before the catastrophe began. She has been so focused on the hospital vigil, like one who has pressed too close to a wall, and cannot see the wall, helpless to know how to begin.

"Thank God for my students . . ."

Though naive to think "*my* students"—rather, individuals who have intersected with Michaela's life at this vulnerable time.

Gratitude for the opportunity to be selfless. To forget *self.*

The teacher defers to the will of others. As in a Zen meditation she must empty herself out and allow herself to be filled by others whose needs are greater than her own.

The seminar room has become an oasis, a sanctuary. So long as the *self* of the teacher is kept at a distance.

Michaela takes a (pathetic) sort of pride in the fact that none of her students has the slightest idea that Michaela's husband is hospitalized. That Michaela's husband is gravely ill. Nor will they, she is determined.

Where is my wife? Why has my wife abandoned me?

Now I have died, no one will love her.

Michaela could weep, these words are so unfair, and condemning.

Gerard hasn't died! She isn't abandoning him, she is only just trying to reach out to others, in the interim. To breathe, an air that is not hospital air, unnaturally cold, recycled air.

Like a fever the desire has seized Michaela, to be *of use.*

As if, offering herself *of use* to others, Michaela will impress an invisible being with her goodness and virtue and be rewarded with Gerard's recovery.

So simple, a child's logic. Yet, Michaela half-believes.

Still, Michaela has spells of weakness, despair. Even on these Thursday afternoons in Albuquerque, where no one knows of Gerard's struggle. Assailed by devastating thoughts like teeming bacteria devouring her flesh.

Deluding yourself. Taking solace in a (false) identity parceled out to strangers.

As if you matter to these strangers, or they to you.

As if anything matters except that your husband is dying, you are failing to save him.

Since the start of the term when Gerard first began coughing Michaela has been losing weight. Her clothes hang loosely on her. (Not unlike Letitia Tanik's clothing on her.) Soft-crepey skin beneath her eyes has become bruised. Out of defiance she has thrown herself too intensely into her students' work, each three-hour meeting is highly charged, exhausting. As if her life depends upon it.

Her voice gives out while she is speaking to the students, her throat feels scraped. She pauses sometimes as if she has lost her way while speaking, like a blind person. She has a new unconscious habit of groping for her cell phone (in her handbag) as if she has heard it ringing inaudibly, vibrating—but when her fingers discover the phone, it is still, without life.

How many times in their marriage have Michaela and Gerard called each other. How many times has Michaela smiled happily in anticipation of hearing Gerard's voice close in her ear—Hello, Michaela? Where are you, darling?—(a question Gerard invariably asks). But now Gerard has ceased calling Michaela, and when Michaela calls Gerard his phone goes directly to voice mail.

Sometimes Gerard's cell phone becomes lost in the sheets of his hospital bed, or has fallen onto the floor, but even when Michaela has carefully positioned the cell phone beside the bed, where Gerard can keep it in view, it is not often that he answers any longer.

You will have to live without me, Michaela.

Since you've abandoned me, that will be your choice.

* * *

TEARFULLY LETITIA INSISTS NO, she does not want to see a doctor. No intention of seeing a doctor. Or informing anyone at the university, or the Albuquerque police.

Her mouth is bitter, downturned. She is close to screaming at Michaela—*No no no. Leave me alone.*

Still, Michaela persists. If not a doctor, Letitia should see a therapist, at least. There is a Rape Crisis Center at the university, Michaela has seen posters. There is Psychological Counseling.

A professional would probably counsel Letitia to avoid encountering her rapist, Michaela tells her. Ideally she should move out of the house they are both living in.

Letitia protests why should *she* move out, *he* should be the one forced to move out.

Michaela tries to explain: if no charges are brought against the rapist he won't be forced to do anything, he'll continue to behave as if nothing has happened. It's important that Letitia avoid him, never talk with him or allow him to talk to her, no telephone calls, no emails or texts. If she decides to file charges such exchanges could be used against her by a defense attorney arguing that she couldn't possibly have been raped by the man since she's on cordial terms with him following the (alleged) rape.

Hotly Letitia says that the rape isn't "alleged." It happened!

Nor has she been on "cordial" terms with the guy since what he'd done to her. She has not!

Patiently Michaela explains: the term "alleged" is a legal term. It will always be used in this way until there is a court case, and an adjudication, and if at this time the rapist is found guilty of rape, it will no longer be "alleged."

Such bullshit!—Letitia cries, disgusted.

"*He* knows, and *I* know. He should take a lie-detector test, that will show who's lying."

The bitterness with which Letitia speaks is a revelation, Michaela thinks. Her hatred for the rapist is contaminated with other, more ambiguous emotions.

"Oh Christ, why don't I just *die*."

The door of the seminar room is opened hesitantly, students are about to enter for the next class. Letitia gives a cry of exasperation and distress, snatches up her bag and rushes from the room. Michaela follows after, feeling protective of the reckless young woman whose face gleams with tears and whose eyes glare and glower.

Does she want others to see? Her shame, mortification?

Michaela follows Letitia along the corridor to an exit. She is reluctant to let Letitia go, and senses that Letitia is reluctant to break away from her.

Utterly new behavior for Michaela, following a distraught student out of a classroom, trying to reason with her. *Take care!*—Gerard might advise her.

She can't abandon Letitia under these circumstances. A rape victim might harm herself, do something irrevocable.

Letitia's anger is a bulwark against breaking down entirely, Michaela thinks. It's her moral duty to help the girl, despite the girl's resistance.

She should not have agreed so readily not to report the rape. But Michaela reasons that she can convince Letitia to change her mind, eventually.

"Letitia? Why don't I take you to an Urgent Care facility. We don't have to go to the infirmary on campus. That would be a very good idea."

Letitia pauses warily. She listens as Michaela explains what an Urgent Care facility is: not an ER, not a clinic or a hospital, nothing to do with the university or with the Albuquerque police. "If you're concerned about the cost, I can pay for it. I have faculty medical coverage, I can arrange this."

Of course Michaela has nothing of the sort: *faculty medical coverage.* As Gerard's wife she is included in Gerard's Harvard medical insurance plan at Harvard but has nothing at the University of New Mexico.

After an exchange of several minutes Letitia agrees reluctantly to be taken to an Urgent Care facility. But only if Michaela promises not to come into the examining room with her, and not to speak with the doctor or nurse after the examination. And not to ask her questions.

To this absurd demand, Michaela agrees. Against her better judgment, but what choice has she? She will hope to convince Letitia to cooperate after the exam.

Thinking—*If there has been a rape, a crime has been committed. A crime will have to be reported to the authorities.*

HOW STRANGE IT FEELS, a stranger beside Michaela in her car! If Gerard could see her he would stare and stare.

Michaela recalls an Urgent Care facility she has often noticed, on Lomas Boulevard a mile or so from campus. She drives Letitia there as Letitia frets and twitches in the seat beside her like an anxious child.

In the waiting room Michaela speaks with a receptionist while Letitia takes a seat in a corner, slump-shouldered, sulky. The spiky neon hair looks particularly incongruous in this setting, Letitia is drawing attention.

Michaela provides her credit card, wondering at her folly. What Gerard will say when he scans the credit card account at the end of the month and comes upon this inexplicable expense: Urgent Care, Albuquerque.

A forty-minute wait before Letitia can see a doctor.

Michaela takes the girl's hand which is limp, damp. Except for Gerard's hand she has not closed her hand around another's hand in some time.

Assuring the frightened Letitia that she will be all right.

All right. All right. No idea what these trite words might even mean.

At first Letitia sits stiffly beside Michaela as if in a state of shock. Each time a patient's name is called she steels herself: but her name is not called. She soon becomes restless again, fretful. Withdraws her hand from Michaela's. Scrolls through her cell phone. Checks her email. Sighing, put-upon and peevish. As if Michaela has brought her to this place for some purpose having nothing to do with her but only to do with Michaela.

At last in an outburst of pique Letitia tells Michaela that she has changed her mind. She doesn't want to be examined—anyway, not right now. She needs to be somewhere else.

Michaela protests: She has waited a half hour, why not a few more minutes?

It's for Letitia's own good to be examined. She may have been injured in some way of which she isn't aware . . . What if she has an infection?

"I said—*I need to leave.*"

Letitia's voice is rising. Others in the waiting room are observing her and Michaela beside her, trying to reason with her, distressed.

(And what is the relationship between the excited girl with the rainbow-streaked hair, and the concerned older woman? Surely they are not blood relatives, that's obvious.)

Letitia leaps to her feet, leaves the waiting room. Deeply embarrassed, Michaela has no choice but to speak with the receptionist, cancel the appointment. (And hope that the credit card charge will be deleted from the system.) She is dismayed with Letitia, she has had enough of Letitia, how difficult to deal with a young person, this young person, like driving an eighteen-wheel truck on a highway, downhill on a steep grade, barely able to keep the wheel steady, danger at every turn.

Michaela follows Letitia outside, into the parking lot. Half-hoping that Letitia will have vanished but when Michaela approaches her car she sees that, of course, no surprise, Letitia is sulking in the passenger's seat.

Letitia's face glows with a radiant fury, righteousness. A sharp odor wafts from her underarms.

For Michaela is to blame, Michaela must be blamed.

In a quivering voice Letitia declares that she needs to be taken home, to where she lives. Now.

"I don't have time for this. Only just makes things worse, I tried to tell you but you wouldn't listen."

Michaela thinks—*She is afraid. I must respect her fear.*

Michaela thinks—*I am the adult, I am responsible.*

"Do as you wish, Letitia. Of course."

Yet still believing that Letitia will come around to her way of thinking, perhaps by tomorrow. Tonight, she will relive the past hour, she will hear again Michaela's calm voice.

Michaela drives Letitia back toward the university, straining to hear Letitia's murmured directions. So exasperating!—Letitia is punishing Michaela by being barely audible.

Very tired, light-headed. After the three-hour workshop. And before that an hour's commute in freeway traffic into Albuqueque. *So tired, I am so tired. When will I have time to die.*

By the time Michaela pulls up in front of the grimy sand-colored stucco house on La Union Street it seems to her that she and Letitia Tanik have been together in each other's company for many hours. They have traveled many miles together.

The residence is a former private house, square-built and graceless, partitioned into rooms for students like other houses on the street. It has three storeys with narrow balconies on the two upper storeys: on the second floor, laundry has been hung to dry, on the third floor a shirtless male figure is leaning against the railing, smoking, drinking from a can. In the waning late-afternoon sun his hair glistens darkly as if it were lacquered. Michaela wonders if this is the person for whom Letitia feels such excited loathing.

Letitia strikes Michaela's arm: "No! Don't stop here! Drive to the corner."

Adding in a rueful voice: "Please."

At the corner several houses away Michaela brakes the car to a stop. Thinking that, if the young man on the balcony noticed her vehicle passing the house slowly he wouldn't have recognized it.

For a minute or more Letitia sits crouched in the seat beside Michaela, panting. Michaela can feel her thoughts rushing and chaotic as a swarm of hornets.

Unexpectedly, impulsively, Letitia reaches out to Michaela, leans over to awkwardly embrace her, pressing her damp face against Michaela's neck.

Such intimacy, so suddenly—Michaela is stunned.

Then, in a murmur, what sounds like *OK, Professor—thanks!* Letitia breaks away from Michaela, slams the car door behind her, and is gone.

So fleeting, and gone.

Michaela stares into the rearview mirror seeing the girl running toward the grimy sand-colored house, with surprising agility. Not a wounded creature after all, Michaela has been deceived.

Watching the rapidly shrinking figure in the rearview mirror, bounding up the front stoop of the house, pushing open the door and disappearing inside.

Michaela rouses herself from a kind of stupor, for a moment uncertain where she is, and why.

An unfamiliar neighborhood, children playing in the street. Vehicles are parked on both sides of the street. Michaela must drive with exaggerated caution as the children's cries turn to jeers in her wake. She feels a crushing loneliness, a dread of what lies ahead.

OK, Professor—thanks! Michaela shakes her head in wonder, she had not expected to be thanked, or embraced.

Nor is *Professor* meant to be ironic, she thinks.

Michaela sees that she has circled the block. Back on La Union and again approaching the sand-colored house.

Slowing her car to see more clearly. Glancing up, surprised to see, unless she isn't surprised, the figure of a girl on the third-floor balcony, approaching the shirtless young man.

Michaela stares. Michaela feels a stab of betrayal. A stab to the heart.

Yet: from this distance, and from this perspective, squinting through the windshield of the rented car that isn't entirely clean, obscured with tiny particles of dust and pollen, a shiny-scummy sheen, Michaela can't be absolutely sure if the girl is Letitia Tanik or someone who resembles her: glaring late-afternoon sun has blinded Michaela, the girl's face and hair are blurred.

Drive away as unobtrusively as possible. Your turn to disappear.

RECOGNIZING HER SURROUNDINGS NOW, Lomas Boulevard leading to the entrance to I-25. Returning to Santa Tierra.

But she is late!—she will be late, returning.

In a crawl of traffic, slowed. It is Michaela's punishment, such sinkage, slippage. On the ocean's floor she is trapped, thick sinuous tendrils curl about her, holding her fast, strangling her.

All that she has kept at a distance for hours rushes at her now like black befouled water, she is powerless to keep it away.

When I died, you were nowhere near.

Where you were, I would never know.

And now—you will be the abandoned one.

14

Respite II

But no. It has not (yet) happened.

Whatever it is that will happen, that will happen inevitably and inexorably and will tear your papier-mâché life in two has not (yet) (evidently) happened.

What relief! Weeping with gratitude, exhaustion. The entire day has swung into dark, it is nearing 8:00 P.M. You are dazed with hunger. Yet the most exquisite happiness swaying in the doorway of room 771.

For your husband has not died in your (clandestine) absence. He has not passed into a coma. He has not *ceased breathing.*

In fact Gerard is lying more or less as you'd left him eight hours before. In his hospital bed on the seventh floor of the Santa Tierra Cancer Center. Saline drip in bruised right arm and in bruised left arm oxycodone. Not (yet) oxygen in a nose tube.

Rumpled bedclothes, which the night attendant will change. Possibly, hidden in the bedclothes, Gerard's cell phone which you'd positioned on his movable tray purposefully so that it wouldn't become lost amid the bedclothes.

Scattered across the bed stray pages from the *New York Times* from which you'd been reading to Gerard that morning in your strained schoolgirl voice so eager to please.

Not so fast, Michaela! Start from the beginning.

The beginning?

Yes! The beginning.

15

Secret Cache

So tired! Her head pounds with pain. A vise is being tightened about her head squeezing her skull out of shape.

It is the unbearable. The unspeakable. Tight ever tighter. And *tired*.

Yet *tired* doesn't translate into sleep. Only *exhausted*.

Can't risk sleeping pills. Can't risk addiction. Not at this crucial time, she must be awake and alert. She is *the wife*.

For addiction to the pills would be immediate, Michaela knows. From past experience. Short intense dreamless interludes of sleep. Waking with such effort, it's like lying beneath slabs of broken concrete. So heavy! Try to throw off with broken wings for arms.

Godamned pills only let you sleep about four hours. Next morning taste in the mouth sour like dried urine.

Gerard did not approve of sleeping pills except in desperate circumstances of the kind in which he now finds himself (trapped): barbiturates, opioids, morphine in ever-larger doses to muffle excruciating pain.

Yet: Michaela has been (secretly) hoarding such medications. Not just since Gerard's hospitalization but before. Years before. A (secret) cache in a handbag she'd brought with her from Cambridge to Santa Tierra, New Mexico, about which Gerard will never know.

Ask *why?* Michaela would protest—*I have no idea*.

SOON, THE PATIENT IN ROOM 771 will be allowed to self-administer hydromorphone (morphine) to control pain. Though (of course) the morphine available to the patient is not unlimited but closely monitored.

Does Dr. McManus have a living will, Mrs. McManus? Please bring a photocopy of this document next time you come to the hospital, will you?

16

A Theory Pre-Post-Mortem

Naegleria fowleri has traveled through their nasal passageways and into their brains.

Burrowed deep into the marrow of their bones.

Riding the crests of tiny waves, warm-coursing blood.

Freshwater heated by the sun, aswirl with muck and teeming with microbes.

An adventure!—they'd thought. Swimming in the sun-warmed mountain lake in the Berkshires, invited to spend a weekend at the country home of friends from Boston.

GERARD HAD SWUM LONGER IN the lake than Michaela. Consequently Gerard has become more infected than Michaela. This is the theory.

Possibly, Michaela isn't infected at all or if she is, it is not with brain-eating *Naegleria fowleri* but with another microbe. (This is another theory, unproven.)

(Until there is an autopsy, or autopsies, nothing can be proven.)

Their hosts, older than Michaela by a decade or more, longtime friends of Gerard, explained apologetically that they rarely swam in the lake any longer, there was too much seaweed close to shore, though certainly the lake was still beautiful. Also apologizing, they rarely hiked in the woods any longer, too many ticks, Lyme disease, friends had been infected but if you were careful, as surely Gerard and Michaela would be, there was no grave danger.

Also—*We're not so young any longer! Can't keep up with Gerard.*

Michaela will long remember Gerard emerging from the lake: water streaming down bare chest, arms, legs flattening dark hairs against his skin like an animal's pelt.

Michaela will long remember how standing in the lake with water lapping against their waists they'd kissed. Gerard had been affectionate, playful. The skin about his eyes unusually pale, and his eyes unusually naked, without glasses.

You know, I love you. My dear wife.

Hope you know that.

Rare for Gerard to utter such words. For Gerard was shy, in the language of intimacy. A brilliant speaker, a sharp debater, far more assured in front of large audiences than at small gatherings, often tongue-tied in his wife's presence. Emotions swept over him, into him. Emotions that could not be named by him did not (in a way) exist. Or could not be acknowledged to exist. Michaela laughed in delight of the man, his fatty-muscled body, folds of flesh at his waist, gut-heavy, though with hard slender legs, ankles.

Faint with love for her husband. Oh!—she adored him.

Though not liking it how, when they swam together in the lake in the Berkshires, Gerard frequently pulled ahead oblivious of her. As sometimes he did when they were hiking together. Even walking together unless clever Michaela managed for them to hold hands. As if something in the future tugged at Gerard, he was helpless to resist. Oblivious not of *her* (she thought) but of the presence of another. A kind of trance overcame the man as if he were drawn by the gravitational pull of private thoughts (a future? but what future? did it include Michaela?) in the languid sun-warmed Berkshires lake in which splotches of light winked and shone like teeming life.

17

Lonely Wife

But how lonely, in the night! Michaela reached out to touch her husband's hand, or wrist, or side, or flank—lightly, not wanting to wake him.

Just to know that you are there.

For if you are there, then I am here.

Not fully awake but frightened suddenly. Needy, shaky. Oh, where was he—her husband?

Blindly she groped for him in the bed. In the night. Panicked not knowing where Gerard was. And what time this was.

Was it possible, she hadn't (yet) met Gerard McManus? All their happiness lay before them, like sunlit land stretching to the distant horizon seen from a small soaring plane?

Yet she was remembering the man, in the future in which he would become her *husband*.

The very word has acquired for her such terrible power, mystery: husband.

Sickness and health. Till death do you part.

How has it come to this, Michaela has become so weak! As a younger woman she'd been much stronger. As a younger woman oblivious of the future she'd exuded an air of confidence, self-sufficiency.

Yet now it has come to seem as if her bones are turning to water. Her sense of herself melting like ice in late winter.

Flashes of ice-water rivulets on a steep shingled roof. Glistening, streaming down in curlicues like snakes.

Michaela was one who hadn't wanted to marry. Boasted not wanting children. Not needing children to extend herself. A false sense of immortality.

Yet now, Michaela is incomplete without the man. Without the husband stunted, disfigured.

Love is the bitter taste. Love is what devours. *You have taken half my soul from me. Now, I am only half a person.*

EMERGING FROM THE SHOWER INTO the steamy bathroom. Unsteady on her feet, wrapping herself in a large towel as if for solace. Seeing on the tile floor, in a corner near-opaque with steam, what appears to be a figure, small, dark, dwarfish—Michaela stops dead, staring. Is it—alive? Something that has crawled into the house from outdoors?

Everywhere in this landscape are lizards, snakes, large glinting-backed beetles. Spiders, scorpions?—deadly venomous creatures.

Michaela sees that the object is inanimate, carved and painted wood: the gape-mouthed potbellied Scavenger God Ishtikini, sometimes called the Skull-God.

Surpassingly ugly, this thing! And why is it *here*?

Michaela recalls how Gerard teased her for not appreciating "exotic" Native American art. He'd laughed at her but he hadn't objected to her hiding the *objets d'art* out of sight. The memory brings tears to Michaela's eyes.

Without Gerard, there will be no one to tease her. No one to chide her, even in pretense. No one to provoke her to protest, and to laugh at her protestations.

In a trance of horror Michaela stands wrapped in the towel, in the heated air, shivering as this realization comes to her. *Alone. You will be so alone.* Staring at the misshapen figure on the floor. She has no idea how the thing has come to be in such a place, and why the sight of it is so upsetting to her.

Then she understands: the ravenous Scavenger God has come for Gerard. But it is blind, its comprehension is stunted, it has come to the wrong place for Gerard.

"Ugly! Evil!"—Michaela is desperate to drag the likeness of Ishtikini to a cupboard beneath the sink counter, where (she is sure) she'd hidden it weeks ago.

How Gerard would laugh at her! In fact, if Gerard were here in the house, Michaela might have suspected that he'd placed the ugly thing in a corner of the bathroom as a prank.

Not that Gerard is one to play pranks on anyone. Certainly not Gerard, and certainly not such a crude prank.

Yet—(Michaela is reasoning wildly)—*if* Gerard were home, and *if* Gerard were behaving out of character (affected by medication, perhaps: steroids, if not opioids), he *might* have played a prank on Michaela.

A more reasonable explanation: a cleaning woman employed by the Institute was sent to the house in Michaela's absence, and cleaned the house, without Michaela's knowledge; for some reason, the woman removed the Ishtikini figure from its hiding place beneath the sink . . .

Michaela hasn't seen any evidence of housecleaning. Michaela is determined not to look around, to see if she can locate any. For this is a logical explanation for the presence of the Ishtikini carving in the bathroom and if Gerard were here, Gerard would likely agree.

Indeed, Michaela knows that Gerard would agree, and in what terms.

Occam's razor: Do not multiply entities beyond necessity. The simplest explanation is (likely to be) the correct explanation.

SHE WILL TELL GERARD ABOUT the Ishtikini figure, she thinks.

But maybe not. No. (*Why* would Michaela tell Gerard anything to confuse and upset him?)

To entertain? To remind him of her, his wife's, disapproval of the ugly *objets d'art*, which had amused him, and provoked him to laugh tenderly at her?

To remind him of the precious intimacy of their marriage, now in danger of slipping away into oblivion?

Michaela will decide when she arrives at the hospital if she will tell Gerard, or not. Much will depend upon Gerard: if he appears to be clear-minded, or confused.

Before leaving the house Michaela checks the other demon-artifacts she'd hidden which include the shriek-mouthed female (subsequently identified as Skli, Goddess of Creation and Destruction) and the squat frog-like creature with the blind pop-eyes (Weyaki, God of Chaos). The leather stag's skull with "real" antlers which (she thought) she'd hidden in the front hall closet she can't seem to find and decides to forget about.

18

"Please Let Us Help You"

No visitors, please!—his condition wasn't *serious.*

No (adult) children, relatives, friends from Cambridge—not yet.

Only just a mild case of pneumonia. Well, maybe a blood clot in a lung. Should be discharged within a few days.

Then, as his condition was gradually revealed to be more serious, indeed critical, he certainly hadn't wanted visitors—for reasons of privacy, vanity.

No no *no.* Not right now.

By and by—maybe. Not now.

Each time she'd tried to reason with him. For those who loved him would want to see Gerard—of course! And knowing that she, the wife, the "new" wife, would be blamed if—if something went terribly wrong, and she failed to contact them in time . . .

"I told you, Michaela. Not now."

"But—when?"

"By and by."

"Especially Lucinda will—" (Lucinda was Gerard's twenty-nine-year-old married daughter living in Seattle.)

"I said—*by and by.*"

This was becoming a refrain with Gerard. A new phrase she'd never heard on his lips before, uttered in a bemused/dismissive tone:

By and by.

I'll let you know.

In the meantime just stop, Michaela. Please.

Trying to reason with him. But carefully—not in a way to upset him. For it's risky to upset Gerard McManus in a weakened state when he isn't altogether *himself.*

Above all you did not want to see the mask of gentlemanly warmth fade from Gerard's face, a look of raw fury coming into the beautiful blue-gray eyes.

No. You did not want to see that.

And if you did, if you have seen it: quickly erase from memory.

Don't oppose him. Don't contradict him. If you love him don't ever, ever provoke him.

STILL, ALARMING NEWS OF GERARD McManus must have made its way back east like airborne spores for one day a Cambridge friend calls Michaela to exclaim into Michaela's ear: "We've heard that Gerard is in the hospital there!—is that true? Shall we come out? Does Gerard want visitors? Do *you* want visitors? Let us help you, Michaela!"

No no *no.* Not right now.

By and by—maybe. Not now.

"But it must be a terrible strain on you too, Michaela. We've heard that Gerard is seriously ill. And you don't have anyone else out there, do you? Any of Gerard's family? No? And where on earth *are* you? Someone said—Santa Fe? New Mexico? Could you air-lift Gerard back to Mass. General, if you have to? Is that a possibility? Though I don't suppose your insurance would pay . . ."

An air of reproach, chiding. And beneath, genuine alarm.

Michaela stammers a reply explaining that she can't talk right now, has to hang up, but the emphatic voice persists: "At least let

Rob and me come out and help *you*. We can cook for you, drive you to the hospital, do errands for you—even if Gerard doesn't want visitors . . ."

Help me? Cook for me?—Michaela laughs. This is funny: most of her food these days is scavenged piecemeal from Gerard's untouched meal trays. Dwarf packages of Cheerios, dwarf containers of (overly sweet) orange juice, apple juice, cranberry juice, dwarf yogurts, Jell-Os, ice creams. Hasn't had what you'd call a *meal*, seated at a table, in memory.

Michaela protests: she doesn't need help, really she is fine, she is *all right*.

"You can't be all right alone, Michaela! It's a terrible ordeal, when a spouse is in the hospital. When it's 'intensive care.' Let us come out and help you. It's the least we can do, you've been so generous with us . . ."

Generous? When? Vaguely Michaela recalls—an incident from her old, lost life in Cambridge . . . Feeling a sensation of panic, that she might be trapped in the present tense by random acts of generosity in the past: accompanying this friend to a clinic for a colonoscopy when no one else in her family had been available, waiting for her, greeting her in the recovery room . . .

"Michaela? Are you still on the line? You haven't sounded well. Please let us help you."

But no one can help us. No one can intrude.

Summoning her strength to rebut the friend's argument. Speaking rapidly, thanking profusely, explaining, on Gerard's cell phone (Madelyn Bronwell had called Gerard's number, Michaela discovered the phone forgotten on Gerard's bedside table, vibrating weakly) that they really don't require help right now, things are going reasonably well and Gerard's daughter Lucinda is planning on coming soon, she'll be staying at the house with Michaela—"It's just a matter now of treatment. All the tests are in, and there's a regimen planned.

Gerard is in good hands here. The medical care in Santa Tierra is first-rate."

Good hands. First-rate. Language so banal, Michaela cannot believe that she is speaking it. Yet, it is the language that comes spontaneously to our lips in such circumstances.

"Still, Mass. General would be so much more—"

"Sorry, we are *here*. Gerard isn't about to be 'air-lifted' anywhere."

Michaela speaks sharply. The friend has more questions but Michaela explains that she can't talk right now, she will call back later. Her voice is cracking, hoarse with the effort not to scream.

After the call Michaela is trembling as if she has narrowly escaped danger. Hoping that none of their other Cambridge friends will call. And no one from Gerard's family.

If these are Final Days these are precious days. No one else is wanted.

19

The Vigil III

No beginning.
  And no end.

SHUDDERING RELIEF IT HAS NOT (yet) happened.

Not this morning. Not this noon. Not this afternoon. Whatever it is that will happen, but not (yet).

Asking where is *my wife?*

(But which wife? Michaela steels herself to hear the wrong name but Gerard is too shrewd to utter any name at all as, she'd sometimes noticed, at large parties or receptions in Cambridge Gerard has begun to refrain from introducing people to one another allowing them to introduce themselves if they wish but risking no embarrassment to himself if he has not remembered their names.)

Demanding to know why is he here? What is this place? Where is his doctor? Who is his doctor? (Dr. T___, from Cambridge?) Why do people here speak with Russian accents? Is this some sort of Fulbright exchange, is the CIA funding the Institute, will he be expected to sign a loyalty oath?

He will refuse, Gerard says. God damn he *will not sign any loyalty oath.*

Shaking his head vehemently to clear it as if the confusion inside might be remedied by shaking things up even more.

Pushing away Michaela's hand when she tries to comfort him.

". . . time to go home. The car is parked in the—what's it called— parking *garage*."

He is becoming fretful. He is becoming excited. He is becoming angry. He is becoming despondent. He refuses to eat: he won't/can't swallow solids. He refuses to drink: liquids make him gag. A spoon lifted to his lips makes him gag, he pushes Michaela's hand away. Makes him angry, and makes him gag. *She, the wife, is making him angry, and making him gag.*

"I told you—it's time to go home. They're not doing a damned thing for me here."

Home. Michaela has the idea that Gerard means, not the glass-walled house on Vista Drive, Santa Tierra, but the brick town house on Monroe Street, Cambridge, where he has lived for most of the past quarter-century.

". . . need to work better, at home. Goddamned interruptions all the time here." Still Gerard is working, or trying to work, on the copyedited manuscript of *The Human Brain and Its Discontents*. But the pages are becoming scattered, in bedclothes, on the bedside table, windowsill, even the floor behind the bed where Michaela has several times discovered them.

Several times she has checked, surreptitiously: the inscription page is still in place—*for my beloved wife and first reader Michaela.* Mornings are not Gerard's best time, for the heavy narcotic slumber of opioid sleep still weighs upon him, until midday.

And midday, and mid-afternoon, are not Gerard's best times for the steady procession of attendants and medical workers exhausts him.

Evening of an interminable day. Dinner brought on a plastic tray, dinner removed on a plastic tray. It has come to seem evident: Gerard is *not himself.*

Nor does it seem evident to Michaela that Gerard's condition is improving or is likely to improve.

In their old familiar life which was the life of just a few weeks before quaint in retrospect as a nineteenth-century daguerreotype Michaela's gentle, gentlemanly husband never spoke harshly to her, never impatiently. Never glared at her as if he scarcely recognizes her.

". . . speaking with a Chinese accent? Are we in Beijing?"

Delirium. Michaela has been warned that Gerard might lapse into *delirium* after days of the oxycodone dripping into his veins.

Drugging, doping. Opioids: opium. A choice between excruciating pain and confusion, grogginess. *Delirium* is the official medical usage but it seems to Michaela a misleading term.

Really it seems to Michaela that her husband is increasingly entangled in dreams. Disturbing dreams. Like a man in quicksand, valiantly struggling, yet unable to pull himself free as a man trapped in a dream cannot open his eyes though he senses—*knows*—that he is dreaming.

". . . without a translator. Train tickets to—is it Uzbekistan?"

Michaela hadn't traveled with Gerard to Russia, East Asia, Africa. Most of Gerard's travels had taken place before their marriage. Now she feels the pang of a double loss: her husband is drifting from her yet he is drifting in the company (she supposes) of another wife, young children.

". . . my passport? Have you seen it? Where is my passport?"

In such a state of *delirium* the usually reasonable Gerard McManus does not wish to cooperate with the medical staff. He does not want more blood extracted from his bruised and battered arms. Especially he does not want to swallow a gallon of ill-tasting GoLYTELY to clear his colon for a colonoscopy and he does not want to endure a catheter in his penis. No! He does not want to be lifted onto yet another gurney and wheeled away descending seven vertiginous floors to Radiology for yet another CAT scan.

How many tests, scans, biopsies has the patient endured! Yet treatment has not yet begun to shrink the cancerous tumors.

Soon! We will zap the small tumors with radiation. And then—

Michaela has tried to comprehend why the aggressive treatment of Gerard's cancer which Dr. N___ has promised, or has seemed to have promised, hasn't begun. As she has tried to comprehend why dapper bow-tied Dr. N___ waited so long before discovering the urethral tumor dismissing the patient's complaint of pain . . . Why, why on earth, an oncologist neglecting to test for a tumor in the stomach or abdomen after complaints of pain, now the tumor has grown *too large to be surgically removed.*

Yet: one more test is needed. Kidney, biopsy.

Unbelievably, one more test. After so many.

Soon then, possibly tomorrow after the results of the biopsy are known: the first of the radiation treatments will be scheduled.

Is that definite?—Michaela asks plaintively.

Is that a promise?—an edge to Michaela's voice.

Searching the seventh floor for Dr. N___ who has been more than usually difficult to find in recent days. He is a tall thick-bodied man with a face impassive as a death-mask and through the eyeholes of this mask small shiny-dark eyes peer warily. Though Michaela ran breathless to the hospital arriving by 7:00 A.M. it seems that Dr. N___ had already made his rounds and had departed.

Wanting to fall to her knees to plead with Dr. N___. *Save my husband!*

Wanting to clutch at his arm, scream into his face. *What are you doing! Why are you waiting! Start the treatment now! Today!*

Not good for Michaela to allow herself to despair. Especially not angry despair.

Not good for Michaela to attempt to leave Gerard's room if he isn't asleep.

Gerard cries: "Wait, where are you going? Don't leave me here!

Don't abandon me! You're my wife, you can't abandon me! Drive the car around to the front! It's in the parking garage where I left it. Here are the keys . . ."

Michaela tries to explain to her excited husband that she is only going downstairs to the cafeteria for a few minutes. She is not leaving the hospital, she is not leaving him. But he can't (just yet) leave the hospital. The treatment for his condition has not (yet) begun.

". . . but what is my 'condition'? What are you talking about? Nothing has been explained."

"Yes, darling. It has been explained . . ."

"Nothing has been explained! What are you saying!"

Gerard has been told this information in excruciating detail as well as having endured it but Gerard seems to have forgotten much that has happened to him since being admitted to the ER. He becomes impatient with Michaela if she speaks slowly and he becomes impatient with Michaela if she speaks too quickly. And when Gerard does hear her it seems that he must be confusing the elusive Dr. N___ with his longtime Cambridge internist Dr. T___.

Another time Michaela explains. But within a few minutes Gerard asks the same questions. Makes the same demands.

"D'you remember where we left the car? In the parking garage? Please go and get it—I don't have any shoes. They won't let me out of here unless you help me. Call for a nurse, I'll start the discharge procedure. Here are the keys . . ."

Michaela is struck to the heart seeing: Gerard fumbling his fingers against the front of the hospital gown searching for a pocket, and car keys in the pocket, except (of course) there is no pocket in the hospital gown, and there are no car keys.

. . . RUNNING, IN THE HOT WIND. Running until she stumbled. Until tears streaked her face. Until her heart burst, she could run no farther.

She ran until her guts ached. She ran until both legs cramped, she cried aloud in pain. Until the throbbing artery in her brain burst like a constellation. She ran out of the hospital, blindly she ran along a roadway. She ran in a place unknown to her where the air was thin as a razor blade and did not nourish her fainting, failing brain. She ran from his incredulous and accusing eyes. She ran from the broken capillaries in his eyes. She ran from her husband's fingers groping for car keys in a nightgown pocket that did not exist. She ran out of the pathos of his pleading words.

Michaela, don't leave! Don't abandon me, stay with me.

If you abandon me something terrible will happen to us both if you abandon me . . .

20

The Experiment

Moments of lucidity. Even now in the Final Days in the gathering dark of rushing waters are islands of sudden bright coherence.

Staring at a cup of meds held out to him by a nurse, mouth softened into a curious smile: "D'you know, Michaela—I don't think the protocols of this experiment were designed with me in mind."

Close by at his bedside Michaela laughs for (she senses) that Gerard has said something witty. In the seventeenth day of the vigil Michaela is beginning to lose her sense of what is *humor*.

Still, she will jot these eccentric words down in a notebook of mostly empty pages. Wanting to recall, cherish, repeat to those who'd known and admired Gerard McManus.

I don't think the protocols of this experiment were designed with me in mind.

Another time, Gerard speaks with Michaela earnestly about Spinoza.

Not for the first time of course. Many times over the years Gerard has spoken of Spinoza with Michaela, always earnestly, and with an air of almost boyish elation. Contrasting the "agnostic" rigor of Spinoza with the "empty abstractions" of Kant and Plato. Spinoza, the very emblem of the solitary, fiercely independent soul.

In the role that came naturally to Michaela as the admiring

younger wife Michaela listened politely to Gerard at such times without really comprehending much of what he said. Now, years later, as Gerard speaks from his hospital bed, in a diminished voice, yet still earnest, urgent, enthusiastic, Michaela tries to listen more carefully and yet does not really understand.

In the notebook writing:

Changed my life. Because changed my way of thinking—the nature of thought.

All things are completed, finite. Contained within eternity. (Spinoza)

Every (physical) substance is necessarily infinite. Every (non)physical substance is necessarily finite.

Happiness is a finite quantity in so far as it is a phenomenon of time, space, & circumstance; but happiness is an infinite quantity in so far as it is a phenomenon of the soul (Eternity).

No idea what this means! Nonetheless Michaela inscribes it carefully in her notebook.

NOT CLEAR WHAT WORDS *MEAN*. If you are losing the one person in your life whom you love, and who has loved you.

One morning regarding her calmly over the front page of the *New York Times* which (Michaela sees in horror) he is holding upside down without realizing. How without his glasses reddened indentations are exposed in the tender skin at the bridge of Gerard's nose and his eyes appear enlarged, the irises dilated.

"My dear wife! You aren't sorry you married me, are you?"

Michaela laughs uneasily, what an absurd thing to say.

"You *are* my wife, aren't you? 'Michaela'!"

Smiling at her. As if delighting in her. But who is *her*? The name "Michaela" sounds questionable.

"Of course I'm your wife, Gerard. Why are you saying such things? You're frightening me . . ."

"You aren't disappointed, I failed you by dying?"

"You—you haven't failed me . . . You haven't died."

Michaela speaks quickly, faintly. It is frightening to her, the way her husband continues to stare smiling at her as if he has never seen her before.

"You will be coming with me, then?"

"Coming—where? Home?"

"Not home. No."

"Yes of course I'm coming with you." Then, not sure what she has agreed to: "Coming with you—where?"

"To the place they will be taking me."

Gerard speaks slowly, matter-of-factly. His eyes are gray-blue, the color of stone. The skin about his eyes is slack, white.

"There is room in these places for 'husband and wife.' You are my wife. There is room for *you*."

"I don't understand . . ."

"But you do. Yes."

RETURN TO THE RENTED HOUSE, collapse on the (unmade, unlaundered) bedsheets.

Exhausted cry yourself to sleep rumbling in something like an open boxcar along a rutted road, jolting your spine, jaws clenched, clammy-slick with sweat, thinking—*So this is Hell; but I am not even there yet.*

As something crawls into your ear—tiny venomous insect, myriad fluttering legs—*almost, you can feel these legs*—and you wake in terror so extreme you can't scream.

21

Orpheus, Eurydice

Since Gerard's eight-month residency at the Institute runs through August, and they have tickets to return to Boston on August 30, it is quite reasonable for Michaela to purchase opera tickets for August 2, the opening night of Gluck's *Orpheus and Eurydice*.

Not an impulsive decision exactly but Michaela finds herself at the Santa Tierra Arts Pavilion where the opera theater is located, which she has not visited before, something like a pleat in time and she has had a break from the hospital, less than an hour, she will allow herself fifty-five minutes, must start back within ten minutes, walking swiftly, running.

Thank you, darling! One of my favorite operas.

Thank you for your faith in me. That I will be still alive.

Certainly Gerard will still be alive, it is not possible that Gerard will not be alive to attend the opera with his wife Michaela. Billions of human beings alive on that (future) date August 2, why not then Gerard McManus. And why not then seated beside Michaela. Once you are born, Michaela reasons, the odds are in your favor to survive.

Before you are born, especially before you are conceived—the odds are decidedly not in your favor.

Therefore, absurd to worry!

Michaela thinks that Gerard, who has a layman's interest in

architecture, will be impressed with the Santa Tierra Arts Pavilion that has been designed to blend with the local architecture of adobe, stucco, sandstone, glass. The Santa Tierra Opera House, featured on the cover of numerous magazines, is a particularly striking building, so constructed that the majority of its banked seats face the San Mateo Mountains, west of the city; performances are timed to begin just after sunset, in the afterglow that precedes dusk.

Thank you for such beauty, Michaela. I love you so much.

The mistake that Orpheus makes, turning to look back at Eurydice and in that instant dooming Eurydice to Hades forever, is an innocent mistake, Michaela thinks. Therefore, terrifying.

She hopes not to make any mistakes. Leading Gerard out of Hades.

Still, it isn't clear what a mistake might be, in life. For in life there is no script, no score. No accompanying music. There is no *author*, thus no *authorial intent*.

It should not have been a mistake to come to Santa Tierra, New Mexico. Yet, Michaela cannot help but think that if they'd remained in Cambridge, Gerard would not be hospitalized now.

High-altitude air, thin and unnourishing. Dust and grit borne on the ceaseless wind, absorbed into the tender pink tissue of lungs.

Coughing fits, a blood clot. (Bacterial) pneumonia.

Yes, but the metastasized cancers must have begun months before.

Cancerous cells, the body turning against itself.

If there is God, cancer is God turning against humankind.

Why?—because that is the nature of God.

Michaela is becoming light-headed adrift in the crowded city square where there appear to be only couples, families. Packs of tourists of whom some are speaking foreign languages.

She and Gerard had planned to hike to the historic district of Santa Tierra together from their house on Vista Drive, a distance of

several miles. They'd planned to visit the Spanish mission at San Gabriel, a local church notable for its painted Mexican murals, the Black
Eagle Antique Indian and Ethnographic Art Show, the Fiestas de
Santa Tierra, the Burning of Skli. (Michaela has learned that the
surpassingly ugly, obscene carving of a female figure with a gaping
mouth, gaping vagina, fingers like curved claws, which she'd hidden
from view in the rented house, is in fact meant to be a likeness of
Skli, a Native American goddess of creation and destruction.) Especially Gerard had looked forward to hiking in Cold Spring Canyon
in the foothills of the San Mateo Mountains and along the banks of
the Rio de Piedras; he'd spoken of visiting the fabled Pueblo Abode
of the Dead in the mountains, accessible only on foot. All these he'd
marked with red-ink asterisks in the *Lonely Planet* guide. So much for
the couple to explore, like newlyweds!

How long ago that seems, now.

Without Gerard at her side Michaela is disoriented, off-balance.
Like a captive creature that has thrown off its leash she feels guilty in
this public place strumming with life.

A captive creature that is also an experimental animal. The door
of her cage has been left open and without being aware of what she is
doing Michaela has wandered out of the cage . . .

Aware of random eyes lighting upon her, gliding over her. Snag-
ging on her like hooks in flesh. Though she has made no effort to
present herself as female, still less a sexual being.

She is thirty-seven years old. She has outlived her youth.

Lanky-limbed, with a narrow upper body, narrow hips. Her
lower lip feels swollen as if it has been bitten. Her tongue feels swollen. Her hair, once abundant, glossy, a rich chestnut brown, is now
sand-colored, dry; brushed behind her ears and kept in place by a
slightly frayed straw hat pulled down low over her forehead. So long
Michaela has avoided examining her face in a mirror, she scarcely
recalls what she looks like.

My beautiful wife! Kiss me.

It has been some time since Gerard has uttered these words, that burn now in Michaela's heart. She is faint with longing, remembering the man's look of stricken rapture that had so moved her at the time when they'd been newly *in love.*

Futile, to be recalling these words now. Cruel.

Missing Gerard! So badly.

Wishing she could slip her arm through his as she did sometimes when they were walking. Take his hand, hold his hand. The most precious intimacy between them (Michaela thought) had been such simple wordless gestures—more spontaneous than their lovemaking.

To be held. Protected. Assured—*I will never abandon you.*

Michaela feels a moment's vertigo, imagining Gerard's arms closing about her. A sensation of horror, that this might never happen again.

Wanting nothing otherwise. If not that, then nothing.

How estranged Michaela feels, in this popular tourist area of upscale boutiques and shops. For there is nothing here that she wants, that can be purchased.

Navajo jewelry, silver and turquoise. Bright-colored hand-woven rugs, glazed pottery, quilts and blankets. Exquisite carved wooden birds, animals, grotesquely exaggerated human figures. Why were animals respectfully depicted, while human figures were made freakish?

We hate and fear our own kind. We know our own kind, their black hearts.

Vendors call to her. Michaela smiles politely at them but doesn't linger. If Gerard were beside her they would visit some of the shops, especially those with craftsmen's workrooms attached. They would examine the many carved objects, sculpted figures. Gerard would probably want to buy one of the humanoid figures, some of them prankishly deformed, as in a parody of Native American iconography.

Repugnant to Michaela, to encounter replicas of the demon-gods whose likenesses she has hidden in her house. The Scavenger God Ishtikini with his coarse black "human" hair sprouting from a grotesquely large skull, swollen potbelly and skinny erect penis . . .

A label explains *Ishtikini takes many forms. Ishtikini is not what he seems. When you think of Ishtikini, think again.*

Without Gerard there is really little that interests her in the world of arts, crafts, gifts, objects. Nothing that could give her a moment's pleasure. Gerard had given her numerous gifts over the years and no doubt here in Santa Tierra he would have selected silver-and-turquoise jewelry for her, which she would have worn with much pleasure. But without Gerard, what meaning did jewelry have? What meaning did anything have?

What Michaela wants is *immaterial*: Gerard restored to health.

Michaela pauses to read a description of *Orpheus and Eurydice* on a poster outside the opera house. How cruel, the legend!

As Orpheus leads Eurydice out of Hades he has to release her hand without explanation as he walks, not beside her but ahead of her; in confusion Eurydice feels this as a rebuke and doubts his love, cries out his name; Orpheus turns heedlessly to comfort her, as a husband would comfort his wife—and in that instant, Eurydice dies.

Because Orpheus so loves Eurydice, he forgets the admonition not to turn back to her when she calls after him.

Even as Eurydice despairs of Orpheus's love, his love for her guarantees that he will destroy her.

The old legends. What is most human in us will be our curse, and will assure our damnation.

ABOUT THIRTY FEET AWAY AT the edge of the square, partly hidden by pedestrians, Michaela notices a bizarre male figure. This person is not in her path but perpendicular to her path. A man of about Gerard's age with a wispy gray beard, disheveled gray hair. Shockingly he appears to be wearing a hospital gown. An IV tube hangs from one of his (badly bruised) arms. Smears of blood on his clothing. His ghastly-white legs are bare and he is wearing paper slippers!

Is this Gerard, somehow? Michaela stares in horror.

Michaela knows that this person isn't Gerard. Could not possibly be Gerard. And yet—Michaela stares.

She would call to him but her throat has shut up. Her swollen tongue fills her mouth, she cannot speak.

Gerard!—the name is choked, inaudible.

There is a surge in the crowd, the forlorn figure in the stained hospital gown is lost to Michaela's sight. Michaela tries to follow after him but has no idea where he has gone.

It feels to her that Gerard in his hospital gown, an IV tube dangling from his arm, is carried away from her as in a rush of water.

Wave upon wave, churning water.

Oh but it's ridiculous! That this (homeless, mentally ill) person could in some way be Gerard, her husband. A distinguished scholar, a Harvard professor, fellow of the Santa Tierra Institute for Advanced Research . . .

But if it is Gerard you must lead him out of Hell. You must not abandon him.

Michaela turns away, shaken. Must leave, must return to the hospital immediately, this is a summons. Walking swiftly, beginning to trot, panting running up the steep hill she soon sees the stucco facade of the Santa Tierra Cancer Center rising before her, majestic.

Rows of windows glittering like eyes obscuring the sky.

The Vigil: Night

At first he'd sent you home at 10:00 P.M. each night. Seeing that you were exhausted, and needed sleep: *Go back to the house, darling! I'll see you in the morning.*

Each day very long. Though not (yet) interminable.

Kissing your hands, kissing your tremulous eyelids, kissing your lips as you leaned over him suffused with love for him.

He'd be fine, Gerard insisted. He'd smiled, even laughed. It is the hospitalized husband's particular pleasure to laugh at the wife's fears for him which are (he is sure!) exaggerated.

He would watch news for a half hour: TV, computer. CNN, MS-NBC, PBS, BBC. He would finish the *New York Times.* Then try to sleep, turn out the lights by 11:00 P.M. Mornings began at dawn in the hospital but no need for you to come before 8:00 A.M.

Though usually, you would arrive by 7:30 A.M.

At that time much was practical, pragmatic: which books he wanted you to bring for him, which tasks he hoped you might do for him, calls to make for him, research to do for him (online, but also at the Institute library). Take-out food (Chinese, Italian, Middle Eastern) it was your task to bring for him, and for you, to eat in place of the (mediocre) hospital food that roused him to such scorn.

But soon, Gerard would cease complaining about the food. Soon, he would cease being interested in food. He would cease asking for books. He seems to have ceased working on *The Human Brain and Its Discontents* whose scattered pages you take care to reassemble and place for safekeeping on a high closet shelf without comment.

Vaguely Gerard says that when he's "out of the damned hospital" he will return to the manuscript and finish it.

You will help him, you assure him.

Yes—*by and by!*

WEEKS LATER IF GERARD IS AWAKE when you prepare to leave for the night he will lift his head from the pillow weakly, plead with you: *Don't leave just yet, Michaela! Stay with me . . .*

Yes! You will.

Of course, you will.

Won't leave him until he has fallen asleep.

Linger at his bedside, holding his hand, stroking his fingers, talking to him, reassuring him, until he drifts into the opioid sleep that has made his skin ashen, his face slack. His breathing erratic, hoarse.

Dilaudid drip in his badly bruised right arm begun at 9:00 P.M., to render the patient unconscious, near comatose.

Not the elusive Dr. N___ (deeply embarrassed by the prospect of his failure as an oncologist to keep his patient alive as he'd seemed to have promised at the outset) but soft-spoken Dr. S___ (palliative care nurse practitioner, female) has explained to Gerard and to you: the choice is between (excruciating) pain but clarity of mind and (narcotized, numbed) pain but a befuddled mind.

Except: if you are in (excruciating) pain, you cannot really be clear-minded.

Then we don't really have any choice, Doctor. That's what you are saying.

I'm afraid yes. Yes, I am afraid—that is what I am saying.

NO END. NO BEGINNING.

Except of course there is: an end.

Sick with guilt each night leaving Gerard. Sick with panic knowing that one morning you might return and Gerard will be gone.

But they wouldn't do that—would they? The hospital has your number(s). They would call to summon you in the night.

Each night you remain longer in the room. Inertia has suffused your limbs. For Gerard does not want you to leave. For Gerard becomes visibly anxious when you prepare to leave. And then it is 11:00 P.M. when the hospital shifts to its nocturnal rhythms. Fewer footsteps, fewer voices, TVs stilled, rooms darkened. Passing darkened rooms on your way to the elevators at the end of the corridor you are ravaged by guilt.

You have come to feel a particular unease, a mounting fear, seeing dusk deepen outside the windows of the room, slow movement of glittering lights miles away at the interstate highway. Lights of the city, lights in the sky, gradually fading as the room's reflections swallow the world beyond the window.

Gerard no longer watches TV. No longer cares for "news"—what once roused him to anger, disgust, dismay seems to make little impression upon him.

And does he want to work on his manuscript any longer today, or should you put it away for him?

By and by.

Not a reply that is an answer exactly. But if you carefully rephrase the question the reply is, simply—*By and by.*

IN A TRANCE OF EXHAUSTION descend seven floors to the near-deserted front lobby. Every detail of the elevator interior—the positioning of the lighted floor buttons, Day-Glo posters advertising the hospital cafeteria and gift shop, dull scratches and scrapings in the walls—is familiar to you as the inside of your eyelids though it is (simultaneously) (immediately) forgotten, erased from your consciousness, the moment you step out of the elevator.

At the long front desk only one receptionist remains at this hour of the night to recognize you as the wife of a patient on the seventh floor: Oncology.

G'night, ma'am. See you tomorrow!

You smile, you wave. Always polite to smile, wave. Though your heart is broken you can smile, wave. Why the hell *not*.

"IF YOU COULD STAY, Mrs. McManus. Maybe—tonight . . ."

Your husband's condition has not improved, it might be said that your husband's condition is worsening so better stay the night. Starting tonight. For sometimes it seems that Dr. McManus is becoming *confused, disoriented*.

Helpful to have a family member in the room at such times—the nursing staff explains.

(Try not to notice that the youngest nurse appeals to you with eyes of extreme unease. *Is she frightened? For God's sake of what—who?*)

Yes but there are no other family members, you inform them. Yes there is only the wife.

Sometimes a very sick patient will eat if a loved one urges him. Please!

Lifting a soup spoon to Gerard's mouth, slowly, cautiously. Spoon clicking against recalcitrant teeth. Easy to spill, take care. Spooning tiny portions of yogurt, cottage cheese. *Your favorite, darling: blueberry. Please try.*

Opens his mouth like a fledgling bird. Starving but cannot eat. Food makes him nauseated. Foods he'd liked well enough just last

week, sliced bananas, Cheerios, apple juice now make him nauseated.

Can't swallow. Gagging. Pushing your hand away.

Enough, Michaela. Stop.

He is forgiving you. Yet, he is (sometimes) (often) furious with you.

YOU WILL KISS GERARD, you will take some solace from the fact,
though it is a minor, mild fact, that Gerard kisses you in return, if but
weakly. And then, summoning your strength to climb up onto the
bed and lie beside him, taking care not to jostle him, not to interfere
with the IV lines in his arms. Snug, snuggling. Curving your arm
over his body, firmly. Your head beside his head on the pillow. Gently
nudging his head. Your breath seeking a rhythm with his.

Declaring that you love him. You will never leave him. You are
his wife—*Michaela.*

The most delicious sleep washes over you. For you are very, very
tired. Shut your eyes, begin the free fall into darkness.

*Love you, will never leave you. Love love love you will never leave
you, that is a promise.*

BEGGING—*BREATHE! PLEASE, DARLING.*

One long Möbius strip of time—interminable.

Since you'd driven Gerard to the ER one morning in late January. Beside you in the passenger's seat complaining in a jocular voice
that you are *overreacting—exaggerating*—as usual. Gerard allows
you to know, between fits of coughing, that he has been humoring
you, that is all.

At the ER they will (he predicts) examine him, run a few tests
and then release him. His problem is nothing more serious than the

damned chronic asthma exacerbated by the hot dry New Mexico air but treatable with medication.

Smile, try to believe. Your husband's illness is entirely your imagination. It is *not real*, it has not the power to *kill*.

Yes but you are grateful that he is humoring you. A husband's love for his wife—*humoring her*.

Sleep on the vinyl couch a few feet away from your husband's bed. For now all pretenses have been torn aside, crumpled and discarded like a sheet of thin crackling paper on an examination table after it has been used. You will stay the night because the nighttime nurses have entreated you. Because you understand, you dare not leave.

Not comfortable on the vinyl couch, too short for your height but no matter: you won't be able to sleep in any case. Conscious of machines in the room. And of your husband's hoarse labored breathing.

Try not to count breaths. Try not to count seconds between breaths.

But where are we? What is this place?

SALINE DRIP. OXYCODONE DRIP. DILAUDID DRIP. Hydromorphone drip. Kidney stent. Pulmonary embolism. Adenocarcinoma. Venous thrombosis. Gastrointestinal consultant. Gallbladder ultrasound. Echocardiogram. CT brain scan. MRI. fMRI. Radiation, chemotherapy, immunology.

Transition to hospice care.

ANOTHER NIGHT, though (yet) the same night.

You are lying on the couch covered by a thin hospital blanket. And a heavy-knit sweater. You are not undressed, you are wearing shirt, slacks, cotton socks. Your head pounds with pain and with a reverberation of pain and you are certain that you haven't slept during the interminable night yet you are being jolted awake by Gerard alarmed and belligerent sitting up in his bed a few feet away though heavily sedated yet Gerard has been wakened by pain or by panic or by terror crying—*Hello? Hello? Hello? What's going on here?*

A voice not Gerard's voice. A voice high-pitched, tremulous with fury you would claim you'd never heard before.

What's going on here? Where is this? Hel-lo! HELLO!

You are very frightened. You have never seen your husband so agitated, his face so contorted. Try to comfort him but he flings off your hand. Assure him that nothing is wrong, you are here with him, you are in the hospital in Santa Tierra with him where he has been ill, but he has been receiving the best medical care . . . In his excited state Gerard doesn't hear you. Staring at you without seeming to recognize you.

You!—you!—you . . .

Before you can stop him Gerard has lifted the sheet from his lower body, seizes the catheter tube and tries to yank it out of the tender stub of a penis. Muttering, cursing as you've never heard him before in commingled fury, despair.

Struggle with the distraught man, grasp his arm, Gerard has lost weight in the hospital but still he is strong, stronger than you and he has the advantage of indignation on his side—*What's this godamned thing! Take this out, get rid of this!* You are astonished, this furious tearful man is not Gerard. You struggle with him, try to explain. Where he is, why he is here. Why you are here with him, you will take care of him . . .

Your gentlemanly husband, Gerard McManus! Unshaven, ashen-faced, scanty gray hair in tufts like the hair of a madman, eyes glaring with hatred of you.

Fuck this! Fuck all of this! You!

Ring the nurse's bell! Ring again, again.

No answer for long terrible minutes as Gerard threatens to throw himself out of the bed, tearing tubes out of his arms, dislodging the catheter. You are sobbing, pleading with him. Reduced to begging him even as Gerard slaps at you, strikes your shoulder with a fist. *You—what are you doing to me! You—who are* you!

At last in a panic you abandon the distraught patient and run out into the corridor. Run, run!—to the nurses' station. Telling a startled-looking nurse that your husband is frightened and excited and doesn't know where he is, you are afraid that he will hurt himself, he will throw himself out of bed—"Please send someone! Right now! Oh please—*help us.*"

NOT ABLE TO STAMMER—*I am terrified of him.*

Terrified of what is happening to him. To us.

23

Prosopagnosia

He'd always been good with faces. Remarkable visual memory for people he hadn't seen in decades, former students, post-docs whose names he could summon within seconds. As a very young child he'd taken pleasure in memorizing mathematical tables—multiplication, division. Later, the periodic table. Vocabulary lists, foreign words and phrases. Maps of the world. Anatomical charts—bones, tissues. Areas of the brain—(and there are many). An acute visual memory for places he hadn't seen in years, trails he'd hiked only once or twice, preserved somehow in his brain with oneiric clarity.

Michaela, whose memory was softer, less defined, impressionistic and wayward and determined more by emotion than logic, envied him, and was at times astonished by him.

Yes, darling. But I've forgotten much more than I've remembered. Much much more!—Gerard laughed, deflecting praise.

(Should Michaela have been hurt by the way Gerard deflected her praise of him? As if she were—merely—flattering an important man, as others might do? A curious sort of modesty, Michaela thought: accepting praise was to Gerard incurring debt, and incurring debt from any source made Gerard uneasy.)

He'd entertained Michaela with tales of a famous neuroscientist friend who suffered from such severe prosopagnosia, or face blindness, he couldn't recognize his own reflection in a mirror or photograph. (Later, Michaela would learn that Gerard's friend was Oliver Sacks with whom he'd collaborated on several projects as a young experimental scientist at Columbia.)

Not recognize his *own face*? This seemed to Michaela hardly believable, in a person (like Sacks) otherwise so highly functioning.

Gerard assured her, it was so. The way in which neurons "recognized" faces was scarcely understood, it was so rapid and usually so accurate.

Prosopagnosia—a neurological pathology in which neurons did not fire, and did not "recognize." Some are born with the condition, some develop it as a result of illness or impairment to a part of the brain. And some simply acquire it with age.

HIS EYES ARE OPEN, *and they move—warily. There is a glisten of intelligence in them. There is the old glisten of irony, self-awareness.*

No. It is a glisten of fear, terror. He has no idea where he is, what he is "seeing."

Perhaps he sees nothing except gradations of light, shadow. He sees "figures"—shapes—that move and dart about, senselessly. Perhaps he no longer hears as he once did. Hearing your voice he does not understand that it is "your" voice or even that it is a "voice."

Seeing you he is not seeing "you"—he is seeing beyond you.

24

Hospice/Honeymoon

Like a (short) thread through the eye of a needle, swiftly in and swiftly out.

Once the word is uttered—*hospice*. A seismic shift, the very air becomes thick, humid.

At the periphery of your vision, a dimming. As the penumbra begins to shrink.

In time, it will become a tunnel. Ever diminishing, thinning. Until the remaining light is small enough to be cupped in two hands. And then, it is extinguished.

For when *hospice* is uttered, it is acknowledged—*There is no hope.*

No hope. The words are obscene, unspeakable. To be *without hope* is to be without a future. Worse, to acknowledge that you are without a future—you have "given up."

When the word *hospice* was first spoken—very carefully, cautiously, by a palliative care physician—it was not clear that either you or Gerard heard it. If you heard, you didn't register it.

A low-grade buzzing in the ears, a ringing in the ears as of a distant alarm, an alarm in a shuttered room. That was all.

Eventually, *hospice* came to be more frequently spoken.

Eventually, Gerard came to utter the words *final days.*

As if shyly. On the phone. So that you would not have to see his face. Or he, yours.

Like stammering *I love you.*

For some, an impossible statement—*I love you.*

But Gerard had managed it, and you'd managed it—not easily, not glibly, but earnestly, tearfully: *I love you.*

I think these might be my final days. Quietly, calmly Gerard had told you.

And so you heard, but hadn't heard. No.

But yes, you'd heard. The walls of the (bath)room reeling around you, you'd almost fainted and struck your head on the porcelain bathtub.

Like a frightened child protesting—*No! Don't say such things, these are not your "final days"* . . .

You could not bear it. Not knowing, at that time, the vast Sahara that lay ahead of all that you could not, cannot bear.

For always, each step of the way, you'd resisted.

Until a day, an hour. Always there is a day, an hour.

When you began to speak of *hospice* yourself.

At first you too were shy, faltering. Your throat felt lacerated within as if by lethal metal filings.

Gradually you learned to utter the two syllables clearly, bravely— *hos pice.*

Soon then, you began to say *our hospice.*

Soon, you began to draw up your vows. Quaintly stated to yourself as if to God, a formal decree.

It is my hope: I will make of our hospice a honeymoon.

My vow is to make my husband as comfortable as he can be.

To make him happy. To make us both happy.

To fulfill whatever he wishes, that is within the range of possibility.

First: a new setting for him. NOT the Santa Tierra Cancer Center.

Our hospice will be in the glass-walled house on Vista Drive. We have signed a lease through the end of August. The living room is flooded with morning light, there is a view of the San Mateo Mountains.

Always there are beautiful sculpted clouds! Gerard will lie propped up in his bed, staring.

Holding hands, we will hold hands. I will sleep beside him holding him.

A hospital bed so positioned that Gerard will always be facing beauty: mountains, sky.

I will scatter seed on the redwood deck outside the window. Gerard will be thrilled to watch the birds . . .

And Gerard loves music! We will bathe him in the most beautiful music through his waking hours.

Holding hands. Listening to Beethoven, Mozart. So long as it is possible I will lie beside him, holding him. Listening together to Beethoven's "Ode to Joy."

Falling asleep together. Head on the pillow beside Gerard's head.

I will bring home art books, his favorite artists, we will look at beautiful works of art together. I will hold his hand, we will look at beautiful works of art together.

His favorite foods . . . Well, we will try!

Perhaps in a new setting Gerard's appetite will return.

I will fly back to Cambridge, Mass., for just one day. Select photographs for Gerard to look through. His childhood, his parents. His family. His first marriage, his children. Eventually, photographs of us together— our marriage . . . We will not be hurried as we look through these precious photographs recording Gerard's life. We will hold hands, we will weep together and comfort each other.

Our hospice will not be sad but joyous, a honeymoon.

Another possibility is to establish our hospice in Cambridge, on Monroe Street. Set up Gerard's hospital bed in his study on the second floor, with a view of the back lawn, trees. A foreshortened view, not a view of mountains, but Cambridge would mean a familiar setting: Gerard's friends, colleagues, students; Gerard's books, both those Gerard McManus had written and those thousands of books that Gerard McManus owned.

(For Gerard is begging to be brought home. Home! Home!—Gerard is pleading. And by home Gerard does not mean Santa Tierra.)

But how to transport Gerard from Albuquerque to Boston? If he is not well enough to fly commercially? A medical transport plane would cost thirty thousand dollars (I have done the research) and then an ambulance would be required to bring him from the airport to the house, and hospice nurses would have to be waiting to take care of him . . . The danger is, it's been pointed out, that a seriously ill patient might be stricken en route, might not survive the journey of an estimated eight hours.

No matter. We will establish our hospice/honeymoon here.

We will be happy here, Gerard's final days.

IN FACT, NOTHING REMOTELY LIKE this happened.

Hospice, yes. *Honeymoon*, no.

The Unbearable

When Michaela was a very young child of three or four it began: the dream of the unbearable.

A sensation of something pushing inside her head. Opening its black-feathered wings wider and wider squeezing her skull out of shape.

Or, a vise around her head. Tighter and tighter the vise squeezing her skull out of shape.

Screamed, screamed until her throat was scraped raw. Eyes rolled back into her head sightless. Skin hypersensitive scalding.

Michaela, wake up! Stop that screaming!

Just a bad dream, it's nothing.

Heaven's sake—stop.

YOU'RE NOT A BABY NOW, *you're a big girl.*

Waking us all up—just stop.

MAYBE IT WASN'T A DREAM. Maybe it was sheer sensation. A rapid and abnormal firing of neurons precipitating acute anxiety, a sensation like convulsion, epilepsy.

(Has Michaela ever been tested for epilepsy? MRI to detect subtle abnormal brain waves?)

(No, and she doesn't intend to. Best not to know.)

For years she'd forgotten. Outgrown the dream. Then, in her thirties the dream has returned.

Hard to determine if you are awake or asleep. And if you are sleeping beside another person, should you try to shield that person from the nightmare; should you try to muffle your panic, your screams . . .

A bad dream, that was all it was. Christ!

(Or was it *life*?)

Sheer sensation of something tightening, ever-tightening, to the point of the unbearable. Squeezing her skull out of shape, eyeballs bulging from their sockets. Never has Michaela been able to describe this dream, if it is a dream, to another person.

Intimacy is a risk. Step by step on ice you can't know: is it thick, or is it not-thick? Is it *thawing*?

The next step you take, will the ice crack beneath your feet and plunge you into freezing water? Making you, along with your terror, something of a fool.

Many times she'd tried to explain the *unbearable* except not to Gerard McManus who'd come late into her life. By which time she'd grown cautious, wary.

Not wanting Gerard to know. To suspect. That Michaela wasn't the radiant-faced young woman he believed she was. That she was not *placid-souled*, as he'd liked to think.

When they'd first met he'd been charmed by her youthfulness, her vivacity. He'd thought she was ten, twelve years younger than her age. *He* was the older man, emotionally battered, wry, a person of some public reputation, that was his role. She could not disillusion this man that she might be older and more battered in her soul than he in his.

BABIES THAT HAD CLUNG TO the insides of her uterus as to life itself. Bleeding out at last in a hemorrhage of suety-thick black blood. Even when she'd wept with relief yet she'd wept also with grief. For such bleeding is a kind of weeping.

The body weeps, that part of the body drains away in sorrow each month. Michaela had been stunned when she'd first begun to bleed at the age of fifteen, later than most of her girlfriends, still somewhat disbelieving that such a thing could happen, especially to *her*.

Interludes in her life when she'd lost so much weight, she had ceased menstruating without realizing. Light-boned, effervescent in her soul. Seeing nursing mothers bare fat white blue-veined breasts to their infants in public she'd stared in astonishment as one might stare at the antics of another species.

Have you ever been pregnant?

Well—not that I know of. No.

But wouldn't you know?

I—I'm not sure. Would *you always know?*

No one knew, she'd told no one. Whom would she tell? A fetus conceived by chance in lonely sorrow has no father.

Pregnancy: a foreign substance has made its way up into the cavities of the body then takes root and grows, grows and grows by degrees forcing the body out of shape.

Something that has crawled into her ear? As she lies vulnerable, unaware? Could be a spider, scorpion, tick. Once inside the ear, burrowing.

Or, making its way up into her nasal passages. Swarming into the brain.

If the brain is lacerated, bleeding. Nowhere for the blood to go. Pressure increases, the pain is excruciating.

As if something too large is being forced inside the skull.

Late-night hours of the vigil in the Final Days, the unbearable has become the very oxygen she craves. As if all of her life has led her to this. As all of her prior life—fear, panic, terror—has been a preparation for this. To cry to the one whom you love *Breathe! Breathe!*—even as breath begins to fail. Yet to cry *Breathe!*—fitting your mouth to his. What words to describe this ordeal, there are no words. Words fail, very breath fails. A high-pitched whistle that becomes ever more higher-pitched, slowly drives the hearer mad. The slowly increasing temperature that results in a boiled brain.

She has failed utterly: in her distraction she'd forgotten to bring her (secret) cache of pills. In the night as Gerard labored to breathe she might have ingested enough pills to convulse her heart yet of course she hadn't prepared, she has not prepared, in any case she would have been discovered slumped on the couch beside her husband's bed, a barely discernible pulse, still alive, rushed downstairs to the ER where technicians would have revived her. For of course no one will respect a naive suicide's wish *do not resuscitate.*

Any way you consider it, a failure of courage and of imagination.

And now, too late. Of course she is going to hold her husband as he dies. Of course she is not going to allow her husband to die alone, unloved. Hours she will hold him, beg him—*Breathe! I love you.*

In her exhaustion recalling how one day her mother asked her almost casually, as if the subject had just come to mind, if she remembered when she'd been a little girl and so sick, she'd almost died: "Your father and I were in the Peace Corps, in Uganda. In our late twenties. We'd committed to some idea of 'public service'—'helping.' But we had a child—you. That wasn't so practical, I don't know what the hell we were thinking. Things were going OK until we all got sick. Then *you* got really sick, some kind of fever, like measles but worse than measles, you were just two years old. Your temperature just kept rising no matter what the doctor told us to do. I remember the thermometer climbing to 102.1 degrees Fahrenheit. You were burning up! I was crying and terrified we were going to lose you, your poor skin was so hot. Sometimes we couldn't tell if you were breathing. Other babies in the clinic were dying—dehydrated. Their little veins were too small for IV lines. The doctor was this bearded American guy who looked like pictures of Charles Darwin except he was only about our age. He'd kind of inherited the clinic, he said. Might've been he wasn't an actual doctor, like an accredited doctor, or licensed, whatever—he said he'd graduated from Penn Medical School but didn't have an M.D. He was a kind, caring guy, turned out to be a morphine addict, but that was later. He hadn't slept for a week, he told us, with this kind of 'plague' like measles. I remember how scared we were, and powerless, kind of hopeless like God had sawed off the tops of our skulls and was grinning down at us. This guy we wanted to believe was an actual doctor telling us that in another few hours we would know, and we said, know what?—*what?* And he said, if your daughter will survive the fever and if she does survive, whether she will survive as the daughter you know."

FINAL DAYS. FINAL TIME. But never do you know it is the final time.

Approaching the hospital. Your mind is a sieve through which such random thoughts flow in a continuous stream. *H'lo, ma'am*—the last time the (morning) receptionist nods and smiles yet nonetheless insists that you sign the ledger as you have signed it unvaryingly for weeks:

MICHAELA MCMANUS 771 ONCOLOGY (DR.) GERARD MCMANUS

Wanting to tell the receptionist—*But we will have our hospice, in our home. Our honeymoon.*

Wanting to explain—*So you won't be seeing much of me, soon.*

But there are no words. Already you are turning away.

Rising in the elevator to the seventh floor. That stunned compliance, as of cattle struck by mallets, rendered unconscious on their feet as they stumble along the chute to slaughter. As the *unbearable* seeps into your brain. Such pressure in your brain! *Breathe!*—you plead with yourself. Dare not faint, Gerard has no one but you.

MICHAELA, COME WITH ME!

There is a place for you. With me.

Canceled

This day, April 14, a notice is taped to the door of the seminar room on the ground floor of Memorial Hall, University of New Mexico at Albuquerque.

DUE TO UNAVOIDABLE CIRCUMSTANCES CREATIVE WRITING 343, MEMOIR (INSTRUCTOR M. MCMANUS) WILL NOT MEET TODAY.

"Good News"

A hospital vigil is notable for sudden interruptions for (often) you lapse into exhausted sleep at the bedside of the patient without knowing where you are or even *why* you are where you have no clear idea where you are, and (often) when you wake there is a pulsing pressure in your ears, inside your head trying to determine: *where, why?*

Not at your husband's bedside on the oncology floor but in another place not known to you though also (evidently) a clinical—chilly!—setting. (Why are hospitals so cold?—it's to discourage the [inevitable] growth of bacteria. Colder the temperature, less bacteria fecundity though never [of course] no bacteria fecundity so long as there is the warm pulsebeat of life.)

Roaring in your ears through which you are having difficulty hearing a doctor's jovial voice.

Good news, Mrs. ___!—there has been a new development in the patient's prognosis.

Good news, Mrs. ___!—bone marrow transplant has been approved provided you are still willing to donate bone marrow for your husband.

Good news, Mrs. ___!—there is a strong possibility that you can save your husband's life.

You are very excited to hear this. Yet, you are terrified.

You are in a conference room in the hospital. Several staff physicians are in attendance whose names are told to you, which you immediately forget. Oncologist Dr. N___ is explaining the marrow extraction procedure which involves a minimum of two hours of surgery under a partial anesthetic, performed by a bone marrow specialist. There is some risk (of course). There will be some pain (of course).

An eighteen-inch needle will be sunk into your hip bone and a minute quantity of marrow extracted.

In fact, as Dr. N___ points out, the "gravest risk" to the donor isn't the bone marrow extraction itself but the anesthesia.

Dr. N___ makes this pronouncement in a voice of such flatness, you understand that it is a witticism of some sort. Or perhaps it is an affectionate reproach. One of the physicians lifts a rueful hand to self-identity—Dr. T___, anesthesiologist.

Another physician is the bone marrow surgeon Dr. R___ who waves at you boyishly.

WEEKS BEFORE YOU'D TOLD Dr. N___ that you would like to donate bone marrow if it would help your husband. At the time Dr. N___ had shrugged off your request as if its naivete had offended him.

Overhearing, your husband had protested—*Don't be ridiculous! I wouldn't allow you to take such a risk and anyway, it isn't going to be necessary.*

You will note afterward how the prospect of weakening, failing, dying is viewed as "ridiculous" by many of the afflicted daring you to contradict them and so indeed you rarely contradict them.

Now, confronted with the prospect of the eighteen-inch needle sunk into your hip bone you are growing faint. You can feel blood draining from your head. In a voice of the most subtle reproach (for he can decipher your panicked thoughts) Dr. N___ says that the bone marrow transplant procedure is far more dangerous for the recipient than the extraction is for the donor: the mortality rate for the recipient is ___ (you do not hear this mumbled statistic) while the mortality rate for the donor is less than 3 percent.

Meaning, 97 percent chance of (donor) survival.

Such excellent odds of survival, you would be shamed into saying anything less than *Yes*.

Though you are shivering. Though you have begun to perspire. You feel a need to grasp at the edge of the conference table, to steady yourself.

Dr. N___ cups his hand to his ear. *What is your response, Mrs. ___?*

I said—yes. I will.

You will—?

—donate bone marrow for my husband.

There! The words are uttered.

Around the table the physicians stare at you, gravely nodding. In their eyes you believe you see respect, admiration. The (brave, good) wife will donate bone marrow for the husband!

Y-Yes.

A legal document is presented to you by a (female) notary public. It is oversized, with numerous pages and addenda. With difficulty you read the small print which even as your eyes move across lines of type fades rapidly, you cannot glance back to reread. And by the end of the (thirty-page) document you have forgotten what you've read.

Sign here, Mrs. ___. The notary public is witness to your signature.

Though your hand is badly shaking you manage to sign your name with a pen provided for you.

Such hoarse breathing! You hope it isn't your own.

Your skin is burning, the fever has made you delirious. Slick clammy sweat on your forehead, in your armpits.

Mrs. ___?—this way.

YOU ARE GREATLY RELIEVED, a (female) nurse's aide will be bathing you. Washing away the sticky sweat, the embarrassing smell of your (female, frightened) body.

Dry yourself in an enormous scratchy white towel, cover your nakedness in a short paper gown that ties at the back. If you sit on the edge of an operating table, the paper gown crinkles and rides up your thighs white as lard.

Absurdly modest for a woman of your age, a woman no longer young but with pretensions of appearing young.

The last of all pretensions is that of being sexually attractive. At least, to someone.

My husband thinks that I am beautiful. In all the world he is the only person who thinks so.

In all of the world my husband is the only person who loves me.

You are urged to lie down on the gurney. You will be transported to Surgery for the procedure. Overhead a perforated ceiling passes in a blur. Your hair falls in tangles over the edge of the gurney. You are helpless on your back as a turtle on its back. You see that you have lost weight since the start of the hospital vigil, you fold your arms across your small flaccid breasts as if to make yourself smaller.

You will be partially sedated, it is (again) explained. You will be partially conscious through the procedure but unable to move. You will not remember most of the experience afterward.

Yes, there will be pain. But if you do not remember pain afterward is it *pain*?

Yes, there will be grief. But if you do not remember grief afterward is it *grief*?

Skilled gloved fingers tap for a vein in the crook of your right arm. Your veins are dehydrated, many (painful) attempts to start a line are made, and fail, before a needle is inserted successfully—*One-two-three! This will pinch!*

A cry escapes your lips. But soon then you begin to float. Though your eyes are not open you see clearly the part-masked faces sur-rounding you in a ring above you, eyes brightly avid with curiosity.

An eighteen-inch needle is held aloft in gloved fingers, shining. Fascinated you observe it descend. A cold sensation on your left pel-vic hip bone, then a piercing pain, and a yet more piercing pain as the needle is inserted deeper, into the bone, into the very marrow of the bone. So extreme is this pain you have no breath to scream. You have no strength to move—you are paralyzed, as it has been promised.

Oh! Oh God help me . . . But your quaint cries are muted, no one hears.

Perhaps there is a surgical error, your brain seizes, your heart fails, you sink into oblivion: die.

Or, fail to die but wake in confusion in Recovery hours later.

Eyes open, Mrs. ___! Eyes open!

Your spine, your neck, and the back of your head ache with pain but your lower body has disappeared in a haze of numbness.

Where is your husband? Vaguely you expect your husband to have been brought to you, to grip your hand and to commend you for being very, very brave.

A sound of crinkling paper, the silly gown you are wearing that is badly smeared with blood has ridden up your thighs.

A sound of muffled coughing. Muffled laughter?

Solemnly you are informed by an embarrassed voice—*Not such good news, Mrs. ___! It appears you were not a viable candidate to donate bone marrow after all. It appears that you are paralyzed from your pelvic hip bone down.*

Stunned silence. You open your mouth to protest but no words issue forth.

More sounds of muffled coughing, laughter. You manage to push yourself up on your elbows, with much effort.

Silly woman! Did. You. Really. Think. That. Through. Any. Pathetic. Action. Of. Your. Own. You. Could. Save. Your. Husband's. Life.

YOU ARE INFORMED: your husband has died, he has been dead for forty-eight hours. The precious bone marrow extracted from your hip bone is in the process even now of being "donated" to another, wealthier, and more important patient.

You are informed: your husband has been awaiting you in the hospital morgue on Level C. You will be taken to Level C now.

Breathe

. . . this tale you tell, tell and retell. This tale you cannot bring to an end. This tale that has entered your own breathing. That is your heartbeat. That has seeped into the very marrow of your bones.

Breathe.
Breathe.
Breathe.
Breathe.
Breathe.
Breathe.
Breathe.

Death Certificate

Of course, the vigil has ended.

The tale you have been telling yourself has ended days ago.

The fever dream will persist but *breathing* has ceased.

In your desperate arms *breathing* has (finally) ceased.

How many hours, days, weeks you'd held your husband! Begging *breathe, breathe* . . .

But you failed him. You were not strong enough to prevail against Death.

Time and date of death: 2:36 P.M., April 13, 2019.

Santa Tierra Cancer Center, Santa Tierra, New Mexico.

Cause of death:

Acute renal failure

Acute hypoxic respiratory failure

Pulmonary edema

Metastatic urothelial cancer

YOU SHOULD MAKE MULTIPLE COPIES of the death certificate, Mrs. Mc-Manus. We usually suggest a dozen or more.

And whatever you do—don't lose the original.

PART II

Post-Mortem

30

The Wound

No, no! It has not (yet) happened.

A misunderstanding. Whatever has happened has not (yet) happened.

Waking from the fever dream stunned amid sweaty clothes. You seem to have fallen asleep on a couch too short for your legs. Sharp pain in your neck, pain the entire length of your spine, left hip bone sharp jolting pain where you'd been lying twisted with knees drawn to your chest.

"Gerard—"

Panicked sitting up immediately to see: your husband is (still) alive in the hospital bed, (still) deeply asleep, (still) breathing.

You feel an immense wave of relief. You could weep, Gerard is (still) alive.

All that has happened, or will happen, has not happened (yet).

So tired! You wonder if bone marrow has leaked from your bones, you have become so weak.

Make your way unsteadily into the bathroom. Right leg bearing most of your weight. In a mirror trying to detect a small circular surgical wound in the left pelvic hip bone but of course there is none but still a dull ache throbs where a wound would be, if there were a wound.

31

Post-Mortem

Mrs. McManus?—you can remain with your husband as long as you wish.

We will be waiting out in the corridor.

Still at the husband's bedside. Sobbing uncontrollably, body wracked in grief.

How useless, grief! As Gerard would observe, the evolutionary advantage in grieving is not self-evident.

Teeth chattering, the air is so cold!

Cannot bear to leave. For how can you leave.

What can be the precise moment, when a wife turns to *leave*.

You are holding Gerard, you are kissing his still-warm face, stroking his face, his crinkly hair.

With a nail scissors brought for this particular purpose you cut a lock of his hair.

In fact, two locks: one that is whitish silver, from his right temple, the other coppery-silver from the thicker hair at the back of his head.

How embarrassed Gerard would be! *Michaela, for heaven's sake what are you doing? Don't let anyone see . . .*

Beautiful hair! You will weep seeing these locks of your husband's beautiful hair preserved forever in a little white envelope hidden in a drawer.

His limp hands you lift in yours, and kiss. These are the hands of a man of good health—one would think: the skin not papery-thin but thick, ruddy.

Draw the blanket up around Gerard's shoulders. Tuck in around his neck. Often Gerard has complained of the cold in this room—he, who'd walked hatless in sub-freezing weather in Cambridge, Mass., no overcoat but only a tweed sport coat, gloves.

Heartily laughing at Michaela shivering in a quilted thermal coat to her ankles . . .

But who will laugh at you now? Who gives a damn about you, now?

Here is the strange thing: Gerard is no longer *breathing*.

Stare at his throat, his chest. Press the palm of your hand against his chest. Lean over, to determine—*is* he breathing?

His eyes are partly open. Blue-gray eyes unfocused as if a transparent film has grown over them. Yet, it seems that these eyes can "see" you—somehow.

As Gerard can "hear" you—somehow.

Whisper to him another time, almost shyly—*Breathe! Can you— breathe . . .*

Shy to beg the man after his long struggle—*Please try, try to breathe, don't give up, don't leave me, I love you so much . . .*

Gerard has not given up—has he?

You have not given up. But you are very tired.

Kiss his lips, that have begun to cool. A wild impulse comes to you, to bite the lips, hard. Gerard will wince, and cry out in pain.

Involuntarily, drawing in breath.

Breathe! Please try . . .

But it has been forty minutes, and then it is sixty minutes. Fascinating, the relentless passage of time.

Here is a riddle: How can there be a single, singular instant that is *the* instant of leave-taking?

For each instant might easily be the penultimate, not *the last*, instant.

Why then would one choose a single, singular instant that is *the last instant*?

You smile, this is absurd. There is no inevitable *last instant*.

The possibility that the vigil is finally over, and that Gerard has finally died, is unacceptable, illogical.

Unbearable thought like something that has squeezed inside your head and is opening its wide wings much too large for the inside of your head.

No, no!—you beg. Whatever it is, it must not open those wide black-feathered wings inside your head . . .

No, it is unbearable. Unfathomable.

And that final heaving exhalation—that sigh.

Always you will hear that sigh. You are hearing it now. The weariness, heaviness.

Breathed his last. Words stark and beautiful and intransigent.

Yet: Why would one breath—out of a lifetime of breaths—be *the last*? How could such a breath be determined? Surely not pure chance? And yet . . .

What would Spinoza say?—the beloved philosopher who'd seemed to believe in a purely determined universe yet seemed to believe, as well, in the human soul?

You are eager to ask Gerard. How Gerard loves to be asked such questions!

Gerard did not at all mind being interrupted in his study—if you had a question for him that merited interruption. *Come in! Come in! What can I do for you, darling?* Leaning back in the creaking swivel chair dangerously far with his hands clasped behind his head, creasing his forehead as he pondered the question, formulating a thoughtful and usually lengthy answer . . .

And come kiss me while you're here.

You are feeling weak, unreal. Shut your eyes and you can hear your husband's voice. Shut your eyes, you can hear your husband *breathing.*

Trying to recall what you'd asked Gerard, over the years. So many questions, and always there'd been answers. But now you can't seem to recall a single question or a single answer.

For you are fascinated, staring at Gerard's face. It is not an impassive face, it is not a "frozen" face—at any moment, it can become animated, life can rush back into the eyes. You are convinced of this. You seem to be awaiting this.

Gripping Gerard's hands in both your hands, to steady them. Otherwise, your hands will tremble terribly.

Yes, you are sure that in the next instant Gerard's eyelids might flutter, his lips might part, he might begin breathing again—his chest heaving into life again . . . Almost you can anticipate the first breath, a sharp intake of breath, the renewal of recognition in the eyes.

Wait. Never cease waiting.

MRS. MCMANUS? MAYBE YOU SHOULD *come away now.*

You've done all you can for your husband, Mrs. McManus.

Now—it's time to take care of yourself.

32

"Widow"

Numbly she makes calls. Yes, it is over. A vigil of weeks, now over. Yes, she is very sorry they were not informed but Gerard did not want visitors. Nor did Gerard want telephone calls. Yes, Gerard insisted.

Yes, they'd planned to transition to *hospice* in their rented house here. But no, that had not happened for Gerard had weakened too swiftly at the end.

Yes, she *is* sorry that there was no *hospice*—no visitors. For Gerard had weakened too swiftly. But no, there was nothing she could do about it then and there is nothing she can do about it now.

"I understand. Yes, it is very upsetting for you. Yes, I know that you loved him. But no, there is no need for you to fly out here. Gerard's request was for cremation. He did not want a funeral. He did not want a 'burial.' There will be a memorial in Cambridge, possibly in the fall. Of course you will be invited. Yes."

RETURNED TO THE ROOM, now the bed was empty and bedclothes removed. A sharp odor of disinfectant brought tears to her eyes.

Hours later. The cardiac and oxygen monitors had been removed, the room was unnaturally quiet. Anonymous. Of no significance that she could discern.

In the doorway she stood, stared. That bed—where had she seen that bed before? Something terrifying about that (empty, stripped) bed.

Something terrifying about (re)entering this room, and seeing that she was *alone* in this room.

For the first time, *alone* in this room. She was inclined to think that it must be a wrong or mistaken room for what could possibly be the purpose of being in this room *alone*?

As she would be assailed by the thought in hours, days, weeks and months to come: What could possibly be the purpose of a life *alone*?

Trying not to think *But where is he. Where have they taken him. What if he is not dead but still alive, he will wake and discover himself—where?*

Trying to fix her attention on the task at hand. Retrieving his things. Clearing out the room preparatory to leaving it forever. This was her mission, she'd insisted upon doing it alone.

Much in the room she would leave behind. All of the flowers including the pink begonias sent by the Institute's administrative assistant Iris Esdras who had been her principal contact with the Institute, and all of the magazines and newspapers accumulated on the windowsill. A few cards from the few acquaintances Gerard had made at the Institute before illness overcame him—these cards Michaela would take home out of respect for the senders though they are strangers to her.

In the drawer of the bedside table were Gerard's glasses, wristwatch, wedding ring, cell phone, Kindle. Immediately she slipped the wristwatch onto her wrist, she slipped the wedding ring onto her thumb. In a narrow wardrobe on a top shelf were Gerard's laptop, more books, what appeared to be the copyedited *The Human*

Brain and Its Discontents. She'd placed the manuscript there herself, for safekeeping, but scarcely remembers. Gerard's clothes on hangers rudely squeezed together in the small space. His favorite blue shirt, he'd worn for a few days in place of a hospital gown! She pressed her face into the shirt, she inhaled greedily. Khaki shorts, T-shirts Gerard had asked her to bring for him but never wore. He'd intended to spend more time sitting in a chair by the window, working; he'd intended to walk as much as he could in the hospital, explore a roof-top garden they could see from the window, when weaker he'd hoped nonetheless to be wheeled in a wheelchair (by Michaela) but somehow they'd done very little of this, time had passed too swiftly, the figure they recalled as Gerard's essential self, his healthy self, was ever rapidly retreating like a figure glimpsed in a rearview mirror as a vehicle speeds away. No need for Michaela to bring the clothes as there was no need for Michaela to bring so many take-out meals Gerard would be incapable of eating and realizing this now her heart was broken anew, she could not bear it.

Michaela, stop.

Just—stop.

She'd frightened Gerard, and then she'd angered him, when she broke down weeping in his presence, as she wept so often when she was alone, hoarse wracking sobs that seized her like a convulsion, face contorted, eyes burning with tears. The first time, Gerard pressed his hands over his ears, turned away appalled, he'd never seen Michaela in such a state.

She'd had the presence of mind to hurry from the room, to spare him. Like a wounded animal hiding in private, in a lavatory.

Of course, your husband doesn't want to see you crying. He doesn't want to know that you are terrified of his dying and he does not want to be terrified of his dying himself nor does he want to cry. So—stop.

He'd loved her less, she thought. After that scene.

Or, his capacity to love had weakened. Like the gauge measuring oxygen retention, faltering, erratic, but slowly falling. Fading.

Squat awkwardly to lift shoes, (soiled) underwear and socks from the floor. All these, stuffed into a bag, along with toiletries— hairbrush, toothbrush, toothpaste, deodorant hurriedly collected.

Toothbrush, deodorant. Michaela bit her lower lip to keep from sobbing.

Discovering then that the copyedited *The Human Brain and Its Discontents* was in a slovenly state: pages bent and mauled, some fallen to the floor amid the (soiled) underwear. How had this happened, Gerard's precious manuscript!

Michaela felt a stab of panic, guilt. If Gerard knew, he would be disappointed in her . . .

No. He would be furious. He'd trusted her!

It had been unspoken between them, that Michaela would safeguard the manuscript, initially until Gerard was well enough to be discharged from the hospital and work on it again, at home; later, when it seemed clear that Gerard would not be able to work on it, ever again. But Michaela must have lost track of it, distracted, distraught.

Seeing now to her dismay that pages were badly out of order. The entire manuscript must have fallen to the floor and someone—(one of the hospital staff?)—had hurriedly, carelessly shoved it together again. What a nightmare if pages annotated by Gerard were missing for, if they were, Michaela would have no way of knowing what he'd written in the margins of the manuscript; there was no computer file for such minute editing.

"Oh, Gerard. Forgive me."

Desperate, on her knees searching for lost pages. Beneath the bed, beneath the bedside table. There was page 93 badly torn, and another—page 261 . . . To her horror Michaela discovered a page so badly stained and torn, it was all but unreadable; another, the very inscription page that had made her so happy, in a corner of the room behind the bed.

Now reading—*for my ife and fir ael*

Relieved to find these pages, ravaged as they are. So grateful!

On hands and knees the widow crawls panting, sobbing. On her belly the widow crawls like a broken-backed snake.

33

Skli

Michaela! Why didn't you call me!
   Didn't I ask you please to keep me informed!
   What a terrible loss! A tragedy!
   Oh my poor, poor dear! Let me hug you.

Iris Esdras swoops upon Michaela like a predator bird folding Michaela in her wings. A buxom big-hipped woman of youthful middle age with a savagely painted face, dyed-black hair parted dramatically in the center of her scalp, exotic scarves, turquoise jewelry, perfume—except her manner is kindly, generous, maternal. No one has touched Michaela with such warmth in some time and so being hugged by Iris Esdras is overwhelming to Michaela, deeply moving if (slightly, somewhat, unmistakably) smothering.

In her hour of need Michaela has been befriended by the administrative assistant of the Institute for Advanced Research at Santa Tierra, the person with whom Gerard most frequently communicated before arriving in Santa Tierra. Ms. Esdras who'd insisted *If you need any help, any information at all—please don't hesitate to call me.*

Though she couldn't have known Gerard well, Iris's shock at his death appears to be genuine. The very *floridity* of her grief makes the widow feel anemic, inadequate. Even her inky-black mascara has smudged with tears.

Hugs Michaela. So hard, Michaela's ribs ache.

Assures Michaela, her *science-historian* husband Gerard was admired by everyone at the Institute. What a tragedy!

Iris insists upon driving Michaela home. They will do some grocery shopping en route. *She* will make the purchases, Michaela can remain in the car. Shut her eyes. Try to rest. Canny Iris seems to have deduced, from a glance at Michaela's haggard white face, bloodshot eyes, and greasy disheveled hair, the effect of the hospital vigil upon her.

No driving for Michaela! Her husband died just that morning, she must take care of herself now.

But arrangements must be made for the "disposal" of the body which is held only temporarily at the hospital.

Iris will help Michaela with arrangements at the Chapel of Chimes Funeral Home and Crematory (which the Institute recommends highly). In fact, Iris volunteers to call the Chapel of Chimes for Michaela, to make these arrangements.

Chapel of Chimes!—Michaela's numbed brain hears *Chapel of Crimes*.

The remains of Gerard McManus, being held in the morgue at the Cancer Center, will be picked up by a representative of the Chapel of Chimes and brought to the crematory.

Ah, Chapel of *Chimes*. Michaela is listening attentively.

And this too dazzles Michaela's numbed brain: her husband is no longer *Gerard*. So long as he'd been breathing, and Michaela had held him secure in her arms, he'd been *Gerard*. But now he has been transformed into *the remains of Gerard McManus*.

Michaela wonders—*But where is Gerard? Is he not "his" body?*

Would Spinoza have known? Is there a spirit that inhabits a body, or is the spirit suffused through the body? And where does the spirit go, when the body fails?

Iris informs Michaela that she has the option of being present at the cremating of her husband's remains and Michaela stares
blankly.

"You can make an appointment. You can be a witness. You don't
'see' the incineration, however—you see the coffin moving on a conveyor belt into a furnace heated to two thousand degrees Fahrenheit,
but beyond that—no. The process takes as long as three hours. You
witness by being present at the beginning."

Michaela quickly shakes her head *no*.

How ridiculous life is, Michaela thinks. Her husband has died
and has left her unprotected and unmoored and here she is calmly
discussing the "disposal" of his body with a stranger. And whether
she would like to witness its incineration. She is staring at a dark-
chocolate mole on the stranger's neck.

As Iris Esdras speaks Michaela imagines that the mole on her
neck is moving. In fact there is a scattering of small moles on Iris's
neck, the size of spiders or ticks, and all of them moving almost im-
perceptibly. (Why does Iris not notice? Does she not *mind*?)

Michaela wipes at her eyes, feeling light-headed. It has been one
of her unbearable dreams recently, she realizes—a swarm of very
small venomous insects crawling over her body as she lies paralyzed
in her bed . . .

One of them, crawling into her ear.

Seeing the look of distress in Michaela's face Iris seizes her hand
and squeezes it, holding the hand against her warm silky bosom.
"You will get through this, dear. We all do—we have."

Michaela resists the impulse to push away. No, no!—she isn't to
be claimed by strangers as one of their own.

As for clearing out Gerard's office at the Institute—(a new topic,
for which Michaela isn't prepared)—Iris assures Michaela that there
is "no urgency" about this. She will put Dr. McManus's books in

boxes herself, she will have the console computer carefully packed, everything delivered to the house on Vista Drive. And no urgency about vacating the house—of course.

Michaela feels a stab of panic. *Vacate the house?*—so soon? She and Gerard had signed a lease for the house, through August. She is sure that they'd jointly signed. She explains to Iris that she isn't ready to leave Santa Tierra yet. She is teaching a writing course at the University of New Mexico in Albuquerque and she is obliged to complete the term.

Also—(though Michaela doesn't volunteer this information)—she can't leave Santa Tierra because Gerard died here. The protracted anguish and agony of her husband's death, his heroism—his spirit. She cannot leave *him*.

If there is a soul, a lost, drifting soul, a soul "released" from its body—surely, that soul would remain here in Santa Tierra.

Though Michaela no more believes in an enduring spiritual life than Gerard or his scientist-colleagues believed in an enduring spiritual life yet somehow, she believes this.

Iris is saying, uncertainly, "Yes, of course, Michaela. You have leased the house until the end of August. But you might prefer to move into smaller quarters, while you teach your course. You might even move to Albuquerque."

Move to Albuquerque! Michaela is appalled. How would this be possible, when Gerard has died in Santa Tierra?

Iris informs Michaela that if she'd like to cancel the lease to the house that could be arranged. Under these "special circumstances" she would not be penalized—"Your deposit would be returned in full."

Michaela protests: "But I don't want to cancel the lease. I'm not ready to move out."

"It will seem like a large house for a single person, Michaela. Living up on the hill can be lonely . . ."

"But Gerard was living there, with me. Just a few weeks ago. It's our last place together. His clothes, his things are there. I will be working on his manuscript there. We had many places we'd intended to visit together in the vicinity of Santa Tierra. I can't—can't—move out, just yet."

"I understand, dear." But Iris speaks hesitantly, for she does not understand.

"I can't leave him, just yet."

"Oh, my dear. Of course you can't."

"I volunteered to donate 'bone marrow' to Gerard. For Gerard. I think that—I think that maybe it did happen . . ." Michaela pauses, confused. She seems to recall a very long needle sinking into her left hip bone. "I think they took 'bone marrow' from me but then, I'm not sure—they lost it . . ."

Iris listens with much sympathy, like one waiting patiently for an opportunity to change the subject.

"Do you think it's possible that, if they find it—the 'bone marrow'—if they locate it, at the hospital, they could—try again? With Gerard? Or"—Michaela falters, rubbing her left hip bone, seeing an inscrutable look in the other woman's face—"is it too late?"

Gently Iris says yes, it is *too late*. She is afraid—*yes*.

But the subject is—what? *Vacating the house*.

Michaela has not given her life elsewhere a thought in weeks. All of the universe has been narrowed to the vigil in the hospital, the siege at Gerard's bedside. Even now she finds herself concerned that she is in a wrong place: she should be in room 771 at the Cancer Center, for Gerard will be upset by her absence.

Terrifying to think that from now on, every place in which Michaela finds herself will be a *wrong place*.

It fills Michaela with revulsion, to contemplate returning without Gerard to the house on Monroe Street in Cambridge, Mass., in which she'd lived with him for the twelve years of their marriage.

The first thing you must do, before you even bring your stupid suitcases upstairs, is kill yourself.

However you can, you will find a way.

Michaela feels something strike her head—hard. She is astonished, confused—is she on the *floor*?

Somehow she has slumped to the floor. Sinking, not falling. Aware that she is fainting yet unable to maintain the strength in her legs. The blow to her left temple is a rebuke.

Iris Esdras is stooping beside her, exclaiming.

Almost for a moment, Michaela thinks that the white-skinned woman with the savagely bright makeup has knocked her to the floor.

Skli. Always hungry for revenge.

"Oh, Michaela! What have you done to yourself!"

Iris is appalled. She has pushed up Michaela's loose sleeves, revealing eight-inch striations on the insides of both arms. Gouges in the white skin which appear to have been made with sharp fingernails, not deep but bloody. The wounds are not fresh but days old and have formed long thin stippled scabs.

Michaela protests: "I didn't do this. I did not do this to myself."

Michaela is humiliated, stunned. Wondering if somehow these wounds are related to the bone marrow extraction . . . And why is this unwelcome stranger leaning over her in the guise of comforting her while at the same time chiding her, examining the lurid scabs on her arms which Michaela has never seen before?—it is all so embarrassing.

Gerard, dismayed by her weeping uncontrollably in the hospital, would be yet more dismayed by this.

"Michaela! You must let me help you."

Iris insists upon leading Michaela into a bathroom, washing her arms gently with soap, treating the wounds with an antiseptic liquid and placing Band-Aids over the long thin scabs. Michaela winces, for there is considerable stinging pain. But mostly Michaela is abashed—this excitable woman will think that Michaela has tried to kill herself, surely she will talk about Michaela to others at the Institute.

That poor woman—Gerard McManus's wife—widow . . .

So distraught, she tried to slash her wrists . . . but not very expertly.

So quickly this has happened, Michaela is trying to understand. Her mistake was letting Skli into the house.

Her mistake—*their* mistake—was entering this house which Skli and the other demons inhabited.

". . . will arrange for you to see a therapist, Michaela. I know several excellent therapists in Santa Tierra. I will not 'report' you—that would not be helpful for anyone. Obviously you've been under a terrible strain for weeks, seemingly with no one to help you, but this is not a solution, dear—what would your husband say?"

Michaela is staring at her bandaged arms. Vivid white gauze, adhesive. Unconvincingly Michaela protests that she'd never seen the long wavering scratches before. She hadn't felt any pain—none. (Until now.)

Had she gouged herself while sleeping, with her fingernails? Or at the hospital, at Gerard's bedside? To punish herself, as Gerard seemed to be suffering? To *suffer with* him?

(But Michaela's nails are dull, broken; she would never have been able to scratch her arms so deeply.)

"I have not 'cut' my arms. This is some sort of mistake."

Iris, driving, makes no response. Michaela says stubbornly, in a louder voice as if Iris were hard of hearing: "I know what you're thinking but you're mistaken. Not even as a teenager did I 'cut' myself. *I did not.*"

With a grim sort of satisfaction, smiling as a mother might smile, a maddening sort of concern shining in her eyes, Iris says: "Well. I will put you in contact with an excellent therapist—a 'grief counselor'—and you can explain to him."

IN THE HOUSE IRIS INSISTS upon remaining with Michaela until Michaela drifts off into an exhausted sleep.

Checking all the windows and doors. Informing Michaela, in a neutral voice, a voice trying not to scold, that Michaela had left the back door unlocked as well as sliding glass doors in the living room.

"You must take better care of yourself, Michaela. The first duty of the widow is to *stay alive.*"

Michaela is floating on a wide dark river in some sort of small boat. Gerard has told her the name of the river for they are to meet there: *Rio de Piedras.* On all sides are shrieks of wild parrots, monkeys. Out of the shadows the demon-goddess Skli emerges. A naked female figure with a shrieking mouth, drooping breasts, a gaping vagina like a wound, and long curved claws for fingers.

Lightly, teasingly, these claws brush along Michaela's arms which are not bandaged now but naked, highly sensitive.

Oh, unbearable! With a convulsive shudder Michaela is rudely awakened.

IMPOSSIBLE TO SLEEP. Michaela's first night as a *widow.*

Though Iris Esdras has departed, the cloying scent of her perfume remains. Almost, Michaela hears the woman's vehement exclamatory voice elsewhere in the house, words indistinct.

Stumbling into the bathroom. Avoids seeing her reflection in the mirror. For already she has been altered considerably, Gerard would scarcely recognize her ravaged face.

Hesitantly, frankly afraid of what she will discover, Michaela checks the cupboard beneath the sink: yes, the malevolent carved-wood figure of Ishtikini is still there, where she'd shoved it.

Except she is sure that she'd pushed it as far back as she could against the wall, ugly face turned away. But now it is facing her, impudently.

Elsewhere, several other disturbing *objets d'art* which Michaela had hidden away remain where she'd placed them including the figure of the demon-goddess Skli. A crude carving of about eight inches in height, mostly wood, with metallic fingers, sharp curved nails like claws. Under a bright light Michaela examines the claws.

Traces of blood? *Her* blood? Not sure.

Michaela would toss the hateful thing into the ravine behind the house except that it is the property of the Institute, as the house that is leased in her name until the end of August is the property of the Institute.

Places the thing inside the closet, shuts the door. Panting, swaying on her feet. Arms swaddled in white gauze, she will have to wear long sleeves when she goes out, to disguise the bandages.

She has been a widow for just nineteen hours.

34

Grief-Vise

In the grip of the grief-vise: all that you will do, all that you will even imagine doing, will require many times more effort.

Lying in your bed in a damp muddle of sheets. Lying with shut arms, legs, head bowed in a paroxysm of dread of what might happen if you move suddenly, "sit up" . . .

Hardly daring to breathe for the grief-vise will tighten around your chest squeezing the very air out of your lungs.

Hearing a telephone ring. A doorbell, repeated.

A voice faint, failing.

Where are we? What is this place?

Where are you? Michaela!

Why have you abandoned me?

35

Chapel of Chimes

"Mrs. McManus?—please come with me."

Mrs. McManus. Your heart sinks. Now there is no *Mr. McManus*, what is the ontological status of *Mrs. McManus?*

The Chapel of Chimes on Alameda Boulevard, Santa Tierra, is a stately dignified stucco building with a gleaming gilt dome, white Ionian columns, a sparkling fountain into which copper pennies have been tossed.

You wonder what the wishes might be of visitors to the Chapel of Chimes.

Too soon! Too soon! Give us back our dead.

Solemnly you are escorted into a large carpeted room containing a gleaming oblong table that could seat as many as thirty people. You are given to understand that funerals/cremations are not usually planned by a single individual but by families.

Waiting in the severely air-conditioned room for a Chapel of Chimes representative to meet with you. Available for your perusal are glossy brochures, tastefully prepared photo-displays of "theme" funerals/cremations suitable for men—bagpipes, hunting and fishing paraphernalia, skiing, sailing.

Also bowling, aviation, *Star Wars*, Elvis Presley . . .

Sudden rude snorting laughter. Is it *yours*?

You push the brochures aside. Through a dark-tinted window you see some sort of frantic activity outside: large dark-feathered birds scuffling about at the base of a eucalyptus tree.

Hearing a dull muffled rhythmic beat. Possibly, the beat of blood in your ears.

And what are you doing here, Michaela?—a voice bemusedly inquires.

Nowhere to be but *here*. For all places are equally unreal.

After what seems like a very long time but is probably only about ten minutes the door opens and a "crematory administrator" enters the room to shake your hand gravely. He is a middle-aged man in a dark suit, necktie, thick-tufted chestnut hairpiece. There is something about his protuberant eyes and just-perceptibly pitted skin that puts you in mind of—who?—Weyaki, God of Chaos?—but in an unperturbed voice he inquires if you have had time to peruse the printed material and if you have any questions and you assure him no, you have no questions, you intend to purchase the most basic cremation for your deceased husband, the plainest "recyclable" coffin, no hobby motifs, no special music. And the plainest "urn."

"Ah, yes! I see."

Weyaki is disappointed, you can tell. A steely light in eyes behind shiny bifocal glasses. Though surely Iris Esdras has informed the Chapel of Chimes that your husband was a research fellow at the Institute, an academic historian for whom a Spartan cremation would be likely.

"There will be a memorial in Cambridge, Massachusetts. In the fall. Gerard was a professor at Harvard."

"Indeed. Yes."

"A prominent professor at Harvard. All his friends—colleagues—are in Cambridge. We really don't know anyone here."

Bizarre to be volunteering so much information in a hoarse stilted voice not your own. As if you owe this stranger an explanation.

It is the most you have spoken in some time. You feel dazed, depleted.

Somewhat chagrined, you'd heard a quaver of boastfulness in your voice. As if, if one boasts of a (deceased) husband, this will make the loss less awful?

If indeed there is a memorial for Gerard in Cambridge in the fall you will select Gerard's favorite music for the occasion: Rachmaninoff's *Vespers*, Beethoven's "Ode to Joy," Murray Perahia playing Chopin, Bach. Though it seems to you unlikely that you will still be alive at that time.

Something distasteful, vulgar about remaining alive under these circumstances.

Weyaki busies himself preparing a contract for you to sign. Rebuffed by his customer the crematory administrator is now all-business, brusque and matter-of-fact. The price of the cremation, he says, including all fees and state tax, will be $2,639.86.

Gerard would laugh for Gerard took delight in commonplace absurdities. Why thirty-*nine* dollars? Why *eighty-six* cents?

Weyaki glances up at you as if you'd spoken aloud. As if you'd laughed scornfully.

All this while you have been distracted by activity outside the window which is a tall narrow dark-tinted window that emits a grudging light. In the near distance there is a stucco wall, and in front of the wall a eucalyptus tree at the base of which something is being attacked, or devoured, by scavenger birds resembling vultures.

Whatever lies on the ground helpless, animal, human—you don't want to look too closely. It must be dead for it is not defending itself against the ravenous birds.

Ah, it's white-skinned, naked—not an animal . . .

Politely Weyaki is asking if you have any questions about the procedure and the contract?

You are staring past Weyaki's thick-tufted hairpiece through the window at the thrashing birds whose wide wings obscure from your view what lies on the ground, helpless to defend itself against a staccato of stabbing beaks.

". . . how would you like to pay, Mrs. McManus? We request that you pay the full amount now, if you can . . ."

You stare, but cannot see. What is being devoured outside the window at the base of the eucalyptus tree, you cannot see . . .

Weyaki turns stoutly in his seat to peer out the window, puzzled that you seem to be staring at something behind him. But he sees nothing.

"Excuse me, Mrs. McManus? Is it—Michaela? Is there something wrong?"

It requires far too much effort to reply to this question even with a simple *no*. You ignore Weyaki, making an effort to wrench your eyes away from the window.

Lift the contract to read it closely as (you recall) Gerard would lift a page from the copyedited manuscript to peruse it when his eyes were no longer in focus.

Another time you'd seen him squinting at the *New York Times*, held upside down.

Never will you recover from the horror of seeing your brilliant husband trying to read the *New York Times* held upside down.

Signing the contract but your fingers are shaking. Steady your hand with your other hand as Weyaki looks on, frowning.

"I'm sorry, I can't—can't seem to . . ."

"Mrs. McManus? Do you need assistance?"

". . . it's just a tremor. It will go away in a minute . . ."

Shielding your eyes with your other hand, from the sight outside the window. Don't allow yourself to look.

ASHEN FACE. BRUISED EYES. SO TIRED!

Breathing breathing breathing that has insinuated itself into your lungs that breathe now in unison with your husband's lungs for his death has burrowed into your life.

EVENTUALLY, THE CONTRACT IS SIGNED.

You have been a widow for eighty-seven hours.

36

The Instructions

As follows.

The widow's mission to assure the husband's safe passage from this world to the next.

During these (crucial) days the soul will wander homeless.

The widow will receive notification when the cremation has been completed.

The widow will appear at the Chapel of Chimes to receive the ashes in an urn.

Embark then with the ashes to the River of Stones.

There, await further instructions.

THIS IS A SURPRISE!—she is not alone.

Waking in the house on Vista Drive chill as a morgue. In that first instant of wakefulness summoning her soul back into her body, which it enters reluctantly.

Turns out that Michaela is not a solitary being as she'd been thinking in (premature) despair and despondency since her husband's death. Though the house is empty of (human) habitation it appears to be filled with an excited agitation of the air like shaken water.

Muffled voices, a chorus of voices. Even laughter.

These voices are familiar, comforting. Though she cannot hear them clearly. A rustling of the eucalyptus surrounding the house. Cries out of the ravine. Her name is spoken, each vowel and consonant given equal weight—*MI CHAE LA.*

Urgent, soothing. Patient, kindly. Melancholy.

The name of the husband is not uttered. That is a correction, the widow surmises.

For the particular individual who has passed away had been given a name only for convenience's sake. A kind of shorthand, or code.

He-who-has-passed-from-you.

He-who-has-been-your-husband.

He-who-will-love-you-beyond-death.

He-who-awaits-you-beyond-death.

37

Hylpe Mi Plz Hylppe Mie

"Of course—I am not going to cancel! I never break my word."

Breathless she hears herself on the phone. Explaining that she intends to complete the memoir course, would not dream of canceling it, nor even missing another class. The *family medical emergency* has been resolved.

In fact, she intends to make up the single class she'd missed. She will explain to the students, today.

Her oasis! While her husband has been in the hospital.

On Thursdays dressing with particular care. Hair briskly brushed, fresh-laundered poplin shirt, white linen slacks with a crease. Upright posture, red-lipstick smile, badge of normalcy.

Optional: white linen jacket, silk scarf knotted at throat.

Out-of-time. Michaela can detach herself *out-of-time* while at the hospital the (endless) vigil continues.

Of course Michaela has memorized all of her students' names. Sleepless nights driving away thoughts of despair, despondency, terror how much more comforting to recite to herself the names of strangers seated around the seminar table, bright faces turned to her.

When Michaela returns to the memoir class on Thursday afternoon not one of these strangers will have any idea why she'd been absent the previous week.

Absurd, such vanity. As if anything matters now that your husband has died.

EVEN LETITIA TANIK WILL HAVE no idea. Letitia, to whom Michaela has written several imploring emails.

> Letitia, I am sorry to have been out of contact. A family medical emergency came up, that is now resolved.
>
> Please keep me updated on your situation.

To this email, no reply.

> Letitia, I hope that I did not upset you the other week & did not put pressure on you. I am concerned for you, still. I was thinking only of your well-being . . .

Nor was there a reply to this email.

> Letitia, I am hoping that we can speak together after our workshop on Thursday. If you have questions for me, please do not hesitate to ask.

And this email also, unanswered.

OH GOD, OH GERARD—*have I made a terrible mistake?*
Please help me . . .

IN A TRANCE OF APPREHENSION driving to Albuquerque.

He hadn't known where she was going on Thursday afternoons, not in the final weeks. She'd ceased explaining as he'd ceased remembering and at last he was too weak and distracted to remember to ask and so she had not volunteered in the hope/expectation that he was not clear-minded enough to register that she was absent from him for several hours and during those hours was *out-of-time.*

Though Gerard is no longer awaiting her in the Santa Tierra Cancer Center yet she feels his disapproval, his hurt. *Where are you, why have you abandoned me?*—for Michaela is a dying man's wife and has no right to be *out-of-time* fleeing from him to another city.

Her proper place is Santa Tierra. Where Gerard's restless soul wanders.

For such reasons she has come to fear driving on the interstate. It is reckless of her, she risks being punished. The grief-vise tightens around her chest in proportion to traffic close about her. Tight, tight—*tight* . . . She hears herself gasping for breath like a fish that has been plucked from the water and tossed onto the sand but if she is very calm the spell will pass, the vise will relax. For the moment.

Traffic thunderous as Niagara Falls and, like Niagara Falls, no beginning and no end. Mammoth trucks passing her (compact, lightweight) vehicle so close on the left, the rental car is sucked shuddering in their wake.

And there is a tug, a distinct tug, of the steering wheel, urging it to the left. Panicked Michaela grips the wheel hard, resisting.

No. No I will not.

Whoever this is urging her to swerve into the left lane of the interstate into rushing traffic must be a prankish sort of demon. Not one of the comforting voices, not (obviously) one of those who wish to instruct the widow in her mission.

God damn no. I will not.

But: guarantee of an instantaneous death.

But: Michaela has obligations to fulfill in what remains of her life.

As if anything matters now that your husband is dead.

WHAT A FOOL SHE IS! And what folly this is.

Unreality rolling in like fog. Polluted air. Almost, Michaela can taste it.

Just breathe. Keep going. For Christ's sake!

Her initial mistake (she thinks) has been the (naive) mistake of the inexperienced instructor: becoming involved with a student. In particular, becoming involved in the personal/troubled life of an undergraduate.

Except, Michaela castigates herself: you can't say that she is really *inexperienced*. Nor is she a young instructor. In the matter of Letitia Tanik she has behaved impulsively, recklessly.

Yet, Michaela is at a loss to understand what she might have done, that she'd failed to do.

How could I ignore her? I could not have ignored her.

Once Letitia told Michaela about the (alleged) rape—no turning back for Michaela.

Recalling with a stab of emotion how Letitia had hugged her, impulsively—burying her face in Michaela's neck. No warning.

(Had that truly happened? When Michaela tries to recall, she isn't sure.)

Then, the shock of driving around the block, happening to see Letitia, or someone who closely resembled Letitia, on the balcony of the residence, approaching the young man . . .

In any case Letitia appears to be absent (again) this afternoon. Michaela is stung by the rejection.

Unless it is not a rejection: possibly Letitia has decided to drop out of the university.

She may have reconciled with the (unnamed) young man—the (alleged) rapist.

She may have had a breakdown. Injured herself. *She may have killed herself, and you will be to blame.*

No one in the workshop takes Letitia's vacant chair at the seminar table. As if the chair is tacitly reserved for the missing person.

Michaela wonders if the space is being *ironically* reserved for Letitia. A signal that the others understand what has happened, and want their instructor to know that they know.

But do they blame *her*?—Michaela wonders.

When Letitia Tanik had been seated in that chair, slump-shouldered, heavy-sighing, sulky and restless, Michaela had been distracted and annoyed by her, wishing that the self-preoccupied young woman hadn't turned up at all. Now, Michaela is anxious that Letitia has not (yet) arrived, it is fifteen minutes past the hour and Letitia has not (yet) arrived, soon the door to the seminar room will be shut.

Badly tempted to ask the other students if they'd had news of Letitia, if anyone in the workshop knows her . . .

No business meddling in the private lives of students.

Oh—but she cared for us!

At least, she cared for one of us.

Blur of faces, quasi-familiar faces, can't remember names, though she'd memorized names, quizzical stares as if the students don't recognize Michaela after just two weeks apart. Fear that they will see through the red-lipstick smile that their instructor has been eviscerated, a husk of a woman, no longer *wife* but *widow* . . . Must impersonate whoever it is these strangers expect. A person *not eviscerated*.

Michaela summons her strength, she will not weaken.

Michaela summons her strength even as it drains from her like rain through outstretched fingers.

Staring at printed student work she has carefully read, reread that morning in preparation for the class, that now looks unfamiliar.

Entire pages unmarked, she is sure she'd annotated with editorial comments. Even her voice is hollow, halting. Her attempt at vivacity—"humor"—is greeted with blank stares. When students speak their voices are muffled and distorted and Michaela is forced to lean forward in an effort to hear what they are saying.

As if a barrier of some kind has arisen between them. Not quite transparent Plexiglas.

Oh, what has happened? Michaela has so loved this workshop, these students . . . Vaguely their names return to her: Melanie, Zora, Wyn, Frankie, Brett, Simon. But which names matched to which faces? Most of the students are older, not enrolled in the undergraduate college. They are mature adults, some of them single mothers, all of them working. Part-time, full-time. They have been eager, earnest. They have been very congenial. They have not disappointed. One of them, a young-old man, appears to be disabled, to a degree: stooped-shouldered, hoarse asthmatic breathing yet has not missed a class, listens intently to his instructor and nods at her every syllable. (Is this Simon? Or—a name she has forgotten?) Indeed these Thursday afternoons have been Michaela's oasis, her interlude of hope. She'd believed that if Gerard could know what her life was apart from him he would approve.

If I am not happy, I have the hope of making others happy. If I am beyond help, I have the hope of helping others . . .

But the students are not so friendly this week. After the long break. As if that break were an abyss: *before, after.*

Before I died. And after.

Their faces are stiff, inscrutable. Zora is frowning at her cell phone which she has positioned surreptitiously on her knee, partly hidden by the table. Frankie is looking sullen, bored. (From waiting? But is Michaela late?) Stoop-shouldered young-old Simon sits with his arms folded tight across his narrow chest, staring past Michaela's head—Simon, usually so shyly friendly toward her. Several persons don't even look familiar to Michaela, who could swear that she'd never seen them before. Not only is she having trouble hearing their voices, but they also seem to be having trouble hearing her voice, squinting and grimacing when she speaks, cupping their hands to their ears, failing to respond to her remarks.

Hello, hello, hello? Hello?

Strange that the young people are sitting at the farther end of the table, crowded together so that they are facing Michaela at the other end. And the table is half-again as long as Michaela recalls.

Hard to believe that a new, longer table has been substituted for the old table.

Hello? Please speak more clearly.

Michaela can hear voices but not words. She can see mouths moving—lips. Trying pathetically to read lips through the Plexiglas barrier. Craning so far forward her neck aches.

Is there something wrong with her ears? An infection? A burning sensation in her left, inner ear . . .

And her own words, muffled by the Plexiglas barrier: Can her students decipher from the contortions of her face, her mouth, her eyes what she is trying to earnestly to tell them?

Hylpe mi plz hylppe mie

• • •

RUNNING COLD WATER INTO A SINK. In the faculty restroom. Splashing water on her heated face which she dares not examine too closely for fear that she will discover how her face is fading. Holding her blue-veined wrists beneath the gushing faucet. Wincing as she stoops, for the grief-vise has left angry bruises around her rib cage.

None of this is remotely real.

You know that don't you?

You are not an instructor at a university. What a joke!

Your husband has not died, it is you who have died.

You who are being punished for abandoning him, brain boiling with fever.

38

Voice Mail Message!

And then, the widow's life takes an utterly unexpected turn.

Yes, it is totally unexpected. Though (yes) the widow should have had more faith.

For though she'd left her cell phone on yet (somehow) it has happened that a call came for Michaela during the three-hour workshop.

Hadn't heard the phone ring, she is sure.

Instructing the nurses at the Cancer Center please call me if there is any news. If anything happens . . .

So they'd called, or someone had called, and though Michaela had made certain that her cell phone was on, she had not heard its hopeful trill, hadn't felt its vibrating, had missed it entirely.

Eagerly, anxiously listening to voice mail now: *This is a message for Mrs. Gerard McManus. There has been a mistake, Mrs. McManus. Your husband Gerard is alive. He has been transferred from the Santa Tierra Cancer Center to . . .* The remainder of the message is garbled, unclear.

Replayed—*This is a message for Mrs. Gerard McManus. There has been a mistake, Mrs. McManus. Your husband Gerard is alive. He has been transferred from the Santa Tierra Cancer Center to . . .*

Again, again and again replayed—*This is a message for Mrs. Gerard McManus. There has been a mistake, Mrs. McManus. Your husband*

Gerard is alive. But he has been transferred from the Santa Tierra Cancer Center to . . .

Desperately Michaela presses the cell phone against her ear, to hear more clearly.

Another time: replay?

39

"No One Can Reach Him"

Long will Michaela remember: driving back to Santa Tierra in the early evening.

A river of lights winking, pulsing. Something awaits her ahead, can't remember exactly what it is but *it is something*.

For to the widow it is *nothing* that terrifies. *Nothing* that awaits.

Her heart quickens, she will drive directly to the hospital. Ascending in the elevator, seventh floor, making her way swiftly and unerringly to room 771 . . . It will still be dinnertime, she can eat with Gerard, leftovers from the tray he has been brought which Gerard will have rejected, inedible hospital food though (as Michaela points out, encouragingly) the applesauce isn't bad, nor is the plain yogurt, and if Gerard wishes she can request apple juice, in fact if the cafeteria downstairs is still open Michaela can run down and purchase ice cream for him, vanilla seems to be safest to offer Gerard lately . . .

But no. No longer. Room 771 is occupied now by a stranger.

None of the nurses would recognize Michaela now. None of the receptionists.

At the hospital now, there is *nothing*.

Must adjust. Readjust. Others have done so throughout millennia.

Where there was something, now—nothing.

So exhausted! Teaching the memoir workshop, that had been such a pleasure for Michaela in the past, had been like pushing an enormous boulder up a hill this afternoon, up up up a hill, no end to the hill . . .

Three hours passing in a blur. Already fading from Michaela's memory as even a troubled dream fades upon waking.

The widow's oasis of (piteous) happiness. This too will be taken from Michaela for her mission is not to assuage her own conscience but to oversee the passage of her husband's spirit into the next world.

Eager to return to Santa Tierra. Not to the hospital, of course, for Gerard is no longer a patient there, instead Michaela will drive to the rented house on Vista Drive where she is living (now) alone . . . Yet not (she understands) entirely alone.

Passing the exit for Placitas she begins to feel it—unmistakably: the steering wheel tugging to the left.

Gripping the wheel tight, holding steady, seventy-one miles an hour, a speed that allows her to keep pace with traffic in the right lane as vehicles pass her continuously in the left lane, a steady stream of vehicles in the left lanes, which Michaela avoids. Yet, invisible fingers contend with her for control of the steering wheel, panicked she turns the wheel back, toward the right, determined to keep a steady, straight course, not inching over into the left lane where her vehicle would be crumpled, crushed within seconds . . .

Instantaneous death. Out-of-time.

Michaela isn't sure that she can prevent the wheel from turning. Her forehead is oozing sweat. Rivulets of sweat down her sides inside the fresh-laundered shirt, smelling of her body, desperately she brakes the vehicle to a jolting stop on the shoulder of the interstate.

She is trembling badly. So exhausted, and so alone!

Fumbles for her cell phone, in her tote bag. The device is slightly different from what she recalls, a kind of cardiac monitor electronically connected to her heart as well as a conventional cell phone.

"Oh, Gerard! Help me."

Relieved to see that *Gerard McManus* is still listed among her contacts.

Hears his phone ringing far away.

Oh, so far away! Michaela's eyes mist over with tears, no idea where Gerard has gone carrying the cell phone with him.

"Darling, please answer. Please, please answer me . . ."

Her heart sinks: a recording clicks on briskly informing her that *Gerard McManus's mailbox is filled, he cannot take any more messages.*

Michaela listens to this message several times, to make sure that she has heard it correctly. To make sure that there isn't more to the message, which she has missed.

In the rental car at the side of I-25 as traffic rushes past thunderous as Niagara Falls in the growing dusk.

"So that's it, then. No one can reach him."

40

Missing

Without Gerard she is beginning to lose Michaela.

Precisely when this began, no idea.

Seeing one morning that parts of her face were missing. And seeing then by accident, startled, astonished, the left side of her forehead seemed to have faded, left eye vacant, left side of her mouth stiff and thinner than the rest of the mouth which was smiling (bravely), the "good" eye focused, resolute.

Later she would discover that part of her (left) arm has begun to disappear. Shadowy bone beginning to be visible through translucent skin.

Examines her (right) hand, only just four fingers which she carefully counts, recounts.

. . . *four, five. (Five? How many fingers should she have had?)*

Placing the hands side by side. Definitely, one is larger than the other.

Broken dirt-edged fingernails. As if she has been clawing at an unforgiving stone wall that surrounds her.

Vividly she recalls Gerard's hand. The wholeness, strength of the man's hand. Comforting thickness of his wrist.

Hairs stippling the back of his hand. Thicker hairs on his forearm, she'd stroked as you might stroke the pelt of a cat.

Love you. Oh I love you!

Beneath the unreality of this world that shimmers, shivers, shudders like ripples on a body of water of an unfathomable depth is the *other world*, which Gerard awaits.

Trying to lift her eyes, to see Gerard's face.

But this face too has lost its clarity. Beginning to fade even as the hand grips hers, hard. And Gerard's voice, deeper than she recalls.

Come kiss me! I've been waiting.

41

Seven Pounds, Two Ounces

Strange: for his ashes, she feels very little.

Bizarre, unexpected—to feel so little.

A call from the Chapel of Chimes. Hispanic accent, difficult to comprehend, low-throaty voice so she (mis)hears for a startled moment—*Chapel of Crimes*.

The impulse is to laugh. When you hear the solemn words *Your husband's cremains* you particularly want to laugh.

The widow drives across town to the Chapel of Chimes to pick up the urn containing the *cremains* of her husband. Alone the widow drives, no one in the seat beside her. Alone the widow fulfills another of the *death duties* custom and the law have established she must fulfill as the widow of a husband newly deceased. By this time Michaela has become a neutral agent, benumbed.

Eviscerated as a (gutted) chicken. No more tears to weep. Tear-rivulets have worn into her cheeks.

Yes of course I would far rather be dead but I am not dead, as it happens.

The urn containing the *cremains* is discreetly encased in a soft maroon cloth bag with a drawstring. To receive this urn Michaela must produce photo ID which a solemn-faced female clerk at the crematory examines carefully as if imposture might be a serious possibility in these circumstances. In addition, Michaela must sign several legal documents though she has already paid for the incineration of her husband.

Such vigilance is curious to Michaela, she is tempted to inquire of the solemn-faced heavily made-up woman—*Is it common that ashes are appropriated by strangers? Is this a particular problem at the Chapel of Chimes?* But that would sound like a joke and it is indelicate to joke at such a time.

Or, it might sound sarcastic and it is bad taste to speak sarcastically at such a time.

Yes it's all ridiculous, what kids call bullshit but please don't worry, I will fulfill my obligations as invariably I do.

Oh, unexpectedly heavy! Michaela feels panic as the *cremains* inside the soft maroon cloth bag are handed to her, so much heavier than she might have imagined. Only seven pounds, two ounces? A man who, only a few months ago, weighed nearly two hundred pounds?

Almost, Michaela fears she will drop the urn. For it is utterly, utterly impossible to believe, that she is holding, in her arms, all that remains of Gerard McManus.

But she grasps the object tight, tight against her chest.

Must be looking very white-faced, sick. The clerk catches her arm and asks if she is all right?

Yes! Michaela assuring the heavily made-up face with a bright faux smile, she is *all right*.

FOR IT HAS BEEN MADE clear to her, Gerard's spirit is restless and wandering and has little to do with the (merely) physical body that was incinerated for several hours in a white-hot furnace being reduced to seven pounds, two ounces of what is called *ash*.

Backseat, front seat?—which is appropriate for the *cremains* of a husband?

Carefully Michaela places the urn in the passenger's seat, beside her.

(But no seat belt! No.)

All that remains of Gerard McManus?—Michaela smiles to think so.

Mere ashes can't contain Gerard's unique being. Not possible.

You know that I am here, Michaela. But I am elsewhere.

On the two-mile route back to the rented house on Vista Drive Michaela takes care to drive with caution. Tremulous and breathing oddly Michaela dreads even a minor accident at such a fraught time.

How bizarre it is, yet how matter-of-fact and ordinary, even commonplace, Michaela is bringing her husband's *cremains* back to a house that was never their home, in an urn, indeed the "economy urn," inside a soft-cloth bag more appropriate for toiletries; and this urn beside her, as if companionably, in the passenger's seat of her car.

Often it had seemed during the hospital vigil of the past several weeks that when he'd struggled for breath Michaela had breathed for Gerard and so now it seems that Michaela is *breathing* for him, still.

Which is why she must keep breathing—deep even rhythmic breaths, to calm him. And herself.

A finite number of breaths required to bring Gerard's *cremains* back to the house, to be placed on top of the bureau in their bedroom.

Still, she feels little. Feels nothing, really. For (she knows) that Gerard is elsewhere, not in the silly cloth bag. Ridiculous!

Ridiculous too, the efforts of Iris Esdras to intervene in the widow's *death duties*. Over-solicitous Iris had volunteered to drive Michaela to the crematory to pick up the *cremains* so that Michaela wouldn't have to go alone "at such a time"; indeed, Iris has kindly volunteered to accompany Michaela on any mission including introducing Michaela to a "grief" therapist, and has several times invited

Michaela to dinner, or lunch, or drinks or tea or Iris's Zen yoga class—*Should you want company at this difficult time, Michaela. Please know that I am here for you.*

Not possible!—Michaela thinks, indignant.

For only if she is alone will Gerard approach her.

Café Luz de la Luna

So lonely!—she could not bear it.

The savage hot winds had ceased. The sky was torn and tattered as gangrene. Heat lightning flashed and faded.

Yet it was only just afternoon, this unnatural twilight. Michaela thought, excited—*The other world is pressing close. It will be easy to step from one into the other.*

She would have to leave the house where it was becoming difficult to breathe. They were instructing her to leave the house. Hurry!—she heard them whispering. In a backpack she carried the manuscript.

The *cremated remains* she would leave behind of course. Placed atop the bureau in their bedroom, inside the soft maroon cloth scarcely identifiable as an object of significance: mere matter.

You know, I am elsewhere.

She knew. She had no doubt.

Swiftly then, descending the hill. At so sharp an angle, the muscles in her calves soon began to ache.

So often she'd made her way down this hill, it had obliterated all other hills in her memory. As the effort of breathing for Gerard had obliterated all other effort in her memory.

(Had she lapsed into the kind of woman who wore a backpack, clothes that looked as if she'd slept in them, whose hair was a windswept tangle? Soon her teeth would have turned yellow, finger-nails and toenails gnarled as talons.)

(Her goddess would be the demon Skli with the gaping mouth, gaping vagina whose ravening emptiness can never be filled.)

At the foot of the hill Michaela turned breathless and bitter away from the high adobe walls of the Institute. Overnight an unreasonable rage on the part of Gerard had filled her, that his office at the Institute had been cleared out and given to another scholar. Books which she'd helped him pack to bring from Cambridge, Mass., placed so specifically on shelves in the office, in alphabetical order, with such hope for the work he hoped to do in the upcoming weeks, had been removed, boxed and returned to him, that's to say to his widow, in the house on Vista Drive.

When would these books be unboxed?—Michaela could not bring herself to imagine.

But why so bitter?—Michaela did not question.

The dead resent the living. For the dead have only the living to honor them.

They were waiting for Michaela to leave Santa Tierra, she knew. Iris Esdras had made that clear. Even as Iris pretended to be Michaela's friend, Iris was hoping to convince her to leave. Vacate the house, return to Massachusetts, we will help you pack, we will make arrangements for you.

But Michaela resisted, Michaela deleted their emails, phone messages.

. . . tried to arrange for the poor woman to see a therapist. Tried to befriend her.

When I tried to hug her she stiffened in my arms . . .

. . . so strange, her skin felt as if it was on fire.

Rare for Santa Tierra the sky glowered like tin. A light rain had begun to fall, the air was porous with mist. On a side street Michaela saw a small café with a terrace, tables with umbrellas. It was a café she'd often passed on her way to the hospital without taking much notice—Café Luz de la Luna. At this hour it was near-deserted. A half-dozen tables, strings of small white lights overhead redundant and foolish in daylight.

Was the café even open? No one on the terrace, no one visible inside.

Here is a good place for us. No one to interfere.

SLOWLY, MICHAELA HAS BEEN GOING through the (badly mangled) copyedited manuscript of *The Human Brain and Its Discontents*.

Slowly, conscientiously, obsessively—in dread of overlooking mistakes, or making mistakes of her own.

She'd assisted Gerard in his scholarly work, in the past. Collating footnotes, proofreading galleys. Retyping pages with pleasure, for she'd genuinely enjoyed her husband's prose. And yes, Michaela had perceived that immersing herself in Gerard McManus's work would be a way into Gerard McManus's heart, a way of making herself indispensable to him, as a wife and closest friend; his first wife, she knew, had not much shared his intellectual interests, and had become estranged from him over a course of years. But Michaela would not so take Gerard McManus for granted, Michaela had other plans.

She hadn't minded loving Gerard more than he loved her. That he was the dominant person in their marriage seemed natural to her. His stature in the world was far greater than her own. His personality seemed to her more developed, more expansive than her own. Certainly he was more intelligent, more educated. He'd been married previously, he had children; Michaela had no children, and had never been married. He'd expressed a concern that he might be exploiting her, her very wish to assist him with his work, but Michaela had protested no, not at all, she was learning from him, she was grateful to him for bringing such happiness into her life.

He'd never seemed to truly believe her, that she was grateful for his love. A kind of beggar-maid, Michaela thought, wryly.

Taking such pride in the dedications in his books—*for Michaela, my beloved wife and first reader.*

(Of course, Michaela had dedicated both her slender memoirs *to Gerard, my beloved husband and first reader.*)

And so, *The Human Brain and Its Discontents* is Michaela's responsibility. There is no one else but Michaela to help prepare this final work of Gerard's for publication at Harvard University Press.

Though Michaela has been going through the manuscript methodically, hoping to repair damage, the manuscript is still far from complete. Not only are individual pages missing, but entire sections also seem to be missing, or are mis-numbered within the text and difficult to retrieve. It seems likely that a number of Post-its with editorial queries have been lost as well as pages that Gerard had annotated in his small precise handwriting. Several chapters near the end contain blank passages and incomplete footnotes as if the author had been in a hurry and intended to fill them in at a later time; in the margins are queries the author seemed to have made to himself (*which? why? how possible?*) which went unanswered. The first ninety pages seem to have been corrected and revised, and read smoothly; beyond this the manuscript deteriorates, the text is erratic and obscure. There are additions to the manuscript Scotch-taped to pages, that have come undone; how many of these may have been lost, Michaela has no way of knowing. Michaela has corrected obvious errors, and rewritten obscure passages to make them clearer. (Of course, she has restored the original dedication—*for my beloved wife and first reader Michaela*—that had become mysteriously mangled.)

Inexplicably, Michaela has been unable to access Gerard's computer file for she seems to have an "invalid" password for him though (she would swear) this is the password that Gerard has always had, as well known to her as her own.

What a nightmare! *The Human Brain and Its Discontents* is an ambitious history and critique of the ethics of experimental science in America, on which Gerard worked for more than five years; it is the first exploration of the subject, and required immense research in numerous libraries and research centers, interviews and meticulous note-taking as well as the preparation of a lengthy bibliography which, Michaela can see, is far from complete.

There is even a new section near the end of the manuscript on the ethics of linguistic anthropology, with an emphasis upon the linguistics of *extinct* and *endangered* languages.

In this fascinating chapter Michaela learns that there are nearly seven thousand languages in the world of which approximately one-half have fewer than three thousand speakers—which classifies them as *endangered*.

If a majority of speakers of a language are elderly, the danger of extinction is compounded.

If a language is written, it will endure (to a degree). If a language is primarily spoken, it can endure only so long as there are living persons who speak it.

Michaela wonders: What would it be, to be the last living survivor of a language?

In a couple, there must be one who outlives the other: the survivor.

Among the indigenous North American languages which Gerard discusses in his book are those spoken by the Comanche, Hopi, Blackfoot, Arapaho, and the Taos Pueblo; Gerard seemed to know a good deal about the Kiwaan language, spoken by less than one hundred Pueblo Indians in the Santa Tierra highlands. He'd applied to the Santa Tierra Institute in order to research indigenous Indian cultures in northern New Mexico, a field entirely new to him.

Linguistics, anthropology, psychology, neuroscience—and philosophy (Spinoza). Somehow in Gerard's brain these came together.

Michaela hadn't understood but had no doubt that Gerard did. She'd been impressed that, at this point in Gerard's career, at his age, Gerard was expanding his definition of scientific experimentation to include linguistics. *The ethics of the appropriation of "subordinate" cultures by the predominant (White) culture.*

Then, in Santa Terria, illness had ravaged him almost immediately. He'd never driven to visit the Pueblo sites, so far as Michaela knew he'd never made contact with Taos Pueblo speakers of Kiwaan. They'd taken just two hikes into the desert and only one hike in the San Mateo State Park. Gerard's very being—physical, mental—had been appropriated by cellular invaders.

At the start, his condition had been misdiagnosed. His symptoms had been misleading. The low-grade stomach pain, that had not yet emerged as excruciating, had been misdiagnosed by the oncologist as mere constipation, forestalling by weeks the crucial scan that would reveal urethral cancer. By which time it was too late for surgery . . .

Oh, why was she tormenting herself with this story again? Again, again, and again this story with so many possibilities, yet with an ending inevitable as a cul-de-sac: inevitable as a sack over the head, blinding, suffocating. Michaela recalls screaming at Dr. N___— *What is wrong? Why are you so slow? Why don't you start treating him?*

Or, possibly she'd only imagined screaming at Dr. N___. Wanting to scream, but the words had stuck in her throat.

Save him. Save my husband. Save his life!

Why are you doing so little? Save his life!

Surely it was malpractice, this delay. But Michaela was too exhausted to feel vindictive, and had not the energy or the spirit for investigating. There'd been no autopsy. And now, mere ash.

In an urn, in the bedroom! Mere ash.

She would bring it back with her to Cambridge, she supposed. The urn in the soft cloth sack, the ash inside the urn, seven pounds two ounces all that remained of Gerard McManus.

Not possible. Michaela is sure.

As it is not possible, that Michaela will ever return to Cambridge, Mass. She is sure.

In lightly falling rain, rain faint as mist, beneath an umbrella at a café table Michaela is trying to make sense of Gerard's argument in lengthy paragraphs, dense prose. The tone of academic writing is discursive, argumentative: a point is being made, against (assumed) opposition. The effect is of a hammer being hammered. Page after page Michaela reads, taking notes. (*Are* these pages numbered correctly? Michaela wonders if something went amiss with the printer.) She is fighting a headache, staving off the moment when she will give in, and take a Tylenol; pill-taking seems to her a weakness, as it had seemed to Gerard before his illness.

Michaela is intrigued by Gerard's research into *extinct* and *endangered* languages. She recalls now his conversations with friends about such languages, and his discussion of a story by Borges, with a poet-friend; Michaela hadn't known enough to participate, and regrets now that she hadn't asked Gerard questions. *Had he been disappointed in her, as he'd been disappointed in his first wife, by her failure to ask appropriate questions?* He'd had an adequate reading knowledge of several languages including French, German, and Italian; he hadn't known any Native American languages, Michaela was sure. His interest in the Kiwaan language was entirely new.

Trying not to succumb to anxiety. She is her husband's only hope. His post-docs are busy with their own projects, his editor at Harvard University Press isn't a specialist in the history of science and has expressed gratitude to Michaela, for whatever help she can provide.

Gerard McManus had been one of Harvard's most distinguished faculty members, he'd been awarded prizes, fellowships, elected to the National Science Academy and the American Philosophical Society, yet these honors had never been quite enough. He hadn't been a vain man, not one who craved superiority over his colleagues and friends, but (Michaela has reason to think) he'd been frightened of his own mortality and may have believed half-consciously that the more distinctions he received, the more he was singled out and honored by the world, the more likely he was not to die as others did.

Michaela hears herself laugh. Or no, Michaela hears herself sob.

"MA'AM?"—A WAITER HAS APPROACHED MICHAELA, hesitantly.

A young Mexican-American waiter, it seems. Evidently the café is open. Or has just opened. The waiter regards Michaela with a wary smile as if his experiences with White women tourists has not always been pleasant.

But Michaela doesn't look like a tourist. She doesn't even look *White*, she thinks. If you look closely her skin is *smudged, sullied*.

She isn't sure how long she has been seated at the table. In her entranced state time moves unpredictably: with glacial-slowness, then in quick leaps and pleats, as if someone is leafing impatiently through the pages of a book. She has made her way through a portion of the manuscript but much of it will have to be examined a second time, and probably a third; she makes little progress, for she keeps finding more problems.

The morning he'd said quietly as one might report the temperature:
"I'm so much weaker than I was yesterday."

Michaela turns the oversized man's watch on her wrist hoping to see the time but the exact time eludes her.

"Ma'am? Is something wrong?"

I am not ma'am. Please.

But of course Michaela is *ma'am*. Michaela is a White woman, and Michaela is *ma'am*. The waiter is no more than twenty-five years old. Whoever she is, she hasn't been twenty-five for a decade or more.

"Would you like to order something now, ma'am, or would you like to wait for your friend to return?"

"'Friend'? What do you mean?"

The waiter glances about the terrace with a quizzical half-smile. As if there is someone in the vicinity of whom he has lost sight. A handsome boy with a narrow fox face. Sideburns, a small mustache. He might be as young as twenty—younger. Michaela wonders what the wary dark brown eyes see, seeing her.

"Was someone here with me?" Michaela is trying to remain lighthearted. Exude an air of caprice. As if she is just joking with him, not menacing him but simply joking with him, not altogether serious.

"Excuse me, did you say—you saw someone here with me?"

Hesitantly the waiter says *yes*. He is not so certain now.

"What did he look like?"

The waiter smiles uneasily. For possibly this is a joke. A White woman's sense of humor? He explains that he hadn't seen her companion very clearly.

"It was a man?"

A man, yes.

The waiter seems anxious to escape. No drink order seems to be forthcoming. He is torn between sympathy for the solitary White woman and a simple wish to escape her.

"Was he tall? With dark, graying hair? A little older than I am? Was he—did he seem—"

The waiter shakes his head quickly, *don't know, ma'am.*

Michaela has more questions for the young man but he slips away from her. Disappears into the café. The afternoon sky has darkened, flashes of lightning illuminate the sky like livid veins. When she looks more closely, she sees that the café is darkened, there is a CLOSED sign in the window.

43

Clinic

My guess is that it crawled into your ear when you were sleeping.

    Size of a pencil point!—got the damned thing out with a surgical tweezers.

    Trouble is, you waited a long time before coming in here, ma'am.

    Did you think it would just go away? An infection, so close to the brain?

Grief Counselor

Like a burst artery it has spilled out into the world.

What had been *the unbearable*, now spilled out into the world.

The old dream of childhood, now it is spread out about you.

Cannot breathe except you breathe in *the unbearable*.

THE BEARDED MOUTH MOVES, GRAVELY. Through a cicada-shrillness words come in broken pieces.

"... natural for you to grieve, Mrs. McManus. Your husband has been gone for less than four weeks ..."

Delicate hesitation at the word *gone*. You sense that the bearded mouth is reluctant to utter such a blunt word as *dead*.

"... but very good for you to keep busy as you have been. Preparing your late husband's manuscript for the press ..."

As if you are a child, a precocious child, in fact a socially maladroit child, needing to be encouraged to behave as other, healthier children behave by instinct.

As if you've accomplished anything significant with Gerard's mangled manuscript. These weeks!

"... from all that I've heard Dr. McManus was a remarkable person, in fact I'm sure that I have read some of his ..."

It is the lipstick-mouth that smiles at the bearded mouth. Polite, encouraging. Behind dark-tinted glasses (mildly bloodshot) eyes are hidden from view so that Dr. M___ cannot exactly *engage* with the client.

Polite smile to encourage the gray-bearded mouth Dr. M___ who means well. For middle-aged drum-bellied grief counsellors displaying framed certifications from the American Association of Health Care Professionals and a master's degree in Clinical Mental Health Counseling from the University of New Mexico on their office walls require encouragement too.

A man of Gerard's approximate age. You should be inclined to be sympathetic.

". . . sounds like a very interesting and important book, a 'history of the ethics of scientific research,' indeed very interesting, Mrs.—Michaela! Your husband would be relieved that you are going to assure its publication . . ."

How dare you speak of my husband. You did not know my husband.

How dare you condescend to me. You do not know me.

". . . 'grief-support group,' meeting once a week . . . several persons—indeed, widows—who have lost their spouses recently . . ."

Given to understand that as a widow you are *not alone.*

Though (in fact) you are utterly, terribly, and irrefutably alone.

". . . important to remain in touch with your emotions, not to deny, suppress, avoid . . ."

Words of logic, common sense. Marketing of banality. *Grief, mourning, need to keep active, see friends. "Support system." Not become a recluse.*

You would appear to be in a near-catatonic state. Numbed, hypnotized. Glassy-eyed hearing these words meant to console, reassure—resign yourself to the *unbearable.*

Yet: your heart has begun beating erratically. Like fingers drumming on a table.

". . . strongly recommend that you have a physical examination . . . caretakers for the gravely ill almost always neglect their own well-being.

"And if I may, I would also like to refer you to a pharmacologist . . ."

A wave of nausea comes over you at the thought of a physical examination: your battered body further violated, something metallic and sharp shoved into your pelvis, blood drawn from your arm (mysteriously) bruised already as Gerard's arms were bruised for weeks, fresh bruises overlapping with faded bruises.

As for a pharmacologist—why, when you already have a (secret) cache of drugs at home to cure yourself of your deep unhappiness?

". . . excuse me, Mrs. McManus?"

You have been staring into space blank-faced, hypnotized. Catatonia a kind of ether suffused through your being.

Waking yourself with a start, as from a bad dream. Rising to your feet too restless to remain seated facing the grief counselor at his teakwood desk.

Quick to assure the startled Dr. M___ that you don't intend to leave his office just yet. But feeling a need to be on your feet, move about a little, reanimate your numbed legs.

". . . of course, Michaela . . . whatever makes you comfortable."

But you, on your feet, moving about the office, seem to be making Dr. M___ uncomfortable. His eyes follow you, warily.

You wonder what Iris Esdras, who'd made this appointment for you with Dr. M___, has told him about you. *Not adjusting to her radically altered circumstances. Not cooperative with anyone who offers to help her. May be self-harmful, suicidal. Has refused to vacate the Institute-owned house and return to her home in the East.*

As a widow you wear white like a bride, refuse to wear black like a vulture. White linen jacket, white linen trousers, pale pink silk shirt, silk scarf knitted at your throat. Impersonating the self-assured woman you'd (once) been.

Showered that morning at 5:00 A.M. rinsing away the rancid smell of animal panic, shampooed and roughly brushed your hair with Gerard's hairbrush brought back from the hospital with his things. Touched by how the brush now mingles your hair and Gerard's hair, silvery, gray, white, coppery-brown, dark-brown hairs tangled together . . .

It is part of your impersonation that you have manicured your (short, blunt) nails before coming to the grief counselor. You have applied makeup to your sallow skin, lipstick to your pallid lips. A Maybelline brow-pencil you'd discovered discarded in a public lavatory you'd brought home to artfully darken your eyebrows.

You intend to *try*. You do not intend to *give up*.

Your wedding ring has become too large for your finger, slips and slides about it. (Gerard's wedding ring you wear on a thin silver chain around your neck, hidden inside your clothes.) And you are wearing your husband's oversized wristwatch that slips and slides about your wrist impracticably, usually you can't see the time.

Which is anyway *widow-time: out-of-time*.

Waiting, on your feet. How long? Telling yourself for Christ's sake *breathe*.

Because you are waiting. Anguish, anxiety of waiting. Continuous state of waiting, expectation. Dare not sleep.

Waiting for—what?

Waiting for what has happened, to happen. The worst that can happen. Or, waiting to learn that *it has not (yet) happened*.

All this while Dr. M___ continues to speak in his voice modulated to placate the (secretly) anxious and (secretly) suicidal even as, in a pose of nonchalance, you have gone to stand at a window overlooking the parking lot.

Why? No one has summoned you.

Except: three floors down, a figure, a male figure, materializes out of the sun-glare.

Peer between the slats of the partly-drawn blind. Suddenly shocked, senses alerted.

A man of Gerard's height, bearing.

Is it—? No. Not possible.

You are stunned, transfixed. Staring between the slats of the blind as your heart begins to accelerate wildly.

". . . why don't you look this way, Michaela? You might be able to concentrate better on what we are saying . . ."

But all of your concentration is fixed upon the lone figure in the parking lot: a man of Gerard's approximate age, height, bearing. He is wearing clothes that are not immediately familiar to you—khaki shorts, a short-sleeved patterned shirt. On his head a baseball cap of the slate-blue color of Stellar's jay's feathers, which is new to you also. But then, you have not seen Gerard in several weeks and have no idea what he might be wearing by now; it would be natural for Gerard to buy a hat like this to protect his eyes from the New Mexico sunshine though on principal Gerard doesn't much care for hats, and certainly not baseball caps . . . And the light is so glaring, you are (probably) not seeing colors clearly, everything seems bleached-out.

"Michaela? Is something wrong?"—there is an edge to Dr. M___'s kindly voice as if even the grief counselor may be losing patience.

You are distracted, you scarcely hear. Alarmed that the man in the baseball cap has turned to walk away indifferent to you staring at him from a third-floor window, not fifty feet away.

But he is aware of you. He is leading, you must follow.

"Michaela? Mrs. McManus? Wait—"

You have snatched up your purse from a table, on your way out of Dr. M___'s office. Hurry, hurry!—not a backward glance. An hour's free consultation scheduled by the Institute, no time for a polite apology to the astonished grief counselor as you half-run out into the corridor, to the stairway and down, out the rear exit panting and stumbling into blinding sunshine desperate to confront your lost husband—*Gerard? Gerard!* But your throat seems to have shut tight, barely can you hear your own scratchy voice calling to someone who has disappeared from sight.

Where has he gone? *Was* it Gerard? You seem to know that you are expected to follow him but—he seems to have vanished . . .

Make your way through the parking lot, along rows of vehicles, all of them unoccupied, unfamiliar. No one. Nothing.

Of course it's possible that the middle-aged man in the baseball cap is a stranger who'd gotten into his vehicle and driven away in the time required for you to emerge from the rear door of the office building—but you don't think so. It is more likely (you think) that he'd entered the office building and taken an elevator—the building is seven floors, a labyrinth.

"Hello? Hello?"—but there is no one in the parking lot.

No witnesses. No one to question. If the man in the baseball cap had just parked his car in the lot you have no idea which car it might be.

Not the leased car, which you have driven here. (The vehicle still registered in Gerard McManus's name.)

In blinding sunshine you stand uncertain. You are very excited—an adrenaline shot to the heart. At the same time you feel ridiculous, unmoored.

Oh Michaela, what has become of you!

You should have come with me, when you had the opportunity.

You were a coward. You will pay for that now.

For an agitated half hour you drift about the parking lot like flotsam idly lifted by an invisible tide. Re-enter the building, make your way along a windowless corridor, exit again by another door, indeed you are unmoored, lost. In the parking lot you consider waiting for the man in the baseball cap to return—but understand that no matter how long you wait in this lot amid a small sea of glittering and glaring vehicles, no matter how long you stand absurd and hopeful in bright sunshine, eyes stinging with tears behind dark-tinted glasses, foolish heart hammering like death, Gerard in his newly purchased khaki shorts and bright blue cap is not likely to return.

Gone.

45

Demon-Goddess

. . . floating on a wide dark river in a small boat, with a small glowering-white sail, no higher than five feet. A shallow river but a fast-running river. In the bruised sky, flashes of heat lighting. Though Gerard has eluded Michaela he has told her the name of the river where they will meet: Rio de Piedras.

But when will they meet?—Michaela is desperate to know.

On all sides shrieks of wild parrots, monkeys. Banks of wild-growing purple wisteria, gigantic lavender bushes, luridly blossoming cactus trees. Out of the shadows the demon-goddess Skli emerges. A naked female figure with a shrieking mouth, breasts drooping past her bony rib cage, gaping vagina like a raw wound. Instead of fingers, long curving talons.

Lightly, teasingly, these talons brush along Michaela's bare arms which are highly sensitive.

Oh, unbearable! With a convulsive shudder Michaela is rudely awakened.

She sits up, stunned. Several minutes are required for her to regain her consciousness, her strength.

She stares at her arms, that are still faintly scarred. Draws a fore-finger over the long vertical scars, shivering.

Michaela had not ever cut her arms. Hoping that finally she'd convinced Iris Esdras that this was so. I am not punishing myself. I am not suicidal.

Barefoot she goes to check the hall closet where the likeness of Skli has been hidden in a shadowy corner, covered by a towel. Satisfied that yes, the ugly thing is exactly where she'd put it, weeks ago. (No need to check beneath the towel!)

And the squat stooping figure of Ishtikini is still in the cupboard beneath the bathroom sink though she can't recall whether she'd left it facing the wall or, as it is now, its small beady leering eyes facing whoever stoops to peer inside.

And come kiss me! I've been waiting.

46

Blindsight

Michaela, come with me!

There is a place for you, with me.

Each day, each hour she searches for him in Santa Tierra. Knowing that he is awaiting her. That possibly he can see her without being able to communicate with her.

(Had he been aware of her in the third-floor window, staring down at him in the parking lot? Had he been constrained, unable to acknowledge her? As Michaela, in the grief counselor's office, stood rooted to the spot for crucial seconds, unable to break free, speechless.)

It is possible that in the other world, the spirits of the dead may be blind. Their senses may be stunted in some way. Had Gerard not told Michaela of cruel neuroscience experiments in which infant monkeys, cats, mice were kept in total darkness until their eyesight deteriorated, and they became blind?—yet in other respects their senses were normal.

And had Gerard not told her about the phenomenon of "blindsight"—a recent discovery of neuroscience that proves that individuals who have suffered damage in the primary visual cortex of the brain can (often) sense an object though they can't "see" it. Claiming not to "see" anything, nonetheless they point without hesitation to the object. Asked why they are pointing at something they claim isn't there, they can offer no explanation.

Michaela wondered at this. How is it possible?

Gerard tried to explain: the eye can be "blind" while the brain "sees"—something we call "sight" occurs, but not to the conscious agent.

But—how is *that* possible?—Michaela laughed, alarmed at the limits of her understanding.

Gerard assured her: much that seems impossible is possible. And much that seems possible will turn out to be impossible.

Michaela thinks of this now—*blindsight*. Something we call "sight" occurs, but not to a conscious agent.

As suffering might occur, unspeakable suffering, but memory is erased in amnesia like raindrops in water, and so there is no *sufferer*.

Alone in Santa Tierra searching for her lost husband.

Wanting to protest—she'd begged to be allowed to donate bone marrow, to save him. But there had been no guarantee that such a procedure would have saved him.

As a widow Michaela is tireless, alert. The widow's life is the life of a penitent bearing her (grotesque, bleeding) heart on the outside of her body. Sleeping only two or three hours a night has sharpened her senses, she believes. *Razor-sharp*. By her count she has been a widow for approximately 750 hours.

No matter her circuitous route downhill from Vista Drive Michaela makes her way unerringly to the historic district of Santa Tierra—the Plaza de la Catedral de Santa Teresa. Here is a ceaseless stream of visitors in and out of the Spanish-style cathedral with its gleaming gilt basilica, tourists crowding one another on the cathedral steps taking pictures with their cell phones. The mood is festive, celebratory. There is a continual flurry of pigeons, white doves. At midday there are no shadows and at dusk shadows are obliterated by dazzling lights. It is Michaela's strategy to appear to be moving randomly among the pedestrians so that if she is being observed she will not arouse suspicion. Yet Michaela is suffused with the zeal of a hunter, scanning the ever-changing scene for the lost husband.

Michaela, where are you?

Why did you abandon me?

She wants to protest: she hadn't abandoned him. There was confusion when he'd seemed to stop breathing. She had held him so long tightly, desperately. She'd breathed for him, into his lungs that were frantic for air, but then something had happened and she'd allowed herself to be lulled into believing that it was for the best, she might leave him, and then return to him; but when she was allowed to return, something had happened in the interim and he was gone.

The stripped bed, the sharp toxic odor of disinfectant that has entered her soul. Glare of white walls. Void.

Futile to protest—*Forgive me, Gerard!*

Hearing again that final heaving sigh. And then—silence.

Michaela has become feral in the past several weeks. She spends as much time as she can outdoors and when she is home—that is, at the rented house on Vista Drive—she is often sprawled in the unmade bed she'd once shared with Gerard in a season of such oblivious happiness, she can scarcely believe it was once theirs; in a dazed and intermittent sleep, punctuated by fits of coughing/sobbing. Often Michaela doesn't dare remove her clothing for there is the vague dread that she will be wakened in the night and summoned to the hospital—*Hurry! Your husband cannot breathe.* (It isn't clear whether the bone marrow extracted so painfully from Michaela's left hip has been preserved, or if it has been allowed to deteriorate. Michaela seems to recall that she'd been informed the bone marrow could only be used if Gerard was strong enough to endure the transplant procedure but then there'd been the confusion of a transfer to another medical facility with a more skillful medical team . . .) Michaela rarely sits down to eat, and never food she has prepared herself—this would be tempting fate: to be called away suddenly to the hospital, to the intensive care room where Gerard is struggling to breathe.

How much more practical then to open a can of Progresso soup which she devours unheated, with a spoon; a can of pumpkin pie mix, also devoured with a spoon; six-ounce containers of cottage cheese, applesauce, yogurt. In the Santa Tierra Cancer Center the wife of the very ill patient had become accustomed to scavenging untouched food from Gerard's trays and so now she eats when the opportunity arises, as feral creatures do. Feral too in her appearance, androgynous-seeming, as well as anonymous: Michaela dresses in a kind of sexual camouflage, long trousers on even very hot days, T-shirts of Gerard's that droop from her shoulders, a scuzzy wide-rimmed straw hat to protect her sensitive skin and dark-tinted glasses to protect her sensitive eyes. In a loose tangle like scribbling from a mad pen her hair falls over her shoulders, uncouth mane of a wild creature. Backpack strapped to her back, shamefully worn running shoes. No one from the Institute would recognize her, identify her as the attractive and even (once) stylish young wife of their colleague from Harvard, Gerard McManus.

If Michaela's memoir students happen to see her in this feral state they would be stunned with dismay, pity, shame. Their professor!

But of course, Michaela has never been their *professor*. Just an adjunct, an impersonation.

In the crowded and bustling plaza Michaela is painfully visible. No one else is alone here except Michaela.

Keenly alert to solitary male figures. Nearly everyone she sees is with at least one other person, most are with families. Her heart aches, she stares with envy. She has no child, and now she has no husband. Rare to see a man by himself in Santa Tierra's city center unless the man is a Latino or Native American, not a tourist or casual visitor but someone who works here.

Rarer still to see someone who superficially resembles Gerard— white, late-middle-age, tourist or visitor—unaccompanied by a wife.

Michaela stares transfixed by women of her own age who are with men, or with families; she feels a twinge of envy at the sight of them, actual pain in her chest. Such women seem to Michaela bathed in light even as they appear to be oblivious of their good fortune.

To take another for granted—Michaela has forgotten what such a luxury is.

She'd never taken Gerard for granted. They had not known each other that long, Michaela had never felt entirely *at ease* with him.

This was the nature of a "late" marriage, she supposed—the knowledge that things might so easily have gone otherwise.

SOON AFTER THEIR ARRIVAL IN Santa Tierra Gerard and Michaela had visited the beautiful Catedral de Santa Teresa, in the city's oldest quarter. At the rear of the church they'd observed the conclusion of a mass, long lines of communicants approaching the altar railing with hands clasped in prayer and eyes devoutly downcast. Forty years, Gerard remarked wryly to Michaela, since his last communion.

Forty years! Yet, he said, he remembered vividly.

The communion wafer—size of a half-dollar, white, very thin, very dry, tasteless. You did not chew the communion wafer but allowed it to melt in your mouth.

And this was the body and the blood of Christ?—Michaela asked.

The body of Christ, not the blood. The blood would be the wine.

Gerard laughed, to indicate the absurdity of such beliefs. Yet his laughter sounded wistful, Michaela thought.

He'd been raised as a nominal Catholic, Michaela knew. Neither of his parents had been devout Catholics. Michaela had attended

Unitarian services with school friends as a girl but had not been taken to religious services by her parents. She had no romantic nostalgia for religion.

If humankind has a religion, Michaela thought, it must be the religion of humanity. Human feeling, human love. Human responsibility.

But *love* is not so readily accessible. The experience of *loving* can be fraught with fear as well as happiness.

Michaela had asked Gerard if he missed his religion and Gerard said no, of course not.

It's truth that we crave, Gerard said. Not delusion.

Yes!—Michaela agreed.

If truth can be a comfort. As delusion can.

He wasn't sure that he had ever believed in God, Gerard had said thoughtfully, but he missed the "certitude" of those days: the *Baltimore Catechism*, the prayer books, rosaries.

The inexpressible solace of a rosary, twined about the fingers. Each bead a prayer, and each prayer heard by God.

You miss the possibility of pleasing someone, or something—for, if you obeyed God, God was pleased with you.

Such a simple religion! Or so it was presented, to children.

Christianity in America is like an endangered language, Gerard thought: the instinct is to preserve it, as the instinct is to preserve endangered species. But maybe that is a futile gesture. Maybe all things are born, flourish, and eventually die, and it's a mistaken kindness to interfere with this cycle.

What he'd really missed, Gerard said, was being a child. Loved by his mother without qualification.

Laughing, and then coughing. (As Gerard was doing frequently since arriving in Santa Tierra.) Michaela didn't laugh but protested that *she* loved him without qualification—"I am the one who loves you now."

Perhaps yes, Michaela was jealous. Is jealous. Of all who'd loved Gerard McManus long ago before he'd become her husband.

Tremulous now entering the dim interior of the cathedral. Oh, what a risk Michaela is taking! Returning to the very place where she'd whispered boldly in a man's ear *I am the one who loves you now.*

Recalling how she'd slipped her hand into Gerard's hand as they stood together waiting for the mass to end, how startled she'd been by the mechanical singsong of the priest's voice, that had sounded almost mocking, like an advertising jingle.

A hot dry air, an air depleted of oxygen, barely stirred by six-foot fans set at strategic places on the stone floor of the cathedral.

Michaela is feeling weak with loss, how often she'd taken Gerard's hand unexpectedly. She had never reached for another's hand in such a way—she'd had lovers but had not so unreservedly loved them, as she'd loved Gerard.

Or perhaps she hadn't had *lovers.* Acquaintances who'd been men, with whom she had slept. (Not many!) But no one like Gerard.

Spontaneously reaching for his hand, to slip her fingers through his. While walking somewhere, or waiting in line. In crowded places. A gesture of childlike affection.

Her heart had swelled, such happiness! To slip her fingers through his.

Because you are my husband. Because no one else has this right.

Inside the cathedral Michaela is feeling disoriented. There is no mass this afternoon—only just rows of pews, glaring-bright stained-glass windows, statues scattered through the church. Milling tourists. Yet, essentially—emptiness.

Michaela tries, but cannot remember where she and Gerard stood. Had they slipped into one of the pews for a few minutes? But which one?

She does remember that they'd admired the life-sized carved-wood statues for which the Catedral de Santa Teresa is renowned in the Southwest. Painted vivid, bright colors, as an imaginative child might paint them, the statues are primitively rendered but none is grotesque and several seem to Michaela quite beautiful. There is the Virgin Mary in a robin's-egg blue robe, her face blandly doll-like, cream-colored; in her arms the Infant Jesus, whose skin is even lighter than hers and whose rosebud mouth is very pink. Only a few feet away, the somber, life-sized likeness of Jesus in resplendent robes, a halo positioned over his head, right hand lifted palm-out in a greeting that looks startlingly vernacular.

In the center of Jesus' chest is a grotesquely exposed larger-than-life-sized heart pierced by a spear and topped with dancing, painted flames.

"The Sacred Heart of Jesus"—Gerard identified the statue for Michaela.

In this depiction Jesus has a gaunt bearded Hispanic face, an expression of impassive and noble resignation. His lips are improbably red, his eyes have been painted shiny-black as a crow's eyes.

But why is the heart *exposed*?—Michaela shuddered.

That's the tradition, Gerard said, a little stiffly.

Yes, but *why*?—Michaela persisted.

Because it's the tradition, Gerard told her. The Sacred Heart of Jesus could not exist if not *exposed*.

Adding then, as Michaela stood quiet: You don't question tradition.

Yes, but *you* did, Michaela pointed out. You've always questioned tradition.

Always, Michaela is flattering her husband. Half-conscious, by instinct. A kind of heliotropism, irresistible.

All the Church is, is tradition, Gerard said. There is no foundation otherwise. You have faith in faith. "The Sacred Heart of Jesus" was a devotion introduced into the Catholic liturgy in the seventeenth century, at the bequest of a nun who'd claimed to having had a private vision of Jesus nineteen days after Pentecost.

A nun! A single, singular woman, making a contribution to the Roman Catholic faith, in the seventeenth century. The nun is long forgotten, but here in the twenty-first century there remains the Sacred Heart of Jesus.

Michaela hesitated to ask what Pentecost is?—not wanting to further annoy her husband.

For no one is comfortable being interrogated about a religion in which he no longer believes, Michaela thinks. Speaking of such things Gerard would be both embarrassed and defensive as he'd been in speaking, obliquely, evasively, of his first, "failed" marriage years before he'd met Michaela.

You don't need to ask, dear. You don't really want to know.

And really, I don't remember. The details are gone and don't concern us.

Examining the garish, crimson-red Sacred Heart of Jesus positioned in the middle of the statue's chest Michaela understands that her question about this tradition was naive. The grotesque heart, the wounded, bleeding and burning crimson heart is the heartbreak that cannot be hidden, the suffering you must endure whether you are Catholic or not.

All who gaze upon this lurid sight understand, feelingly. As they understand the broken body on the cross.

Michaela swipes at her eyes. But no more tears!—she vows.

Since Gerard's hospitalization she'd cried more than she had cried in the first thirty-seven years of her life. Usually, hidden away alone. Where no one can see or hear her. She is stricken with shame now, she'd broken down in Gerard's presence, he'd had to endure his wife's (premature) grief.

Stumbling to a pew, to sit for a few minutes and try to summon back her strength.

Hide her face in her hands like a communicant humbling herself to accept the sacred wafer.

But where are you, my dear wife. I am waiting for you.

BLUR OF WHITE-FEATHERED WINGS!—on the cathedral steps doves flutter noisily up beside Michaela beating their wings uncomfortably close to her face.

Michaela waves the doves away, shielding her face until they are gone.

Recalling how, months ago, white doves fluttered about their heads as she and Gerard exited the cathedral, also. Tourists could not be dissuaded from scattering bits of bread on the cathedral steps for the birds that arrived in thrumming swarms as if eager to be photographed.

Michaela is not sure what to do next. Where to turn. She has not (yet) sighted a tall solitary male figure who might quicken her interest. Virtually everyone she sees is a tourist, here in Plaza Square in the heart of the Old Town.

At the southern end of the square is the gleaming new Santa Tierra Opera House from which in a burst of manic enthusiasm Michaela acquired two tickets for a performance of *Orpheus and Eurydice* in early August.

That had been on a harried April day that seems now a lifetime ago. What had Michaela been thinking!—of course, poor Gerard could not have lived so many weeks. And if he had, he would not have been in any condition to attend the opera.

She blames the oncologist Dr. N___. Bitterly. If but for Dr. N___, whose incomprehensible slowness had allowed the fatal urethral cancer to grow, and grow, Gerard McManus would now be alive. Michaela believes this to be a fact, indisputable.

She hasn't seen the (expensive) opera tickets since and guesses they are lost.

There is the Café de Palomas Blancas where on one of their first days in Santa Tierra, Gerard and Michaela had stopped for lunch.

Walking in the historic district hand in hand for the first time. Breathless from the altitude, somewhat light-headed, giddy. It had seemed like a honeymoon then. The Santa Tierra adventure.

Michaela swallows hard. How has it happened, she has become a ghost haunting her own, lost life . . .

Michaela requests a table on the café terrace though (she knows) the waiter would prefer to save the table for a couple, and seat the solitary Michaela inside the cafe; but this table is near the table at which, months ago, she and Gerard sat. Almost, Michaela can see them: Gerard reading to Michaela out of the Santa Tierra guidebook, in which he was making annotations. When not immersed in his work Gerard brought to leisurely activities the same sort of attention to detail he brought to his work.

Faint with memory, feeling her eyes mist with tears. How close she is to that other table—yet, strangers are seated there, and not Gerard and Michaela.

Michaela is tempted to ask waiters at the Café de Palomas Blancas if they remember her and her husband from weeks before, but no, of course no one would remember.

No one cares about us, except us. No one cares about *me*. Except *you*.

Even if she doesn't see Gerard it's possible, with the logic of blindsight, that her brain will "see"—register—his presence. And if Gerard doesn't see her—(as he hadn't seemed to see her peering down at him from the grief counselor's window)—he might yet "see" her with another part of his brain.

For such reasons Michaela does most of her work on the copyedited manuscript outdoors, in public places. She has become too restless to remain in the house on Vista Drive, that contains odd, untraceable odors, as of rancid food, rotted meat, faint feculent gases though each room (Michaela has made sure) has been thoroughly cleaned, and she never prepares food in the kitchen; the refrigerator is virtually empty. For some reason the grief-vise grips her tighter indoors: sometimes she has to sit down, gasp for air, stricken like an asthma-sufferer . . . Until the grief-vise releases her, and oxygen flows again into her lungs.

How much better to work outdoors, amid a bustle of strangers, anonymous in their eyes, thus invisible. And if Gerard discovers her, it will give him pleasure to see how devoted she is to *The Human Brain and Its Discontents*.

He couldn't have been happy with the neglected manuscript, those final two weeks in the hospital. Michaela is eager to reassure him, she will prepare the manuscript for publication as he'd wished.

You can't let me down, Michaela. I have only you.

Another reason for taking the manuscript everywhere she goes is that Michaela doesn't want to risk leaving it behind in the house. Like leaving a candle flame, or a living thing—you dare not risk its extinction.

Also, Michaela worries that the Institute will try to evict her. Move her things out onto the road, in her absence. Or worse yet, destroy her things.

Seek out Gerard's manuscript, and destroy it.

Michaela has come to see that *The Human Brain and Its Discontents* may be a masterpiece. And, in its questioning of (White) academic appropriation of native languages, it might be heretical. There is good reason for rival historians to wish to destroy it.

Michaela has been alternately excited by, and discouraged by, her progress with the manuscript. Sometimes it seems that work she'd done one day has been lost the next. As she has located misnumbered pages within the manuscript she seems to have misplaced other pages. Post-its have disappeared, and with them precious editorial queries. Some of Gerard's marginal notations are not decipherable, and some have faded. Those paragraphs in the later part of the manuscript which she has revised to make clearer seem knotty and obscure to her when she rereads them, as if in her absence Gerard has stubbornly, perversely, reverted them to their earlier state.

She has been working on the manuscript for months—or has it been years? The fast-approaching deadline is just nine days away.

If you need an extension, Michaela . . . Just let me know.

But Michaela doesn't trust Gerard's editor. Michaela doesn't trust the Harvard University Press. She is concerned that, using Gerard's death as an excuse, they will postpone or even cancel the publication of his book because of its controversial nature.

This concern, Michaela wants to shield from Gerard. As she'd breathed with him in the hospital, matching her breath to his, and as she'd eventually breathed for him, substituting her (stronger) breath for his, so it seems to Michaela that she can give life again to Gerard through her work on the manuscript. Immersed in his words, as in his very brain. And so it is particularly distressing to Michaela to discover lapses and errors in the manuscript which she is certain she'd corrected, which she must correct again.

Carefully Michaela spreads the manuscript onto the café table. It is not ideal to work on a table this small, but Michaela can manage. In such places she feels that she is part of the flow of normal life. She is not a solitary individual, a woman who has lost her husband, thus her place in the world; amid swarms of tourists, Michaela is protected by anonymity.

A widow must have an escape hatch.

This widow has enough pills to kill a herd of elephants.

Michaela laughs. An abrasive voice, new to her. Good!

Whenever Michaela can, she laughs. Her laughter sounds like hoarse choking. Croaking. The sound a crow might make mocking human laughter.

"Ma'am?"—a waiter approaches, as if Michaela had summoned him. Not so deferential as the young waiter at the Café Luz de la

Luna. Older, closer to Michaela's age, standing close to her, smiling/sneering down at her.

"Shall I bring you another glass of wine, ma'am?"

Has Michaela been drinking wine? She'd meant to order seltzer water. Lifting her glass, surprised to see that it's nearly empty, and indeed it is a wineglass containing what appears to be (white) wine.

Not good to be drinking at this hour of the afternoon. A solitary woman, at the Café de Palomas Blancas. In white-hued sunshine that makes her eyes ache even behind dark-tinted glasses.

Shut her eyes and she can imagine: Gerard is sitting across from her.

Or, Gerard is coming to meet her in a few minutes. (She checks her wristwatch: but it is Gerard's wristwatch. For a moment she can't comprehend why she is wearing Gerard's wristwatch.)

Michaela thanks the waiter but doesn't order another glass of wine. Instead, seltzer water. With mock politeness the waiter inquires: lemon, ma'am?—or lime?

Michaela laughs, the question is so absurd. *Your husband is dead, do you prefer lemon or lime?*

"Lime. Thank you."

"*Gracias, señora.*" Shifting to Spanish, tourist-Spanish, is a rebuke of some sort, which Michaela will ignore.

She will leave the impudent waiter a sizable tip. Surprise him with her generosity. That she is a *White woman*, that she is an *American*, a *gringa*, he has no right to judge her without knowing her.

Small gusts of wind arise, blowing tiny bits of grit across the plaza. Michaela wipes at her eyes. She has been squinting at the manuscript for nearly an hour, she has made very little progress. Reads, rereads the same paragraph(s). A sensation ripples over her skin of anxiety, dread: she is being *seen*.

But when she glances up, she sees no one. No one whose eyes engage hers.

Michaela has come to believe that the man outside the grief

counselor's building had indeed been Gerard, and that he'd been drawn to her, and was waiting for her; but she'd failed to identify him. She'd been filled with fear, she'd held back. A part of her had resisted knowing who he was, and that she must go with him. She'd thought—*Of course that isn't Gerard. Gerard has died, his remains have been incinerated* . . .

As soon as she'd articulated this thought, Gerard had "died" a second time, and had vanished. She is sure that this is what happened, but also that it is an insight possible only in retrospect. At the time she'd been too confused and frightened to know what was happening.

She'd been doubting, yet hopeful. For to doubt is to hope. Where there is no doubt, there can be no hope. Recalling bitterly from the hospital vigil, hope is what most wounds us.

So many days of hoping. Weeks. Willing the man for whom she was responsible to live, to breathe. Her soul had consumed itself in the effort, as in a blazing inferno.

It was not Dr. N___'s fault of course. Death had invaded their lungs like a malevolent breath, unstoppable.

Michaela glances up, shades her eyes—sees an older man in a wheelchair, being pushed past the café by a boy of about twelve. The (portly, flush-faced) older man *is not* Gerard—(she sees at once)—but Michaela feels a wave of compassion for him, not love but the possibility of love. For he is someone else's husband, if not hers. As if she'd become a wound—raw, implacable—her own heart exposed in her breast garish and absurd as the Sacred Heart of Jesus—that would bleed, bleed without end, out of pity for all who suffered, as Gerard had suffered, in her desperate need to alleviate their suffering and in this way, her own.

She would never comprehend how swiftly—how brutally—their situations had reversed. Gerard the protector and comforter, the stronger; Michaela the indecisive, hesitant, weaker. Within weeks, days, it was Michaela who must protect and give comfort, and Gerard who was dependent upon her. *My wife. Don't abandon me, take me out of here . . .*

So badly she'd wanted to be her husband's caretaker in the hospice. She'd planned—they'd planned—a beautiful honeymoon, which would be their hospice. There would be music, and flowers. Fresh flowers each day. Holding hands, kissing. Only tender words not recriminations, expressions of despair. No more bloodwork, "vital signs." No more hunting for the elusive oncologist sporting the bow tie. *Fuck him. Who needs him.* However long and however bravely Gerard would continue to live, Michaela would live, too; and when at last Gerard began to surrender his life, when there was no alternative but that Gerard must surrender his life, Michaela would prepare for her death, too.

Unhurried. Unharried. Utterly private. A beautiful death, guaranteed by a plethora of painkillers, sleeping pills Michaela has been hoarding for years with the instinct, as methodical as it is grim, of a squirrel burying nuts in the earth for its own survival in an (unfathomable) future. As many of these pills and capsules as she could tolerate swallowing with mouthfuls of water, she would take at precisely the correct time.

A singular death, shared by wife and husband. As in the prime of their lovemaking they'd been one person, transformed in a joy so extreme it lay beyond language, even imagination.

But that hadn't happened. Nothing like that had happened. Cruelly, something else had happened, the stunned survivor is still trying to understand.

"GERARD!"–YOU WAKE FROM A HAZE of sorrow seeing your husband across the sun-drenched plaza, staring in your direction.

You will recall afterward—he must have sighted you first. His gaze on you waking you like an electric current rippling through your body.

Is this Gerard?—a man of Gerard's approximate age and height, standing very still and observing you with unusual interest.

Your heart begins to beat rapidly. You are in dread of this person, this stranger, calling out to you—*Hello! I think we've met—you're Gerard McManus's wife?*

If so identified, you would shrink away in pain. Your lips shrinking back from your teeth in a grimace.

But the man who resembles Gerard is too gentlemanly to call to you across the plaza. Indeed, he seems not to recognize you after all. But something about you has attracted him, unmistakably.

He is taller than Gerard had been, leaner, with a somber yet affable face and the slightly sunken eyes of one who has been ill. His jaws are unshaven even as he exudes an air of dignity; he wears a short-sleeved white cotton shirt, blue-striped seersucker trousers that fit him loosely; in the bright sunshine he is hatless, his eyes squint.

A smile tugs at the corner of his mouth—shy, tentative—inquisitive—as Gerard used to smile at you in the early days of your knowing each other. So tender a smile, you feel your heart constrict in pain.

Not knowing what you are doing you rise to your feet, you approach this man like a woman in a dream.

It is expected that you will shatter. You, the wife, revealed to be so weak. Clutch at the man who'd been your husband, lose your composure utterly. Wanting only to throw your arms around him, collapse into tears. But you will not succumb, like Orpheus: too much is at stake.

A delicate moment like passing a thread through the eye of a needle. The slightest misstep, all will vanish.

The bright-hued air has narrowed, you are making your way through a sort of tunnel. Around you the sound of voices, music, traffic has become a buzzing roar. Your vision has weirdly sharpened, even as it has greatly narrowed. There comes a sudden clamor of horns—rude, jarring: you have stepped into traffic, at the edge of the plaza, and might have been struck by a vehicle except the driver brakes to a stop just inches away from you, shouts at you in a vexed voice.

Gerard hurries to you, seizing your arm and pulling you to safety—"Excuse me! Take my hand . . ."

Not Gerard's deep-baritone voice as you recall it, nor is this something Gerard is likely to say to you; in actual life, Gerard would have scolded you, and wouldn't have smiled.

Michaela! Watch where the hell you're going!

Yet: there may be an impediment of some kind to prevent Gerard from seeing you clearly and knowing who you are. A scrim of moisture over his eyes. A blurring of his vision.

Roughly he has pulled you up onto the sidewalk, out of the cobblestone street. For an awkward moment he continues to clasp your hand—a small-boned hand, in a larger hand.

It is nothing like you remember, this handclasp. But yes, it is everything you remember.

The vigorous Gerard, before opioids dulled his soul.

The sexually alert, warmly aroused Gerard, before the shadow of his death unmanned him.

Though it seems that this Gerard has been ill he is (evidently) now a convalescent. His head has been shaved (for surgery?), his hair has grown back thinly, metallic-gray. Unsteady on his feet like one who must monitor his strength but he'd managed to make his way quickly to you, to pull you out of the street and save you from injury. You see with relief that this Gerard is straight-backed, he has not (yet) been broken by pain and by the narcotic dulling of pain.

Is this the man you'd seen from the grief counselor's window? Is this the man you'd held in your arms, for so many hours?—urging him to *breathe*?

One of the walking wounded. So many.

You are so deeply moved, agitated, you are having difficulty seeing Gerard's features. As you'd have difficulty seeing your own reflection in a mirror, looming close. You are aware that he isn't wearing
the slate-colored baseball cap today but this might be to suggest that
time has shifted—if it is another time, it is another Gerard. Such
seismic shifts are beyond your comprehension. The short-sleeved
white shirt might be familiar but you're sure you've never seen the
seersucker trousers before—unless there's a seersucker suit, of a by-
gone era, at the back of Gerard's closet in Cambridge, predating your
entry into his life.

"Do we know each other?"—Gerard smiles at you quizzically.

"I—I don't know. Do you know *me*?"

Gerard's bemused eyes drop to your feet, rise again to your face,
as if assessing. Something like recognition hovers beneath his consciousness like a shadow beneath the surface of water.

"Will you tell me your name?"

"'Michaela.'"

"'Michaela!' A beautiful name."

You have never considered "Michaela" a beautiful name. Rather,
a variant of "Michael."

As if a woman might be a mere variant of a man, with a minimal
identity of her own.

You ask Gerard his name and he tells you but it is a disappointing name, a common name, you register only that it is *not Gerard
McManus.*

(Later, it will seem significant to you: he hasn't asked you your
last name.)

But you are speculating: if this person is indeed Gerard, he is a
Gerard who exists in the present time, and so he is not the Gerard of
several weeks ago. It is likely that a kind of veil or film shields him
from you now. He is of the *other side*, he could not be identical with

the man who'd been your husband; certainly, he would not have the identical name since he cannot have had the identical history of the man who has died.

"You ask if I know you, Michaela. Well, to 'know' can be a kind of intuition. To 'know' can bypass facts altogether."

This man is excited by you, flattered to have attracted the attention of a woman some years younger than he is though (it seems) he is also made uneasy by you, staring at him with such unabashed wonder and yearning.

In such a place, it's likely to suspect that a woman behaving so oddly has been drinking, or has taken drugs. Possibly, she is mentally unbalanced, with her bedraggled hair, rumpled clothing, staring eyes, a homeless person.

Still, Michaela thinks: it can't be so very uncommon that individuals seem to recognize one another in public places, in crowds, in festive settings like the Plaza de la Catedral de Santa Teresa on a Saturday afternoon in May. Women, men. The sexually deprived, and the sexually rapacious. Random sightings that throw sparks, explode into flame.

This man with the unshaven jaws has been a man whom women have adored, that much seems evident. His mouth is a sensual mouth, it yearns for intimacy. Though there is no ring on his left hand. How strange it is, how unnatural it seems, and cruel, that this man seems to have become a solitary and bereft being.

Your wedding band is too large for your finger. It slips off, you retrieve it, a half-dozen times a day. You see that this man has glanced at your ring several times, thoughtfully.

He knows. He remembers.

Awkward for you to speak to each other but awkward to remain silent also. If you did not know each other—if there were not the curious gravitational pull between you—by this time you would surely have turned away out of embarrassment. But you continue to gaze at each other, uncertainly, as if each is waiting for the other to speak.

He asks if you are staying in a hotel in Santa Tierra and you tell him no, in a rented house on Vista Drive. But he seems not to have heard of Vista Drive.

"The house is near the Institute—the Institute for Advanced Research at Santa Tierra. You've heard of the Institute?"

"'Institute for . . .' No. I don't think so."

But yes, he is remembering. Something.

What you are seeing (you realize) is a side of Gerard McManus that has been hidden from you for the twelve years of your marriage. A man who might strike up a conversation with a strange woman on the street, excited by the prospect of the unknown and not made uneasy by it, and by her curious behavior; a man seemingly at ease with his own sexuality. You recall that in your life together Gerard wasn't at ease with most women; at least, those who weren't professional women. He'd lacked a capacity for "small talk"—trivial exchanges seemed to embarrass him.

Indeed, silence had seemed more natural to Gerard, often.

But if you'd slipped your hand into his, and clasped his hand tight, he responded warmly, at once. And if you leaned down to kiss him as he was sitting at his desk . . .

But that is the husband I love. That is the man who loves me.

And now it seems clear that this man, the man with the shaved head and sensual mouth, is older than the Gerard you recall, who was only forty-eight at the time of his death; this Gerard is a decade older at least. He has been afflicted with illness—but not a fatal illness. On his left arm, just visible beneath the shirtsleeve, is a tattoo of some kind—you are shocked to see this since (of course) your Gerard never had a tattoo on his left arm, or on any part of his body.

You recall that in a later chapter of *The Human Brain and Its Discontents* Gerard refers respectfully to the "encryptic" and "codified" language of body ornamentation, i.e., tattoos, in Native Americans; among the non-Native population, where tattooing seemed to him arbitrary and exhibitionistic, Gerard was likely to be disapproving.

The cathedral bells are chiming the hour: 6:00 P.M. The sun is still high in the western sky. You feel a sick sort of excitement, yearning for dusk, night. For how much easier to take this man back with you to the house on Vista Drive and to take him to bed with you once again, than to comprehend who he is, what he is, what you are to each other.

Your companion seems to sense this. He looms above you leaning close. In his eyes are minute broken capillaries, that have discolored the whites of his eyes and given him a jaundiced look.

"I was about to stop for a cappuccino, Michaela. Will you join me?"—the question is oddly formal, as if much depends upon the answer.

Quickly you say *yes*. You would like that very much.

Your Gerard had loved cappuccino. You'd brought him several cups in the hospital, in those last, hopeful days before it became clear that Gerard could neither eat nor drink anything with pleasure but only with a nostalgic memory of pleasure, and finally without even that solace; and finally, he'd never tasted a cappuccino again. (A grim sort of relief you'd felt when at last you'd asked him if you should run to a Starbucks a few blocks away to get him a cappuccino and he'd said with a melancholy shrug—*Thanks darling but no. No more. Don't bother.*)

But this man is vigorous, forceful. Remembering nothing of the terrible weeks of the vigil. Daring to touch your elbow with an air of gallantry as he leads you out of the cathedral square.

So it must be relived?—the early, awkward stages of your love for Gerard, and Gerard's love for you? Not in Cambridge, Mass., but in Santa Tierra, New Mexico?

You feel a wave of panic, that love could not possibly bloom a second time.

Considering the unfathomable odds against an individual's birth, no individual could ever be (plausibly) born a second time.

And so, no love could be (plausibly) born a second time.

No choice but to walk alongside this Gerard. You cannot imagine the remainder of the night without him, as you could not have imagined, only a few weeks ago, the remainder of your life without him. It is exciting to you, it is unnerving, how this Gerard looms above you, and seems to be brushing his arm against you as if inadvertently; originally, in Cambridge, Gerard had been courtly with you, often lapsing into silence as you chattered nervously.

Wild laughter threatens to spill from your mouth. You have laughed so infrequently in months, you are fearful of an eruption of hysterical laughter now.

For it is funny, how this Gerard is more verbal than your Gerard had been when you'd first met, which causes you to be more silent. Curious too how you hear in this Gerard's praise for the beauty of Santa Tierra and the San Mateo Mountains an echo of your Gerard's praise months ago.

Beauty, uncanny.

Monumental and surreal . . .

But the air—so thin!

You hear yourself laugh, though there is nothing particularly funny about these remarks. That they are an echo of the other Gerard's remarks, that is what's funny; but there is no way to explain this. (For this man, this stranger, has never heard these remarks before, of course; to him, his observations are wholly original, and your reaction verges upon insulting.)

Why is everything that is happening between you and him so funny, suddenly?—so terrifying?

Wild laughter of adolescence. Female adolescence.

Crazed-flamy laughter of the (female) groin.

Unbearable desire, channeled into a tiny cusp of tissue and that tissue comprised almost entirely of nerve-endings.

Yet, carelessly touched, roughly touched, all desire pulsing inside that sliver of tissue dies within an instant, and vanishes as if it has never been.

Try to recall: making love with Gerard McManus. Tenderness, clumsiness. A maneuvering of bodies no longer young, agile. Embarrassed laughter. Forgiving laughter. For there had to have been a first time and yet, your memory is smudged-blank as a whiteboard carelessly wiped.

Because you are not yet in love with each other. It is all provisional, still taking shape.

You are excited, and you are apprehensive. Walking with this stranger who is leading you—where? You have left the brightly lit plaza square behind. You are in a neighborhood of narrow streets. Though you are not saying much to your companion—(your tongue feels thick, an impediment in your mouth)—a conversation between the two of you is taking place; the air close about you is charged with static electricity. More and more tense this electricity is becoming, like pent-up desire, approaching the unbearable, a terror of release.

You feel a stab of desire, sharp between the legs. You have not felt anything like this in weeks—months . . . Much of your body has died, and has atrophied. Your skin is a sort of white husk, there are fine white grains of powder at your hairline. If eviscerated, you would be exposed as hollow inside, like a mannequin. Your blood has long ago dried up, into a gritty sort of powder. But you only smile, you don't really miss *life*.

Easier to be posthumous, in fact. Oh, far easier!

But now you realize: you are being confronted with your husband Gerard on an altered plane of being. Here is an older Gerard whom you'd never met who is Gerard's essential self, his purest self, not (yet) shaped by his relationship with you.

No wonder you are so uncomfortable with each other, and yet so hopeful, so tremulous with desire: it is all still *taking shape*.

You stop for cappuccinos at an outdoor café with a littered terrace. The sun has begun to bleed into the sky like a broken egg yolk. You regard each other shyly, with wonder. You are laughing, your companion must have said something witty. His eyes are discolored by broken capillaries yet they are beautiful eyes. He asks if you are alone in Santa Tierra and you tell him no, you are not alone. He reaches out to touch the oversized man's watch that slides around your wrist. "Do you have a husband, Michaela?"—the question is a subtle sort of accusation.

You tell him that you are still married to your husband. But your husband isn't in your life right now.

As if you've told him a riddle. He is looking bemused, suspicious. Glisten of perspiration on his forehead that is more creased than you'd thought at first, as the lines beside his eyes and mouth are deeper. Lifting the small white cappuccino cup to his lips, his hand betrays a tremor. No man wants to be played like a fool—if there is a foolish miscalculation, a sexual blunder, it had better be on the part of the woman, not the man. For the woman, in this case, has purposefully attracted the man to her; she has sent him unmistakable yet (possibly) fraudulent signals. He isn't angry, however. He isn't angry yet. He asks about Gerard—carefully he refers to Gerard as *your husband*—and you tell him that your husband was an historian of science, on the faculty at Harvard. It occurs to you that this is a piteous boast. *Was* invalidates the boast. Your companion is listening, frowning. He leans forward on his elbows on the table, which is wobbly, annoying. How difficult to take seriously a sexual drama that unfolds atop a wobbly table! You have been curious about the tattoo. You can make out what appears to be a cobalt-blue wing—(a bird's wing?)—(an eagle's wing?)—on the ropey muscle of the man's left bicep. In a near-swoon you wonder if this man has tattoos elsewhere on his body.

But he too has almost died. He has almost crossed to the other side, you see in his bleeding eyes.

Impulsively you reach out to close your hand over the hand of your companion. For a moment he is too startled to react then he closes his fingers around yours, firmly.

"If we could just sit like this for a while. Please."

You sit, clasping hands. Monumental masses of cloud drift westward, obscuring the sun and turning the sky to flame. A sensation of great calm comes over you.

After a while you say, quietly: "You are Gerard—aren't you? I think you must be."

"Who is 'Gerard,' dear? Your husband?"

"*You* are my husband, I think. I mean—you might have been."

Your companion laughs, a flush rising roughly in his face. His unshaven jaws glint silver. His speech is oddly formal, as if he is translating it from another language. "I'd be delighted if you were my wife, Michaela. But, well—life has dealt me other cards."

For a while you sit in silence, still clasping hands.

Your heart beats quietly, calmly. You tell this man how you'd held him in your arms in this very city, not so long ago. You'd assured him that he would not suffer, he would not be alone. You held him for hours as he struggled for breath, and then ceased breathing. And you'd held him longer, to assure that he was protected. You need to know—was he aware of you? Those final hours? Or did it all come too late?

Your companion considers these questions. He does not seem surprised or confused by them. Yes, he says slowly. He was aware of you—he'd never doubted you.

He calls you "Michaela"—as Gerard might have done, in a whisper.

Recalling those final minutes you begin to cry. The final breath of a man's life. The final, heaving sigh.

Recalling the horror that swept over you, which you cannot put behind you. When you'd realized that the man you held in your arms had ceased breathing.

The tortured breath, the long effort, the heartbreak of that (futile) effort, you will never forget. The heroism of which human beings are capable, which must be endured, and which is unfathomable even by those who bear witness.

Yet, your remembering this heroism does not bring comfort to the man who has suffered. *Breathed his last. In your arms.*

Except now, in this sidewalk café in Santa Tierra, there may be a respite.

A pleat in time. A clasping of hands. *This* is *Gerard—but he doesn't know that he has died.*

You understand: you must not acknowledge his death or, like Eurydice, he will "die" a second time. He will vanish from you, you will lose him a second time.

You have been shivering, convulsively. Your teeth chatter. You hear yourself declare to Gerard that you love him more than ever. You grip his hand tightly, you lift his hand and cover it with kisses.

The knuckles of that hand, covered in coarse hairs.

He is astonished by you. He is alert, aroused. He says: "You'd better come with me, darling."

He leaves several bills on the table. He pulls you to your feet. You stagger against him, he closes his arms about you for a moment before you push back, regain your composure. You'd felt his heartbeat—you'd felt his desire. Your face is flushed with blood, your eyes leak tears. You are crazed with a desire to take him to the house on Vista Drive. You would lie with him in your arms another time, you would comfort him again, breathe into his lungs again, and this time you would not ever surrender him.

But he has other plans. He scarcely listens to you. Pulling you across a street, into a shabby market selling food, live chickens and goats, sweet corn in bushels, pottery, weavings and carvings, turquoise jewelry, artwork.

He is excited and aroused, not so gentlemanly as he'd seemed. He lives here somewhere—does he? Not a tourist, like you.

Leading you past vendors' stalls, some of them grated shut for the night. There is a strong smell of alcohol, spilled food. Shrieks of laughter, a blaring car alarm that sets your teeth on edge.

"Not too much farther. C'mon!"—tugging your arm, fingers circling your wrist.

Faces here are not illuminated by the bright festive lights of the plaza square. You have begun to hear a harsh sibilant speech, no language you recognize.

Not English, and not Spanish. (Kiwaan?)

The sky has darkened with immense clouds shaped like galleons. Beyond the mountains there is a horizontal stream of liquid fire, so beautiful your eyes are flooded with tears.

You have been walking some distance, you are out of breath. There are few other White tourists here. Dark-skinned men with somber faces are predominant. Dusky-skinned, olive-dark-skinned. Very black hair, inky-black. Very black eyes with no pupil, only iris.

Your companion continues to pull you along the littered street. You could not dissuade him now if you wished. It is certain that he lives nearby. He rents a room in a hotel nearby. And not one of the gleaming new hotels near the cathedral. You stumble at a curb as something white-blurred flies at you—a soft clumping against your face. The man who resembles Gerard curses and strikes the flailing white dove with his fist, breaking its neck immediately so that it plummets to the ground, twitching.

You have no time to recoil in horror. You have no wish to provoke that fist to strike your face.

As your companion urges you along you have a glimpse of crude paintings, carvings. He has brought you to a Native American market. Animals with blunt protruding muzzles, small greedy eyes, curved tusks. Animals with savage bared saliva-glistening fangs. Predator birds, coiled serpents with gleaming coins for eyes. Weyaki, God of Chaos, in the shape of a fat squat pop-eyed bullfrog. Find yourself staring at crude drawings of white-skinned people—White men, White uniformed men beating dark-skinned persons with clubs, knocking them to the ground, kicking ribs, bellies, faces.

Uniformed soldiers on horseback shooting rifles point-blank at Indians who have already fallen to the ground. Slaughter of Indian women and children, naked bodies heaped together. A pueblo village, a flaming cross.

Grinning White faces, skull-faces. Mouths dripping blood.

White women with red labial lips, chalky-white skin, spots of rouge on cheekbones like clowns. White women teetering in ridiculous high-heeled shoes, tight-fitting clothes accentuating their bony chests, pelvises, pointy little breasts. Is this how they see us? you think. Is this how they see *me*.

You are out of place here. You don't belong here. The eyes of dark-skinned strangers light upon you, indignant.

White bitch. White butcher.

Race murderer!

Turn away, frightened. Hatred for you glares in their eyes. Try to protest it wasn't you, isn't you, not you who are the *race murderer*. Yes it is true, you are a *White woman*, but you are not a *race murderer*— not you!

Music has been driven out of the air, the air is filled with shouts of derision, loathing. Try to turn back but a fist strikes your face causing you to stagger. You sink to your knees. Blood splashes onto the loose T-shirt you are wearing, dripping from your nose. Your companion whom you've trusted in the pathos of your need has turned against you, in disgust of you.

Is this Gerard? Your husband? Pushing you from him, publicly repudiating you?

Call after him—*Gerard!* As a terrified child calls for a parent—
—*Don't leave me here! Don't leave me here alone!*

Within minutes the sky has darkened to night, the air is thin and cold. The sun has disappeared beneath the horizon. A glaring-white moon has risen. No mercy for the *race murderer*!

The lights of Santa Tierra are miles away. You have been brought to the edge of the desert. Shivering convulsively you have been brought to the altar of the cruel Skull God of the high desert plateau—the demon-god *Ishtikini*. Pueblo-god of toothless laughter, god of eyeless sockets, beast-god, god of bone-piles, scavenger-god, cannibal-god poised to devour the body's organs as life ceases to pulse through them: heart, brain, lungs, kidney, liver, stomach, intestines, genitals.

The demon-goddess Skli runs shrieking at you. Her talon-fingers claw at your face. Blood drips from between her legs. Arms grip you tight, tight around the rib cage, scarcely can you breathe as Skli jabs her razor-sharp talons between your legs, up inside you in a scalding spasm of pain.

Cries of a wounded and terrified animal, terrible to hear.

You are left to fall, fall heavily, ignominiously on the ground wetted with your dark-oozing blood. Too weak to cry for help or even to lift your head.

47

Dawn

Wakened by a din of wild parrots in the ravine behind the house! Sounding as if they are being killed but when Michaela ventures out onto the deck barefoot and (who knows how haphazardly) clothed she sees nothing except a fleeting flurry of wings, vivid-green, bloodred in the foliage below.

Very still she stands listening. Leaning against the railing, gazing down.

Waiting to be told—what? Mesmerized by savage cries, as by the savagery of grief.

UNDERSTAND: YOUR HUSBAND IS DEAD. *He is not coming back. But you are alive. You must return to your own life.*

48

The Good Widow

"Yes. I understand."

That morning, when the phone rings, Michaela answers it instead of ignoring it as she has done for weeks.

Instead of shrinking away in dread. Pressing her hands over her ears, running from the room.

Later, she begins to make calls herself. Belated calls, she hopes *not too late.*

Unopened mail (forwarded from Cambridge, Mass.) dumped onto a table in a room she rarely enters, shunned for weeks she begins to sort into several piles.

Trembling hands, racing heart, has to urge herself *Breathe!— breathe* but she does not falter, she does not faint though her blood pressure has become dangerously low in recent weeks, often she has to lower her head between her legs, at her weakest she has had to crawl up the stairs to the second floor of the house *wounded by grief, crazed by grief, broken by grief as a snake upon whose vertebrae a giant boot has stomped.*

Understanding: soon it will be time for her to leave Santa Tierra.

Soon, time to vacate the house on Vista Drive which has been leased through the month of August.

And soon, time for Michaela to assume her responsibilities as the widow of Gerard McManus and as the executrix of the estate of Gerard McManus whose Last Will & Testament is to be submitted for due process in the Middlesex County Probate Court, Cambridge, Massachusetts.

"YES. I AM SO VERY SORRY. I have been out of communication, I have no excuse . . ."

It has been weeks, she has failed in her duties. She has allowed herself to succumb to grief. She has allowed herself to deteriorate mentally, physically. Failed to open crucial letters and so she has failed to mail copies of her husband's death certificate to their lawyer's office. Failed to return crucial telephone calls, emails since in the time required to even make a decision returning such calls and emails she is likely to have lapsed into an open-eyed dream recalling in painful detail how for years she and Gerard shopped together at the Safeway on Massachusetts Avenue using two carts, for efficiency's sake separating just inside the store (Michaela to begin with fresh produce, Gerard to begin with fish and seafood) and meeting at the checkout counter, where Michaela was invariably first, as Gerard required time to select particular items like cereal, coffee, orange juice, and did not care to be "rushed"; how Michaela laughed at Gerard, for feeling obliged to declare that, in the Safeway, as elsewhere (museums, for instance) he did not care to be "rushed" which (Michaela understood) was a way of chiding her for moving too swiftly, as an impatient child might do; how on a good day, they would have remembered to bring their own (cloth) bags for the groceries into the store: crimson tote bag from the Harvard Coop, green tote bag from Greenpeace, two or three other tote bags of no consequence at the time and charged with consequence now, that these scraps of rag have outlived Gerard Mc-

Manus; how companionably the couple loaded their groceries into the trunk of Gerard's Subaru Forester; how, at the house on Monroe Street, to which, as usual, Gerard had driven them, they carried the groceries into the house through the side door, from the garage; how, in the kitchen, they unloaded the bags, cans in cupboards, perishables in the refrigerator, bananas in a fruit bowl on the counter; how beautifully choreographed their movements, "Gerard"—"Michaela"; at the same time, how totally oblivious they are of their movements, and of the astonishing fact that they are together, and that they are alive; that is—"Gerard" and "Michaela" are *alive together*. Long entranced minutes are required for Michaela in the rented house on Vista Drive in Santa Tierra in the third month of widowhood to perceive this astonishing truth, and yet more minutes are required as the widow stares at this "Gerard" and "Michaela" seeing that they are talking about something, since entering the kitchen they have scarcely ceased talking about something, smiling, laughing, but what is the subject?—what so engrosses them, as Gerard places a bag of frozen peas in the freezer (which, Michaela sees, he is putting in the wrong place, not in the freezer drawer with other frozen vegetables but on the [door] shelf with frozen bread—but she will not correct him now, she will wait until later, when Gerard isn't around to observe), as Michaela stands on her toes to arrange cans of soup with their labels facing outward on the third shelf of the cupboard beside the refrigerator; but the widow can't hear what they are saying, she can see their mouths moving, she can hear the murmur of their voices; she is filled with distress that she can't know why Michaela is laughing, shaking her head in that way that signals disbelief with something (improbable, playful) that Gerard is saying, and in Gerard's face that small, tucked-in smile, signaling that he knows he is exaggerating, of course he isn't serious, as Michaela knows that he isn't serious and so they laugh together, in that instant so deeply bonded and so clearly husband-and-wife, the widow in the rented house on Vista Drive begins to sob helplessly, hopelessly for all that she has lost that is irretrievable . . .

More crucially, the widow has failed to open certified letters sent to her from Gerard's attorney pursuant to the Last Will & Testament of Gerard McManus for which she has been named executrix as she has been named executrix of Gerard McManus's manuscripts, archives, and personal library of twenty-six thousand volumes.

Failed even to (re)read the (thirty-two-page) will, emailed to her from the attorney's office. (Of course, Gerard's will should contain no surprises for Michaela: they'd had their wills drawn at the same time, a decade ago, updated four years ago, with the same attorney, and with most of the same provisions in each will.) (Is Michaela's Last Will & Testament also thirty-two pages long? She has not seen it in years, and has no idea.) Well, the widow cannot explain what has happened to her. When Gerard had so clearly depended upon her.

Naming *my wife Michaela* his executrix. His principal beneficiary. Entrusting her with his priceless manuscript.

His children, her stepchildren. Her in-laws.

"Hello? This is Michaela. Yes—me . . . I'm so sorry . . ."

Always a hazard to speak with Gerard's family, friends, those who'd loved him yet Michaela remains dry-eyed through the ordeal and does not stutter or stammer, much.

". . . he'd asked me to tell you he loves—loved you . . ."

Choking, unable to continue. For Christ's sake *Breathe!*—*one damned breath after another.*

Likely that her tear ducts have atrophied. Grief drained from every pore like oily sweat.

Too complicated to explain to Gerard's family that at the start of his hospitalization she'd begged him to allow her to contact them but he'd refused. Pride, or whatever it had been. And soon then, too late.

Still, no one accuses Michaela. Not the daughter, and not the son. Indeed, each exhibits surprise and relief that their negligent stepmother has called, at last.

". . . yes, he wanted to be remembered to you. At the very end, he . . ."

None of this is remotely true. In his misery, in the opioid delirium of his final days Gerard had barely been conscious of Michaela cradling him in her arms, kissing his forehead.

". . . said how he loved you, he was so sorry he hadn't wanted visitors . . ."

To be a good widow, as to be a good wife, one must learn how to lie convincingly.

As Michaela recovers her sane self, she will recover her (atrophied) ability to lie.

It is unnatural for Michaela to speak with Gerard's children, relatives, close friends, since invariably in the past it was Gerard who did most of the talking with them, and not Michaela; and it is unnatural to Michaela to seem to be speaking for Gerard as if he can't speak for himself.

Strange, to be speaking the name *Gerard* so frequently. As if Gerard were somewhere distant, or was in some way incapacitated.

"Yes. You are correct. Gerard had updated his will just a few years ago. So I think that this will is . . ."

Hearing the voice calm and matter-of-fact as if her life has not shattered, collapsed at her feet.

Is most of life imposture?—Michaela wonders.

Only when she'd been sick, after Gerard's death. Then, Michaela had not been an impostor.

Others have managed to survive such losses, however. Now, it is Michaela's turn.

Her body has been sick, her bowels leaking a watery excrement, swollen pulses beating in her legs, flashing stabs of pain behind her eyes. It has required too much strength to bathe—a shower, far too agitated—scarcely has she troubled to wash her hands after she has used the bathroom.

For why?—no one gives a damn if your hands are swarming with bacteria.

But now she prepares to take a shower. If she intends to persevere with her life, to fulfill her duties as a widow, she must at least take a shower, rid her body of the sour animal-odors of grief, despair. Scalding water, soaping between her legs where the demon-goddess Skli had thrust her razor-claws to draw blood, humiliate.

A raw wound, between her legs. Michaela touches herself cautiously and is surprised that her fingers come away unbloodied.

A bruise on her lower jaw, where the fist had struck.

(Had it been Gerard who'd struck her? She remembers the look of fury in his face, stunning to see. Never before in their life together had Gerard come close to striking her.)

Disconcerting to see hairs in the shower drain, hairs in the bristles of Gerard's hairbrush. Each time Michaela washes her hair, brushes and combs it, an excessive number of hairs come out.

Weight-loss will result in hair-loss, Michaela knows. In her feral state she'd gotten into the habit of eating while standing, eating what she can hold in her hand, not taking time to prepare food out of an embarrassment to be eating alone, as an animal eats alone.

Steamy mirror in which her head is lowered as a beast's head is lowered before the lethal blow to the skull.

Shadowed eyes peering at shadowed eyes, appalled at how exhausted she looks, how sickly-pale her face, that would have dismayed Gerard.

My beautiful girl.

What have you done to yourself!

". . . as soon as the will is probated. Absolutely."

Michaela has learned from their attorney in Cambridge that Gerard's estate is "frozen" until his will can be probated by the Middlesex

County Probate Court. Gerard's and Michaela's joint bank accounts are (partially) frozen until the will can be probated. This is customary procedure, nothing to be alarmed about. (Michaela is assured.) But it is crucial to make an appointment with the probate court as soon as possible, E. L. Erickson tells her.

"Certainly, yes. I—I will fly back as soon as . . ."

Michaela's voice hovers uncertainly. *Fly back*—where?

She will never return to Cambridge, Mass., she knows. Never return to the house on Monroe Street where she would be struck down dead if she stepped inside.

". . . things are finalized, here."

Finalized. What a word! Michaela's lips twist in a sneer.

For all her resolve in the past several days Michaela has been unable to force herself to (re)read Gerard's will. The horror she'd felt years ago in Erickson's office as she and Gerard were signing their names on their wills before witnesses returns to her now.

How correct you were, to be horrified! Terrified.

How absolutely correct, to understand that these documents signal the end of your existence.

YET: THERE IS SOMETHING VERY important about the widow returning to the house on Monroe Street, Cambridge.

Except she cannot seem to recall what it is.

The first thing you must do, before you even bring your stupid suitcases upstairs, is kill yourself.

However you can, you will find a way.

Of course!—there is a distinct way for there is a garage attached to the house as there is not a garage attached to the rented house in Santa Tierra.

Michaela can stuff towels around the windows in this garage and beneath the sliding door to guarantee that exhaust billowing from the car will not leak out. She has read that death by carbon monoxide inhalation can be astonishingly swift—within three to five minutes in ideal circumstances, in a secured garage.

Easily then, Michaela can swallow a handful of sleeping pills from her cache of pills, drink a glass or two of wine, relax behind the wheel of the car listening to Gerard's favorite radio station WCRB-FM (classical music), and drift off to sleep as the motor runs with lethal quiet undetected for far, far longer than three-to-five minutes.

Yes darling. Come!

Your hand in mine.

*   *   *

THERE IS SOMETHING IGNOBLE ABOUT *inheriting*. Something demeaning about *surviving*.

Strange, Michaela has scarcely thought of Gerard's will. Of an inheritance. *Her* inheritance—the thought fills her with unease.

Vaguely she recalls that Gerard's will had been a conventional one. Most of his estate to the *surviving spouse*. Several other, smaller bequests to Gerard's children and to charitable organizations to which he'd been donating for years.

". . . thank you but no!—that isn't necessary, Lucinda. Everything is under control."

Must discourage the earnest (step)daughter who lives in Seattle from flying to Santa Tierra, to help the (step)mother. As if, after all she has endured, Michaela needs help, now!

All that she will do, she will do alone.

Please please please—*alone*.

Feeling panic, that Gerard's relatives will take it upon themselves to come to Santa Tierra, to accompany Michaela back home.

Though Michaela is grateful, she supposes, that Gerard's family seems to have forgiven her (inexplicable) behavior.

As if Michaela had died too. But Michaela had not died.

"We weren't sure what to do, Michaela," Lucinda is saying, hesitantly, "—you never returned our calls or emails. We had no idea how ill Dad was until an administrator from the Institute contacted us. She said she was a 'close friend' of yours and that you'd given her permission to keep us informed about Dad . . ."

Michaela listens with mounting astonishment.

"I never gave anyone permission to talk about Gerard to you! I don't even know the woman."

"She said she was a friend of yours—'Iris—'"

"No! She's not a friend of mine."

"She said—"

"No!"

So upset, Michaela breaks the connection.

So upset, Michaela ignores the phone ringing as Lucinda calls back. In an instant Michaela is coldly furious, raging. She has not felt such emotion in months.

Stumbles out onto the redwood deck leaning far over the railing, hands over her ears.

No no no no no.

Eventually, when Michaela lowers her hands, it's only the cries of the wild parrots in the ravine below that she hears.

NEXT DAY, MICHAELA CALLS THE (step)daughter to apologize and explain: she is not in need of help right now.

In her new, sane state Michaela repents of the behavior of the other Michaela deranged by grief as a rabid wild creature. *But no more.*

The (good, sane) widow means to fulfill her obligations. She has roused herself from the death-spell, she will not succumb again.

Bill-paying. Writing checks. No more mundane way of (re)connecting with the world.

In the widow, the mundane and the penitential merge.

In the widow, the mundane and the unbearable merge.

For Michaela has discovered a folder of (unpaid) bills in Gerard's desk in the rented house. Bills forwarded from Cambridge, set aside by Gerard when he was stricken with pneumonia, soon forgotten as he struggled for his life.

It was Gerard's routine to pay bills online, near the end of the month. Now some of these bills are past due. Among them, Gerard's medical insurance.

How mortified Gerard would be, Michaela thinks. That he'd failed to pay bills. Failed to do the common ordinary routine tasks he'd done so capably as a husband.

Failed you by dying.

A grim task, paying bills. And now newer bills, soon to be a deluge of bills from the Santa Tierra Cancer Center . . . But writing checks can be a solace in a time when nothing matters for writing checks is invariably a solitary activity, one does not miss a spouse while writing checks which Michaela can do, she reasons, until the money runs out and if/when the money runs out that will be a clear sign that Gerard has been preparing for her, that her life has run out.

I'm here, I won't leave you, darling Michaela.

I have your hand. I am waiting.

THE MOST SOMBER OF THE WIDOW'S TASKS as it is the most absurd, and the most heartrending: bringing her husband's ashes home with her to the house on Monroe Street, Cambridge, where he'd lived for many years.

If Gerard and Michaela had known, when they'd left the house so blithely in January: that one of them would not return but *be brought back* in an urn . . .

Michaela wants to laugh wildly. But laughter in the widow is a prelude to hysterical weeping, thus not advised.

Vaguely the (adult) children have spoken of "scattering Dad's ashes"—in the Catskills, in a mountain stream behind a cabin in Roxbury once owned by Gerard's grandparents which (all the relatives agree) was Gerard's "favorite place in all the world."

Michaela has heard of this mythic place in the Catskills, no electricity, no indoor plumbing, long since purchased by strangers, but during the twelve years of her marriage to Gerard, Gerard made no effort to revisit Roxbury, preferring to travel abroad in the summer; but Michaela has not objected to these plans to which she has politely listened.

In fact she has no intention of allowing Gerard's ashes to be scattered anywhere, like debris. What a crude custom!

Though understanding—*These are just ashes. These are not Gerard.*

Lying in bed in the house on Vista Drive from which she is soon to be expelled rehearsing in her head how she will carry the urn containing Gerard's *cremains* onto the plane with her. She will not check the urn with luggage. She will not ship it. She will not risk its loss.

At the security check she will present the urn for inspection.

This urn contains my husband's ashes, I am bringing back to our home.

Somberly, respectfully the widow will be waved through security.

No doubt, one of the NSA officers will murmur that he/she is *sorry for your loss, ma'am.*

As other passengers bring small dogs onto airplanes, in carrying cases that can be slid beneath the seat in front of them, so Michaela will take the urn, the ashes, the *cremains* of her late husband onto the plane with her, to slide beneath the seat in front of her.

How ridiculous our lives, Michaela thinks, appalled.

When the *person* is reduced to *matter*—obscene.

How much less shameful just to die. And how strange, so few others have thought of this, or have had the courage to act upon it.

That stab of guilt in the gut, a kind of nausea, that the widow is still alive while the husband is dead.

Yet as Michaela (compulsively) rehearses the scene she begins to see that not all of the airport security officers are behaving respectfully toward the widow. Indeed, one of them is frowning suspiciously at the urn inside its maroon cloth bag, placed for inspection on the X-ray conveyor belt.

Though Michaela has notified several officers that the urn contains a man's *cremains* and though the urn is clearly stamped *G. Mc-Manus. Chapel of Chimes, Santa Tierra, NM*, the NSA supervisor tells Michaela sternly that the urn will have to be opened for inspection.

Worse, it falls to the widow to open the urn as several security officers look on. Michaela has never yet opened the urn, has not wanted to gaze upon its contents, has never felt sufficiently strong enough to gaze upon its contents, and so has no idea how to open the damned urn for the lid is securely in place.

Twist the lid? Pull at the lid? Pull *hard*? Michaela's face is flushed with vexation, anxiety, guilt.

(Will none of the security officers help her? *Not one?*)

At last, Michaela succeeds in prying off the lid. Quickly shuts her eyes, cannot bring herself to look upon what is inside, that has been combusted and reduced to seven pounds, two ounces.

Security officers examine the contents of the urn by stabbing a pen into the ashes, a gloved forefinger, groping, stirring. Michaela is upset by these crude actions but dares not object. She is dismayed to be told brusquely—*Ma'am? We'll have to ask you to step over here.*

There is some question about the contents of the urn. Despite the ID stamped onto the urn.

. . . have to ask you to wait here, ma'am. Until we can determine exactly what is in this receptacle.

Do *cremains* resemble some type of narcotics? A kind of cocaine, hashish?

Michaela is allowed to rummage frantically through her carry-on suitcase to find the Chapel of Chimes Crematory receipt. This she shows to the NSA officer who scrutinizes it at length but shakes his head gravely.

Ma'am there's no way for us to know if this document pertains to this receptacle. Or, if it pertains to the receptacle, if the prior contents of the receptacle might not have been emptied out, and another substance substituted.

At which point the widow begins to weep those helpless tears she has usually kept private.

Wracked with tears, the human face flushes, swells. As the eyes become puffy, vision narrows.

To weep so rawly, so openly—a kind of nakedness.

So ashamed! Lying in her bed sweating, miserable unable to sleep Michaela foresees a contingent of security officers called, a detainment as fellow travelers look on bemused.

An analysis of the urn's contents by a forensics laboratory might require days, a week. Weeks. During which time Michaela cannot be allowed to fly. (Where will Michaela actually *be*? She would have had to vacate the house on Vista Drive; this lurid scene would be taking place in the Albuquerque airport.) Indeed, Michaela may soon be arrested on suspicion of conspiring to smuggle a controlled substance onto an interstate flight.

WIDOW OF RECENTLY DECEASED HARVARD PROFESSOR ARRESTED

SUSPECT IN DRUG SMUGGLING RING

So sweating! miserable!—by this time Michaela has given up trying to sleep.

Oh Jesus!—just die.

Kill yourself, stop this charade. You have a cache of pills for just that purpose.

No. She has changed her mind. She will not plan to bring Gerard's ashes onto the plane. She will have to pack the ashes in her (checked) luggage. A new and riveting idea will be to bring the urn into the garage with her, when she asphyxiates herself at last back in Cambridge; she will set the urn in the passenger's seat beside her, in the car in the garage in Cambridge as it fills up with thin gray clouds of exhaust, to music played by Gerard's favorite classical music station WCRB-FM.

And come kiss me, I'm waiting.

49

"Save Yourself"

You recall having told them *No thank you.*

Politely firmly telling all of them *No please. Stay away.*

Yet: the doorbell is ringing. After a pause, a sound of knocking.

Recall having locked the door (of course) yet to your horror you hear the door being pushed open—"Hello? Michaela? Are you there?"

Throaty female voice, familiar. Yet for a moment you cannot identify it.

Early that morning wakened by the vise tightening around your chest. Gasping for breath. Cries of wild parrots in the ravine, confused with your own racing thoughts.

Not expecting an intruder to *drop by.*

A spy from the Institute. Adamantly you'd told them *no.*

Now crouching in the bathroom. Disheveled, only partly dressed. The last thing you want is a visitor. An intruder.

In the bright-lit bathroom you'd been making an inventory of the cache of pills. Sleeping pills, painkillers. Plastic containers lined up on the counter beside the sink. Accumulation of years.

Enough to kill an elephant.

Feeling a thrill of apprehension, anticipation. For you are undecided what to do about the pills. In one scenario, the prudent one, you flush the pills down the toilet, careful to flush them in small enough portions so that the toilet doesn't become clogged. In another scenario, the more exhilarating, you bring the pills home to Cambridge, Mass., with you carefully secured in your carry-on suitcase.

Prior to the airtight garage, asphyxiation by carbon monoxide. Hours of a running motor, music lulling you to sleep.

"Michaela, please answer me! It's Iris . . ."

Of course, the voice is the voice of Iris Esdras. You are filled with rage, dismay.

The voice quavers with concern and with the thrill of such concern which is coercive, intrusive. Iris Esdras to whom you'd explained that you would not be home if she dropped by, you would not be home whenever she dropped by. Yet now, Iris has pushed her way inside the house. Iris is determined to help you, she has said. She is determined to prevent you from hurting yourself further, she has said. (For Iris is convinced that you have cut yourself, injured yourself in secret stealthy ways that are worsening.) Now, she is standing just outside the bathroom door and you see to your dismay that the door is unlocked and it is too late for you to lock it for if you do, Iris will know that you are locking it and that you are behind the door only a few inches away from her.

Appalled, you see the doorknob turning. Iris isn't pushing the door *open*—yet. Iris is just (discreetly) checking to see if the door is locked.

If locked, the situation might be an emergency. So Iris would conclude. A dramatic intervention might be required: calling 911.

Sirens on Vista Drive, early morning before the sun has fully arisen. Medics breaking into the house, laying their hands on the crouching cringing weeping partially-dressed woman backed into a corner of a bathroom . . .

No choice then but to open the door. As if you've only now become aware of Iris calling to you.

"Ah, Michaela! Thank God you are—all right . . ."

Genuine relief in the woman's white-powdered geisha face. In the heavily made-up eyes. Steel yourself for the smothering embrace.

". . . worried about you, dear!"

Dear. When has Iris Esdras started calling you *dear.*

You are limp, unresisting in her embrace. Your arms hang at your sides like a puppet's. You can think of nothing to say that is not craven, accommodating. You do not want trouble, you want merely to be left alone.

For Gerard keeps his distance, when others are near.

A smell of talcum-powdered flesh, cosmetics. Glisten of red-painted fingernails. Iris Esdras has a face vivid as a poster. Indian-black dyed hair parted in the center of her (very white) scalp and drawn back into a tight chignon. She holds herself with the aggressive aplomb of a flamenco dancer though she is a solid woman with fleshy bosom, hips. She wears floating scarves, ankle-length skirts, nubby tops with dipping necklines that reveal the tops of large gelatinous breasts. Her shoes are golden open-toed sandals, her toenails polished and glittering.

You assure Iris that you are all right but Iris is doubtful. She grips your thin shoulders, peers into your face as if peering into an abyss. She will prepare breakfast for you, she says. You are too thin. You are not well. She will make calls for you—the Institute will pay for your return flight, business class.

You thank Iris but try to explain that you are not leaving Santa Tierra just yet. There are several things that Gerard has asked you to do, you will do for his sake. You have your own commitments in Albuquerque.

Iris shakes her head skeptically. Commitments in Albuquerque? Iris is bemused, doubtful.

You ask Iris to do a favor for you: would she please take away from the house, this very morning, the ugly carvings of demon-gods you discovered when you'd moved in and have hidden from sight . . . One is here in the bathroom, beneath the sink, and two others are in the hall closet. Ishtikini, Skli, Weyaki . . . You are not sure how to pronounce their names.

Iris laughs and assures you that no other Institute fellows have ever complained about the art in this house, or in any of the Institute houses. Usually they are delighted with their accommodations and furnishings. What exactly do you mean, Iris asks: which "gods"?

You tell her: the Scavenger God, the Goddess of Creation and Destruction, the God of Chaos . . . You believe that they are Pueblo gods.

No, Iris says. Those are "prank gods"—"shadow gods"—not authentic Pueblo gods.

But what does that mean? you ask her. Not "authentic" Pueblo gods?

Iris shakes her head, amused. As if trying to explain the hierarchy of Pueblo gods to you would be hopeless.

All you need to know, Iris says, is that the sculpted figures in this house are not meant to represent *real gods*. The demons you've named are frequent subjects for art because the "higher gods"—the "authentic Pueblo gods"—cannot be embodied in figures and so the "lower gods"—Ishtikini is a favorite, and the female Skli—are popular.

You wince, hearing the names spoken aloud. You beg Iris: "Just take them away, please."

Iris's sharp eyes have dropped to your bare cringing feet. She sees, for how could those sharp eyes fail to see, that your toenails are long and jagged as burgeoning claws. She sees that, though you may have showered recently, it was not sufficient to make up for weeks of self-neglect, a patina of grime is detectable between your toes.

Iris points out, reasonably, that if you are planning to vacate the house soon, what difference does it make if there are "ugly" carvings in the house?

You say, stammering: "Please—just take them. Now."

You have begun to tremble badly. In the bathroom mirror you see your ghastly-white face. You see yourself stoop to open the cupboard door beneath the sink. You see Iris Esdras's savagely made-up face hovering above you, staring. You see both your hands gripping the Ishtikini figure with the grotesquely enlarged skull, howling mouth, pencil-thin erect penis, a figure made of dense, dark carved wood that is surprisingly heavy for its size.

You see your hands lift the sculpted demon above Iris's head and bring it down swiftly and hard. Taken by surprise the woman screams softly, a cry of disbelief. As she staggers and begins to fall she claws at you, pulling at your clothing, falling heavily onto the tile floor that is already blossoming with red splotches. From above you see that her skull has been broken, the chalky-white scalp has been torn, a flap of skin is hanging loose . . .

You stare down at her. Your brain feels as if it has been utterly annihilated. At a little distance in the mirror Gerard observes, waiting.

You know better than to look for him. If you turn your head he will vanish.

Come to me now, Michaela.

You have done all you need to do here.

You turn back to Iris Esdras who stands peering quizzically at you.

Iris is saying again that the "prank gods" should be no problem, just leave the carvings where they are if you find them ugly. These are harmless folk carvings, some find charming and others find "ugly."

Iris goes on to explain that she will be happy to help you ship boxes and to make arrangements for your flight home. The Institute will provide a business class ticket if you vacate the house by the first of July—

You interrupt: "Please go away. Take this with you, and go away. Now."

The ugly Scavenger God is in your hand. Both your hands. You thrust it at her.

When Iris hesitates you tell her: "Then go away yourself! Save yourself."

50

The Examination

Lie down! lie down flat on your back! on the examination table relax!

Relax muscles, relax bones! Relax brain spilling thoughts like lukewarm water out of a tremulous paper cup!

In the paper gown thinly covering nakedness, relax!

Your first duty is to keep yourself alive.

AT LAST YOU HAVE MADE an appointment with Dr. W___.

Dr. W___ has been recommended to you by Dr. M___.

Dr. M___ was recommended to you by (your friend) Iris Esdras.

Very low blood pressure, Dr. W___ has discovered.

Rapid heartbeat. "Excitation."

Temperature above normal (99.9 degrees Fahrenheit).

Bloodwork will show anemia, potassium deficiency.

Weight loss, considerable. Skin: pallor, clammy.

You have been feeling faint, feverish. Light-headed. Prone to sudden headaches, eye aches. Flashes like heat lightning may indicate a lesion in a brain artery. Your inner ear throbs. Your inner ear is crazed with itching. You are tempted to thrust a sharp wire into your ear canal—anything to stop the itching. *Are you burning up alive? Is grief a firestorm, burning you up alive?*

Dr. W___ listens to your lungs with a stethoscope. Chest, back. Dr. W___ instructs you to cough.

Dr. W___ listens to your heart. (Heartbeat accelerated!)

Circles your ankles with his (gloved) forefinger and thumb to determine if ankles are swollen.

An EKG is administered by a cardiac technician. (Chilly) electrodes affixed to your chest, throat, abdomen.

Then, an echocardiogram. (Chilly) electrodes affixed to your chest, throat, abdomen. To more precisely record the murmuration of the heart and to detect the (possible) presence of a blood clot.

Lie down, lie very still. Breathe don't breathe.

Forty-seven exacting minutes and for part of this time you can listen to the eerie *swishing* of the heart and if you wish (you do not wish) you can stare at a screen to see the wraith-like *swishing* of the heart.

A leaky valve, no doubt. A broken heart.

Lying very still breathing and not-breathing, breathing and not-breathing, for there is a space between breathing and not-breathing, a caesura. Lie still, alert and alive. *The first duty of the Good Widow is to keep herself alive.*

Begin to hear beneath and beyond the *swishing* of your heart a deeper, more labored, more painful *swishing*. Begin to hear hoarse labored breathing.

A familiar breathing. Terrifying, that breathing.

You hear, and you tell yourself—*No. It is not.*

For you'd held him as he'd died. As he'd lapsed into not-breathing, and died. You'd held him, you'd died with him, yet you have continued to live, your life is a curse like a blinding light glaring without end, eyes without eyelids condemned to blindsight.

Willing to concede by this time, weeks after your husband's death, and weeks after the incineration of his remains at the Chapel of Chimes Crematory, that Gerard is no longer living. You do not—yet—

say to yourself *My husband has died.* You do not say *My husband is dead.* But you are able to say *My husband is no longer living.*

Still the breathing is getting louder. At first it seems to be coming from beneath the examination table but now it appears to be coming from another direction. From a vent in the wall? From the echocardiogram monitor? From a ligature in the air?

A chuffing sound, thick, dense. A struggle of air, a strangle of air, terrible to hear. As if what is breathing is breathing against volition, wish. As if very breathing is itself a torment. As if *breath* is a torture like nails being pounded into flesh. As if what is *breathed in* is something other than mere air.

Poor Gerard!—having to breathe a kind of viscous substance, a liquidy gas, putrescent-green, through his nostrils, lungs.

Gerard is struggling, suffering. You cannot bear his suffering.

It is not our own suffering but the suffering of others that destroys us. Not our own deaths we dread but the deaths of others whom we do not wish to outlive.

"No. Stop."

You sit up, suddenly. In the midst of the test you can no longer bear being touched. You can no longer bear listening to your heartbeat and to the struggling breath that now pervades the room.

Push away the instrument in the startled nurse's hand. Tear at electrodes with your nails, flinging them from you.

You are crying soundlessly. Your face has crumpled like a papier-mâché mask.

Whatever words the nurse is speaking to soothe you, ignore.

Dr. W___ has been summoned but by the time Dr. W___ enters the room you have thrown on your clothes haphazardly, you have kicked the paper gown aside, you are prepared to leave.

Exit—you think. *Exit, exist.*

Not quick enough to escape. In Dr. W___'s office panting, sweating though the air feels refrigerated.

As in the hospital morgue where your husband was taken. Where his *remains* were kept until delivered to the Chapel of Chimes Funeral Home and Crematory.

Dr. W___ is Asian, of that mysterious age between twenty-nine and forty-nine. His skin is unlined, his eyes are very dark. With his expression of compassionate incomprehension he smiles at you as you struggle to explain to him why you are desperate to leave before the echocardiogram is concluded.

"I—I don't think—that I should be here," you stammer foolishly. "I think—I should be somewhere else . . ."

"Yes? This is—where?"

"With my husband Gerard."

"And your husband is—?"

"My husband is not in Santa Tierra."

"Then he is—where?"

"He might be in Santa Tierra but I don't know where."

Dr. W___ regards you with searching eyes. Like one trying to decipher a foreign language.

"He wants me with him. I—I am going to him soon."

"But can that not wait, Mrs. McManus, until after the test?"

This is so reasonable a query, in a voice so softened with concern for you, you can only repeat, in a whisper: "But I want to be with him, too. I—I should be there, now."

Sick with guilt. Shame.

The first duty of the widow is to join her husband.

We are on earth to assuage each other's loneliness.

Nowhere so lonely as Death.

Feel your head lighten like a balloon filled with helium. You are feeling giddy suddenly. Soon, this ordeal will be over!

"Mrs. McManus, do you have family? Of your own? A parent or parents you might contact?"

Family. Parents. Your brain is struck blank.

On the farther side of the abyss, your loving parents, not yet elderly, though on the brink of elderly, whom you cannot contact as one bearing contagion cannot contact the living.

"N-No. I don't think so. I mean—I'm not close to them. I don't want to worry them. I can't put the burden of—what has happened— my grief—onto them . . ."

"Friends, then? Back home?"

You shake your head. *Friends. Back home.*

The farther side of the abyss, of no more meaning to you than strangers would be.

"I belong *here*. There's nothing for me *there*. I am only just waiting to see where—exactly—I am expected to go."

Whatever the significance of these words, that seem to you a calm statement of fact, frowning Dr. W___ feels compelled to make a decision for you: arranging for you to be admitted to the ER in the hospital adjoining this building.

"You will be transported there by wheelchair, Mrs. McManus. You're in an excitable state, your safety is at risk."

Coldly you regard Dr. W___. Gerard would be impressed by your calm, your hauteur, as you decline to be admitted to the ER.

Very firmly you decline, you do not give your consent, never will you consent to be admitted to this or any other hospital, you will sign no papers and if anyone tries to restrain you, you will sue.

You will walk out of this hateful place now. They can't keep you.

It is against the law to restrain an individual against her rights! You know your rights as a citizen.

Dr. W___ tries to "reason" with you. But you have lost interest in Dr. W___.

Indeed you are able to stand. Though you are shaky on your feet you are able to walk, your legs move with the ease of a puppet's legs swinging free of gravity. You are fully in control of the coordination of your limbs! Hold yourself straight and tall recalling how in

Gerard's New Mexico guidebook the hiker is advised to make himself as straight, tall, large, impressive as possible if confronted by a mountain lion, and to make aggressive noises, to frighten the animal away.

Under no circumstances run from a mountain lion—it is advised.

You and Gerard thought this was funny. Very funny. You laughed together, delighted.

Under no circumstances. Run.

Make your way out of Dr. W___'s office without running.

You cannot recall having seen this labyrinth of (windowless, fluorescent-lit) corridors before. Yet, you seem to know that there will be an elevator ahead . . . If you keep in motion, if you ignore the calls in your wake—*Mrs. McManus?*—*Michaela?*—you will step outside into the sunlight within a minute or two.

Walk, run in the sunlight. Run, run! Never look back.

In the parking lot no idea where you have parked the car or even if you have a car or, having a (rental) car, which car it is but hoping that, wishing to believe that if you see the car, if your hungry eyes move onto the car, you will remember.

Michaela, this is too hard on you! Come to me now.

There is a place for you, darling. With me.

51

"Take Me Home"

Here is the key, Michaela. Bring the car around, I will meet you at the front of the hospital.

Gerard has been fumbling at a pocket, seeking the ignition key. Fumbling to find a pocket in the hospital gown but there is no pocket, there is no key, except indeed Gerard has found a key which he presses into your hand, and you take it from him sobbing with relief that your lives have been so profoundly altered, in just this instant.

Not a key which you recognize but you clutch it in your fingers as if clutching life itself and next thing you know you are outside in thin, cooling air, it is dusk, headlights are coming on, you find yourself climbing the concrete steps of the parking garage adjacent to the Cancer Center panting with excitement and with hope, Gerard's words ringing in your ears—*Bring the car around!*

Many times in recent months you have found yourself in parking lots searching for a car but this is the first time, you believe, that you have the ignition key in your fingers, thus proof (you think) that indeed there is a car; though you are uncertain which car is yours and Gerard's among rows of vehicles that seem to stretch out of sight . . .

If you see the vehicle, you will recognize it. If you press the remote control, lights will be activated.

Shrewdly you think: a Massachusetts license plate will be easy to identify amid New Mexico plates.

But then you realize: the car Gerard has rented has New Mexico plates. Not Massachusetts.

Search for the car, short of breath, anxious. It is crucial to keep in motion so that the vise around your chest can't tighten and begin to suffocate you.

But it makes you very anxious, that Gerard is waiting for you. By now he is waiting impatiently for you, you must not let him down.

All love is betrayal under extreme conditions. For love is not strong enough to endure extreme conditions.

But then, to your astonishment and relief, you have found the car—the lights have come on, the car has leapt into life.

Drive the car out of the garage. Careful, for the lane is narrow. There are posts oddly positioned. To your chagrin despite your caution you have scraped the passenger's side of the car against a post for you can't see through the side mirror very clearly.

Tell yourself—*The mirror is the past. The past is lost.*

Tell yourself—*You can't go there! You have no way there.*

Somehow you manage to descend the many levels of the parking garage, you manage to exit the parking garage, you are forced to turn right, to be routed around the block, and these are lengthy blocks; several frustrating minutes are required for you to approach the front of the hospital where Gerard has been waiting for you, and then you see that Gerard isn't there, you see a succession of strangers pushing through the slow-turning automated doors, blurred faces of strangers, but not Gerard; you are filled with anxiety, you have no idea what to do, your husband is not here . . .

Then, there is a sharp rap on the windshield.

You turn, and now you see Gerard standing close beside the car, on the driver's side. But this is not the Gerard you expect to see.

Your husband's hair that is usually so carefully brushed is disheveled, patches of scalp are exposed. He is in a stained hospital gown that falls scarcely to his knees, and he is barefoot. His cheeks are gaunt, he has lost weight. His eyes are bloodshot glaring at you. It is terrible to see how angry your husband is with you, how disappointed. For you have taken a very long time to bring the car around to the front of the hospital, it seems.

To your dismay you see that Gerard is pulling a gurney bearing IV lines, Dilaudid dripping into one bruised arm, a saline solution into the other bruised arm. But he begins pounding the car windshield with a fist, furious.

Let me in! Let me in! Take me home!

52

The Lonely

So lonely. Lonely to be touched.
    Lonely to be held, protected. Named.
    So lonely have made an appointment with Death.

MY GUESS IS, IT CRAWLED *into your ear when you were sleeping.*
    Fever, inflammation, itching—has to be a bacterial infection.
    This advanced, close to the brain, danger is encephalitis.
    Why'd you wait so long to get medical help?
    Where've you been all these weeks?

53

Revelation in the Form of a Dove

On the eve of your final class meeting in Albuquerque.

Out of nowhere the news comes before you can protect yourself.

In the form of a white-feathered bird plummeting from the sky, striking your face before you can protect yourself—*Letitia Tanik has died*.

You are stricken with remorse. You are stricken with guilt.

Wanting to know more but there is no one to ask.

Letitia Tanik has died.

But how, why? You have no idea.

The news has come to you terse and enigmatic as a riddle. You understand that you are expected to guess this riddle but you are unable to comprehend it, you are sickened with guilt, the nausea of guilt, now it is not just Gerard whom you have failed but the young woman as well, whom by now you have nearly forgotten.

Waking from sleep coughing, choking. Face wet with tears.

Recalling how Letitia hugged you in your car, pressed her warm face against your neck. *Thank you, Professor!* No one has touched you so intimately and with such feeling in a long time.

Lying in bed dazed with remorse. For certainly—it is possible that Letitia has died. Very possible, that Letitia has committed suicide.

You hadn't known how to talk to her, you'd lacked the skill. Hadn't known how to persuade the distraught young woman to save herself.

Since the day you'd taken her to the Urgent Care facility you'd never heard from her again. She'd never returned to class. She'd never replied to your emails. You'd decided not to report the incident for you'd promised Letitia that you would not.

And so now in bed trying to summon the strength to get up which is always the greatest effort of the day as if Sisyphus were hauling up the hill not a boulder but his very self.

Forgive me, Letitia! I have failed you, too.

54

"Thank You for Changing My Life"

Driving to Albuquerque for your final class meeting.

At last!—the end of the term. After which you will be free to leave New Mexico forever.

After which you will be released from New Mexico forever.

And so you take care to drive in the right lane of I-25. Exactly at the speed limit.

For the (ghostly) tugging on the steering wheel continues. A gravitational pull to the left.

Michaela, this is too hard on you! Come to me now.

There is a place for you, darling. With me.

Torment yourself on the drive from Santa Tierra to Albuquerque thinking of the ways in which you might have plausibly helped Letitia Tanik. Except you'd failed out of ignorance, cowardice. For shyness is a form of cowardice. Not wishing to intrude.

Not wishing to incur the young woman's anger.

Not wishing to acknowledge that there are some things we cannot do as there are some people we cannot help.

Your head ringing with the accusation—*Letitia Tanik has died.*

The ontological mystery of Death: that the dead vanish and never reappear except in dreams. They are gone from us, and we cannot see them, speak with them, touch them, breathe for them. No matter how we yearn for them.

Maneuver your vehicle along I-25, staring straight ahead. Though your eyes well with tears, and the steering wheel continues to tug to the left, stare straight ahead.

"PROFESSOR!"—A FAMILIAR VOICE, as you are about to enter the stucco classroom building for the final time.

A girl is approaching you on the walkway, smiling hesitantly. You can't see her eyes—oversized sunglasses with very dark lenses, and white plastic frames, obscure half her face. She is wearing a long-sleeved shirt of some thin, gauzy apricot-colored material, a shadowy bra beneath, white cord shorts that fit her sizable thighs snugly, open-toed sandals. Glittering loop earrings swing from her earlobes, her mouth is bright red and glossy as a face on a poster. Her nails, like her toenails, are polished bright red. Her hair is dark brown, shiny-dark-brown, cut very short, punk-style, shaved at the nape of the neck.

YOU STARE UNCOMPREHENDING. Then you see—Letitia Tanik!

Not dead as you'd dreamt her only the night before but vivid in life, standing before you like a chastened child.

You are suffused with surprise, relief.

"Letitia! It's—you . . . ."

Letitia laughs, embarrassed. Clearly she is pleased, perhaps flattered, that you remember her name, and (judging by the look on your face) you are deeply moved to see her.

"Professor, I hoped I'd catch you before the workshop. First time I've been back on campus in a while but—I wanted to see you . . ."

In a cascade of words that sound rehearsed, yet sincere, Letitia apologizes for having stopped coming to the workshop, and not answering your emails. She insists that the workshop was very important to her. *You* are very important to her.

Apologies aren't necessary, you tell Letitia. So relieved to see your student alive, you can't stop smiling foolishly.

She has a medical leave from the university, Letitia says. She was able to convince the family doctor in Las Cruces that she'd some kind of breakdown like mononucleosis, she'd returned home to her parents' house where she slept a lot, and her mother fed her, "mononucleosis" is something they could understand, they could research online, and you treat "mono" by mostly just resting so that was OK— "If they had some other idea, like my mother might've, or my sisters, what was going on with me, they didn't say anything. They wouldn't, to my face." Letitia laughs, wiping at her eyes.

You ask if Letitia's doctor in Los Cruces actually examined her. If he'd done bloodwork. But Letitia shrugs off your questions.

You tell Letitia that she's looking much, much better. Obviously, she is feeling better . . .

Yes. Much better. She *is*.

Like a dutiful student Letitia tells you that she tried to keep in touch with several other writers in the workshop: she felt "really bad" to let them down, and to let you down; being in a workshop means supporting other people's work but it was this "really shitty time" in her life that wrecked so many things for her, and hurt other people like some friends she lost because she just couldn't see them or even talk with them 'cause she didn't want to answer their questions and they'd see that she was behaving in a weird way.

You tell Letitia that she doesn't have to apologize. Of course, you understand.

Embarrassed, Letitia tells you that she can't come to the workshop that afternoon, either. Someone is waiting for her, she just can't.

Someone waiting, just can't—vaguely Letitia gestures in the direction of a parking lot.

You feel an impulse to laugh. *Of course*, Letitia is going to miss this final class even as she is insisting how she'd loved the class, how much she'd learned from you and how grateful she is . . .

Letitia shrugs evasively when you ask what has happened to her since you'd last seen her.

"Well—some things. Lots of things."

"What does that mean, Letitia? 'Lots of things'?"

Letitia laughs again, blushing. Clearly she has no intention of telling her professor what is making her laugh so shrilly.

"But—you have a medical leave? Until the fall?"

"Maybe longer. That depends."

"You are coming back to school, though? You're not going to quit permanently, I hope."

"Well—that depends."

Your former student is determined not to contradict you for to contradict you would be to protract the conversation which has become awkward as if the two of you have met on a narrow walkway and must maneuver past each other without touching.

"But you are—all right, Letitia?"

"I told you, ma'am. I'm OK." Letitia is beginning to sound edgy, as if you are treading too close.

All right. OK. A kind of code. You are each speaking in code but neither you nor Letitia is certain what is being communicated.

Still, you are vastly relieved. *Alive, alive. Letitia Tanik is alive!*

Less than an hour before you'd been sick with guilt. Thinking that you might have saved the young woman's life and had failed to save it would have poisoned the remainder of your own life after the loss of your husband.

That you must still expiate—that loss. During this long day in Albuquerque you will avoid thinking about it.

As Letitia continues to speak you understand that, to her, you are an adult—an adult with authority. She has no idea of your unimportance at the university, or in the world. She sincerely believes that you are a "professor"—you are an adult with power of some kind. You have written two memoirs, you have published two books. Some of the students in the workshop have read these books and perhaps Letitia is one of them, for at the start of the term she'd been highly vocal, she'd participated enthusiastically in the workshop. You are like no one Letitia knows and so you are not to be trusted, not fully.

Yet, you are a figure to be placated. Even now she must placate, seduce you. It is her way of relating to a stranger.

You have hesitated to ask Letitia about her rapist. *The* rapist.

Letitia has been waiting for you to ask. What has become of the engineering student, if anything; did she ever report him, or talk to anyone about the rape beside you? Did she really see a doctor, did she get a proper gynecological exam? You doubt that the assailant has been charged with the crime, or even questioned by police officers. You sense this.

At least Letitia isn't living in the same residence with him. (Or so you suppose.)

Yet: when the mist of grieving has cleared you've found yourself seeing again the shirtless young man leaning on the third-floor balcony railing, you recollect him leaning indolently, a beer can in hand; you recall another person, a young woman stepping out onto the balcony to join him, or confront him—you hadn't seen clearly enough to identify.

She has gone back to him. The rapist.

You feel a sinking sensation. Can this be true?—you don't want to consider it.

But it's not for you to judge, you think. Not for you to accuse.

You are unable to ask Letitia about any of this. Or why she'd failed to answer your emails.

You don't want to seem prying. You don't want to sound accusa-tory, disapproving.

Letitia is eager to change the subject. She has learned so much from the workshop, she claims. She has learned so much from *you*.

"Like, encouraging us to keep journals. That changed my life, ac-tually. I mean—I knew about journals but never started one. I guess I thought—how could you leave anything out? How could you stop writing a thousand pages? Like—*Anna Karenina? War and Peace?* Once I started, I was afraid I couldn't stop. The words just poured out. This thing that happened to me—you know—maybe I have written a thousand pages but it's online, not in an actual journal someone could find. I couldn't come on campus 'cause I was sick, I mean ac-tually I was pretty sick, some days I hardly got out of bed, I was so tired, it was like mononucleosis actually. But I've been writing, I know it's too late for the course 'cause you're giving me an incomplete, you were really, really nice about giving me an incomplete but maybe, if this is OK, this story I wrote, if it's, like, worth an A—or a B—you could give me that grade instead of the incomplete? Is that possible? I know I've missed classes—I know that. I guess you can fail a course by missing classes, like a seminar once a week, each time you miss it's like missing three classes, right?—I know that. I take responsibility for that. But anyway, here's this"—Letitia hands you a manuscript of about thirty pages, you catch a glimpse of the title "Urgent Care." "It's, like, a part of something longer. Not a memoir—more like a fictional story. You know, 'made up.'" Letitia laughs giddily.

It is eerie: looking at Letitia Tanik you can see in her dark glasses only your own wraithlike face, in miniature.

Almost 3:00 P.M., the start of your workshop. Several students have passed you and Letitia on the walkway, headed into the build-ing. They glance curiously at you, and at Letitia; they will have noted Letitia's shiny dark hair no longer streaked with neon colors, but they have not lingered to speak to her, or to you.

You wonder: Do they know about their classmate Letitia? Has she confided in any of them? Have they suspected—something?

But what happened to Letitia, does Letitia herself really know?

How to give meaning to a narrative. When the nature of what *has happened* isn't clear even to the person to whom it *has happened*.

You prepare yourself for Letitia to hug you as she'd hugged you in your car, dare not breathe waiting for Letitia to hug you another time but (you are not disappointed: you've steeled yourself) already Letitia is turning aside with an embarrassed murmur—"Thank you for changing my life, Professor. OK?"

In the end, a trite phrase. Wave of her hand, wan lipstick-smile, someone is waiting for her elsewhere and Letitia has to leave.

* * *

"NO ONE!"

On this final class day, a stunning sight: none of your students has showed up.

Entering the seminar room on the ground floor of Memorial Hall and discovering to your dismay, chagrin, shame—no one is there . . .

The long oval table takes up most of the (empty) room. On the floor, a discarded paper bag out of which a food-stained paper plate has slid. There are several shoulder-high windows with dingy panes that glare with a vague opaque light.

Though you can see that no one is here, no one is likely to arrive, you enter the room, drop your book bag on the table, stand staring, thinking, smiling inanely.

What a fool you are! You've come on the wrong day.

A day late, the course has ended.

Some of the students came, not many. They went away again.

You will never see them again.

NO: THERE HAS BEEN A MISUNDERSTANDING.

You re-enter the seminar room, it is another time. The Plexiglas barrier between you and the others has vanished, like a spell lifted.

And soon now, the memory of the Plexiglas barrier will seem to you just a dream. A bad dream, among many.

You are (still) upright and alive and the proof of it is, when you enter the seminar room on the ground floor of Memorial Hall there are figures—faces—arranged around a long oval table awaiting *you*.

At first, the faces are blurs, smudges. You cannot identify the faces by their features—*there are no features.*

Then, as you stare, the flat smooth blurs begin to "fill in"—become "familiar"—as if by an effort of your will; to your relief their names return to you as well with a sort of liquid magic—*Melanie, Zora, Trev, Frankie, Brett, Wyn, Simon . . .*

And here, another surprise, that leaves you stunned and blinking away tears: these smiling strangers have brought a large untidy bouquet of daisies, goldenrod, Queen Anne's lace, and hollyhocks for you! To celebrate the conclusion of the workshop, it seems.

They are fond of you—are they? These individuals? Almost shyly murmuring—*Hi, Michaela!*

(For you have encouraged them to call you "Michaela"—not "Professor" and not "Mrs. McManus.")

Smiles come fluttering at you like butterflies. Laugh in delight as your eyes fill with tears. Truly you are thrilled, grateful thanking these thoughtful persons for the flowers which have the look of flowers haphazardly gathered by hand, snatched from a wild field and all the more precious for being wild. Rapidly your brain calculates: you will bring the bouquet to Gerard in the hospital. You will surprise Gerard in the hospital. You will hope that Gerard hasn't noticed your absence and that he will be warmly surprised when you return as if you'd just stepped out of the room. For this is still a time when your husband can appreciate flowers though (possibly) it has become a time when the very beauty of flowers is wounding to the eye jaundiced by illness. Perhaps there is something repugnant and cruel about bringing beautiful flowers to the terminally ill . . .

Thank you, thank you! Oh, I love you . . .

Not an outburst you dare. Just—cannot.

But—this air of celebration, congratulation. As if your students understand how you have protected them from your broken self. The contagion of your despair, the (devastating) fact that language is a futile adversary against death, you have kept from them and in this way you have given them hope.

Yes. I can do this again. One more time.

And if it is done by me then I am the person who has done it—I am that woman.

You feel like a swimmer who has bravely—recklessly—plunged into a river that seemed placid at shore but turns out to be moving swiftly, far more swiftly than you can navigate, bearing you helplessly downstream. Flail your arms and kick wildly to elude the undertow, with tremendous effort manage to swim to the farther shore and emerge staggering, exhausted and your lungs burning—but on your feet.

If he could know, Gerard would be proud of you.

Always he'd supported your work: writing, teaching.

Those years of marriage when your husband loved you and was your closest friend and (yes) would have sacrificed his life for yours, would have wished for you to outlive him.

Over now. Must move on now.

Kick, flail your limbs!

For this final workshop you've brought the class macaroons from a bakery in Santa Tierra, clementines and bunches of South American seedless purple grapes, "organic" nuts and lentil chips, seltzer water.

You've brought plastic cups, paper plates and floral paper napkins to be passed about, gaily. Suddenly, a party! Frankie has brought cup-cakes with pink frosting, she'd baked herself.

Trev has brought two six-packs of Coors beer. Zora has brought two six-packs of Diet Coke.

How foolish it seems to you now, you'd imagined that these in-dividuals had grown hostile to you. Recall how you couldn't seem to hear them through the Plexiglas barrier, they couldn't seem to hear you. Last night you'd lain awake for hours dreading that no one would show up for the final workshop.

Frequently this semester you've overheard students making plans to meet outside the workshop, to further critique their work. You've brought strangers together into a little community that, though in-spired by you, will exclude and outlive you.

Take pride, Michaela. Try.

Your mission in the West is ending, you think. A (single) plane ticket has been purchased. Boxes have been packed, sealed. The (un-tenanted, empty) house on Monroe Street, Cambridge, awaits its (newly sole) owner.

The garage attached to the house awaits. The vehicle purchased in Gerard's name which has become your property now.

Try to recall the interior of the garage. Try to recall how airtight it is—you suspect, not much. The rattling overhead doors have never closed against the pavement floor—there must be an inch, two inches gaping.

You can't leave New Mexico, however, without making a pil-grimage to the several sites marked with asterisks in Gerard's *Lonely Planet Guide to New Mexico*. These are not mere tourist landmarks but (possibly) junctures with the *other world*—the boundary between worlds will be thin there. Passing from one into the other will not require a superhuman effort. It will not be "unnatural." It is likely that, if you have the courage, you will be able to confront Gerard's spirit and accompany it into the *other world* as you've been instructed.

Calmly you think such thoughts even as you oversee your class with something more than your usual presence of mind. For such thoughts are a comfort to you.

For even dread, if it is a dread specific to you, is a comfort to you.

SIMON KHRAW, ONE OF THREE MEN in the workshop, has accumulated, by his account, more than three hundred pages of a memoir of his childhood and adolescence titled *Life-in-Progress*. This afternoon he is submitting the third chapter, a continuation of an account of childhood pulmonary illness (bronchiolitis) within a barely functioning working-class household in Albuquerque, narrated in a dry, droll manner.

In a tense quavering voice Simon reads a section describing how by the age of ten he'd nearly died several times, had to be rushed to the ER at Albuquerque General Hospital, even intubated, with the consequence that his parents came to resent him, grew indifferent and even abusive to him. He recounts having overheard his mother complain to a relative when he was just nine: "Mom said sure, I love Simon, but I'd be lying if I didn't say we'd all be kind of relieved if he just— 'passed away.'" Simon laughs shrilly, pressing his fist against his mouth.

This is a shocking revelation. No one will look at Simon. Since you are seated near him you reach over—instinctively—and place your hand lightly over his hand, which is trembling.

Simon gives a little start. His impulse is to snatch his hand away but he resists.

There is a pained silence. Though there have been poignant revelations in the past in the workshop you have not ever touched anyone, that you can recall. (Letitia Tanik was an exception, but you had not touched Letitia in class, in front of witnesses.)

Soon then, the moment passes. Discussion begins as usual, as if nothing out of the ordinary has occurred.

BUT WHAT HAVE YOU DONE, *Michaela? Why?*

Often you've noticed that Simon seems to avert his gaze from you, even when you address him directly in the workshop. Curtly he will murmur *Yes, right. OK. Thanks!*—his expression stiff, impassive as he takes notes on a laptop.

Other times, you see his glassy-green eyes sliding sidelong onto you, when he might guess you aren't aware.

How old is Simon Khraw? Impossible to determine.

A boy's features squeezed inside the ruin of a middle-aged face.

Youth, eagerness, hope squeezed inside defeat, resignation, resentment.

Simon invariably wears a short-sleeved white cotton shirt to class, chino shorts that fit him loosely. On his wrist an expensive-looking digital watch with a black blank face of the kind that have to be touched to reveal the time as if secretly, to the wearer.

His skin is curiously unlined yet the skin itself appears to be desiccated as parchment paper. His eyes are alive, alert, wary, like the eyes of a hyperactive child, slightly protuberant. His tightly wavy sand-colored hair gives him the look of a store mannequin: artificial, prissy. But when you look more closely you see that his hair is receding, his angular hands tremble with what might be anxiety, or eagerness, or impatience. A nerve appears to be frozen in his left cheek, that doesn't allow expressiveness on that side of his face, and you feel, or imagine that you feel, a pent-up intensity in Simon's lean body, that yearns to discharge itself.

Passages in the memoir speak of courses in computer science at Cal Tech but no years and no ages are given. Certainly Simon is no longer *young*.

Illness has aged him, prematurely. Illness and the fear of illness.

Simon is one of the better writers in the workshop but he isn't a workshop presence. If he were absent, probably no one would miss him. (*You* would not miss him, as you would miss your more vocal, outgoing students who call you Michaela casually, and smile at you.) Out of shyness or perversity Simon speaks rarely and then in terse and elliptical remarks as if he were thinking out loud. It's possible—probable—that Simon with a degree from Cal Tech considers himself superior to his classmates in the workshop, most of whom don't have college degrees; or, as an insecure male Simon is self-conscious in the presence of attractive young women to whom he is invisible.

Arrogant/insecure. Stubborn/withdrawn.

In fact the other writers respect Simon, though they exude little warmth in his company. When his work is discussed he is stiffly polite, typing away compulsively on his laptop, resisting even praise as if he can't trust it; he rarely smiles. Yet he thanks each person for having read his work and offering criticism; he never fails to thank you at the end of the workshop; with a shy sort of aggressiveness he has shaken your hand—"Thank you, Mrs. McManus." (He has never called you "Michaela" as the others do.)

A handclasp, a stranger. A faint shudder has run through you, dismissed in an instant.

You have seen Simon on his way to class walking slowly and with deliberation, with a cane, while younger, more agile and indifferent students bypass him.

He has not missed a single class meeting.

You have seen his eyes drift upon you sidelong, inscrutably.

Does he imagine a special rapport with you? Does he imagine that he is in love with you?

Not possible! He has no idea who you are.

By the end of this final workshop two other memoir chapters have been presented and critiqued in detail, sympathetically but rigorously. Most of the party food and drink has been consumed. The festive air still remains, like a party balloon just slightly deflated.

Three hours of intense discussion leave you exhausted but exhilarated, enlivened. You feel as if important work has been accomplished.

Your mind has not drifted off as it has sometimes done. You realize that for these three hours you have been too concentrated on the class to feel sorrow, anguish, dread.

You have not had a single thought of Gerard.

COMFORT OR SELF-TORMENT?—rehearsing what you will/would say to Gerard about this final class of yours, that has meant so much to you. As any befouled air would mean much to a person desperate to breathe.

How you will report to Gerard. Bright chattering news, the exchange between spouses. For your life will fade into oblivion if you don't report it to the husband.

Wanting to tell Gerard, not boastfully but with an air of hope, that your memoir students have brought presents for you, quite surprising you.

Not just the vase of flowers but also cards, a stack of cards, and an elaborately wrapped object kept in hiding beneath the table until the end of class—oddly shaped, large as a watermelon with something protruding at the top, covered in silvery paper that makes a crackling sound as you unwrap it.

And what is this?—you stare, too stunned to smile.

Pueblo Indian, it's explained to you.

From the reservation at Cases Grandes, renowned for its artists . . .

The thing is a (life-sized) stag's head ingeniously fashioned out of myriad layers of worn leather strips, held together by staples that resemble tiny glittering seeds. The eyes are opaque glass orbs while the battered and discolored horns appear to be "authentic."

Hear yourself thanking the students for the gift in a bright appreciative voice. Hear yourself admiring the sculpture for its originality, ingenuity. Your voice gives out, you swallow hard to keep from choking.

"A memento from New Mexico. To take back home with you, Michaela."

"Some of us drove out to Cases Grandes, last weekend . . ."

You stammer thanks. Oh, sincere thanks!

Your fingertips are tingling. You glance down and see to your horror that the tiny glittering seeds in the leather stag's head are in fact ticks—living ticks. Awakened from their slumber by the heat of your flesh several have crawled onto your hands.

Surreptitiously you try to shake off the tiny insects no larger than mites. You don't want your students to see—you don't want to embarrass them or disappoint them even as you are thinking with a part of your brain how crucial it is not to allow ticks to burrow into moist, hidden parts of the body—armpits, crotch, inner ear. The nape of a neck beneath thick damp hair.

You open the cards now, before the students depart. You are touched by several cards that are handmade, in bright primary colors, cheery, affectionate—*Dear Michaela, Thank you for changing my life!*—the words shimmer in your vision, like tears.

Briskly then the oval table is cleared, cleaned. These are adult students who pick up after themselves; several are mothers, accustomed to cleaning up after everyone. Paper plates, plastic cups, napkins and leftovers, emptied Coors and Diet Coke cans are gaily tossed into the trash. Final farewells, handshakes and hugs. The women students hug you—"Thank you, Michaela!" You are dazed by a vision of the glorious Michaela who has changed the lives of others even as her own life has collapsed like a punctured balloon.

Keep in touch—you tell them.

And—*I will miss you. Send new work.*

Soon, all have departed. Simon Khraw seems to have been the first to leave, perhaps before you'd even unwrapped the leather stag's head. *He* had no part in the folly, his indifference indicates.

Nor has he left you a card. Good, you think.

Of the writers Simon is both the one whose manuscript is the most promising and the one from whom you hope not to hear in the future.

Manage to cover the leather stag's head with the crinkling silver paper for you cannot bear to look at the ugly thing. As soon as the corridor outside the seminar room is totally empty you will carry it into a restroom to drop into a trash container.

(But—are the ticks swarming? Feel something crawl rapidly up your arm. A tingling sensation in your armpit.)

(A tingling sensation in your left inner ear.)

The vase of daisies, goldenrod, Queen Anne's lace and hollyhocks you will bring back with you to Santa Tierra. A challenge to position the vase in your car, on the floor in the backseat, buttressed by books so that it won't tip over and spill its contents. But you will try because the wildflowers are beautiful and you cannot bear to leave them behind.

BLINK IF YOU CAN HEAR ME.

Blink if you are (still) alive.

Stare into a restroom mirror to discover—your face has been restored!

Parts of your body that have been missing for months appear to be missing no longer, a shoulder, a finger or two, the left side of the mouth.

A swath of hair, an earlobe white as the petal of a daisy. Cautiously you take a deep breath. *Is* the spell over?

Reasoning with yourself: you'd been a man's wife and you'd loved your husband very much but now you will be living without him.

"You can live like this, Michaela—exactly as you've lived today."

So Gerard might counsel her. When he realizes that he has died and that you have not (yet) died.

"Yes you are broken—defeated . . . But you will not seem so to others and so you must not reveal your heart to them out of mercy—for them."

Not a whole life. Never again a whole life. A half-life. The widow's *half-life*.

"But it can be your life from now on."

Your heart is suffused with warmth, hope. A sensation small, delicate and fleeting as a moth's wings.

You can. You will.

You vow.

55

Half-Life

Shaky-legged, leaning on a cane, he is making his way to a bus stop bench on Ascension Drive at the outer edge of the campus.

Sitting heavily on the bench as if his knees have given out.

And the cane, slipped from his fingers striking the sidewalk, rolling.

He is very tired, or dazed. Such fugues come over him after periods of intense concentration. With difficulty straining to retrieve the cane on the ground for no one is coming to help him, no one is nearby.

If he dies this very hour, he will die alone. Slumped on the bench at the bus stop, a cane clutched between his knees, useless.

LEAVING THE PARKING LOT YOU recognize the slumped figure on the bench at once: Simon Khraw. White shirt, chino shorts.

You have a choice of exits from the lot. Easily you can avoid Ascension Drive if you wish and exit onto another, smaller roadway.

So much easier to pretend that you don't see Simon Khraw, as he hasn't (evidently) seen you. But you feel sorry for the man with the young-old face and so (against your better judgment) you take the exit that will bring your vehicle close beside him at the bus stop.

Lower your window, call to Simon—"Simon? Hello! May I give you a ride home?"

May. Not *can.* For it's a delicate matter, you understand, offering a "challenged" person help he hasn't indicated he wants.

Simon glances up from his laptop, startled. For a moment he doesn't seem to recognize you in your vehicle, and you wonder if his eyesight is poor. Then, embarrassed, or annoyed, Simon quickly shakes his head *No thanks.*

If you looked closely perhaps you'd see that Simon's parchment-pale skin has darkened with blood. Or perhaps his face remains impassive, semi-paralyzed.

"No? Are you sure, Simon? Really, it's no trouble . . ."

Simon. Calling the man by name seems aggressively teacherly, proprietary.

No idea how far away Simon Khraw lives but you don't intend to give up so easily. This is the widow's *half-life*—making yourself vulnerable to others, offering help that might be rejected out of pride.

As you'd offered assistance to Letitia Tanik, whatever came of it in the end. *Try. You must try.*

It isn't pity you feel for Simon Khraw. You don't think so. Sympathy, perhaps. *And the way he has looked at you.*

So matter-of-fact are you in offering Simon a ride, so sensible and without a hint of doing a favor for a person who looks as if he could use one, as if you'd driven Simon home in your car many times and this evening is nothing out of the ordinary, you are able to overcome the man's (seeming) reluctance, and soon Simon is limping to your vehicle, hoisting himself inside with a pained grimace.

Winded and wheezing from struggling to walk just a few yards. Has to be grateful for the ride though he is also chagrined, chastened.

You know from Simon's memoir that his form of bronchiolitis is incurable but not "progressive" as lung cancer would be. He has good days, and he has bad days. He has days when he has to breathe pure oxygen from a portable canister, and exertion is difficult, and he has days when he can breathe more or less normally, and walk without a cane. (You have seen this "mature" student striding along the walkway almost gaily—once, twice this term.) Hot gusts of wind are bad for Simon, bearing grit and pollutants; cool clear air is good for him. You gather from his memoir that he is estranged from his family and has acquired an attitude of "stoic indifference" toward them—not very convincing, you have thought. Though Simon's painfully candid and unsparing memoir doesn't reveal whether he lives with anyone, or has any "intimate" relations with anyone; not even if he has a caretaker, someone responsible for his well-being.

His breathing is a sound like thistles being shaken. You are hesitant to ask if he is all right, such a question might offend him . . .

Curtly Simon informs you that yes, he is *all right*.

"When I get tired some kind of 'spell' comes over me. But only for a few minutes. It isn't *crucial*."

As if he has been reading your thoughts, and has not liked them.

Giving you directions to his house three miles away Simon speaks tersely as if under duress. In such close quarters you feel shy of each other: the instructor and the student.

In an academic setting there is no *physicality*. The understanding is—*minds, not bodies*.

In the front seat of your car entirely different circumstances prevail than in the seminar room. Suddenly, Simon Khraw is *close*. Impossible to ignore the man's labored breathing, his nervous proximity. Wavy chestnut-colored hairs on his legs that are lean, not obviously muscular.

And—what are your (relative) ages? The aura of authority hovers about you, unavoidably. As an older student Simon might naturally resent an instructor who is younger than he, as well as female.

You think—*He is uneasy with me, as a woman. This might be a mistake.*

Yet once begun, the scene must play out. As you drive, Simon gives directions. He is careful to keep his voice level, neutral.

No escaping what you have impulsively set in motion out of loneliness and the perversity of loneliness which is a terror of being alone and being not-alone like the systolic beating of a single heart.

Even as you are aware of the (tense, excited) stranger beside you, you are thinking of how you'd first come with Gerard McManus to his house on Monroe Street. Feeling between you had quickly strengthened, within a few days. He'd purchased your books and read them both overnight and wanted to speak with you about them. Which had frightened you for such a reaction was not like other men you'd known of whom one or two had never troubled to read a word you'd written as if in knowing you intimately they knew you in a way that bypassed your books and rendered them redundant. Invited by (smiling, excited) Gerard to step inside the gaunt handsome old brick house and a wave of panicked vertigo came over you as if you were stepping into your own future, helpless to resist.

The gravitational pull of the future—is it? Swept up in a great seething wave, tossed and spun and deposited a distance away, spent and gasping on the sand.

I am here. I am here. But—where?

The first surprise is that Simon Khraw lives in a house in a neighborhood of single-family residences and not in a duplex or an apartment building. The house at 227 Armand Street is a small wood-frame bungalow like others on the street, near-hidden behind wild-growing cacti and sagebrush, with blinds drawn to the windowsills. The front lawn is thinly covered with raked gravel and storm debris. In the waning light it appears that the bungalow has been painted an eerie bluish color that glows just perceptibly, as if radioactive.

"Thank you, Michaela. It's very kind of you . . ."

Michaela sounds unnatural in Simon's mouth, as if he has forced himself to utter a taboo word.

Eyes averted Simon struggles to get the passenger's door open and maneuver his legs out without dropping his cane. He is also carrying a book bag that thumps against his knees. His breath comes quickened, harsh and petulant. But you are not about to leap from the car and come around to the passenger's side of the car, to assist him.

Prepare to drive away but no, Simon is leaning down to peer back into the car at you through the lowered window. Asking with a pained grimace if—maybe—you'd like to come inside for a few minutes before driving back to Santa Tierra? He can offer tea, coffee, wine . . .

You are touched by this invitation, so awkwardly uttered. By the grimace in Simon's face, and the hope in his eyes.

Of course, you quickly decline. *Thank you Simon, but— no. I can't.*

In fact you hear yourself say, "Well. I guess—for a few minutes . . ."

WHEN THERE IS NOWHERE ELSE TO GO. *No one awaiting you patiently or impatiently.*

No one wondering where you are. If you are alive, not-alive.

For the room on the seventh floor of the hospital has been cleared and cleaned and disinfected and there is a stranger now in the bed that had been your husband's for so long you'd have thought the mattress had shaped itself to his mortal body.

• • •

TEETH CHATTERING WITH COLD. Except it is not cold but ninety-two degrees Fahrenheit.

Though this is a harmless decision, you are thinking.

Impulsive, heedless—harmless.

Visiting a student. An adult student. Officially, when grades are handed in, a former student. For only a few minutes. A person you will never see again.

As if entranced. *You* are entranced. From a distance Gerard is observing his widow in disbelief, disapproval.

What on earth are you thinking, Michaela?

I am your husband. I am waiting for you . . .

Once out of the car cannot change your mind foolishly and climb back into the car! Not while Simon Khraw is watching you.

Once out of the car and boldly following Simon along the walkway of colored faded finely cracked concrete there is no retreat. The scene must be played out.

Fact: terror of the empty house in Santa Tierra awaiting you has overcome a lesser fear of this lesser house as terror of the deceased husband has overcome a lesser fear of Simon Khraw with his ravaged young-old face gazing at you with squinting adoring eyes.

Someone to adore you, again. A tawdry transaction.

Following the man as in a trance. Such weakness, the impulse of a moment. Thrill of dread, exultation. Certainly you can have no (genuine) wish to follow a stranger into a bungalow with drawn blinds.

Slovenly cacti, overgrown sagebrush and lavender exuding such a sweet smell, you feel a moment's faintness.

Odor of recklessness here, confused with the odor of lavender.

Worse, odor of desperation.

But now, you are inside the house. The door has been (quietly) shut behind you.

Nervously Simon apologizes for the condition of his house. He hasn't had a visitor in—how long?—possibly a year . . .

The interior of the bungalow shimmers with filtered and refracted sunshine. You are made to feel vertiginous as if finding yourself in the interior of a body amid the heat of living body-organs.

Blinds have been drawn over the living room windows to keep out the oppressively hot New Mexico sun. Low-thrumming window-unit air conditioners, not central air-conditioning, operate minimally.

Stale air, a smell of—can it be birds? Parakeets, parrots? Cockatoos?—you see a scattering of feathers, some of them bright-colored green and red, others filmy-white, on the carpet. You hear excited bird-chatter from another room.

Simon, your awkward host, has set his book bag down on a table. He rubs his thin hands together, unconsciously. Stares at you with glassy-green narrowed eyes as if you inhabit a blaze of light overwhelming to him. The improbable has happened, has it?—and now what?

Clearly Simon hadn't expected you to accept his impulsive invitation any more than you would have expected to accept it.

Smiling at you, smiling hard, flush-faced as an abashed child. The man's teeth are somewhat small for an adult male, not altogether even, or particularly white; you envision an individual who flosses his teeth compulsively, with a grim sort of joy.

Without thinking to invite you to be seated Simon stammers can he get you tea? coffee? apple juice, cranberry juice? ginger ale? wine?

Wine seems anomalous here. You cannot imagine drinking *wine* with Simon Khraw alone in this place.

Or, maybe: iced tea?

Yes. Iced tea. You are both relieved, this is a very sensible suggestion considering the heat.

Simon continues to shake his head in wonder, smiling as a child might smile at a riddle. It's very hard for him, he says, to comprehend the fact that you are actually here in his house.

Though he'd dreamt something like this, he tells you. A few nights ago. And at the beginning of the memoir course in January.

Like what?—you ask hesitantly.

That you are actually *here*. In his house, in this place. As you are now.

Not that he'd seen your face clearly in the dream. He had not. But he'd known it was you . . .

Gerard would have mused on the subject: how the dreaming brain seems to "know" the identification of a person who in the dream does not bear any resemblance to the actual person.

Hear yourself laugh. Skeptical laughter. Nervous laughter. Still your teeth are chattering with cold.

Wanting to think that in even your distracted state you exert some small sexual power over him, the man. He who has been your student for fifteen weeks whose work you rigorously "critiqued" as if you were superior to him.

Wanting to think—*This is not a mistake. Not to be regretted.*

But Simon does not seem resentful now, or in any way hostile. Perhaps you have misjudged him all along. His eyes are glistening as if he is deeply moved, on the verge of tears.

He adores you. That is why to your shame you are here.

Simon has more to say but he is breathless suddenly. Excuses himself to go into the kitchen, to prepare the iced tea. Peppermint tea, he promises.

Forgetting (again) to invite you to sit down. So, you are left by yourself, relieved. Drifting about the small living room with its faded but warm colors, sagging sofa, worn cushions, Navajo carpets and wall hangings, bookcases crammed with books including textbooks, photographs of familiar scenes you might guess have been taken by Simon himself—sculpted sand dunes, desert vegetation, mountain trails, mountain peaks, vivid-blue sky. On a tile ledge beneath a fireplace, a guitar that looks as if it is used, not-new. On a nearby table amid a stack of books is one of yours—the first memoir, with the pale green cover that suggests either a filigree of fern-leaves or lacework . . .

Feeling for a moment confined, trapped. If Simon has read the memoir he has inhabited the interior of your truest self, no display of the widow's altruistic *half-life* will deceive him.

Thinking—*But I can leave at any time. I would not even need to explain.*

Escape! Leaving a scribbled note behind propped up on the fire-place mantel.

Probably just as well we never see each other again.

Just as well, cut knotty complications at the start.

But you make no move to leave. You anticipate peppermint-flavored iced tea, your throat is dry with thirst.

That perpetual wind, wind-gusts, bearing tiny bits of sand and dust breathed into your lungs. *Thirst is an honest emotion.*

Peering at your wraithlike reflection in a small smoky mirror on a wall. Curious what it is, Simon Khraw sees in you, or of you.

Shocked to discover that a part of your face has (again) begun to fade away like a watercolor bleached in bright sunshine.

Simon returns in a glow of anticipation carrying a tangerine-colored plastic tray with glasses, iced tea in a pitcher. You guess that the peppermint-flavored iced tea has come from a bottle in the re-frigerator and this is a relief—he has not been fussing in the kitchen. He has merely dropped ice cubes into glasses, poured in peppermint tea from a bottle, affixed a sprig of mint to each glass. Gingersnaps spread on a platter, shaken out of a box. Simon chattering, nervous. Touching to see that he has taken time to wet his hair and comb it, just a little—tight-wavy sand-colored hair that gives him the look of a store mannequin, near-handsome in a white dress shirt.

You sit. Facing each other on a cushioned rattan chair, a cush-ioned rattan sofa. Pleasurably self-conscious, hopeful. Raising your voices to be heard over the thrum of the air conditioner, a conversa-tion to be recalled haphazardly afterward as a juggling act in a circus might be recalled in wonder that it was performed at all, not whether it was performed with skill.

Politely, discreetly your host does not inquire after your (private) life. He does not point out your book on a nearby table, he will not ask you to inscribe and sign it. He is thoughtful, circumspect. You are made to acknowledge that he is an intelligent person, and there is

a certain craftiness in his intelligence. Perhaps he knows very well—
(perhaps all your students know)—that your beloved husband has
died just a few weeks ago, possibly he'd read of the death in a local
newspaper. But Simon intends not to make you feel uneasy. Simon
entertains you with an account of the vicissitudes of his work—*Khraw
Software Consulting, Inc.*

Yes, he'd almost gone bankrupt, initially. But he is doing better
now—much better.

As Simon speaks—less halting now, on the cusp of boasting, and
how relieved you are that Simon has something of which he can boast,
as a woman might be grateful for a man's virility not for her sake but
for his, that he will not be sexually humiliated in her presence—
you listen politely, yes you are impressed as you are meant to be impressed. You see with a pang of sympathy how chronic illness has
ravaged the man's youth even as it has kept him young, unused.

If you wish you might seize his heart in your hand.

Squeeze and squeeze his (virginal) heart in your hand. If you
wish.

You are often laughing, the two of you. Like conspirators. Simon's
sense of humor is fey, unexpected. You have not laughed in so long,
your throat is scraped with the effort.

The peppermint-flavored iced tea is delicious. The gingersnaps
are slightly stale but delicious too, your mouth floods with saliva. But
you are soon satisfied, you have soon had enough.

Neither of you speaks of the memoir workshop. Simon does not
wheedle praise from you, and you don't offer praise. It should be evident from your remarks through the term that you consider Simon a
very good writer, that's to say a promising writer, and there is something irrevocably condescending about the word *promising*. So you
avoid it.

Nor do you speak of anyone in the memoir workshop. Indeed,
you and Simon might have met just that afternoon. Within the hour.

Simon Khraw might not have been "your student" at all, only an interesting individual you'd encountered at the bus stop.

He does speak of his health, however. Impossible for Simon to avoid speaking of this subject. Eager for you to know that his chronic condition is "in remission." It has been "in remission" for several years. Of course there have been "episodes"—occasionally. Not serious enough to necessitate a trip to the ER—at least, not usually.

Revolutionary research into lung-ailments like bronchiolitis, emphysema, lung cancer is being done at the Salk Institute, Johns Hopkins, UC-Berkeley. He is hopeful, Simon says, of an *89 percent recovery* of his lungs' capacity to breathe, one day.

A normal life, then. One day soon.

You listen in fascination. You are enthralled by these words. You feel a sensation of great tenderness. An urge to take hold of the man's nervously gesticulating hands, to calm them. An urge to squeeze his hands between yours urging him—*Breathe! Breathe!* You will promise to protect him, you will hold him in your arms when he needs you, you will not abandon him in his hour of desperation.

By remarks Simon has made, you gather that he is probably in his late twenties. If twenty-nine, he might pass for thirty-nine, or older. But only if seen from a certain angle. Certainly he isn't Gerard's age as you'd (almost) thought at first. Here is a young relative of yours, unidentified until now, needy, very needy, demanding of attention, yet sweet-tempered, adoring and loyal; terrified of aloneness, the struggling to breathe when alone, suffocating in his bed, strangled in the night, alone. *You, you must save him. That is why you are here.*

You feel a sensation like a powerful sedative washing over you, melting away your defenses, your resistance. Hearing hope quivering in another's voice. You believe everything and anything that Simon tells you, as you'd believed the extravagant plans of the dapper bow-tied oncologist Dr. N___, a Napoleon eager to zap tumors into oblivion, snatch back a dying man from oblivion, vividly you recall the dapper Napoleon seeming to promise you that your husband might be saved while (privately) knowing that before he'd stepped into the ER he was beyond saving. You believe everything and anything that Simon Khraw is telling you for essentially you believe nothing, you have lost faith not only in *cutting-edge research* but in faith itself. Yet, you register hope in your smiling face. You reflect hope, as in a reflective surface. You might joke—(one day: if you become an intimate companion of Simon Khraw)—of donating bone marrow to prolong his life, if bone marrow might prolong his life. A cleansing of the afflicted one's very being, away with the old DNA, hose in the new, begin again with a new immune system, a virgin birth, you are a widow and your life is a half-life anyway, why not seed yourself into the body of another. Simon will remain in remission for the remainder of his life or he will not remain in remission for the remainder of his life. He will recover, to a degree—he will learn to pass for "normal." Or, he will gradually deteriorate and die prematurely, unless he deteriorates fairly quickly and dies prematurely.

All this you believe, equally. All possibilities.

Find yourself staring at a Navajo rug on the floor at your feet. The rug is somewhat faded but you admire the rich subtle browns, the hue of wheat, the hue of a young deer's coat, russet-brown and russet-red, earthen brown and oatmeal-white and the deepest black, a rug that is a work of art, a rug that is a puzzle, in which jagged sawtooth patterns intersect with one another in geometric precision. For all of life is such intersecting, such possibilities. Until, as it passes through possibility, life becomes something other than life, and is called Death.

In a lowered voice as if someone might overhear Simon is telling you of an encounter with a priest when he was twelve years old.

Warning the boy not to become bitter, angry, not to turn against God because of his illness so for a long time he'd tried damned hard not to be bitter, angry, not to turn against God until one day when he was fifteen and collapsed in gym class unable to breathe and had to be rushed by ambulance to the ER it had come to him unmistakable as snakebite: why the hell shouldn't he be bitter, angry, and turn against God—"Seems like I've earned it."

When you leave Simon's house you see how Simon stands very still waiting for you to touch him in farewell as (perhaps) you'd touched his hand in the workshop but you ease from him smiling, bright-smiling in eagerness to depart, to escape his yearning eyes, don't dare touch him, certainly not embrace him as the women students in your workshop embraced you.

No, not even a handshake of farewell. Too risky.

"Well. I hope you will let me be your friend, Michaela . . ."

Awkward as he follows you outside into the cooling air of early evening. As he follows you to your car at the curb. Out of a pocket Simon extracts a letter, a letter sealed in an envelope, exceedingly awkward now, dry-lipped, dry-mouthed, he'd meant to give you this at the end of the workshop but had been too shy. But now, he's beyond shyness.

"I'm thinking hell, I wrote it. So why not."

56

The Adulteress

Driving home on I-25. In the night.

Lesser traffic now but nighttime construction has narrowed the interstate to two lanes as in a highway winding through Hell.

Grinding yellow bulldozers, rapid percussive *beeping*, headlights of gigantic rigs blinding your eyes. Cautiously you creep along at twenty miles an hour in dread of an accident.

In dread of retribution. The adulterous wife.

WHEN YOU ENTER THE HOSPITAL ROOM—what will you see? Will your husband be conscious, will he be unconscious, will he recognize you and will a smile break over his face or will he turn blank frightened eyes to you . . .

Your heart stops, considering. A chill oily sweat breaks out over your guilty body.

Returning to Santa Tierra in the night. Nearly 11:00 P.M.!

Never have you been absent from the house on Vista Drive for so many hours. Exiting I-25 shivering with guilt, anxiety. Passing signs for Los Alamos, Santa Fe somewhere in the distance.

. . . will he lift his arms to embrace you one final time with all the strength remaining in his weakened body or will he stare at you with cold

furious pit–eyes, will he demand to know where the hell you've been? Will
he try to speak and fail, too exhausted to speak, too exhausted for the flut-
tering eyelids to remain open . . .

On Vista Drive slowly ascend the curving road. Utter darkness in
the prestige neighborhood above the Institute. Below, scattered lights
of Santa Tierra glitter frivolous and inconsequential as Christmas
tree lights.

Approaching the house all but indistinguishable in the dark. That
house. *The* house.

A house you'd shared with another person. Unaccountably now,
an empty house.

You are feeling uneasy. Approaching a darkened house in which
plate-glass windows shimmer in the reflected light of your headlights.

The house should not be totally *dark.* You'd left lights on while you
were away—as Gerard always did. And a radio turned on, to mimic
human voices.

But now, the house appears to be totally dark. You wonder if the
radio has been switched off, too.

Mouth dry as ashes. You, the adulterous woman about to be
found out.

In the driveway in the car, engine running. Curiously lethargic,
leaden-limbed. For perhaps it will be a mistake to enter the (darkened) house having been away an unconscionable number of hours.

(The idling vehicle is outdoors and not in a confined space. Exhaust lifts skyward, harmless. Not a chance of carbon monoxide poi-
soning to put you out of your misery.)

Tingling sensation in your left ear as a white-hot forbidden
thought burrows ever closer to your brain.

Let me be your friend. Love me!

Swallow hard, sick with guilt. Shame.

Wanting to protest—*There was no adultery. There was not a touch-*
ing of hands. There was—nothing.

Wanting to protest—*I am a widow, a widow has no husband. A widow cannot be an adulteress.*

Already on the jolting drive back to Santa Tierra your memory of Albuquerque has begun to fade. Heat-haze like a dream, fading.

The excitement and elation of your final class—the faces of your students. Their precious names, you'd memorized—fading . . .

Eerie-blue-tinted bungalow on Armand Street nearly hidden behind ragged cacti. Blinds to the windowsills, like sightless eyes.

Those (illicit) hours you'd spent in the company of a stranger. In need of caretaking, in need of (your) care. *Michaela, let me be your friend.*

All fading. Harmless as white-tinged exhaust in the open air.

THE RIDDLE: IF YOU ENTER the Santa Tierra Cancer Center you will not be allowed past the reception desk.

For somehow it has happened: if you enter the Santa Tierra Cancer Center and ascend in an elevator to the seventh floor (Oncology), if you make your way along the corridor to that room, that singular room of all rooms in the world, it will not be Gerard who awaits you in the bed in that room.

The bed, the room, the corridor, the elevator, the receptionist at the reception desk, the facade of the Cancer Center—all (continue to) exist. Yet, Gerard does not exist.

Very difficult to understand that if you search for Gerard in all the rooms of the world for the remainder of your life you will never find him.

A mental effort like trying to comprehend imaginary numbers. A riddle that hurts the brain.

Inside the house, a faint odor of something earthen, rotted makes your nostrils pinch in warning. You switch on lights quickly including the very lights you remember switching on before you'd left for Albuquerque in the early afternoon.

The house is deathly silent. No radio is on though (you are certain) you'd switched on the radio also—an affable chatter of voices following you out the door.

Thinking of how in the spinal cord viral death bides its time until awakened by the weakening of the immune system.

How we carry our deaths inside us. Snug, stealthy in the spinal cord.

And here is another strange thing: the lights are not adequate to illuminate the rooms. As if a scrim were between you and the objects in the rooms rendering them blurry and imprecise as objects seen in water.

The demon-gods have sucked away the wattage in the lightbulbs— literally! An assault upon your reason more devious, because so subtle, than a violent assault.

You'd begged Iris Esdras to take the ugly carvings out of the house but Iris merely laughed at you.

Months before, Gerard had laughed at you, too.

Into the house you've brought the vase of flowers your students gave you. Fallen petals leaving a trail in your wake.

So long you've been away from the house! *Adulteress.*

Into the house the book bag crammed with student portfolios and slipped into the bag among these the sealed envelope from Simon Khraw thrust into your startled and unwilling hand.

This envelope you will never open.

This envelope you intend to never open.

This envelope you vow you will never open but will nonetheless place on the bureau in your bedroom sealed and unread.

Evidence of the widow's innocence.

Cherish the letter. But not read the letter.

In a few days you will pack away the (unopened) envelope into the carry-on suitcase you will bring with you on the return flight to Boston. This envelope forgotten in a pocket of the suitcase where (perhaps) it will remain unopened and unread. Long after you've returned Monroe Street, Cambridge.

Discovered one day among your things in the bedroom of the house by the heirs of the house.

Except you have no heirs. Gerard was your only heir.

You will not discard the envelope from Simon Khraw entrusted in your hand but you might lose it and if it is (hypothetically) lost you will feel a pang of regret, yet relief: for you will not then know what Simon has written to you, that seems to have meant so much to him and might tear at your heart if you knew.

If unread, the letter will disappear utterly from your consciousness.

Possibility cut off at the source.

"HELLO? HELLO..."

Your wan voice, in the empty house echoless.

In mimicry of Gerard who would return home calling *Hello? Michaela? Are you home?*—a note of urgency in his voice.

Though at more ebullient times—*Hello hello hello, darling! I'm back.*

You'd hurried to greet him. No matter how briefly he'd been away.

A pleasure to greet a returning husband as if anticipating a time when the husband will not return, thus such returns are precious.

Such thoughts, plaguing you tonight. Staring into the (lighted) rooms to assure yourself that you are alone, there is nothing to fear.

But it is aloneness, that is fear.

Disappointing, the flowers aren't so beautiful now. Hardly any point in bringing them home. If you'd meant to boast to Gerard, how popular you are with your students, the ruse has fallen flat.

Might've tossed the vase and the flowers into the trash, with the surpassingly ugly leather stag's head.

Now, a stink of brackish water on your hands, clothing. Somehow, dripped onto the carpet.

Thinking—*Is it Death that has entered this house . . .*

Pour out the remains of the discolored water into the kitchen sink, run cold water to flush away the smell. Dispose of the vase, flowers in the sturdy green trash container by the side of the house.

So many weeks, you haven't yet adjusted to the thin cold air of Santa Tierra. You haven't adjusted to the high desert. And how cold it has become, since midday the temperature must have dropped fifty degrees . . .

Prepare for bed by kicking off your shoes beside the bed. Sleeping in your clothes, or most of your clothes, a habit you'd acquired when Gerard first entered the hospital in anticipation of a ringing phone interrupting your sleep—*Mrs. McManus? Your husband is in critical condition, come to the hospital at once.*

In fact, this call never came. For you were already in the hospital at the final days of your husband's death.

Lying very still on the bed. Willing your breath to continue, not to cease, for there is much that Gerard expects of you even now.

Yet gradually, you weaken. Your eyelids quiver, your fingers lose their grip. The phone rings, you are paralyzed to reach for the receiver even as you hear a low rapid machine voice— *. . . did not die after all . . . transferred to a rehabilitation clinic . . . records (temporarily) misplaced . . . please call this number to arrange for bringing him home . . .* But you can't decipher the number, the message breaks off.

Lying on the bed, hands clasped over your chest. Not *in*, but *on* the bed. As the crucial distinction might be made between lying *on*, and not *in*, the grave.

. . . please call this number to arrange for bringing him home . . .

Your brain has gone blank. If you move your thoughts will spill over tasting of brackish water.

Dare not move and dare not allow yourself to think of the next day. It is night now, a starless night. The prospect of the next day fills you with horror.

And after that day, the next. And *the next*.

An interminable future. Your vision will fail, the horizon is so distant.

For now, your teaching has ended. Now, you are cast adrift upon a brackish sea.

You try to recall the pleasure of teaching. Only a few hours ago, in Albuquerque. And your pleasure when Letitia Tanik approached you declaring herself alive.

A pleasure not without a certain degree of nervous excitement, yet riveting, mesmerizing. Thrumming with life as an organ is engorged with blood.

Your hope that, for all the misery of your (secret) life, you have touched the lives of some individuals who would otherwise be strangers to you.

You smile. Try to smile. A grimace distorts your mouth.

He'd thought you were beautiful. He'd gazed at you with loving eyes. He'd never seen the widow's ghastly smile, at least he has been spared such a sight . . .

Yet more pitiful, a widow's vanity.

You are hearing: a harsh *chuffing* sound somewhere in the house.

Uneven breathing, an impatient sound like rushes being shaken. In fact you have been hearing this sound for some time but have wished to think it was only the wind.

Where is this sound? Inside the house or possibly in the ravine behind the house?

Restless wings, churning wings. A murmuration of black-feathered birds.

Fully awake. Fists rubbing your eyes. The *chuffing* is a kind of laughter. A kind of scorn. The pathos of your hope, your naivete in imagining that you might find consolation in work.

As if a life lived with strangers could compensate for the emptiness in your heart.

Muffled laughter, you are so pathetic.

A softer laughter, you are so pitiful.

Rise from the rumpled bed which you've scarcely changed in weeks. For what purpose, what defiance of futility, fresh-laundered pillow cases and sheets without a husband. Staggering on your feet stunned to see that it is 4:00 A.M.

Haven't you slept, all these hours? Your brain is buzzing like fluorescent tubing. The harsh labored breathing coming from somewhere nearby.

"Gerard?"—your voice is low, guarded.

You are seized with fear, yet hope. It has been very hard to accept that Gerard has abandoned you.

Of course: you understand that it isn't likely to be Gerard in the house for since April 13 Gerard is considered to be *deceased*. There are multiple copies of "his" death certificate. "His" ashes are stored in this very room in an urn inside a soft-cloth bag.

Yet, the breathing that assails your ears very closely resembles Gerard's breathing in the final terrible hours of his life.

Understand: Gerard's breathing has never ceased. Though escalating in difficulty, with ever more pauses between breaths, it will never cease.

Cautiously you leave the bedroom. Open the door to the corridor, the sound of the breathing is immediately louder.

Alarmed to see a thin band of light beneath a door at the farther end of the corridor, where there'd been no light earlier when you'd gone to bed. That room once designated as Gerard's study, rarely used, since Gerard preferred to work at the Institute when he'd been well enough to work at all.

"Hello? Is someone there? Who—who is there?" Your voice is faint, tremulous.

On shaky legs making your way toward Gerard's study. The band of light beneath the door. Trembling convulsively, shivering with cold, rivulets of sweat dripping down your feverish face which is a face of shame for out of cowardice you have abandoned your husband who has only you to bring him to the *other world*.

An adulteress, basking in the adoration of strangers. A widow, hoping to deny her responsibility to the dead.

As you approach the room at the end of the corridor the breathing inside is becoming louder and more labored like the breathing of a great wounded beast. Lengthy pauses between breaths, gasping for air—hoarse, hissing, excruciating to hear.

Terrified of approaching the door yet you must approach the door. Gravity pulls you toward the door. Halfway there your knees begin to buckle. Stagger forward to kneel in front of the door, dare not open the door but only press your burning forehead against it.

Forgive me, Gerard, I am not strong enough.

I am going home. I am going away from here.

HOURS LATER WAKING DAZED and stiff on the hardwood floor, partly dressed, barefoot. No idea why, what has drawn you here. Your neck throbs with a foolish sort of pain. Your eyes are tender and raw as if you'd been staring for hours into a blinding light.

Surprised to see that the time is so late, past 7:30 A.M., usually you are awake before dawn unable to return to sleep. But there is relief this morning—the house is very still. Except for the cries and calls of birds outside, and the dull drumbeat of your blood, all is silence, calm as a sky of the most airy feathery cirrus clouds.

57

The Approach

Come to me, Michaela. I am waiting.
This is the crossing-over place.

LESS THAN FORTY-EIGHT HOURS REMAINING in Santa Tierra.

Transfixed by the (digital) clock moving in one direction only.

The boarding pass bearing your name has been printed and is laid out on the bureau beside your passport. House keys, car keys you will need when you return to the house on Monroe Street, Cambridge. Clothing you will wear on the flight is laid out on a chair in your bedroom. You have even engaged a hired car to pick you up at Logan Airport as ordinarily Gerard would have done. In a giddy sort of excitement your heart beats at the prospect of the *return*.

A *return* executed by Michaela McManus, alone. A wife who has rarely traveled alone since becoming a wife. Who has never alone executed a *return*.

Gerard's books have been carefully boxed, shipped via UPS. Boxes of clothing shipped. More than half the suitcases packed—Gerard's, and yours. Today you will finish emptying drawers, closets. The house will be cleaned—you insist upon cleaning it yourself.

The demon-gods—*prank gods*, as Iris Esdras has called them—

you plan to return to their original places in the house on the morning of your departure; until then, they will remain out of your sight.

Out of sight, out of mind.

Out of mind, out of sight.

Out of mine, blindsight.

Yes! Soon you will be free of the *prank gods*, and will never see them again.

MICHAELA, COME!

Midday must leave the house, can't breathe.

Drive to the Arriba County Historical Museum twelve miles north of Santa Tierra. One of several sites marked with an asterisk in Gerard's *Guide to New Mexico.*

One of those places likely to be *crossing-over places* if such places exist.

Despite the sweltering summer sun you are feeling hopeful. Soon, soon!

This terrible loneliness must end, Michaela. It is time.

Alert and aware of being (possibly) observed. When a human presence is nowhere it is everywhere.

(If *he* is observing you—what does *he* see?)

At the Arriba County Historical Museum you must park a quarter mile away since the parking lot is partially under construction. Half-jog through sunshine quivering like the heat-waves of a kiln so that by the time you arrive at the museum rivulets of sweat are running down your forehead, sides and you are panting.

Hurry, hurry! You have delayed so long.

At the museum entrance, a wheelchair ramp beside the stone steps. Your attention is drawn to a man of Gerard's approximate age, in a wheelchair, stiffly erect as if in pain or in the anticipation of pain, being pushed up the ramp by a sulky boy of about eleven; something about the man in the wheelchair is familiar to you, the set of the shoulders, the high-held head, even his casual clothing, short-sleeved plaid shirt and khaki shorts. His face is partly obscured by a visored white cap that seems new to you and fits his head oddly.

Seeing that the boy is having difficulty pushing the wheelchair up the ramp you inquire—"May I help?"

Risky, interfering in the lives of strangers. The scowling boy surprises you by muttering *Thanks!*

Curious, the wheelchair isn't motorized. Or its mechanism is malfunctioning. With effort you push the (heavy, bulky) wheelchair up the ramp and into the museum through automatic doors. You are grateful to be of use. So frankly and without ambiguity *of use*. As you have not been *of use*, in recent memory.

Recall Gerard having been transferred to a rehab clinic, not deceased but wrongly discharged from the Cancer Center and (somehow) wrongly placed in a rehab clinic unknown to you. A simple (if egregious, unconscionable) mistake of the kind common in an era of computerization. Astonishing that all along Gerard has been alive without your knowing in a parallel world inaccessible to you . . .

Which is only logical: if Gerard had not ceased to exist on April 13 of this year but had continued existing, his appearance now will differ to a considerable degree from what it had been on April 13.

Yet—with a pang of disappointment, but not actual surprise—you see that the man in the wheelchair is not Gerard after all. The man scarcely resembles Gerard, a decade younger, thirty pounds heavier, lacking Gerard's gentlemanly manner, something insolent about him but (still) you feel a frisson of emotion guessing how strangers who happen to glance at the three of you in this (fleeting) moment will be led to think—*Wife, husband, son.*

In that fleeting moment, a rush of pride. That you are not alone, you are not unloved, you are not a pathetic left-behind wife but indeed someone's wife, yes and someone's mother. Only look!

Unlike the boy who thanked you for coming to his assistance the man in the wheelchair barely acknowledges you: a shrug of his shoulders and a grunt as he takes possession of the wheelchair himself, turning the wheels with deft hands rapidly and impatiently, speeding away.

Because he does not love you. He does not even know you.

At the ticket counter purchase a single ticket. But when you are about to enter the first exhibit you realize that you've been given two tickets, you are holding two (adult) tickets in your hand not able to recall if you'd paid for two, or only one. No way of knowing without going back and asking the ticket seller, you'd scarcely noticed the price and hadn't troubled to take the receipt.

One ticket you present to a museum guard, the other you crumple into a pocket, abashed.

The historic museum with its exhibits, installations, and endlessly looping videos of rough-hewn frontier life is a popular tourist destination, its major exhibits crowded with visitors, families with children including very young children in strollers. The most-watched videos reenact battle scenes, skirmishes involving volleys of arrows, gunfire. Clashes between dark-skinned indigenous people and colorfully costumed Spanish conquerors. Uniformed U.S. soldiers pursuing Indian adversaries, firing rifles. Videos of cowboys on horseback, cattle roundups. Rodeos. Stampedes. Galloping horses. Find yourself staring fascinated at fellow museum visitors. You feel envy, awe. Strangers bound together by the simplest urgencies—tending to the (endless) needs of children. But also by random remarks, glances, frowns, smiles as if nothing were so crucial in life as the rapport between family members, a soft-sticky cobweb joining individuals together who otherwise might have little interest in one another; indeed, might be repelled by one another.

No other single individual in sight. Only you.

And in the eyes of these others, you are invisible.

Not loved, no one. Nowhere.

If Gerard were here, he would explore the least crowded exhibits first, on the third, top floor of the museum: archival materials including treaties, maps, and diaries; displays of primitive knives, spears, bows and arrows, arrowheads; rusted implements, beaded ornamentation, leather moccasins, feather headdresses once belonging to chiefs of Apache, Navajo, Pueblo Indian tribes. He would study daguerreotypes of Indians, white settlers, U.S. military, Pueblo villages, and burial sites. Works of art, sculpted objects, frayed woven things, life-sized replicas of tribal dwelling-places complete with steam rising as if it were smoke from woodfires. He'd look skeptically at a waxworks display of melancholy vacant-eyed mannequins, red-stain-skinned males and females, adults and children, in a diorama meant to represent *Fort Still Apache Village Life circa 1847.*

Gerard would take time to read information posted on museum walls, he would rent headphones to listen intently to audio recordings. When you became restless with the need to move on to another room, Gerard would linger.

Sometimes, you became impatient. You are stricken with the keenest envy, if only you could become impatient again with your husband . . .

Reach impulsively for his hand, only inches away from yours. Clasp his slow-responsive hand in yours, grip it tight.

How is it possible, you are alive and I am still dead!

But no: you mean to say *How is it possible, you are dead and I am still alive . . .*

In the next exhibit you read of millions of indigenous persons slaughtered by Spanish conquerors, colonists. You read a lurid history of exploitation, enslavement involving the Roman Catholic Church. Jesuit priests, Catholic missionaries, Spanish missions, churches erected in the wilderness, to tame the wilderness. You read of Indian children removed from their families, forced to live in Catholic orphanages, tribal names changed to Christian names, forbidden to speak their native languages. You read of Indian children escaping the orphanages, returning home or trying to return home. Killed while escaping, or suicides. An untold story of American colonial past: the suicides of children. Military-led massacres, lynchings. Scalpings. Villages burnt to the ground. Deaths by contagion: smallpox, measles, syphilis, tuberculosis. In 1491 there was believed to be a population in North America of 145 million indigenous people, by 1691 the population had been reduced by 95 percent.

That is, 138 million indigenous people exterminated.

Genocide! Centuries before the word came into existence.

None of this is surprising to you. None of this should be surprising to you.

Known to you but forgotten, in a haze of the approximate and the guessed-at like the distance between Earth and the sun measured in light-miles you've memorized only to forget, in that category of the known-forgotten, or rather the forgotten-known.

Through bulky earphones you listen to a recording of Pueblo Indian children interviewed decades ago. Perhaps these were children abducted from their families and forced to live in Catholic orphanages where terrible things were done to them, and where they did terrible things to themselves, the children speak in halting English, voices so high-pitched you can't decipher their words, and sometimes their voices crack and fail and you hear only static and weeping.

Unless it is you who is weeping? Wiping foolishly at your dripping eyes, sad slack mouth.

Glancing about, but no one is observing you. No Gerard.

This terrible loneliness. Cannot bear much longer.

NOTHING TO HOLD YOU IN THE Arriba County Historical Museum for obviously Gerard is not here.

Yet even as you chide yourself *Gerard is not here* you invite the antic possibility that *yes indeed, Gerard is here.*

On the second floor of the museum amid a din of recorded "Apache war chants" you sight the man in the wheelchair who'd behaved so rudely toward you an hour before. No longer pushed by the sulky child (who follows after him at a little distance, looking bored) but propelling himself through an exhibit of many-times-magnified Apache war masks looming floor to ceiling. As you stare the wheelchair-man lifts his head to peer at you from beneath the visor of his cap and you are jolted by the cunning malice of his gaze—*It is Gerard peering at you, but without recognition.*

While unmistakably Gerard's, it is a gaze that both "knows" you and does not acknowledge you as worthy of attention, significant. This Gerard gazes upon you with the crude, sexually-assessing eyes of a random male. He never met you at the concert in Cambridge (perhaps) but (perhaps) he'd glimpsed you among the audience that night. Or, he'd glimpsed you in Cambridge. The most fleeting of glances, an (impersonal) male assessing an (impersonal) female encountered in a public place. Behind the facial mask is a brain that (evidently) recognizes your face but without a context to provide meaning: you, who have been married to Gerard for more than twelve years, and love Gerard deeply, are something less than an acquaintance to this Gerard who has never known you intimately and would not feel a moment's grief if he learned of your death.

It is shocking, stunning. To see Gerard's gaze turned cunning, malicious. That the man is not Gerard, and yet *is Gerard*, is overwhelming to you. As a father might gaze upon his own child not knowing that he is his child, unmoved if the child's brains are bashed out before his eyes . . .

Stand there helpless, staring. As the stranger in the wheelchair propels himself brazenly past you amid Apache war chants so loud and so terrifying in ferocity, visitors to the exhibit wince and clap their hands over their ears.

Desperately you want to appeal to this man, beg him—*But, Gerard, don't you recognize me?—your wife Michaela. We love each other, we have been married to each other for twelve years . . .*

But you know that such an appeal would be futile. This Gerard is not your beloved husband. He is not your friend, he does not wish you well, you would be an annoyance to him, you are not even sexually attractive to him, barely you register with him as *female.* And the Apache war chants would drown out your plaintive words in any case.

NOT DISAPPOINTED! INDEED, RELIEVED.

Eager to leave the Arriba County Historical Museum but on your way out you discover an exhibit titled *Indigenous Gods & Demons of the Southwest* which draws you to it despite your better judgment.

A minor exhibit, in an alcove off the mezzanine. A windowless dungeon-space that has drawn few other visitors. Overhead fluorescent lights bleach shadows and give to the displayed objects a curious flatness like that of cartoons.

The sort of exhibit, with much historical material posted on the walls, that Gerard would have liked. The figures range from simple line drawings of the kind a gifted child might make to elaborate carvings and sculptures that might qualify as "art." All exude an air of the primitive and the exalted. You feel hairs stir at the nape of your neck as you draw closer.

Immediately you recognize the Scavenger God Ishtikini with his grotesquely enlarged skull-head, staring eyes and potbelly, pencil-thin erect penis. The largest figure of this demon-god is a carving that stands, in a peculiar crouch, with bent knees, about twelve inches in height; the most menacing is smaller, constructed of scrap metal and slivers of broken glass, with small beady eyes that seem to shift in their sockets, fixed upon the observer. Another Ishtikini carved from birchwood is identical in its malevolent expression with the carving you have hidden beneath the bathroom sink in your rented house.

Can't stop from shivering, shuddering. In a description of Ishtikini you learn what you hadn't known before—that the "insatiable" demon-god has the power to burrow into living bodies, jackal-like, devouring brains, hearts, entrails, genitals.

Ishtikini (Zuni Pueblo Indian Scavenger God, Skull God) is both god and demon: ravenous appetite that is never satiated.

Skli is represented in several lewd figures, drawings and sculpted pieces, each more grotesque than the other. You have to imagine that only a man could create such obscene visions of the "female"— a shrieking O of a mouth, drooping breasts like a sow's teats, a garish-bloody vagina. It's surprising then to discover a cartoon strip by a contemporary Navajo feminist artist who presents the demon-goddess as an action heroine like Wonder Woman, with oversized designer sunglasses, bright-red lips, sharp-pointed breasts like missiles, naked except for thigh-high leather boots with three-inch heels that reach nearly to the bloody gash between the legs—quite a brazen sight! In cartoon panels *Our Skli SuperGoddess of Creation & Destruction* is pictured seizing white-skinned adversaries, both female and male, biting off their heads and eviscerating them with sharp talon-claws gleaming with red nail polish.

You make an effort to admire this appropriation of the demon-goddess by a young woman artist. Try to smile, no personal harm is meant against you, certainly not *you.*

Also transformed into something of a comical figure is Weyaki,

God of Chaos, the pop-eyed bloated-frog demon-god claimed to be responsible for the woes of the world. Weyaki, who seems sexless, has never appalled you quite as much as Ishtikini and Skli.

At the end of the exhibit is the figure that has most baffled you: the life-sized stag's head constructed of layers of leather crudely stapled together, with glassy eyes and "authentic" stag's horns . . . A demon-god like the others? "Prank god"? You'd never learned its name, if it has a name.

You duck beneath the rope separating visitors from the exhibit. No guard is nearby to reprimand you, all you want is to read the caption beneath the stag's head but the words are faded, indecipherable.

Touch the leather head as if petting it. Examine the glittering seed-sized staples holding it together that appear to be, here, merely staples, and not (as you'd imagined in the seminar room) living ticks. It seems to be a feature of the stag's head that it has been clumsily assembled and is glaringly artificial and absurd, as if in mockery of Native American artwork; the "authentic" horns are, then, a further mockery?—or, a cry of dismay?

The natural appropriated by the artificial. The sacred appropriated by the profane, obscene.

But you aren't sure. Can't know. The grief-vise is tightening around your chest.

All of the demon-gods are a torment to you, regarding you with their sinister/vacant eyes. Hard not to believe that they have been lying in wait for you here, for all of your life.

But why did Gerard bring you to them?—Why did Gerard want so badly to come west, in what would be the final phase of his life? That is the riddle.

Become aware that your fingertips are tingling. There is a rapid ascent of something too small to be seen by the naked eye, myriad things no larger than pencil points, running up your arm as you stand before the stag's head blinking and staring and trying (futilely) to comprehend . . . Whatever you are trying to see, you cannot *see*.

Soon then, numbness spreads and you cannot *feel*.

INNER EAR. INFECTION, BACTERIA. Close to the brain.

Blink if you hear me? Michaela?

Blink if you are (still) alive.

58

Bell Tower at San Gabriel

Come, Michaela! Higher.

Climbing spiral steps. Hurry!

Ferociously blinking your eyes. Tears in your eyes. Dust, sand in your eyes.

In a bell tower beside an "historic" adobe church, steep stone steps worn smooth, uneven and slanted beneath your feet like eroded rock.

It's the beautiful old Spanish mission San Gabriel de Isleta. Founded in 1597 by Franciscan fathers. Weatherworn adobe church, walls and bell tower and cemetery, twenty-foot wooden cross visible for miles across the violet-hazy desert plain.

Why you'd driven here. Drawn by the cross. Seven miles west of Santa Tierra.

What is a cross but outflung arms. Semblance of a torso, something that has managed to stand upright, outflung pleading arms.

Gerard had marked with an asterisk the Mission San Gabriel de Isleta in the guidebook.

Higher, higher. Hurry!

Out of breath climbing the spiral steps. Turning so tightly, steps so narrow, you are feeling giddy like a child turning in circles.

Hot gusts of wind blowing hair dry as straw into your eyes, mouth. Sucking your breath away.

Stark and beautiful at a distance the bell tower is not so beautiful close-up. Desert rock, what Frank Lloyd Wright called *desert masonry*, beginning to crumble. Bits of calking litter the steps, bird droppings and the delicate skeletons of small birds, shards of tiny white bone underfoot.

Wince, stepping on these tiny white bones!

Already you are winded. Already feeling sharp pains in your thighs.

Your legs are accustomed to running on flat surfaces, not climbing steep steps. Your lungs are (still) not accustomed to thin air.

Pain can be no deterrent. Pain is to be expected. Gerard's most anguished moments were in silence, he would not scream aloud or whimper as the long needle sank into his abdomen releasing the contrast material . . .

You are determined to reach the top of the bell tower before you are stopped. An impulsive decision, you hadn't time to deliberate—ducked beneath the rope downstairs, ignore the warning sign—

BELL TOWER CLOSED FOR REPAIR

UNSAFE DO NOT ENTER

In the distance he is waiting. Except you are not certain in which direction.

Why you are here, you believe. Why you have been urged to climb to the top of the bell tower, to *see*.

(Waiting for a sign.)

For the promise is, the terrible loneliness will end.

The terrible loneliness will end this very day, possibly.

This very hour. Possibly.

The time of *crossing-over*.

Waiting for you, these weeks. He will protect you. Fold you in his arms so you are still. So you cannot despair as you have been despairing, devouring your own guts. So you cannot do (further) injury to yourself.

He will forgive you for betraying him, for having forgotten him. (But you want to protest—you'd never forgotten him!) Fleeing the *crossing-over* out of cowardice.

Come, Michaela! Higher.

Less than twenty-four hours before you will be leaving Santa Tierra. Your boarding pass has been printed, most of your (and Gerard's) luggage has been packed. Tags on suitcases neatly identified. You will use your passport for ID.

In your carry-on suitcase, the (yet-unopened) envelope from the needy young asthmatic man in Albuquerque which (you vow) you have no intention of opening yet which (you concede) you cannot bring yourself to discard.

I hope you will let me be your friend, Michaela.

You are feeling dizzy, thinking such (unwanted) thoughts. Unless it's the thoughts that are thinking you.

Invasion of the brain. Something soft-liquidy, warm-viscous, formless, heedless has eased, seeped its way into your brain.

And the high desert air, thin as a razor blade. Breathe, breathe!— that is the commandment.

Insufficient blood to the brain. Insufficient for the brain to repel the (ravenous) invasion.

Danger is, should your foot slip on the smooth-worn steps turning so tight upon themselves . . .

Through crude windows in the tower wall you can see the mountains—the San Mateo Mountains. From this location the mountains look different from what you recall in Santa Tierra, steeper, less defined, partly obscured by the violet heat-haze like a dream.

Nearer the bell tower, the Rio de Piedras—River of Stones. An ugly river, strangely—not reflecting the (hard blue western) sky but gray-shimmering as an immense snake, restless in sinuous movement.

Midway between the San Mateo Mountains and the Rio de Piedras is Cold Spring Canyon State Park which Gerard has also marked with an asterisk in the *Lonely Planet* guidebook.

Often in Santa Tierra, before his illness, Gerard had spoken of hiking in the mountains and canyon trails. You knew he'd had knee trouble, a mild stenosis of the spine, Gerard's days of ambitious hiking were behind him but still he'd wanted to hike one of the shorter trails in Cold Spring Canyon with you. Before he'd become ill.

Together you'd studied photographs of hiking trails through the canyon. Steep granite walls tinged with indigo, vertical striations in the rock, like ancient hieroglyphics. Warnings of rattlesnakes, mountain lions. Flash floods in the event of sudden rainfall. Shortest hike is five miles, starting from the trailhead beside the Rio de Piedras.

As you climb the stone steps you are approaching the open sky. The top of your skull is lifting. Dazzling light! High filmy cirrus clouds like fading thoughts.

Begin to feel a sensation of vertigo, nausea. The grief-vise returns suddenly grasping your ribs, squeezing.

Sudden impulse to turn back . . .

Don't be afraid, Michaela.

Nothing to fear, Michaela.

Is Gerard waiting in the distance? From the top of the bell tower you will wave to him with the happy abandon of a child waving to an (invisible) parent.

Shading your eyes, desperate to see where Gerard is . . .

Below, a voice lifts sharply: "Ma'am! Excuse me!"

And: "The rope is here for a reason."

A guard has detected you in the forbidden bell tower. A young Mexican-American. If he intends to be sarcastic in his speech the sarcasm is diluted by his politeness.

This guard, possibly the sole guard at Mission San Gabriel, you'd hoped to elude. You'd sighted him when you'd first entered the church pretending to be among a group of tourists led by a Native American guide.

Almost, you'd climbed out of the guard's sight. Only a few more steps before you reach the top of the bell tower. Open sky, fierce winds.

Michaela, hurry!

Michaela, I am waiting.

But the sharp-eyed guard has followed you up the steps. Raising his voice, sternly: "Ma'am? I said—*the rope is here for a reason. The bell tower is not open.*"

You are calculating: Can you make it to the top of the steps before the guard stops you? Would a young Mexican-American man dare seize your arm?

Stand panting and light-headed at the waist-high railing pressing yourself against the railing shading your eyes staring into the distance awaiting a sign as the wind whips against you greedy, impatient . . .

But, no. You have stopped climbing the steps. A dead stop, sudden.

What are you doing, Michaela? After coming so far.

His voice is flat with disappointment, disapproval. But you have no choice, you have come to a halt. For a long moment trying to catch your breath, unable to move forward or back.

I can't, can't. Can't go forward.

Forgive me, Gerard. I have failed you another time.

You have turned, you will descend the steps. Meekly, like a guilty child who has been caught in a blatant misdeed.

Apologizing to the guard. Explaining that you'd intended just to take pictures with your cell phone as you'd done at other missions, in other bell towers, with no trouble.

But the guard isn't easily placated. He is upset, your behavior seems to have alarmed him.

". . . must have seen the sign, ma'am. Signs all over. When the wind is blowing like this, especially there is danger of an accident at the top . . ."

Accident at the top, a plunge over the railing. No guard wants death on his watch.

If the bell tower were truly dangerous wouldn't there be some sort of partition nailed over the entry to prevent tourists from climbing the steps?—that could be your rationale for ducking under the rope. But you don't dare suggest it.

Retreat, return to the ground floor. Apologize again to the guard. Speak clearly, smile at him. Do not further antagonize him.

Wanting him to know that you are indeed just a presumptuous tourist, a pushy White woman, a heedless *gringa*, ignoring signs and warning ropes because that is what *White privilege* has conditioned you to do; you are not a desperate woman, a woman maddened by grief intent upon risking her life in a fierce hot wind at the top of a tower; he has not narrowly avoided witnessing this woman fall to the ground, cracking her skull, spilling her brains on the much-trod pavement beneath the tower . . .

No. That did not happen, and was not likely to happen.

Make your way (unhurried, casual) out of the church. Past a side altar where small squat lighted candles flicker in the draft and a single woman, white-haired, kneeling, her thin hands covering much of her face, has come to pray.

By now your heartbeat has slowed, the wild anticipation has subsided. You have become a deflated balloon, no longer at risk.

Hoping that no one has been observing you. A noisy busload of tourists has arrived at the front door of the church, preparing to swarm inside.

Ma'am! The rope is here for a reason—Gerard will laugh when you repeat these words.

One of those comical catch phrases that echo through a marriage until eventually neither spouse remembers its origins. Only that wife and husband are bonded together by such memories, the more trivial the more endearing, enduring.

Pause to push several bills into an urn for donations to the Mission—five-dollar bills, a ten-dollar bill. Your penance.

In the gift shop pretend to be interested in purchasing something. Pretend that you are a typical tourist. Not shaking, trembling, forehead oozing sweat, as the adrenaline rush subsides suddenly very tired, weak-kneed. Instead stare at the merchandise. Hand-tooled leather goods, silver and turquoise jewelry, prayer cards picturing a young dark-eyed Saint Gabriel. Miniature adobe replicas of the Mission San Gabriel de Isleta. Postcards, brochures, maps. T-shirts, caps. Sierra Club books, Audubon Society books, *Spanish Missions of the Southwest: A Pictorial History*. Children's books, cartoon book titled *A History of the Latino Holocaust*.

Step out into the bright gusty air. You wonder if the guard is reporting you—to whom? And why?

But he doesn't know your name. No one knows your name. No one knows where you are. In all of the world there is no one (now) who knows where you are or has the slightest interest in where you are.

No purpose to your life. No compass.

59

Rio de Piedras

But of course there is a purpose: you know what that purpose is.

The trailhead at Rio de Piedras is three miles away. Drive there directly, no need to seek a sign from Gerard.

ARRIVE AT COLD SPRING CANYON State Park suffused with hope, yearning.

Because the other places have been absent of him. Of those places marked in the guidebook with an asterisk, only the trail at the river remains.

Because it is time, you are certain. The *crossing-over* time.

Less than twenty hours before your flight to Boston from Albuquerque. And so, what will happen must happen, now.

As if you'd known beforehand, you are dressed for hiking. Though you are not wearing hiking boots (as Gerard would have insisted) you are wearing running shoes and cotton socks.

Khaki shorts, one of Gerard's white T-shirts loose-fitting on you. On your head, a hat with a brim to protect your eyes from the sun.

White-hot sunshine, in the canyon! Though the sky is beginning to be mottled with clouds, not so glaring a blue as it had appeared from the bell tower in Mission San Gabriel.

Hikers are assembling at the trailhead a quarter mile from the glittering Rio de Piedras, just visible in the distance. A loose confederation of (White?) individuals led by a swaggering-macho Native American guide whose straight black hair falls to his muscular shoulders, held in place by a red headband.

In all the visual field, nothing so vivid as the red headband.

At first, the guide appears to be young, in his mid-twenties. When you look more closely, however, you can see that he is middle-aged, at least forty, with a thickened face, hard-muscled neck, legs. His manner is aggressively friendly, his eyes shine with a teasing sort of merriment gliding over the hikers, and over you, as if counting, assessing.

"Hello! Can you all hear me? My name is—"

Harsh brusque sound resembling *Kwer-vo*. A bird's cry.

"—your guide today for our climb into the canyon and to the Pueblo burial site . . ."

As you recall Gerard had particularly wanted to see the Pueblo burial site which is, according to the guidebook, accessible only from the five-mile canyon trail.

You are feeling anxious, excited. Faint with anticipation. It is evident to you, Gerard is here somewhere.

Fact is, if Gerard is anywhere, Gerard is *here*.

(Not among the hikers, however. Not likely. He will be waiting for you on the trail.)

The swaggering-macho guide with the name harsh as a bird's cry is giving instructions in hiking protocol to the assembled hikers: never wander off alone in the canyon for you can become lost within minutes, make sure that you have a full bottle of water when you set out, if you begin to feel heated or light-headed on the trail *do not continue*, in the event of sudden rainfall *do not continue* . . .

Always in these steep-walled canyons there is a danger of *flash floods* from sudden heavy rain. But, as *Kwer-vo* announces, the weather report for this day is "clear"—"safe."

In fact, the sky is not so clear, entirely. Ribbed clouds above the mountains, glinting-gray like mineral. Still the sun shines unimpeded.

He will be leading them into the canyon in seven minutes sharp, the guide warns. Hikers should use restrooms while they can, stock up on supplies.

In the Canyon Lodge hurriedly you purchase a bottle of Evian water and a package of trail mix—nuts, raisins. Can't recall when you've eaten last. You are feeling light-headed but with anticipation, hope.

The lodge is air-conditioned yet heat seems to be radiating from your body. Beneath your hair the nape of your neck is slick with sweat. Do you have a (mild) fever? Grief has so settled in your bones, you cannot recall a time when you were not burning with it. A fever is the frantic effort of expelling the enemy from your bloodstream.

No one to oversee your health, well-being any longer. No one who gives a damn about you.

Fact is, you are angry at Gerard for abandoning *you*. You have not abandoned him.

In a women's restroom press paper towels soaked in cold water against your face.

Except the water out of the faucet is lukewarm not cold. Cheap paper towels soak through and dissolve within seconds.

Terrible loneliness. Your bitter heart.

Cannot make your way alone on the trail . . .

"Ma'am? Is something wrong?"—a presence has appeared beside you, with a concerned female voice.

Evidently you have been behaving strangely—possibly, swaying on your feet.

Yes just slightly light-headed. Flushed with fever.

Quickly assure the solicitous woman that you are fine. Embarrassed but yes, fine.

Avoid her eyes. Avoid pity. Especially, self-pity.

In a sharp voice insisting—"Yes. I am *all right*."

You hurry to join the hikers. You will keep the red headband in sight.

Uneasily you have been wondering if Gerard knows that you are scheduled to leave New Mexico in the morning. If Gerard understands that this is your final chance for the *crossing-over*.

A curious fact: you believe with a part of your mind that (probably, almost certainly) Gerard is waiting for you somewhere along the canyon trail while at the same time you understand that Gerard is dead, Gerard has become (mere) ashes already packed in one of the larger suitcases and tenderly protected from spilling by having been wrapped in Gerard's terry cloth bathrobe by your hands.

Yet, the logic is unassailable: if Gerard is anywhere, Gerard is *here*.

It seems likely too, the guide with the name harsh as a bird's cry will have something to do with the *crossing-over*.

The guide's straight black hair and defiant swagger remind you of the Scavenger God Ishtikini.

You begin to wonder if the guide *is* Ishtikini.

Deftly you make your way along the trail bypassing slower hikers. At the outset, the Canyon Trail is not challenging: flat, at least ten feet wide, with just a scattering of small boulders, a clear path. Keeping a steady pace you pass couples, families with children . . . You wonder at the wisdom of parents who bring small children onto this rocky trail which will soon turn arduous.

Sacrifices for Ishtikini, is that what we are?

Smile to think so. Grim logic.

You are an experienced hiker, but only to a degree. You have never backpacked. You have camped out only as a girl, in summer camp. Never have you hiked a really long and challenging trail—seven miles was your limit, long ago in the Adirondacks. Nine, twelve miles through labyrinthine trails in the San Mateo Mountains would be impossible for you.

In his youth Gerard had backpacked in Yosemite, Yellowstone, Bryce Canyon. But not in recent years. Not since knowing you.

You are feeling very fit! In the restroom mirror before the intrusive stranger interrupted your reverie a feverish-radiant face had floated, a surprisingly youthful face, the face of a woman not (obviously) stricken with grief though somewhat thin, malnourished.

A face radiant with hope. A face ravenous with hope.

Would Gerard recognize you after so many weeks?—almost shyly you wonder.

There is something of the bride about you, you realize. A virginal bride. So many weeks, months since you have lain in your husband's arms. So many weeks, months since your husband has entered your body in love, penetrated your soul.

What marriage is, this penetration of the soul by the soul of another in which bodies are but the medium. You can recall now only dimly such lovemaking as if it had taken place in a previous lifetime.

Make your way along the trail at a steady pace. While the trail is still wide enough, pass slower hikers. (It is always a joy to pass slower hikers!)

Kwer-vo will always be ahead of you, you cannot catch up with him, no one can catch up with *Kwer-vo* who leads you and the other (White, Caucasian?) hikers deeper into the canyon. *Kwer-vo* with his broad muscular back, legs so hard-muscled as to be almost deformed, glaring-red headband amid the sere and muted colors of the canyon.

Do not glance sidelong at hikers when you pass them. Your impression is, their faces are blurred, indistinct as faces glimpsed through wavy glass. If they speak to you, their words are blurred. Ignore them.

Keep the guide in sight. He will lead you to Gerard, that is all that matters.

Hot gusts of wind at your back.

AN HOUR INTO THE CANYON is the first stop: the Pueblo Abode of the Dead.

By this time the trail has descended into a maze of boulders, stunted mesquite. Steep canyon walls blocking sunlight. A harsh mineral smell. Weaker hikers have turned back, only a few hardy hikers remain.

Stunning now to come upon a sudden declivity in the trail dropping some fifty feet to an open area like an amphitheater. *Kwer-vo* identifies the site of an ancient Pueblo "sacrificial altar" and "burial catacombs" predating even the Spanish invasion in 1540 and long-abandoned by the time of English settlers in the region in the late nineteenth century.

Try to imagine seeing this extraordinary sight for the first time. As the original Pueblos must have done. Making their tortuous way through the canyon, turning a corner and coming upon what looks like a gigantic gouging in the earth for—what purpose?

Has to be a purpose.

To the primitive mind, no accidents.

"To give you a sense of scale," *Kwer-vo* says, "—remember that New Mexico wasn't admitted into the Union until 1912. This Pueblo burial site dates back to 1512."

Murmurs, exclamations. Nervous (White) laughter. Hairs stir at the nape of your neck.

Present-day Pueblos living at Taos (or elsewhere) do not descend from the Pueblos who'd once lived in this region, *Kwer-vo* says. There are more than one dozen Pueblo Indian tribes in New Mexico and each speaks a language that differs significantly from the others though there is a common (extinct) root.

"Yes, I am a Pueblo Indian—but I am of the Kawa tribe."

Kiwaan. The "endangered" language in which Gerard was interested.

You wonder if *Kwer-vo* wants to distance himself from the ancient

Pueblos who'd practiced human sacrifice. If he wants *gringos* to know that they were not his ancestors and he doesn't speak their language.

Kwer-vo laughs often as he addresses his listeners. But when you glance at him you see that there is little mirth in the man's face.

He has been wounded, perhaps he is a U.S. military veteran. His hard-chiseled face is scarred, his (hairless) jaws appear battered. You see that he is missing part of his left ear which has been inexpertly repaired, replaced with a synthetic flesh-colored material that fails to blend convincingly with his own skin.

You allow other hikers to descend into the burial site before you follow, cautiously. In such circumstances Gerard would urge caution. The sun is beating on your head, it would be easy to slip on loose rocks. You have not slept well the previous night, your vision is softening at the edges. A turn of your ankle, a fall that sprains a wrist, cracks a skull—*No.*

You are relieved to see that most of the Pueblo site is off-limits to hikers, protected by fences. But how annoying that hikers are swarming daringly close to the ruins, taking pictures with cameras and cell phones.

Selfies! A Pueblo sacrificial altar behind a fatuous grinning face.

Uneasily, you have been aware of *Kwer-vo* watching you. When he isn't addressing the hikers his scarred face settles into an expression of affable aloofness, disdain.

One of the hikers asks *Kwer-vo* if stains on the altar are human blood and *Kwer-vo* retorts—"No. The last sacrifice was hundreds of years ago."

Still, stains are visible. Pictures are taken.

Again, you see *Kwer-vo* watching you. Aware of you.

Because you are the lone single woman remaining on the trail? Or—because you are known to him?

You don't want to think that the Indian guide has a particular interest in you, a sexual interest. That he is curious about *you.*

A faint stirring in the pit of your belly, not sexual desire so much as the nostalgia of such desire, its loss.

But I am not a woman any longer. I am a widow.

You have a fear of humiliating yourself, a woman without a husband, an abandoned woman. A woman seeking male interest from any quarter.

Through rocks encrusted with thick layers of sand there emerge here and there totems of the dead. Some are abstract shapes and some resemble humanoid figures. Or, the abstract, weathered shapes are all that remain of the human shapes after centuries.

In the hill beyond, you see the faint outlines of cell-like hollows in rock, as in a gigantic hive. Hundreds, thousands of these hollows. Was this a primitive pueblo dwelling, or was it an extension of the catacomb?

The living, the dead. At the *crossing-over*, each is indistinguishable from the other.

The ghastly fact overwhelms you, like filthy water rising to cover your mouth. The burial site is all of the earth, wherever you step there is Death.

Heat-lightning in the sky. Without anyone seeming to have noticed the sky has become mottled with rain clouds.

Still, sunshine prevails. Shafts of sunshine, illuminating patches of the ruined altar.

One of the hikers remarks ruefully to the guide that the Cold Spring Canyon hike is "damned more strenuous" than the guidebook had promised. He isn't sure if he can complete the five-mile trail, might have to turn back soon . . . Good thing that all the women and kids turned back by now.

All of the women? You wait for *Kwer-vo* to point you out, the exception.

Another hiker jokes that it's just as well the children have turned back, if there's child sacrifice here.

A glimmer of a frown passes over *Kwer-vo*'s face for (of course) this chatter annoys him but (of course) he is a salaried guide, he is obliged to consider inane remarks seriously.

Kwer-vo replies that it isn't "one hundred percent clear" just who was sacrificed at this site. Mostly, sacrifices were believed to be animals. And "captives"—"enemies."

Is this true?—you wonder. In the Arriba County Museum you'd learned that Pueblo children as young as infants were occasionally sacrificed to Ishtikini and other gods. For what would be the point of sacrificing anyone but the most precious beings to your most precious god? Would a god settle for anything less?

But you are not going to contradict *Kwer-vo*, who speaks with such authority.

Also, *Kwer-vo* points out, marriage ceremonies took place here as well. Funeral ceremonies. Baptisms. Not just *sacrifices.*

Marriage! You hear this with great interest.

You drink from the Evian bottle, that trembles in your hand. Water no longer chilled but unpleasantly warm, water you envision seething with microbes, bacteria. The interior of your mouth is coated with a fine film of dust that extends into your throat, lungs.

Is that the plan? Marriage. Then—the crossing-over . . .

For you have been seeing Gerard. Without wishing to acknowledge that you have been seeing him.

What had Gerard called it—*blindsight.* The brain sees what the eyes register. Though the brain cannot always name what it is that the eyes (blindly) register.

You have not wanted to look closely at your fellow hikers. Sidelong glances, no more. At the Arriba Museum you'd noticed also— the faces of people around you had become blurred, imprecise. And now at the burial site, you are experiencing a kind of tunnel vision, you can see only straight ahead, fixedly; your peripheral vision has vanished.

Staring at one of the hikers, his face in profile, vivid and unmistakable: Gerard.

You are stunned, in that instant unable to move. A white-hot sensation passes over you leaving you feeling faint. The hiker who has kept closest to *Kwer-vo* since the start of the hike, whom you have not attempted to pass, is Gerard—until now you have only seen his back.

But of course, now it seems obvious: *Gerard.*

Vaguely you'd expected that your husband would be waiting for you on the trail somewhere ahead. Or at the burial site.

And so here you are, at the burial site. But Gerard has been one of the hikers all along, and you had not realized.

Of course, Gerard is altered since his long hospitalization. He is not so tall as he'd been—though he is still *tall*—and though he has maintained a steady pace on the trail he appears to be walking with a slight limp; you are made to recall how in the hospital that he'd been walking, when he was still able to walk, in the corridor on the seventh floor, with a slight limp, and you'd laughed in astonishment for in those (early) days you'd been often astonished, surprised, disbelieving; and such responses often provoke laughter, sharp laughter, startled laughter, frightened laughter, and you'd heard yourself ask your husband why, why on earth was he *limping*, since when had he begun *limping*, oh God—what was this *limping*—and Gerard had said, wounded, as if your careless remark had indeed stung him, that he had always had a slight limp, his right knee had been injured decades ago, but you'd never seemed to notice before because he tried to disguise it, and because you had not been "prepared" to see him limping.

But now on the canyon trail Gerard has been limping, unmistakably. He is one of the older hikers though he is still "fit"—impressively.

You see that Gerard is wearing a short-sleeved white shirt which you believe you recognize, and hiking shorts, and on his head a familiar beige cap . . . You'd packed these articles of clothing, you think, but possibly not. Or, what is more likely, these articles of clothing were left behind in the Cancer Center when Gerard was transferred to a rehabilitation clinic where (vaguely you recall) his record was lost in a computer crash . . .

Your heart seizes: Why does Gerard not seem to see *you*?

Why does he keep so rigidly turned from you, refusing to acknowledge *you*?

(Though certainly he is aware of you. He has glanced at you repeatedly, you have not noticed. Between Gerard and *Kwer-vo* there is some sort of understanding.)

Gerard will be your bridegroom here, is that it? And you have been brought here to be his bride?

Unlike the civil ceremony in Cambridge, Mass., performed by a clerk, with only a few relatives as witnesses, this ceremony will be a sacred ritual in a place of unearthly beauty and strangeness.

Yet, you hesitate to approach Gerard who continues to stand alone, his back to you. Clearly now you can see that he is awaiting you. He is awaiting something. He is the only hiker who has not been prowling about the ruins taking pictures; he is not (evidently) carrying a camera. (But you have packed Gerard's camera! Carefully as the ashes have been packed, wrapped in clothing.)

Strange, to be stricken with shyness. Or perhaps it is fear. You stand rooted to the spot about thirty feet from Gerard, as hikers continue to swarm about the site like ants, occasionally obscuring your view of your husband . . .

Above, on a promontory overlooking the site, but a few feet back from the edge so that he can't be easily seen by the hikers, *Kwer-vo* is squatting on his heels smoking a cigarette in swift drags. He has turned his head slantwise, as an animal might do when it eats quickly.

You are shocked to see anyone smoking in the canyon, and particularly the Indian guide; you are sure you'd seen signs forbidding smoking here. For weeks there has been a fire hazard warning in Santa Tierra and vicinity.

Ishtikini takes many forms. Ishtikini is not what he seems.

When you think of Ishtikini, think again.

HIKERS ARE CLIMBING BACK TO the trail. An arduous climb, much longer than it had appeared to be when they'd clambered down.

Kwer-vo is beckoning to them, to you. Hurry!

He has decided to turn back, it seems. Not to continue after all. For there is likely to be rain, possibly heavy rain. A flash flood in the canyon.

Kwer-vo admits, the weather report was mistaken. He is grim, yet cheerful: "As we say in my language—*Thsussa pia*. 'Sorry-sorry.'"

Is this authentic? Kiwaan speech? Or is the (Indian) guide with the brash red headband mocking his anxious (White) listeners?

The first drops of rain are falling—heavy, languid. Eagerly the hikers turn back toward the trailhead.

However, Gerard is not turning back with the others. Defiantly Gerard continues along the trail without a backward glance.

This too is shocking to you. But you have no choice, you must follow Gerard, at a distance of about thirty feet.

Kwer-vo calls after you in a voice registering alarm: "Wait! Ma'am! There's danger of heavy rain, I am advising all the hikers to return to the lodge . . ."

But *Kwer-vo*'s alarm doesn't sound very sincere. As his apology for the erroneous weather report seemed similarly flat, bemused.

You understand: the Indian guide is giving you and Gerard permission to move on, apart from the others. *You* are singled out for a special destiny, you and Gerard.

You will have *Kwer-vo*'s blessing, daring to separate yourself from the other, inconsequential hikers.

And so, you ignore *Kwer-vo* calling after you. Follow Gerard along the trail, hoping to catch up with him. At the juncture with the sacrificial site the trail has widened to about five feet though it looks as if it will soon narrow again in a jumble of boulders and mesquite.

Shyly now you call to him—"Hello? Gerard? It's Michaela. I'm behind you . . ."

Shy, excited. Trembling with love of the man, and fear of him.

"Gerard? I—I'm behind you . . . Let me catch up with you."

But Gerard doesn't seem to hear. Though surely he must hear a voice calling his name . . .

He doesn't slow his pace so that you can catch up with him, however. It will be your task to overtake him.

Because he is leading me to the crossing-over place.

Because I must follow him, unquestioning.

Recalling Gerard's anger when you'd taken too long to bring the car around to the front of the hospital. His rage, incredulity when you'd first spent the night in his hospital room, he'd tried to remove the catheter from his penis and you dared to try to stop him . . .

But Gerard appears to be much calmer now. He is straight-backed, determined. He must have heard you calling to him for he is acknowledging you, lifting a hand in greeting, though without turning his head more than partway.

You can see him, you can recognize him, in profile. But he does not turn to meet your gaze.

He would like to. But he cannot.

You must trust him. Trust is love.

There is the commandment, not to turn around. Not to address the loved one. You must not expect Gerard to treat you like a child. *Trust.*

Ominous thunder. A sound of collapse, many miles away. Still, the darkest rain clouds are not (yet) overhead.

Rain in discrete drops like plump purple grapes. Though there are *raindrops* there is nothing (yet) like *raining*.

As the trail narrows and becomes difficult again Gerard keeps a remarkably steady pace. You don't recall your affable husband hiking with such urgency in the past. You are panting, trying to keep pace with him. Where once the two of you often hiked side by side when the trail was wide enough now Gerard forges ahead.

Recalling with a twinge of loss how you'd often held hands, walking together. Along the Charles River. In museums, on city streets. Usually you were the one to clasp Gerard's hand in your own, and Gerard would then squeeze your hand in turn.

Though Gerard rarely initiated holding your hand, yet he responded warmly when you held his.

My dear husband. My darling.

Why won't you wait for me . . .

Your eyes are still watering from the sun, that has caused them to ache. Though now, the harsh bright sunshine is softening as clouds are blown in overhead, a kind of scrim or mist will soon obscure the sun.

"Gerard? Please wait for me . . ."

You are not begging. Perhaps you are pleading, making a case as a wife might plead with a husband, not unreasonably. But Gerard continues to walk/limp at a swift pace. His back is straight, adamant. His head is held high. You would think that this hiker is familiar with the somewhat treacherous trail, he must have hiked it previously.

Slip-sliding downhill. A trail is most treacherous in a steep descent.

Beside you, scarified canyon walls, of the hue of burnt blood.

Odors of stony earth, mesquite. On the canyon walls are curious striations like ancient hieroglyphics, scribblings in a mad hand.

Raindrops plump as grapes begin to lose their discrete shape. No longer raindrops now, just rain.

Sheets of rain. Pelting rain.

Desperately you call for Gerard to wait for you. You are panicked, that you will slip on wet rocks, fall and injure yourself. But you cannot see where Gerard has gone, the glimmer of white, his shirt, has vanished . . .

Offer yourself to Ishtikini. Then, Gerard will forgive you.

You are aware: if rain continues to fall so heavily, within minutes the steep narrow canyon will fill with rushing water.

You'd been warned. How many times warned. Signs on the trail, signs in the Canyon Lodge. You'd seen, yet did not see.

Already your shoes are soaked with rain. Your clothes are soaked, your hat, hair.

Wanting to protest, Gerard has never been so cruel to you in life. Never has he left you behind on a trail. Never has he ignored your cries, pleas.

Yet you stumble along the trail, ever downhill. Almost, you wonder if you have taken a wrong fork in the trail, confused by rain.

If you have lost Gerard forever.

So long you have been yearning for your husband, now you will join him. Unless he eludes you, even now.

Darling love you so much.

Follow me, trust me.

Give me your hand darling. Hurry!

But you seem to be lost. You can't reach Gerard, can't seize his hand, he is somewhere ahead of you, you are panting, exhausted. You who'd prided yourself on being a fit person, in excellent condition for your age, a runner, a serious walker, what vanity!

No way to avoid boulders blocking the trail, you must crawl over them.

Legs bleeding from myriad scratches. Lungs aching, face wet with tears lost in rain.

You have been hearing it behind you, not wanting to acknowledge what you are hearing: rushing water.

It is not believable to you, that Gerard would abandon you to the canyon. To the Scavenger God. For isn't there a sacred bond between you, wife and husband, annihilated together in the *crossing-over*?

In the distance, a glimpse of white. Gerard's white shirt so far away, you despair.

Calling—"Gerard! Gerard! Wait for me . . ."

You have to realize, you can't follow Gerard in a straight course. Must return to the previous fork in the trail, and take the fork you'd not taken, at the point at which you'd made your (near-fatal) error. If only it isn't too late, there is time yet to remedy the mistake.

A bitter fact: though you see your husband in front of you through sheets of rain yet you can't go directly to him, to make your claim. This is the bitter fact.

It is perplexing to you, that Gerard continues to hike with such urgency, even in the rain. Even though he knows (must know) that you are following him. His limp doesn't interfere with his stride but seems to be accelerating it. To compensate for the limp he moves with more agility. He is stiff-backed, unyielding. Recall how in bed that night in January, perhaps it was the night everything began, the unraveling, the stumbling, the desperate plea *Breathe!*—he'd feigned sleep when you'd wanted so badly to hold him for he'd wished for the oblivion of sleep more than the love of a wife at that moment in your lives.

Wanting to protest—*But I love you so much.*

No life without you.

Still you persist in believing that if you can only catch up with Gerard and force him to look you full in the face, he will acknowledge you as you are begging him to acknowledge you. The words will be torn from him—*Michaela! Of course, I love you too.*

You must make Gerard understand, you have repudiated the world for him. You had wanted to donate precious bone marrow to him, the closest approximation to the soul. And now, the *crossing-over time.* You are prepared to surrender.

But sheets of rain are blinding you. Your hair, your clothes are soaked. You are shivering, your teeth are chattering, this is such folly. And where is Gerard?

You have been running, stumbling in the rain. Always a mistake to run on a rocky trail yet you are running and in the rain you fall, fall hard. You have turned your ankle, you are whimpering with pain.

In terror you hear rushing water behind you. Not the beating of pulses in your head but dark water rushing between nightmare canyon walls.

"Gerard! Wait! It's me—your wife . . ."

Your screamed words are arrows, you've struck the man.

Arrows in his (fleeing) back.

It isn't clear, will not be clear if in the exigency of the moment Gerard is aware of you or if he has simply heard your voice, a voice, a voice of such anguish and yearning he cannot any longer deny it, and so in that instant weakness overtakes him like a net, abruptly he pauses in his flight to turn, to turn to you, at last to see *you*, revealing the precise face of your husband exactly as you remember him, an expression of despair, yet of love, that sucks away your breath in the instant before the rushing water overtakes you from behind and you are gone.

BUT THERE IS NO GERARD, *there is no guide. There is no one.*

Alone you are choking, panting, swallowing water. Filthy water rising to your thighs, belly, chest. Churning water, knocking you off-balance.

You slip, you clutch at nothing, you fall. Trying with all of your remaining strength to lift yourself out of the crazed-rushing water. Within minutes it has risen by five feet, you have gambled and lost. You are a foolish gringa, *you will die in this remote place. Close by, the Rio de Piedras is rising also, by inches, feet. Heavy rainfall, bursting from the sky. You have grown faint, exhausted. Your limbs are leaden with fatigue. You are losing consciousness. You are losing the bright scintillant thread of yourself. The life that has been* you *since your birth, you are losing, that life is dimming, flickering, suffocating, drowning. Try to lift yourself with herculean effort, every molecule in your being straining to live but—your strength is not enough.*

And then, unbelievably, you are on your feet—another time, on your feet—even as your feet are swept away beneath you; even as you clutch at a rock to hoist yourself erect. For nothing matters except that you can breathe—Breathe! *Even as a wicked rush of water pummels you like a mauling lover, throws you against rocks. Your skull is cracked like an eggshell. Your brain floods with black blood from burst arteries. Your last cry is strangled, inaudible*—Help! Help me, Gerard!—*but there is no one.*

In this instant annihilated. Gone.

60

The Departure

Awaiting the taxi that will take her to the Albuquerque airport for her 11:00 A.M. flight to Boston Michaela has read more than once a terse column of newsprint on the front page of the *Santa Tierra Post*.

Suitcases (packed, locked, labeled) waiting in the driveway. Michaela waiting on the front stoop of the house on Vista Drive.

Yes, seven pounds of cremains have been packed in an urn. Gerard's manuscript, notes. In one of the zippered pockets, the (yet unread) letter from Simon Khraw.

Faint with relief. Laughing with relief. Breathing deeply as she has rarely allowed herself to breathe in Santa Tierra, now the grief-vise seems to have vanished entirely.

Bruises at her rib cage will heal, in time. Those (inexplicable) scratches on the insides of her forearms, thin strips of scab soon to wither away, drop off.

Michaela is grateful to be leaving the house on Vista Drive that has been a petri dish of simmering nightmare memories. So grateful!

Though the sky is clear as washed glass, transparent and nothing behind it—not a thing. A smell of lavender envelopes her, sickly-sweet as ether. From out of the ravine behind the house cries of wild parrots which (she supposes) she will miss back home in Cambridge.

Stupid suitcases. Why bother bringing them.

The rented house, property of the Santa Tierra Institute for Advanced Research, is shuttered, locked! Michaela will never again set foot in the house. What relief to step out of the house at last, put the keys in an envelope left in the mailbox for Iris Esdras.

(Innocently she'd misled Iris Esdras. Telling her that she, Michaela, was not leaving for the airport until 11:00 A.M. and so if Iris wished to drop by, as she'd several times said, she might come at 10:30 A.M., and Michaela would like very much to see her and say goodbye . . .)

Inside the house, in their "secure" places, one of them unceremoniously draped with a towel, the demon-gods left behind.

No more. Never again.

Gone!

Michaela has been sipping coffee out of a mug. Black coffee, a solace. Michaela has been scanning the *Santa Tierra Post*, daily delivered to the house but which she'd ignored during the several months of residing here.

Appalled to discover in the lower left corner of the front page, a brief article headlined:

UNIDENTIFIED WOMAN DIES IN FLASH FLOOD, COLD SPRING CANYON

Arriba County rescue workers discovered the body of an unidentified woman hiker in Cold Spring Canyon yesterday afternoon, a casualty of a flash flood following yesterday's record-breaking torrential downpour.

The unidentified woman has been described by the Arriba County medical examiner as Caucasian, with medium-brown hair, in her mid-thirties, weighing approximately one hundred five pounds, height five feet seven. No wallet or ID was found on her person. Most of her clothing had been torn from her in the flash flood and has not been recovered.

Water was found in the woman's lungs but her death was believed to have been caused primarily by extreme trauma to the skull as well as blood loss from multiple lacerations.

Park employees informed rescue workers that the woman had continued on the trail after hikers had been instructed to return to the trailhead. Soon after this, the trail was closed. Park employees searched for the woman hiker without success until they were forced to turn back because of flooding.

No vehicle belonging to the unidentified woman has been located so far at Canyon Lodge.

Flash floods washed out sections of several Arriba County roads and shut down several miles on Rt. 25 for much of yesterday. Nine persons have been hospitalized following flooding-related accidents but the only fatality reported so far has been the unidentified woman hiker in Cold Spring Canyon.

The Arriba County sheriff requests that if anyone has information leading to the identity of the storm victim they should please call 505-493-2201.

Michaela reads, rereads this article. She is appalled, chilled.

It seems to her particularly sad, the woman is unidentified. No ID, no wallet. Clothing torn from her.

Her family must be missing her. Someone must be missing her.

A terrible death in rushing water, between pitiless canyon walls.

Quickly Michaela folds up the *Santa Tierra Post*, puts it aside. Never will she read the *Santa Tierra Post* again.

Her hands are shaking. A chill has come over her. But it is useless to be upset over a stranger who by now, a day later, has perhaps been identified . . .

The taxi has arrived! Michaela leaps to her feet, overjoyed.

The trunk of the taxi has sprung open. Michaela helps the driver lift suitcases into the trunk, her strength is surprising to the young Hispanic. And two suitcases are set in the backseat beside Michaela.

"Albuquerque Airport, ma'am? Yes?"

Yes! The first morning of Michaela's new life.

61

A Voice Out of a Fever Cloud

A hand is gripping yours. Warm dry hand gripping your slippery humid hand.

Whoever it is urging you—*Breathe!*

Leaning over you begging you—*Breathe!*

Blink if you can hear. Blink if you are (still) alive.

Blink squint try to see who it is leaning over you begging—*Breathe!*

Darling love you so much have your hand

Will never abandon